Frederick Thickstun Clark

The Mistress of the Ranch

Frederick Thickstun Clark

The Mistress of the Ranch

ISBN/EAN: 9783743317970

Manufactured in Europe, USA, Canada, Australia, Japa

Cover: Foto ©Andreas Hilbeck / pixelio.de

Manufactured and distributed by brebook publishing software (www.brebook.com)

Frederick Thickstun Clark

The Mistress of the Ranch

THE MISTRESS OF THE RANCH

A Novel

BY

FREDERICK THICKSTUN CLARK
AUTHOR OF "ON CLOUD MOUNTAIN" ETC.

NEW YORK
HARPER & BROTHERS PUBLISHERS
1897

THE MISTRESS OF THE RANCH

CHAPTER I

Phœbe Ellen bounced off the train and squared herself on the depot platform, one foot in advance of the
other.

"Well, where is he?" she demanded.

Anny, having remained till a full stop made her descent from the car less spectacular, had to walk some
distance down the planking before coming up with her
sister. They appeared of about the same age, but Anny
was not so blond, and her eyes were larger and calmer.
Her mouth, too, wore a look of habitual repose, while
Phœbe Ellen's always seemed quivering under the strain
of aggressive speech.

They halted side by side near the station building, with
their oil-cloth satchels in their hands.

"Not a waggin in sight!" continued Phœbe Ellen,
stabbing her eyes into the distance on all sides. "Didn't
he say he'd meet us to the train? Wasn't them his words?
Where's that letter? Oh, ye needn't hunt it up. I
know he said he'd meet us to the train. I've seen folks
in my time 't didn't know a promise from their own lazi-
ness, 'n' made shore they was doin' all they ever said they
would when they sot aroun' wonderin' why folks wa'n't
satisfied. Well" (she deposited her satchel on the platform with an energy which seemed to distrust the ability
of gravity alone to perform that function), "here we be,
but where's Sam Tinker?"

Her attitude of challenge included everything in sight, even the mountains. They looked serene and passive and altogether manageable, as was fitting and proper, considering the presence in which they found themselves. On the whole, Phœbe Ellen concluded that she had no quarrel with the Rocky Mountains. But Sam Tinker—where was he?

Anny understood when she was expected to answer her sister's questions. She said nothing now. Her eyes were upon the retreating train, which was coughing its way toilsomely up grade. It disappeared with a final switch of its dragon's tail behind a spur of the foot-hills, and her eyes wandered out to the mountains.

"I like 'em," she meditated. "They look like they had big, kind thoughts."

But Phœbe Ellen had begun again.

"Anything I hate, it's foolin' with a promise; 'n' it's 's common 's whiskers. Well! They ain't no promises in heaven, fer they ain't no men there—that's a comfort. *Tinker!*" She repeated the word with a forced calm. "Ye might know by the name ye never could tell where to put yer finger on 'im. Tinker! Shall we set down 'n' wait? The very name o' that man goes agin me. It means wait, it spells wait. Half the folks in this 'ere world seems to think all the other half 's got to do 's to set aroun' a-prayin' fer 'em to keep their 'p'intments 'n' smirk 'n' look happy if they show up afore doomsday. Well, if Sam Tinker comes 'n' finds *me* a-waitin', he'll want to bile the greetin' he gits from me. It won't be tender!"

Anny withdrew her eyes from the mountains.

"Mebbe suthin' 's happened," she suggested. Her voice contrasted agreeably with the nipping and eager tones of her sister.

Phœbe Ellen took up the word in a voice of acute objection.

"What *could* 'a' happened ? He said he'd be 'ere, 'n'
that orter settle it. He 'ain't no bizness to let nothin'
happen. If he seen anything happenin', he orter 'a' flaxed
aroun' 'n' hendered it. Let's go 'n' ast the depot-man if
he knows."

She seized her satchel once more, and, with a sudden
turn, advanced upon the station-master. Her stride was
martial, she looked determined to return with her shield
or upon it. The man was trundling a truck down the
platform, and he vibrated from head to foot in sympathy
with the rumbling of the vehicle. Anny moved in that
direction, too. She always looked as if dragged in the
wake of her sister on one of the minor waves of that strong
individuality.

"Say, you, there—you depot-man!" called Phœbe Ellen, flourishing her satchel. The official stopped and
faced about, leaning against the slant end of his truck.
He had a mottled complexion of chemical pink, which
was still further complicated by numerous freckles of various degrees of brownness. Several tufts of week-old
blond beard were discoverable on unexpected corners of
his face.

"Ye mus' be the Thompson gals, I reckon ?" he inquired, with some awkwardness, pushing his hat forward
and brushing up his soft yellow hair behind.

The girls stared at each other as if trying to decide to
what extent the greeting was supernatural. Phœbe Ellen
recovered first. She always did.

"How 'd *you* know ?" she demanded, with a warlike
fling of her head to one side.

The depot-man grinned. He was more at his ease than
his first sheepishness would have led one to suppose.

"Oh, they's little birds aroun' in these parts," he remarked.

"'N' they talk, do they ?" snorted Phœbe Ellen. "'N'
they live aroun' the depot, do they ? 'N' they wheel

trucks 'n' git funny with strangers, do they?" She gave a scornful exhalation and drew her right shoulder up to her ear. "Well, say, now, 'ud ye mind comin' down off'm the bough fer a minute, Birdie, 'n' tellin' us whether they's sech a man livin' in these 'ere parts 's Sam Tinker?"

The depot-man still grinned, but he answered with a sort of roseate meekness which was probably his form of apology.

"I didn't go to do nothin' to rile ye," he said, first rubbing his nose and then the back of his neck. "It was Sam hisself 't tole me 'bout ye. He said he'd be 'ere to the arternoon up train to meet ye."

Phœbe Ellen fetched a long breath, as if here at last was a clew.

"Oh, he did, did he?" Then suddenly making the depot-man responsible, "Well, then, why ain't he 'ere?"

He scratched his ear in perplexity.

"Give it up!" was his final answer, with an outward fling of his hand. "Mebbe he's dead."

Phœbe Ellen stiffened herself.

"He'll wish 't he was when I lay eyes on 'im! Won't I give it to 'im? Oh no!"

The depot-man's smile was so genial that in spite of herself Phœbe Ellen's mouth relaxed. There were humorous lines in her face when she was not frowning.

He adjusted his truck parallel with the cracks in the platform, as if there were some special virtue in that arrangement, and took time to meditate. "When Dan Thompson died over there on the Rio Grande, he left his property to his sister Anny. Now, which o' these is Anny, I wonder?"

Aloud he said:

"Sam was over yistiddy, 'n' he tole me he'd be 'ere to-day afore you was. Suthin' must 'a' happened. He allus keeps 'is word."

Phœbe Ellen snorted again.

"A Tinker 't keeps 'is word!" She suddenly turned on him with a malicious smile. "Is yer reel name Birdie?" she inquired. She cocked her head and examined him with one eye half closed.

The depot-man twisted his heel into a knot-hole and looked confused. But he went on wondering. "The talker mus' be Anny. The other un 's fatter 'n' purtier, but she don't look so sassy."

But aloud he said, with his peculiar pink acquiescence:

"I reckon they ain't no use tryin' to keep my name from ye if ye're goin' to make yer home in these parts. They call me Pinky." He withdrew his heel, grew redder as he examined it, then rubbed his neck softly with his left hand.

His air of deprecation had no effect on Phœbe Ellen.

"Pinky?" she cried. "How purty! I 'spected if 'twan't Birdie it 'ud be Daisy, or Petunia, or suthin'. But Pinky! How sweet! Jes' the name fer a feller 't 'ud b'lieve anybody named Tinker could keep 'is word!"

Pinky's blood overflowed his features in a purple flood, but presently his freckles emerged into view once more, like a lot of corks bobbing on rough water.

"'Tain't my reel name," he explained. "My reel name 's Rose—Dick Rose. The fellers 'ere is terrors fer nicknames, 'n' it didn't take 'em a minute to see 't my name 'n' my color went together, 'n' that fixed *me*."

"Pinky Rose!" murmured Phœbe Ellen, examining him from head to foot and all too obviously connecting the luridness of the name with the luridness of the man.

"*I* don't keer," declared Pinky, with grinning defiance. "*I* ain't a-goin' to run fer office."

"Nor git married?" inquired Phœbe Ellen. "Well, I b'lieve ye!" Then with a backward jerk of her blond head, "I ain't a-goin' to pick no quar'l with yer name— I'm a gal o' peace 'n' harmony, 'n' I keep my feet off'm my neighbors 's long 's they don't lay aroun' permisc'us fer me to stumble over. So ye stan' up fer Sam Tinker, do ye? I'm int'rested in *him*." Her emphasis was exclusive. Pinky felt it, and resolved to say nothing more about himself. "Ye know he's goin' to look arter the ranch fer a while."

"She *is* Anny," thought the depot-man. He had no comprehension of Phœbe Ellen's habits of assumption and appropriation. "Yes," he said, aloud, "Sam tole me how yer brother Dan-made 'im promise to stay a year 'n' look arter things."

"Yes, 'n' this is the way he begins. Oh, *I* know his kind—small pertaters 'n' few in a hill. Look at the trick he's gone 'n' played on us fust off! He'll want us to kiss 'im how-d'ye-do, won't he? Like 's not he'll be 'spectin' a bokay 'n' a chromo fer ever comin' 't all! It's lyin'—that's what it 'ud be called back East there in Nebrasky!"

"Oh, not lyin'," Pinky argued, in meek expostulation. "This ain't a kentry o' liars—the boys stan's by their word, they ain't cowards. 'N' Sam—"

"Sam's a little George Washin'ton with tin wings, ain't he? Lor', is this heaven? Sis, does this look like heaven?" She swept her masterful glance along the dreary alkali park and back to the unwholesome excrescence of half a dozen huts which constituted Eden City.

"It ain't heaven, 's I knows on," replied Anny, with the pretty, serious drawl which was her distinctive form of speech. "But they may be honest men 'ere, fer all that. I'm glad Sam Tinker's honest," she added to Pinky. "Brother Dan was mos'ly a good jedge o' folks."

"Sam 'll treat ye square," said Pinky.

"He will!" put in Phœbe Ellen, with emphasis. "I'll keep my eyes on 'im. I never yit seen a man 't I'd trust 's fur 's I could throw 'im by his coat-tails. If he 'spects to git ahead o' *me*, he'll have to git up airly in the mornin', I kin tell 'im that. I kin run that ranch myself, on a pinch. I looked arter the place back East there in Nebrasky, 'n' I kin do it 'ere, arter I git used to the erry-gation 'n' sech."

She turned on the depot-man with abrupt question-ing.

"How fur 's the ranch from 'ere, anyhow?" she asked.

"Seven mile."

"I made shore I 'membered. That ain't bad. When we git lonesome we can come over 'n' have a visit with ye."

Pinky accepted this mark of favor with open delight.

"That's right! Come over—come over often. It ain't heaven 'ere, 's ye said yerself, if it *is* called Eden City. Still, it might be wuss. W'y, if this 'ere kentry had plenty o' water 'n' good people, it 'ud be a reg'lar para-dise!"

"So 'ud hell," was Phœbe Ellen's laconic retort. She intended nothing funny or irreverent, merely a statement of fact; but her speech so doubled Pinky up with laugh-ter that she was obliged to laugh, too. She always looked less thin-lipped and more likable when she laughed.

"Ye might come over to the ranch 'n' visit *us*, arter we git settled," she said, after he had sobered down. "We'd be glad to see ye—wouldn't we, sis?"

The pretty sister smiled acquiescence.

"Queer how they don't call each other by their fust names," reflected Pinky. "I ain't heerd 'em do it yit." Aloud he said, "Oh, I'll come over, shore. Pete Haw-kins—he lives there in the fust cabin to the left—he takes my place when I want a off-day. He's got the post-office, 'n' runs a s'loon 'n' dry goods 'n' groceries. I've seen 'im peekin' out fifty times or more sence ye come—he's powerful bashful. That's why he wa'n't 'ere when the train come in, though they was sev'ral kegs fer 'im. He knowed ye was comin', 'n' ye couldn't 'a' dragged 'im over with ropes. He says 't a man 't kin stan' up 'n' face a gal 's a genyus. He allus laffs at me 'cause I do it so easy. He calls me a doode."

Phœbe Ellen looked him over from the tips of his cowboy boots to the crown of his cowboy hat, fixed her eyes upon each separately, then deliberately traced the surging blood from his cheeks to his temples, from his temples behind his ears, and thence, as it seemed to him, half-way down his back ; then, woman-like, at the moment when he expected annihilation, she spared him.

" Wot d'rection ort that Tinker o' your'n to come from, anyhow ?" she inquired. " Somehow I've took a turble hatred o' that man !"

Pinky pointed with a thin, freckled hand.

" Ye see that foot-hill spur joggin' out there jest above the ruff o' the s'loon ? Well, the road comes down the farther side o' that. Goin' over, ye have to climb up 'n' down all the way, but down mos'ly ; then all to wunst ye turn a sharp corner, 'n' there ye be in a green valley lower down 'n this, with mountains all aroun' 'n' a river in it. That's the Rio Grande." He gave the name a drawling English pronunciation. " It's jest a little river there, but it's orfle clear 'n' purty. 'N' the ranch is one o' the best in the State. Everybody says so."

" I'll be glad to live in a green kentry," spoke up Anny. " I useter git dretful sick o' Nebrasky."

" I'm glad it's dif'rent from Eden City," declared Phœbe Ellen. " This is wuss 'n Nebrasky."

" No," said Anny, softly. " They ain't no mountains there."

"Some un 's comin' down the foot-hill road," said Pinky, suddenly. " Jes' by the low end o' the mesa—see ?" He was shading his eyes with one hand and pointing with the other.

" Is it that Tinker o' your'n ?" asked Phœbe Ellen.

She seemed determined to hold him responsible for the transgressor.

"They ain't no one else in these parts 't drives a buckboard with one gray hoss 'n' a mustang. Yes, it's Sam."

"Well, I'm ready fer 'im," said Phœbe Ellen, shutting her lips tight.

WПILE waiting for the delinquent to come up, Phœbe Ellen's eyes wandered over the shabby, tent-roofed cabins, the brush palings, the sordid yards with their accumulations of tin cans and beer bottles — the whole human effort which affronted Nature and which Nature was too feeble to resent. A burro set up its braying just beyond the track. A melancholy hen close by Pete Hawkins's saloon was mourning over an egg she had just dropped in the dirt. The yellowish gray of the park was blotched here and there with the leprous inflorescence of alkali ; the only bit of color to be seen was an occasional bunch of cardinal cactus, as red as if the ground had been stabbed and the blood had oozed out and coagulated. Man should have left the place alone ; for in subduing it he had admitted the devil as a partner. But on all sides the mountains rose, showing that beyond the " city " limits God still reigned.

Pinky went on meditating. " I've seen Sam Tinker in some mighty ticklish places in my time, but never in a row with a woomarn. If a feller was to jump on 'im fer a fist-fight—well, that feller wouldn't jump much afore he'd be laid out ; if it was pistols, I'd bet dollars to chewin'-gum on the sun a-shinin' through the other feller fust ; but a woomarn—what kin he do ? 'Ll he turn tail 'n' run ? The idee o' Sam runnin'! But wot else is tey fer a man to do ? He can't fight—he can't stan' 'n' take it. Think o' Sam Tinker runnin' away from anything with two legs ! 'N' the heiress—look at 'er. That's wot my ole mother useter call facin' a frownin' world."

Phœbe Ellen had deposited her satchel once more upon the platform, and had taken her stand in front of it in an attitude of battle. She stood very straight, her arms folded tightly across her breast, her back hollowed in, one foot in advance of the other. There were hard wrinkles from the corners of her nose to her mouth, and her lips looked very thin.

Anny stood considerably in the rear, fully aware of the gravity of the situation, but conscious of the futility of interference. She was frowning, too, but with anxiety. Her eyes looked helpless, and now and then there was a deprecative tremor about her lips.

The wagon drew nearer down the winding road. The dust rose in a hazy yellow cloud, hiding the horses and vehicle at times, then floating away into filaments and wreaths, and disappearing in final faint sun-glimmers. A little beyond Pete Hawkins's saloon the driver became visible—a huge creature in a gray sombrero, bending the shoulders of Hercules carelessly over the loose-held reins. He wore overalls and a brown mining-jacket with copper rivets at the corners of the pockets. Now he straightened his shoulders and lifted his head in an attitude of attention, examining the occupants of the platform with interest.

Pinky sent him a lusty greeting.

"Hello, Chris'mas! Fin'ly got 'ere, have ye? Train's come 'n' gone half a hour ago!"

Before answering, the man took time to bend back the brim of his hat into an impromptu halo, and his countenance, thus relieved of shadow, took the sunlight in a generous gleam. It was a full, strong face, inspiring respect by the manly completeness of its physical outline as well as by the evidence of soul behind it. There was strength of will in the projecting chin, and gentleness in the upward curve of the mouth at the corners. He had a complexion of ruddy brown, through which his eyes gleamed kindly. His level brows looked as if they seldom frowned, and never without good reason. His mouth had broadened in response to Pinky's greeting, displaying a set of perfect teeth beneath a heavy brown mustache.

"Hello, yerself!" came back the answer, in a voice which had a healthy depth of lung behind it.

And presently Sam Tinker was backing his wagon against the planking in a position for the women to mount easily from the rear. Then he flung the reins over the dashboard, straddled the two seats at two slow strides, and with a third came down upon the platform with a force which shook that structure to its base.

"Well, hello!" he called out, in ponderous welcome to the two women.

But he was confronted by silence—and Phœbe Ellen with her arms akimbo.

"Well!" was her greeting, shrilly pitched, while she drew herself in at the waist and leaned forward as if pecking at him with a long, sharp bill. "So ye've come, have ye?" She straightened herself with a jerk and stood stiffly, glaring up at him.

He was so big that he had the advantage over her even in a combat of words; for length, breadth, and thickness have tongues of their own and speak even before they are spoken to. The smile slowly faded from his face, and he looked down at her with grave examination, as if still uncertain of the spirit of her greeting. But the battlesome attitude, the shrill voice, the twisted mouth, the hysterical defiance of a woman in a rage, left him no long occasion for doubt. He pushed his hat a little farther back—the movement displayed a tangle of moist brown hair close-packed against a low forehead—and, settling the weight of his body easily upon one leg, extended his examination from her face to her dress and thence to her feet.

The carelessness of his movement and pose brought the

fire into Phœbe Ellen's eye.   She began with apostrophic scorn :

"So this 'ere's wot it means to take the live-stock o' a ranch 'thout seein' 'em, even when it's a dead brother 't recommends 'em !"   Her furious glance left the cowboy in no doubt as to whom she referred to as live-stock. "This 'ere's the kind o' cattle I'm 'spected to pervide paster 'n' fodder fer, 'cordin' to my dead brother's wishes, 'n' git nothin' in return but the right to stan' aroun', wearin' my legs short with waitin', while they're kickin' up their heels somers with joy on the range !   This 'ere's wot it means to take hired men on charity, askin' nothin' in return but to be treated white fer it !   This 'ere's the way the hired han's lays out to come it over me from the start, imposin' on me 'count o' my weakness fer my dead brother, 'n' settin' theirselves up above me, showin' me they mean to run things to suit theirselves !   This is the sort—"

"Ye're Miss Anny, I reckon ?" he asked, still eying her with the placid curiosity which marked him as her superior, and which made her blood boil.

Here Anny herself seemed on the point of interposing, but Phœbe Ellen got in her word first.   She had no intention of denying her identity, but she meant to establish herself once for all as her sister's equal in authority.

"Well, if I ain't, ye kin take it fer granted I know 'er idees.   Wot d'ye mean, anyhow, by not gittin' 'ere till hours arter ye said ye would ?   'Ain't ye got no sense o' promises ?   Reckon I'm a picter in a frame to be sot down 'ere on the platform till ye happen to come 'long 'n' cart me off permisc'ous ?   Don't ye know wot a lady 's like, to leave 'er sprawlin' 'n' straddlin' aroun' in public like this ? If this 'ere's a spec'men o' yer ways 'n' doin's, if this 'ere's the line ye 'pose to fight it out on, I want to tell ye right now we'll have to part comp'ny, 'n' the sooner the quicker

—see ? None o' *my* money goes to s'port that kind o' shif'lessness—'n' ye kin jes' bear that in mind."

Sam Tinker waited till she finished, gave her a final comprehensive glance, then turned to Pinky.

"That her trunk ?" he asked, in an emotionless tone, pointing with a huge index finger to a receptacle in pressed zinc a little way up the platform.

Pinky nodded. There was something unusual in the cowboy's face, but the nature of the expression was doubtful. Even Phœbe Ellen began to feel it and to shift uneasily from one foot to the other.

" I'll git a plank, 'n' we'll roll it into the back o' the buckboard together," said Pinky. " It's turble heavy."

But Sam answered, composedly, " No, ye needn't mind. I reckon I kin manage it."

Phœbe Ellen, who knew precisely how heavy that trunk was, inwardly chuckled as the giant marched up to it and tested its weight by pulling at one end. " He'll have to call on Pinky 'n' mebbe both o' us gals," she thought, with glee. " That 'll make 'im drop 'is tail-feathers, I reckon !" But her amazement grew to the splitting-point as he solemnly spit on his hands, rubbed them together, then, spreading his legs Colossus-wise, seized the trunk by the middle, lifted it with a quivering of the muscles of the hips such as one sees in a horse straining uphill, and, settling it comfortably on one shoulder, marched down the platform, and deposited it endwise in the rear of the wagon.

" Is he the devil ?" asked Phœbe Ellen, more of herself than of Anny, but loud enough for the latter to hear. " It took me 'n' you 'n' the hired man to load that into the waggin to home, 'n' then we had to end it over 'n' over up a pair o' planks." She advanced a little closer to the giant, his supernatural strength, whether as man or devil, compelling her respect. She intended to say something in approval, but before she had time to open her mouth he turned on her and said, with an utter lack of emotion of any kind:

"Well, I reckon it's time to wish ye a good-arternoon, Miss Thompson. Pinky 'll pint out the way to the ranch fer ye. I'll ride over in the mornin' myself fer my things. Good-arternoon!"

Then he turned his back and strode away.

Phœbe Ellen's eyes widened on the retreating figure. She began a series of inarticulate exclamations.

"Well! Say! Lookee 'ere!—"

Her jaw dropped. Her face had a stunned, relaxed look.

"He—he—where's he goin' to?" she finally demanded with a half-gasp, turning to Pinky.

Pinky was grinning with enjoyment, either at her discomfiture or at Sam's way out of his difficulties.

"Looks like he was goin' over to Pete Hawkins's, don't it?" he answered. "But I d'know. It may be Wilcox's —Wilcox 's a friend o' his, 'n' he hangs out in the nex' shanty. No, it's Pete's—see?"

"I'll pay 'im out fer that," Phœbe Ellen muttered. "I never was treated so afore—never!"

She looked quite pale.

"Wot d' ye reckon he's goin' to do over there?" she inquired.

"Take a observashun fust thing, I shouldn't wonder."

"A observashun?"

"Through the bottom o' a whiskey-glass. Sam's a thirsty soul!"

"But—he'll come back?"

"I didn't git the idee he would. He didn't look it."

"He said suthin' 'bout ridin' over arter his things in the mornin', didn't he?" She evidently distrusted her own memory of what had transpired.

"That's wot he said," Pinky confirmed her.

"But he's got to come back *now*—he's my hired man—

he's *got* to come back ! I—I'll discharge 'im 'n' git 'nother if he don't come back. I'll set 'im a-packin' if he don't come back ! I'll—"

" 'Pears like he'd gone 'n' discharged hisself," remarked Pinky, in his half-deprecatory way. He was no longer grinning, but seemed wholly intent on the fair stranger's troubles. "I took it that was his way o' settin' hisself a-packin'. Anyways, that's my idee."

"But wot's the matter ? Wot's he mad at ? Can't a gal tell a hired man when he's gone 'n' done wrong ? This is a purty kentry !"

"Well, 'tain't our way out 'ere to swoller much 't don't taste good, 'n' that's a fact. 'N' Sam kin do as he likes— he's got a ranch o' his own down in Las Animas. He's jes' nachelly left ye to look out fer yerselves. *He* won't be walked over by nobody."

"But yell at 'im—call 'im back !" cried Phœbe Ellen, just as the giant was entering the saloon.

"Ho, Sam !" shouted Pinky, with ready obedience.

The huge figure turned with deliberation.

"Come back a minute, will ye ?"

The giant considered. Then, as if he had made up his mind after weighing all the pros and cons, he retraced his steps with ponderous slowness.

"Well, 'ere I be," he remarked, pausing a little way from the platform.

"She wanted a pow-wow," said Pinky, jerking his thumb in Phœbe Ellen's direction.

Sam turned his large face full upon her. It was a face capable of only one expression at a time, and that of some big, incomplex emotion. Just now his look told of nothing except a desire to know what she wanted. His resentment—if he had any—lay below a simple, serious inquiry as to what was expected of him.

Phœbe Ellen met his composure with inward trepidation. There was something compelling in his unresentful simplicity—it gave him an advantage which would have been impossible to the boisterous anger she had expected. In calling him back she was prepared to meet him with concessions ; a loss of personal dignity counted but little with her in the cause of her interests, and she had seen in a flash that her interests—by which she really meant Anny's—depended upon retaining this man in her service. But the look of him as he stood there, huge, unmanageable, indifferently inquiring, overcame her with a sudden rage. She had never before felt herself in the presence of a master, and this cowboy's attitude of cool superiority galled her like deliberate insult. She flung aside consequences in the impulse towards satisfaction which with her meant fight.

"Well!" she cried, bridling like a mettlesome horse and hiding an involuntary quavering in her tone by a forced use of breath. "So ye reckoned ye was goin' to run off 'n' leave me, did ye ?" Even to her own ears this interrogation seemed feeble, but she could think of nothing better. "It's plain ye don't know my kind—but ye will afore ye git through with me ! Now, lookee 'ere ; ye 're my hired man, d' ye see ? 'N' if ye know wot's good fer them big bones o' yourn, ye'll toe the mark I make fer ye. Git up on the front seat o' that buckboard, now, quicker 'n th' Lord 'll let ye, 'n' take them reins 'n' drive us over to the ranch. D' ye hear ?"

Sam Tinker looked his antagonist over with a careful attention which had no contempt in it, but possibly a hint of amusement; took time to make up his mind that a direct reply would be a useless waste of energy, then turned to Pinky with massive composure.

"Don't yell arter me ag'in," he said. "I'm thirsty." And he started once more for the saloon.

Phœbe Ellen, beside herself with rage, rushed after him, shouting and brandishing her fists. But the unheeding figure marched on with elephantine dignity, and the heavy feet came down with dull regularity on the dry adobe soil. She might as well have expected to order one of the mountains in her direction and have it obey. Finally she stopped, helpless, red in the face, furious, flinging herself, one might say, in two directions at once.

But he was still within tongue's reach of her.

"Come back!" she screeched. "I tell ye to come back! If ye don't, I'll—I'll—" Then, with an hysterical realization of the uselessness of threat, "*Why* won't ye come back?" she finished, on the verge of tears.

He turned with a smile more masterful than anything that had preceded it.

"Oh, I'd jes 's soon tell ye why." His voice was calm and slow. "I'm used to the devil in breeches, 'n' I know how to fight 'im; but in petticoats"—he spread his huge hands towards her, palms outward, wagging them slowly to right and left—"in petticoats, excuse *me*." And with a leisurely stride he disappeared in the saloon.

Phœbe Ellen came back and sat down on the platform. She was pale, with anger partly, but with some other emotion as well.

"I wish to th' Almighty I was a man," she said, after a long moment, more to herself than to her companions.

Anny said nothing, but—

"Wot 'ud ye do?" asked Pinky.

"I'd kill that critter—that's wot I'd do!"

Pinky stroked his chin and brushed up his yellow hair behind.

"It's the only way ye could git ahead o' 'im," he said, with a grin.

CHAPTER III

Phœbe Ellen braced her elbow against her knee and propped her chin in her hand. When a woman of lively tongue and slow sensibilities is forced to face the consequences of her eloquence, she is in for a long period of meditation. The lively tongue has run ahead of self-interest, and it takes time for the slow sensibilities to catch up; and when they do they are not always equal to a proper readjustment of moral speed. Phœbe Ellen was as surprised at Sam Tinker's transformation into an antagonistic force as if her ordinary processes had turned to acts of thaumaturgy, and a demon with a will of his own had been evolved instead of the compliant genius of her expectations. She could not understand it. She was accustomed to scolding, and to the settlement of ends by that means. It had not occurred to her that there might be natures to whom such a settlement was impossible, and to whom the employment of such means was an affront. She had applied her ordinary little match to what seemed the ordinary little pile of kindling-wood, and that an explosion occurred was no more to be accounted for than are any of those outbreaks which we prepare against ourselves in the egotism intended to forestall such result.

Something of all this was manifest to Pinky, who, realizing that there was no more fun to be got out of the situation at present, busied himself about some freight on another part of the platform. It was mostly kegs.

As for Anny, she had seated herself on a candle-box at a distance from the station building—a coign of vantage from which she could see the mountains on all sides.

They took her eye with an enchantment which was new
to her, and she was content to look up at them and wonder and adore. She found a rapturous satisfaction in
tracing the outline of the peaks against the cloudless
blue ; here an abrupt upward notch in the sky-line, there
a carefully rounded dome, and there again a steady, even,
heavenward slope, up which she could almost feel the
high winds racing. The gulches made purple havoc of
the shadows all along the foot-hills, and stretches of distant pines sent murky ripples up ridge and mesa.

For some time a student of physiognomy would have
discovered in Phœbe Ellen's face nothing but a look of
mingled anger and surprise. But gradually this expression gave place to a droop of self-distrust in the muscles
about the mouth and chin. Then she began to look
about in search of her sister.

"Sis !" she called, when she had discovered her.

Anny removed her eyes from the white peaks with a
vacant effort at attention, and for a minute did not seem
to understand.

"Come 'ere a minute !"

She arose and moved forward, the look of wrapped contemplation gradually giving place to her habitual expression of friendly interest.

"We're in it, ain't we ?" Phœbe Ellen said, with a faint
little smile which betrayed the shattered self-confidence
beneath it.

Anny took up a standing position at her sister's side.

"It looks that way," she admitted, without referring
to the folly that had brought them into their difficulties.

"Well, wot be we goin' to do ?"

It was so seldom that Phœbe Ellen made any appeal
except to the obedience of those around her that Anny
was immediately touched. She was unaccustomed to the
sight of that somewhat vixenish face with the lips tremulous and a flaccid droop about the chin. Anny's sense of

humor was strong—the whole situation had been a mixture of tragedy and comedy to her—but her sympathies
were stronger.

"Never mind," she said, soothingly. "Never mind."

"He don't mean to come back," Phœbe Ellen announced,
in a hollow tone.

"We'll find a way out," said Anny, cheerfully.

"We can't go on a-settin' 'ere ferever." Phœbe Ellen's
pronoun was oblivious of Anny's standing posture, as was
her following remark. "This 'ere plankin's gittin' tired
a'ready. I'd like to be movin' on."

"So 'ud I," assented Anny.

"But we can't start out alone—"

"I reckon we could find the way."

"Oh, we could find the way fast 'nough—I ain't afeerd
o' that. I was thinkin' o' wot we'd do arterwards."

"Arterwards?"

"Arter we got to the ranch. A ranch out 'ere ain't
like wot 'tis in Nebrasky. We got to have some un
aroun' 't's used to things."

"We *couldn't* 'tend to it like we orter, all to wunst,"
assented Anny, in her slow, even drawl.

"Oh, I know it!" groaned Phœbe Ellen, dropping her
hands between her knees. "They ain't 'nother soul 'bout
that ranch 't kin run it—Dan's letters used to say so ; 'n'
if we go to run it ourselves, we'll run it into the groun'.
He's *got* to go back till I kin git the hang o' things. We
can't git 'long 'thout 'im."

"No," acquiesced the even voice.

"'N' arter I larn the ins 'n' outs I'll fire 'im s' quick
it 'll make his head swim ! I'll set the dorgs onto 'im—
I'll pitch 'im into the river ! But how to git 'im back ?
He don't need to work, 'cause he's got a ranch somers o'
his own. To think o' him over there this minute, fillin'
his skin with whiskey, while we— But the herders is all
used to mindin' 'im—wot if they was to leave in a wad if

we was to go back 'thout 'im? Lots o' cowboys won't mind a woomarn—Dan used to say so. 'N' I *can't* look arter the cattle 'n' errygation 'n' the range till I larn the workin' o' things. Wot be we goin' to do?"

"It's plain 'nough to me wot orter be done." Anny's words had become positive, but her tone was as mild as ever.

Phœbe Ellen was in a melting mood. People always are when they extend helpless arms to be lifted out of their scrapes.

"I've knowed ye to have idees," she conceded, almost with tears.

"In fact, they ain't but one thing to be done," continued Anny.

"Well, let's hear it."

The pretty, drawling voice articulated with a distinctness which might have belonged to a more incisive utterance.

"Go over to the s'loon 'n' call 'im out 'n' tell 'im ye're sorry."

Phœbe Ellen stiffened her neck, glared, snorted, drew down her mouth, gave her head a sideward fling, and clamped both hands around her knee.

"Well!" she said, in a fatal tone. "If that don't beat the speckled Jews!"

"It 'ud work," persisted Anny, gently.

"Work! Tell 'im I'm sorry! Well, if that's all the idee ye got, 'nough 's been said." She waited a moment for Anny to expatiate on the advantages of her plan, but as no argument was offered, she went on in a modified tone, "Tell 'im I'm sorry! I reckon I see myself!"

"Then I reckon I might 's well set down, too, 'n' make myself to hum?" inquired Anny, with unruffled serenity.

"I reckon ye might, if that's all ye got to offer; 'n' ye might 's well make up yer mind to set 'ere till the crack o' doom, too, though this plankin' 's orfle hard. Tell 'im

I'm sorry !" The energy of the repetition suggested a feebleness of resistance which Anny was not slow to understand. It even implied a familiarity with the idea before it had been presented.

"Well, ye was wrong, now, wa'n't ye, sis ?" the younger sister said, persuasively, laying her hand on Phœbe Ellen's knee.

"Wrong ? Never !" cried the latter, tightening her mouth and drawing away.

"Well, a leetle bit quick, then. Ye'll have to own up ye was a leetle bit quick."

Phœbe Ellen, who wanted to be coaxed, denied the charge in a fainter voice.

"I wa'n't no sech thing—ye know I wa'n't !"

"Ye orter 'a' give 'im a chance to speak up 'n' 'splain."

"He orter 'a' took the chance when he seen how mad I was."

"No; ye didn't give 'im no show 't all. Ye begun on 'im afore he had time to open his mouth. That's where ye was wrong. Ye acted like ye was reg'larly sp'ilin' for a fight, 'n' he seen it 'n' kep' still. Ye was on the wrong side through the hull bizness, sis. Ye know it yerself, only ye're mad 'n' won't own up."

"He hadn't no bizness to be late, nohow."

"How d' ye know that ? Ye orter 'a' ast 'im 'n' made shore. 'N' if he hadn't no 'scuse, 'twa'n't sech a turble sin, arter all. Half a hour's waitin' didn't hurt us. Ye've kep' us 'ere longer 'n that right now by bein' cranky 'n' drivin' 'im off. Now ye've got one o' two things to do: git into the waggin 'n' start, or go over to the s'loon 'n' tell 'im ye're sorry."

"I won't never do that." The tone was very feeble.

"Then wot's the use o' waitin' 'ere ? Why not jump in 'n' be off ?"

"Wot's the use o' startin' 'less Tinker goes 'long o' us ? He must have whiskey 'nough in 'im to float a ship by this. The ranch 'll go to everlastin' pot 'thout 'im — I know 'twill. He's jes' the one to boss the cowboys 'n' look arter the crops 'n' cattle—it's 's plain 's the shoes on yer feet !"

"Oh, they ain't no question o' his bein' jes' the man we need ! But if we've got to worry 'long 'thout 'im, why not climb in 'n' lick up ? *This* ain't no good."

" 'D ye see the way he lifted in that trunk ?"

Anny nodded.

"Tell 'im I'm sorry ? I'll see myself farther fust ! 'D ye reckon he looked so orfle mad ?"

"No ; only like he wouldn't be walked over."

" 'D I walk over 'im ?"

Anny smiled.

"No, but ye tried."

The sarcasm was lost on Phœbe Ellen. She was too oppressed by her predicament to think of anything but a possible way out of it. Suddenly she was struck with a bright idea.

"Lookee 'ere, sis," she cried, "*you* go 'n' tell 'im ye're sorry !"

"Me ? He don't know me from Adam. He never even looked at me wunst."

"I reckon I *did* take up most o' his 'tention," reflected Phœbe Ellen, not without pride. "But ye kin tell 'im who ye be. Tell 'im ye're my sister—that 'll fetch 'im. He'll 'member me !"

"But I ain't done nothin' to be sorry fer," objected Anny.

"Wot's the differ ? If he wants some un to say they're sorry, ye kin do it a heap purtier 'n wot I kin. Come, now. Trot along !"

"Why, I'd jes' soon, 's fur 's the doin' o' it goes," said Anny, still smiling. "But wot's the use o' wastin' time like that ? Ye're the one 't done the wrong, 'n' ye're the one 't 'll have to make it right."

“I don’t see the differ. It’s all in the fambly.”

“’Tain’t a fambly affair, nohow. He’ll see the differ, ’n’ ye would yerself in his place.”

Phœbe Ellen sighed.

“Ye’re shore ’twouldn’t go ?”

“Shore.”

“O’ course I won’t ’pollygize to ’im,” Phœbe Ellen declared. “I can’t. I never done sech a thing in my life.”

“Ye might ’a’ begun airlier, that’s so,” remarked Anny, always with her gentle smile. “But it’s never too late to mend, ye know.”

At this point another brilliant idea struck Phœbe Ellen.

“Lookee ’ere, I’ve got jes’ the thing !” she cried.

“Well, wot now ?”

“Go over ’n’ tell ’im *I’m* sorry ! Tell ’im I said I acted mean, ’n’ I’m sorry fer it !” Phœbe Ellen was quite jubilant over her ingenuity. “See how quick he’ll come down !”

But Anny understood this only as another evasion of the main issue. She shook her head.

“’Twon’t do, sis, ’twon’t do,” she declared.

“I don’t see why.”

“’Cause ’twon’t sat’sfy ’im.”

“He’s a queer un if *that* won’t sat’sfy ’im ! How d’ ye know ’twon’t ?”

“I seen it in ’is face.”

Phœbe Ellen sniffed.

“Ye must ’a’ been lookin’ at ’im powerful hard to see the like o’ that in his face !”

“Ye seen it there yerself, if ye’ll only stop to think. He won’t take no beatin’ round the bush—ye’ve got to git right down to bizness with *him*. Wot’ud he do with a ’pollygy from me, anyhow ?”

“’Pollygy !” repeated Phœbe Ellen, with a scornful

groan. "I'll never do it 's long 's I have a mouth to screech with or nails to claw—never! How kin I? I don't know how! Ye don't reckon he's gone 'n' sneaked out o' the back door over there jes' to git away from me, do ye? How *kin* I 'pollygize if he's gone afore I had the chance? I b'lieve the man's tuck a hatred o' me from the start, 'n' made up 'is mind afore he seen me 't he'd leave!"

"No—no," soothed Anny, who saw her sister yielding.

"I can't see 'im from 'ere."

"He's somers inside. Go over 'n' see."

"But if he shouldn't be there?"

"Then ye kin come back 'n' no harm done."

"'N' if he was to turn up 'is nose at me?"

"He won't—he won't!"

There was a silence, during which Phœbe Ellen's face grew solemn.

"If he was to turn up his nose at me, I'd never fergive ye fer it, sis—I never could!"

Anny stifled a furtive smile, but said nothing.

"I d'know wot makes me hate to do it so—it's jest a matter o' bizness, arter all."

"Jest a matter o' bizness, that's all," repeated Anny.

"'N' I'm used to bizness—I've allus done it fer you 'n' me both. I'm shore I don't keer wot he thinks o' me."

"'Course not!"

"I ain't no call to want to show off afore 'im, 'n' I wouldn't do it if I had. But oh, sis, wot if he *should* turn up 'is nose?"

"I'll go bail he won't!"

"'N' wot if he shouldn't excep' my pollygy? Sis, I should die!"

The position of the sisters had been momentarily reversed. Phœbe Ellen's strength had become weakness, and Anny's weakness strength.

"He'll except it," declared the latter.

"If he don't, d' ye know wot I'm goin' to do?"

"No. Wot?"

"I'm a-going to lay every bit o' the blame on *you!*"

Anny had expected some dreadful threat, but at this anticlimax she laughed out.

"Well," she assented, "I kin stan' that."

"'N' if he does except—"

"Then ye kin take all the credit to yerself." Anny's pretty smile was visible again.

Phœbe Ellen was too far gone by this time to resent anything short of downright abuse.

"Ye'll go over with me, won't ye, sis?" she pleaded. "I kin never face that man alone!"

"No. Ye kin talk easier if I ain't there."

Phœbe Ellen realized the truth of this, and urged the point no further. She rose slowly.

"I don't see 's they's any use o' kickin' agin wot's boun' to be," was her comment, as she gained her feet. "When the men gits on their high hosses, I don't see who's left in the world to take 'em down but the wimmin. It's only a matter o' bizness, anyway. Wot do I keer wot he thinks o' me?"

And she began to edge her way towards the saloon.

"O' course I won't 'pollygize," was her final declaration, flung over her shoulder for Anny to catch as best she might. "I'll jes' tell 'im I'm sorry I acted mean 'n' won't do it agin. Further 'n that I jes' won't go—so there! 'N' if that don't suit 'im—"

The succeeding words were lost as she dragged herself saloonward. But she was still talking to herself. "Who'd 'a' ever pictered *me* in sech a fix?" she muttered. "Gittin' down on my marrer-bones 'n' crawlin' afore a *man!* Well, they ain't no sense in half doin' it. If I kinder stan' aroun' on the edges o' my dignity he'll never come back. 'N' he's *got* to come back—I want 'im. No, I got to swoller the hull pill—it 'll only taste bitterer to bite it in two. Wot a fool I was to tackle 'im at fust! I might 'a' knowed by the looks o' 'im I couldn't use 'im fer a sidewalk. If I get out o' this scrape, I'll never try to come it over 'im agin !"

Near the door of the saloon she straightened herself.

"Now fer it," she said to herself. "Hull hog or none!"

Another step brought her to the threshold. She leaned over and peered inside.

It was dark in there—so dark that coming in from the glare of the sun she could at first see nothing but shadows within shadows. A noise directed her attention towards the back of the room. A man opened the rear door, letting in a momentary flood of light; it illuminated a scared masculine face with a billy-goat beard, turned wildly in her direction before the door closed, and hid it from view. "That mus' be Pete Hawkins," thought Phœbe Ellen, to whom his existence outside Pinky's description suggested analogies. "Afeer'd o' a woomarn! If Sam Tinker was like that I could soon bring 'im aroun' !"

Her glance wandered peeringly around the little room. It was shabby, fly-blown, unwholesomely odorous. There was an irregular wedge of cheese under a wire-screen box, around which defunct flies lay thick as over-ripe blackberries on the grass in August. Overalls and tin pails were strung together along a rope above the deal counter; there were canned goods, sugar-barrels, cracker-boxes, sombreros, miners' boots, and whiskey-kegs, all mingled together as in the nightmare of an orderly shopkeeper. On the left was a high table which served as bar. Over this the only occupant of the place was leaning, or, rather, sprawling, his chest touching it, both forearms extended along it, his fingers clasped. It was Sam Tinker, and his face was towards her. Evidently he had concluded that her coming was an event not worthy of the attention of his whole body, for he did not move or recognize her in any way except with his eyes.

"Come out a minute, will ye?" she asked, in a tone intended to be only conciliatory, but which was in fact appealing. His face was utterly impassive as he gazed back at her, and she could not imagine what expression it would finally assume. Some sort of insensibility, of course; the big heavy features looked to her excited imagination as if covered with rhinoceros hide. Or would he frown? Or would he laugh? Or would he turn away without answering her? Or would he stare back at her forever with that look of thick-skinned comfort? Lest any one of these dreadful things should happen she supplemented her request by a "Please," which was tremulous in spite of her.

The giant considered during a moment which seemed ages. Then he heaved his shoulders up from the bar, the right one first, adjusted his hat with leisurely self-possession, hitched up his overalls, thrust his thumbs into his belt, and got under motion.

When he reached her side on the door-step he still said nothing, but with the sunlight upon him he looked more sentient and impressive.

"Ye wanted some more talk?" he finally inquired.

"I—I wanted to—to—yes, they was suthin' I wanted to —in fact they was suthin' on my mind," she stammered, twisting her hand into the folds of her gown and kicking at a tuft of yucca which happened to be growing near. There was an embarrassed meekness in her manner which he rightly judged was new to her.

"Well, here I be," he said, smiling slightly at some thought of his own.

The smile reassured her, though she did not understand it.

"I wanted to own up 't I was mean to ye." Her voice was scarcely audible, but it showed that she was suffering to the quick of her sensibilities. "I've had time to think it over, 'n' I know I didn't use ye right, 'n' I'm sorry fer it, 'n' I'll take keer it don't happen agin."

The words were masculine in their simple directness, but the tone gave them a distinct feminine effect.

The smile faded out of the giant's face and he regarded her gravely, as if to make sure of her sincerity. Then he said, just a hint of a smile returning to the corners of his mustache:

"Oh, ye want me to go back?"

"I do!" breathed Phœbe Ellen.

"Well, see 'ere, now," he said, settling himself with ponderous comfort upon one leg. "I'd jes' 's soon go back. Dan wanted me to stay with ye a year, 'n' I promised 'im I would, 'n' we was pards. But I want to tell ye one thing."

Phœbe Ellen's eyes sharpened upon his, eager for concessions.

"I'm willin' to give a 'count o' myself 's long 's I'm in yer pay—only I want the chance. I've got a mouth on me 't kin talk if ye'll give it time, 'n' it kin tell the truth, too, so 't ye kin depend on it. I've got to be treated white —see?"

"I'll treat ye white," Phœbe Ellen promised, humbly.

"Come on, then."

And he swung along ahead of her towards the station.

"The gray cast his shoe 'bout half-way over," he explained to her, as she trudged along in his shadow. "It took time to fix it."

"I orter 'a' ast wot kep' ye," said Phœbe Ellen, still chewing her humble pie.

CHAPTER IV

PINKY and Anny had drawn close together to watch the result of Phœbe Ellen's manœuvring.

"She's got 'im!" cried the depot-man, as the conference in front of the saloon broke up. "She must 'a' come down wonderful to git around 'im so soon. Why, he's grinnin'!"

"I shouldn't wonder if she done it funny," was Anny's way of accounting for that phenomenon.

Phœbe Ellen came bobbing along in Sam's wake, and looking as if she expected to be greeted by shrieks of derision; but there was nothing to hurt her in the way she was met by Pinky and Anny. On the platform the four of them drifted into one of those provisional groups which a disrupted social element forms as by a newly developed centripetal force, and which always have an air of potential rearrangement into more natural and comfortable relations. It is the attempt of society to make believe that nothing has happened contrary to the gregarious instincts which hold it together.

By no effort of her own Phœbe Ellen found herself in Pinky's neighborhood. She looked pale, as if her descent into the Valley of Humiliation had left her exhausted. She talked a little, though with an effort. Pinky devoted himself to her. She had torn her dress near the bottom, and graciously accepted his aid in pinning it up. She made some complimentary remarks about the weather, and Pinky told her this was only a sample of what Colorado could do; she would get the whole piece as time went on. Pinky hardly knew how he liked her best—defeated and deprecating, or confident and aggressive.

Sam busied himself about the horses, after the seemingly purposeless manner of drivers the world over who understand their business. He adjusted a buckle here, a strap there, pulled the mustang's mane into shape, and examined the foot of the gray from which the shoe had been cast on the way over.

By the same subtle law which had brought Pinky and Phœbe Ellen together on the platform, Anny strayed around in Sam's direction. He was bending over the foot of the gray at the moment, and when he rose he faced her unexpectedly. He had not noticed her before, and the pleasure of his surprise made a look of slow dawn in his features. She was very pretty in her brown sun-hat trimmed with red-clover blossoms, and with her blond hair visible in fluffy curls around her forehead. She was greatly like her sister, but her cheeks had more color, her body more curves, her eyes more light. She looked warmer, more approachable. He paused, gazing at the womanly apparition with frank appreciation.

They stood thus for a full moment, she flushed but not deeply embarrassed, he boldly but respectfully admiring. She had approached him with the intention of saying something in condonement of her sister's temper, but his frank enjoyment of the sight of her kept her silent. She was not sure that she was altogether pleased with his direct, satisfied gaze; but certainly she was not offended. She half wished she had not tried to say anything by way of apology; what if he should discover in her blushes the fact that she thought him handsome? Finally he said, patting the gray absently with his big, steady hand:

"Ye mus' be 'er sister, I reckon?"

The pronoun required no antecedent, and Anny nodded.

"Ye look like 'er," resumed Sam, after another leisurely survey of her from head to foot.

"Everybody says so," acknowledged Anny. She was afraid her looks might be disagreeable after his conflict with Phœbe Ellen. But his next words reassured her.

"Everybody's right. Ye look like 'er—with improvements." He began his speech gravely, but finished it with a twinkle.

Anny smiled, still not quite easily.

"Ye'll like 'er better when ye know 'er," she said. "Her bark 's wuss 'n her bite."

Sam shifted his bulk from the left leg to the right, and propped his elbow against the neck of the gray.

"Was it a bark or a bite I got?" he inquired. His smile started in his eyes and ended in the corners of his mustache.

"A little o' both, I reckon. Anyway, I'm glad she brought ye back with 'er."

"So be I—*now*." His eyes put a large meaning into his speech.

She went on somewhat hurriedly:

"I know 'twa'n't fer her sake—nor mine—'t ye come back. Dan wanted ye to look arter us—he writ us afore he died how he'd got ye to promise to have an eye on us fer a year. 'N' I know ye don't have to work out—he told us 'bout that, too. I wanted to tell ye I knowed how things was, so it wouldn't look like I was ongrateful."

Her gravity was reflected in his face and speech as he answered:

"Thankee. I'll do wot I kin. I keerd fer Dan. I was with 'im when he died."

He had removed his elbow from the neck of the gray and was again patting him absently.

"He was buried near the house, wa'n't he?" Anny finally asked, in a low tone.

"Jest a little above, under the pines."

"Pore Dan—pore Dan!"

"He was 's straight a man 's ever put spur to heel,"

said Sam, his tone softening as if not to make a discord with the grief in hers.

"Some day ye mus' tell me all 'bout it." The tremor in her voice showed that the tears were not far behind. Sam was moved, too, not only by the memory of his dead friend, but by a sense of having come unexpectedly into a heritage of large and precious acquaintance with that friend's sister.

"Ye mustn't mind sis's bossy ways," Anny went on, drying her eyes furtively on her handkerchief, and changing a subject which was rapidly becoming too much for both of them. "She's used to doin' 'bout as she likes, 'n' don't know jes' where to draw the line."

"I sha'n't mind now," Sam assured her.

She smiled up at him suddenly as she tucked her handkerchief into her belt.

"Oh, she'll never tackle *you* agin," she said, with a soft little laugh.

By this time Phœbe Ellen had crawled into the back seat of the buckboard, where she was sitting with a chastened look. Pinky was still in attendance.

"What d' ye reckon they're talkin' 'bout?" she asked, in a low tone, jerking her head in the direction of Anny and Sam.

"Dunno."

"Mebbe it's me." Phœbe Ellen sniffed.

"I can't hear," Pinky declared.

"Mebbe he's tellin' 'er all 'bout wot I said over to the s'loon, 'n' they're laffin' over it together."

"That ain't like Sam. He wouldn't do sech a thing."

"It ain't like sis, either," said Phœbe Ellen, with a sigh of relief. "Looks like they're powerful int'rested in each other, though, don't it?"

"Well, why not? Sam's a likely feller."

Phœbe Ellen snorted.

"'S if 'twas a question o' his bein' a likely feller! I

wonder if he's goin' to stan' there all day gossipin' with 'er? It's time we was on the way to the ranch if we want to git there afore midnight."

"Mebbe he's gittin' stuck on 'er!" cackled Pinky.

"Stuck on 'er!" Phœbe Ellen's voice sounded so high and hard that Pinky looked at her in surprise.

"Why not?" he asked, innocently.

But catching his glance, she began to laugh. She laughed quite boisterously, but, though Pinky joined her, he failed entirely to see the point of the joke.

"Shall I see wot they're talkin' 'bout?" he volunteered, when she had sobered down a little.

Phœbe Ellen stopped laughing as suddenly as she had begun.

"'S if it made any differ to *me* what they're talkin' 'bout!" she said, flinging her head back haughtily.

Then she was unaccountably silent. Pinky wondered what there was in his offer to anger her—she had first showed an interest in the conversation of Anny and Sam, and he had intended only to please her. "Wimmin is queer," was the axiom by which he settled the question. "They're nice, though," he supplemented, with his eyes upon Phœbe Ellen.

In fact, she was thoroughly impatient to be gone—it filled her with an unaccountable rage to see how absorbed Sam and Anny had become in each other—but she would have been torn by pincers before asking a favor of that cowboy after the way he had treated her. If he chose to wait till doomsday before starting for the ranch, he might, for all of her. He had mastered her once, and she had no intention of giving him another opportunity.

She kept up a desultory conversation with Pinky—if that cowboy could get so absorbed in talking to Anny, she would show him that Pinky knew how to admire, too!— but it was an effort. She realized with a suppressed fury that Sam had the advantage of her throughout, for his eyes never wandered in her direction, though she often looked to see. At last, however, he came around to the side of the wagon and assisted Anny in.

"He needn't be so mighty keerful o' 'er," whispered Phœbe Ellen to Pinky. "She ain't eggs. She wouldn't bust if she was to slip 'n' take a tumble."

Then she became vociferous in her invitations for Pinky to come over and visit her. One would have thought that she had been hungering and thirsting during a long term of years for his society, and that, having found it, she never could have enough of it. She was *so* glad she had met him ; she couldn't think how she would have put in the long period of waiting at the depot if he hadn't been there to talk to. And couldn't he manage to come over next Sunday ? Couldn't he manage to come over every Sunday ? She would be more at leisure then than on other days, and they could have *such* fun ! But he must be sure to come, Sunday or any day ; she wanted to know him better, he was one of her kind. And—

"Be ye ready ?" inquired Sam Tinker, twitching the lines with one large, impassive hand. For all she could see, he had heard never a word of her gush over Pinky; or if he had, he showed no resentment.

"Oh, ready—yes," replied Phœbe Ellen, resolved to try once more. Then turning to Pinky, "Wa'n't it lucky we had sech a chance to git 'quainted ? I swan, 'pears like I'm tickled mos' to death with bein' belated, bein' that's how we got to know each other. Let's shake han's fer good-luck to a better knowin' o' wot nice folks we be. I reckon I'll have to go to house-cleanin' 'bout 's soon 's I git to the ranch, but ye'll allus be welcome. Come often, 'n' bring yer knittin' !"

"Got mos' through ?" inquired Tinker, glancing back at her with a slow, enigmatic smile. .

The wagon drove off amid Phœbe Ellen's renewed invitations and Pinky's shrill acceptances. "Remember!"

she shouted. "Sundays anyway, 'n' other days when ye kin!" When the widening distance swallowed up her shrieks and his quavers, she contented herself with waving her handkerchief, rising high in her seat that Sam might enjoy the spectacle of her new-born friendship, even though his face was turned the other way.

"Ain't he nice?" she inquired of Anny in a loud voice, when she at last seated herself for good. "I d' know when I've been so took with a man 's wot I be with him. 'N' I allus did like the name o' Dick! It's s' much nicer 'n yer old Bible names!"

At that a slow grin dawned on Sam Tinker's face—she could see it by leaning to the right and peering around his shoulder. The grin widened, and Phœbe Ellen fell to wondering if she had made a fool of herself a second time that day. Following out this thought, she became silent and preoccupied, and at last angry. One can manage to play out his part after a fashion, regardless of the disapproval of the audience; but when one's faith in himself begins to fail, it is time to ring down the curtain and put out the lights.

Anny and Sam, however, found plenty to talk about. She had a hundred questions to ask about the country through which they passed, learned to distinguish the buffalo-grass on which the herds pastured, was properly surprised at the soapy qualities of the yucca root, and became an expert in differentiating mountain sage from sage-brush. She had a pretty, interested way of asking questions which Sam thought charming; and his well-considered answers impressed her as opinions of weight and importance. By-and-by their conversation wandered back to the death of her brother Dan, and Sam described with grave simplicity the burial just above the ranch on the mountain-side. All the cowboys and cowmen of the region—there is a vast difference between what is represented by the terms—had been present, and old

man Halstead had read the burial service. Anny's face
grew very sorrowful as she listened ; it seemed pitiful
that he should die at such a distance from all his kin ;
she would have come at once had she only known ; but
Dan had a horror of what he considered being a burden—
as if she would not have been easier in her mind to her
dying day had she been at his side through it all and min-
istered to him.   She wanted to know if grass and flowers
grew up there where he was buried.   She had brought a
little cinnamon rose-bush on purpose to plant there, and
a white lily bulb, and some seeds ; and when she was told
that they had heaped a great pile of stones above the spot
to keep the coyotes from digging, she sat for several minutes crying softly behind her handkerchief ; and Sam
looked back at her with a pitying comprehension of her
grief, saying simply :

" I keered fer Dan, too."

And in that community of loss both recognized the
growth of a friendship which, though sudden, was likely
to last.

For a little way beyond the spur of the foot-hills from
which they had seen Sam Tinker emerge the road wound
up a desolate cañon, waterless and split into transverse
gulches, among whose rocks even the pines refused to
grow.   There were queer cracks and chasms in this riven
world—tumble-down mountains with their ruins all about
their bases, displaying caverns whose depths only the
eagles had explored, and thrusting forward high flat sur-
faces which had been scooped by the storms into hollows
and troughs.   Finally the road came out upon a summit
which hardly seemed a summit at all, for there were lof-
tier elevations all around, shutting out the distances and
narrowing the horizon to a series of peaks and plateaus
which looked close enough to be touched.   From that
point the highway began to descend and to become less
desolate.   It passed into a stretch of mountain woodland,

where mingled pines and aspens made a cool green light along the ground, and the rocks, also clothed with pines, were brilliantly red and yellow higher up. Huge bowlders had rolled from the cliffs, and here and there formed what seemed impassable barriers ; but by a sudden dodge the road got past and went on winding downward among the trees. A tiny rill of water appeared beside the way. It grew to a noisy stream, edged by willows and alders and bordered by small tracts of hardy grass where the cañon widened and gave meadow-room. Now and then the stream plunged down a precipice with an audible thrill which made one's nerves tingle ; but at a distance the sound became a dreamy monotone, and the wind blowing it down the cañon seemed laden with slumber, as if it had traversed acres of Indian poppy - fields. The cliffs became strangely like castle walls with loop-holes and crenulated towers ; one beheld a natural bridge spanning an arch of blue sky. There were queer likenesses of faces in the profiles of the crags ; monsters, too—a lion's head, the outline of an elephant's back, a sphinx's calm forehead turned heavenward, indifferent to human questioning. There was something dreadful in the narrowness and height of the horizons ; the gulches suggested the beauties and terrors of an unknown world.

Phœbe Ellen sat silent through it all, listening to the conversation between Anny and Sam. She was as completely out of it as if she had not existed. She was conscious of a gradually increasing sense of indignation. Sam Tinker had crushed her, and was gloating over her humiliation. She longed for an opportunity to assert herself, to impress herself upon the moment, so that he would remain in awe of her forever. But occasion was not propitious ; and even had she seen her way to some violent act of self-assertion she would have failed to grasp it, in the assurance that somehow he would get the advantage of her. Only once did her displeasure manifest itself, and that was when he took a pipe and a bag of tobacco from his pocket and prepared to fire up.

"Objeck to smokin'?" he asked, over his shoulder, after he had rammed the tobacco in with his forefinger and packed it with his thumb.

"Not a bit," was Anny's cordial answer.

But at this point Phœbe Ellen's longing to assert herself overcame her discretion, and her pent-up anger exploded.

"Well, *I* do !" she cried. The noisy fierceness of her tone was funny, and she half comprehended its absurdity. "I hate it !"

Sam scratched a match on his overalls and applied it deliberately. Then he took two or three leisurely pulls, and, after making sure of the draught, tightened the reins with a suddenness which brought the horses to their haunches.

"Whoa !" he cried.

"Good land !" cried Anny. "Anything broke? How ye skeered me ! Wot's the matter ?"

He jerked his head towards Phœbe Ellen, who was directly behind him.

"She don't like smokin'," he answered, in a matter-of-fact tone, as he flung an enormous puff in Phœbe Ellen's direction, "'n' I didn't know but wot she'd like to git out 'n' walk the rest o' the way." They remained motionless for two or three minutes in the middle of the road. "Hey ?" he finally asked, half turning, as if to catch Phœbe Ellen's answer.

Her reply came after another moment of silence.

"Ye kin drive along," she said, in a faint voice. "*I* kin stan' it, I reckon. I'm learnin' to stan' anything !"

And as the horses started once more she resolved in her heart more firmly than ever to let Sam Tinker alone as long as his services were necessary on the ranch. But he and Anny went on talking as if nothing had happened. They were getting acquainted with a vengeance. She wondered why Anny didn't climb over on the front seat in order to be closer to him. "They might whisper to each other then," she thought, bitterly.

Down, still down they went among the gulches. Here the foot-hills parted, as if to reveal the awful purple stretches of pines on distant mountain-sides; there the shadows of clouds made gorgeous blue daubs along the red and yellow mesas; close at hand the trees looked like black splashes among the rocks, as if a battle of literary Titans had taken place there, and the ink from broken bottles had not yet dried. The pines and aspens grew thicker and thicker on the uplands; the willows and cottonwoods hid the hurrying water; the rock-maple sent its projectile-like curves throughout the long line at the foot of the cliffs, as if a fairy army were opening its batteries upon the road; clematis twined over tree trunks and low shrubs; sweetbrier sent its cool incense up from shady places.

"This 'ere's suthin' like," said Anny, with a long breath of satisfaction. "Ye kin breathe 'ere. Ye kin look aroun' 'thout feelin' sorry ye ain't somers else."

"It's purtier still to the ranch," Sam assured her.

"Is it fur yit?"

"Only a little ways. Ye turn a rock 'n' come right on it all to wunst—a little above it, 'n' it lays all afore ye, like it was spread out a-purpose to be looked at."

"I know I'll like it," said Anny, with a fervent glance around her.

The road narrowed. One wheel of the wagon was in the current for a little way. A steep scramble down one side of a miniature waterfall, a plunge into the cool green shadows of the cottonwoods, a whirl to the left around a spur of rock, and then—

"Here we be!" cried Sam Tinker.

CHAPTER V

THE valley lay all below them, narrow and irregular and green, beginning as a fall where the rocks split and let the river through, below which a pool whirled its foam and bubbles among conflicting currents, and still farther down expanded into shallows and ripples and noise. Below that the stream uncoiled its silvery length along the green of the lowlands, and was lost to the eye among distant willows before it disappeared from the landscape in the stately curve of the valley which bounded the view on the south. Just now the water was dulled by the afternoon shadows, and the only gleam visible was the white of the shallows here and there among the trees; but had it been earlier in the day the current would have sent forth a flash so sharp as to hurt the eye and oblige it to turn for rest towards the pine-clad ridges and the blue sky.

The stream they had been following took a sudden turn to the left and plunged into the bottoms, where its course to the river could be traced by willows and alders and a tenderer growth of grass. There were mountains on every side, stopping up both ends of the valley and sheltering it as if taking thought of its peace and comfort. The summits took the shapes of towers and walls and domes; pinnacles and Gothic arches and flying buttresses produced the effect of Cyclopean architecture in ruins. There were rows of sculpture, too, set high on the rocks —stately statues of men and women in crudely carved drapery, and busts of Titans defying heaven—moulded by the random chisel of the Storm in those mad moments when he dashes to his work with the floods in one hand and the lightnings in the other.

The sun still took the mountain-tops in flashes of green and gold, and brought the pines on slope and ridge into sharp relief against the sky. The valley was all in shadow, but who can describe the distances made plain by those shades of luminous obscurity which always fill sheltered spaces where the light is dropped down by reflections from the upper air? At the lower end of the long "open" the peaks were only dreams of mountains; the foot-hills on the west were so heavily and softly purple that they seemed to have been woven with a velvet nap; the nearer distances were purple, too, with aerial touches of gray and violet along swell and hollow. The pines made the slopes all soft and feathery, here black, there purple, there green —even yellow where the sunshine still lingered on the heights.

On the bottoms were outlined angular spaces under cultivation. An oat - field thrust its sharp corner to the highest point of the irrigation ditch, clear to the edge of the cliff, and thence stretched to the river in widening lines, a mottled expanse of sensitive gray which seemed to thrill with a nervous ecstasy as the wind passed. The coarse, wholesome green of potato - tops gave utilitarian value to a stretch of black soil near the willows by the river. Farther up-stream, enclosed in a neat brush paling, was a garden-plot whose contents, with the exception of several lusty rows of pea-vines, could not be determined in detail at a distance, but which inspired a joyous confidence that everything good grew there in its season and tasted better for having absorbed the pure air and water of the mountains.

The ranch buildings were placed on a slope well back from the river, and shaded by the hills at morning and evening and by the pines at noon. Their irregularity was in itself picturesque, making them one with the rocks and

trees among which they were scattered. They were built
of logs with adobe chinking, and roofed with slabs and
thatch. There were so many barns, all so low, and lying
at such queer angles with each other, that their builder
might have been some primitive architectural giant, who
in a frolic had played jackstones with them after their
completion. There was a wagon-shed, a hen-park, a pigpen with a princely domain for a rooting-ground by the
river ; there were long rows of stanchions under a thatched
shed ; and several big corrals, built of mighty logs at the
base, and slanting up to top-rails of little saplings, were
visible at irregular distances from the barns. One saw
scattered stacks of hay, straw, and alfalfa, the overflow of
last year's abundance. The home ranch, as the dwelling-
house was called, was long and low like the other buildings, but forever distinguished by a shingle roof and a
veranda. The pines cast an austere shadow about the
place, and just above it a small stream dashed headlong
down the rocks and disappeared in the irrigation ditch
above the oat-field. The entire spot looked clean and
cool, as if the dew had just washed it.

Anny laughed out, drawing in a slow breath, and ex-
haling it with the sound which follows a gasp of pleasure.

"It's lovely !" she cried, with kindled eyes. "Ain't it
lovely, sis ? 'N' it looks like it was well took keer of.
See how tidy 'tis aroun' the straw-stacks! Dan used to
say that was a sure sign o' a keerful rancher. Don't ye
like it a'ready ? It *is* dif'rent from Nebrasky."

Phœbe Ellen set her jaws before answering.

"It 'll do," was all that could be got from her.

"It's the purtiest spot atop o' God's green airth," declared Sam Tinker, as solemnly as if repeating a *Credo*.
"'N' not only that, but they's money in it. 'Tain't developed yit—but jest you wait!" His enthusiasm compelled
him to speak more rapidly than usual, and for greater

convenience he took his pipe from his mouth. "We've allus raised three crops o' oats a year—we let 'em seed theirselves jest afore we cut 'em, 'n' the errygation does the rest. They ain't no sech thing as a failure o' crops—the place is pertected from cold 'n' wind, 'n' we kin turn on the water when we like. Be ye a perfessor?" he asked, suddenly turning to Anny.

"A perfessor?"

"A church member, ye know."

"Oh no," smiled Anny, wondering what was coming next.

"I was goin' to say if ye was, ye'd feel kinder lost out 'ere on the Rio Grande."

"Why?"

"Ye wouldn't have nothin' to pray fer. Our rains never las' more 'n a hour or so in the arternoon, 'n' the groun' 's dry 's ever afore night. 'N' when we want rain we jes go up to the head o' the ditch 'n' turn it on. It's a powerful savin' on a man's pants."

"Oh," Anny laughed. And it was evident that he enjoyed her appreciation of his joke, though he only smiled.

When she had laughed sufficiently she began her questioning anew.

"Where's the herds brother Dan used to write s' much 'bout? I don't see a single steer nowheres aroun' the valley."

"They're scattered all through the hills. They don't hang roun' the ranch much, 'n' we don't want 'em. The ranch is eighteen or twenty mile long, ye know, 'n' broad correspondin'—they have room 'nough 'thout trespassin' on the home ground. They like it better to wander off, 'n' so do we."

"But don't they git lost?"

"It's got a fence round it, the ranch has—it was finished last fall. But they do sometimes wander off."

"The fence gits out of repair? I should think the wires 'ud pull loose."

Sam's pipe had gone out, and he finished it by knocking out the ashes against the wheel, loosening the stem, and restoring the dismembered apparatus to his pocket.

"Sometimes they git cut," he said.

"Cut?" repeated Anny. "But how?"

"The rustlers does it."

"Oh, the cattle-thieves."

Sam nodded.

"'N' if ye ketch 'em?"

"We deckerate the nearest evergreen with 'em."

"Oh," said Anny, with a shudder.

"'Tain't s' common 's 't used to be," Sam hastened to say. Then, with a true Westerner's estimate of the enormity of cattle-stealing, "But it sarves 'em right, damn 'em! It sarves 'em right!"

Anny changed the subject hastily.

"I should think the cattle 'ud freeze out on the hills in the winter."

"Oh, they would if they stayed up on the higher levels. But they's lots o' sheltered places with grass 'n' water. They come into the valley then, too—lower down; 'n' it's allus mod'rate 'ere. That's why we've got the crops fenced in—it don't do to have 'em trampled on, even when they ain't growin'. It's rare we lose any stock by freezin'. Though they 's fool steers the same 's fool humans, 'n' they ain't no tellin' wot sort o' cold weather they'll wander into." Phœbe Ellen tightened her lips as she wondered whether she had better make a personal application of this bit of wisdom. "But they've ketched sight o' us from the home ranch — see?" he went on. "That's Leatherhead wavin' both arms 'n' feet out in front o' the verandy." Sam had taken off his sombrero and was waving it in answering greeting.

Anny laughed softly. She was in a mood to be pleased with everything.

"Leatherhead!" she repeated. "It's mean to call 'im that. O' course it ain't his reel name."

"I d' know wot his reel name is—I never thort to ast. We jes' call 'im that, I d' know why. He'd be a fool if he couldn't cook."

"Mebbe that's why," smiled Anny. "'Pears like we was overlookin' everything, clean on top o' the world." Then with a sudden change in her voice, "'N' Dan's grave—kin we see that from 'ere?"

Sam swept his calm eyes along the valley to the buildings, and there seemed to be peering in among the shadows.

"I kin see jest where myself, but I d' know 's I kin p'int it out. Ye see the big round rock jest a little way up from the nigh corner o' the verandy, with the pines all around it?"

She brought her eyes on a level with his pointing finger.

"Yes—I see."

"'N' the big pine in the middle o' the group?"

"Yes."

"Well, it's right under there." He lowered his hand to his knee, where it rested, ponderous and immobile, palm downward. "Ye can't see the heap o' stones—it's in shadder. It ain't two minutes' walk from the front door. Dan had the place all picked out—he used to go up there 'n' lay down in his blanket fer hours, afore he got so he couldn't leave the house. It's a purty spot, if a body wants to set down 'n' look aroun'. Often when I've got a bit o' harness to mend, or when I want a quiet pipe all by myself, I go up there."

"A gal could take 'er sewin' 'n' stay all the arternoon," said Anny. "I kin jes' think wot 'twould be like."

Sam nodded gravely. And after a little meditative pause she continued:

"It 'll seem like gittin' clost to Dan. I know he'll like it."

Her glance wandered from the pine grove up the road along which they would have to pass. A little in front of them the entire mountain-side looked as if it had been overturned by a plough.

" Ye ain't agoin' to try to raise crops on that hill-side, I hope ?" she inquired. " How'd ye manage to plough it, anyhow ? Kin ye git water up there ?"

Sam moved his big hand from his knee to the seat beside him, gouged his knuckles into the wood, and thus turned so as to face her.

" Oh, that's las' spring's landslide," he said.

Anny was inclined to laugh, but he looked so grave that she sobered up instantly.

" D' ye have 'em every spring ?" she inquired.

" Oftener."

She opened her mouth and eyes simultaneously.

" Every spring, 'n' often atween times. Look down b'low there 'n' see wot a lot o' the mountain 's dumped itself into the valley."

" It mus' be orfle when it's goin'," shivered Anny, peering over the road's edge and down the slope. " Tell me wot it's like."

" 'Tain't like nothin' but jes' wot 'tis—a hull mountain-side 't 's took a notion to go tobogganin'. But it goes —how it goes ! 'N' it don't stop till it's had its fun. Ye see, they's a stretch o' soil 'long there—reel adobe soil, too—'t ain't got no rocks nor trees nor nothin' to hold it in place, 'n' bein' it's purty steep, every wunst in a while it gits up 'n' moves off."

" I shouldn't like to be anigh it when it got under way," remarked Anny, still with her eyes upon the " dump."

" It ain't never done no harm yit," said Sam, " fer no-body hain't happened to be in the way o' it when it got on a tear. The soil mus' be purty deep to keep it up year arter year like it does; but I reckon they ain't s' much peels off 's wot we think."

"If anybody happened to be in the way o' it when it got started," asked Anny, still gazing down the mountain-side, "wot'ud it do ?"

Sam's face grew solemn.

"Bury 'em alive," he answered.

"Bury 'em alive ?" repeated Anny, in a hushed voice.

He nodded gravely.

"So deep, too, 't they couldn't never be found till Jedgment Day. Nobody 'd know where to dig fer 'em."

"What a orfle thing !" murmured the girl.

"Ye see, the road runs right crossways o' it, 'n' that's allus seemed to me sorter like flyin' in the face o' Providence. The jar o' drivin' over it might easy set the hull thing into motion. It never has, I know ; but I've allus made shore it might. If it should start off when a team was passin' — well, the nex' thing seen o' *them* 'ud be when Gabriel got arter 'em with his trumpet 'n' led 'em home to glory. I tole Dan more 'n wunst jest how it looked to me, 'n' he 'lowed I was right, 'n' meant to turn the road higher up—ye see, it could be easy made to run off there to the right, above them rocks. 'N' then they wouldn't be no danger."

"We kin fix it," said Anny, with her deliberative nod.

"Somehow Dan allus found suthin' else to do, with the crops or the live-stock, or suthin'. 'Ye 'll wait too long,' I used to tell 'im. 'Ye'll wait till some un's killed afore ye'll reely see the need o' it.' But I never drive acrosst the place 'thout feelin' thankful when I'm over. 'N' I ain't never been 'cused o' bein' nervous, neither."

They paused a moment for him to point out the various buildings and speak of their uses, and to call attention to one of the ranch dogs which was bounding up the road to meet them ; then he gathered up the reins preparatory to driving on.

"Wait a minute!" cried Anny, suddenly, clutching his sleeve. "I want to git out 'n' walk."

He turned with a look of smiling question.

"How silly!" snapped Phœbe Ellen. "Wot freak's gone 'n' struck ye now ?"

"It ain't but a step," persisted Anny, "'n' all down-hill."

"Oh, 'tain't the distance I objeck to," explained Phœbe Ellen, in a biting tone. "It's the idee. *Wot's* the meanin' o' it ? Flopdoodlin' in 'n' out o' a waggin like they wa'n't nothin' perm'nent nor settled in the world !"

Anny looked abashed but determined.

"Is it silly ? Well, mebbe 'tis. But—I want to go to the house by way o' Dan's grave. The idee come to me all to wunst, 'n' I know he'd like me to kerry it out. The fust thing I do, I'd like to put some flowers on that pile o' stones—it seems sech a dretful thing to be buried under a pile o' stones, sis—" Her voice wavered and broke. Phœbe Ellen made no further objection, and her grim face visibly relaxed as her eyes wandered back from Anny to the pine grove where her brother was buried.

"I'll help ye to 'light," said Sam, his strong features taking an added degree of strength from his approval.

"No, don't mind," Anny replied, and she was out upon the ground before he fairly knew what had happened.

CHAPTER VI

THE wagon rolled down the slope. The dog from the ranch, facetiously named Investigator, came up with wagging tail and lolling tongue, and, after a lusty greeting from Sam, went on to make Anny's acquaintance. Sam looked back once, and saw the two moving soberly along above the road, already on the best of terms and thoroughly approving of each other, as good dogs and good people always do. Anny was gathering Mariposa lilies, and bunching them in her left hand by their long stems.

"Dan liked them posies best o' all," Sam reflected. "Queer 't she should strike 'em fust off to fix up his grave with. 'Pears like she gits at things the right way 'thout bein' told. That's everything in a woomarn!"

He crossed the landslide and went considerably beyond without turning to look at her again. But he had the picture of her in his mind, holding her bouquet a little aloft as she bent to add to it, while Investigator observed her with grave interest, as if it were his affair, too. Imagination was not Sam's strong point, but he had never received a more vivid impression than that of the young girl, stepping lightly upward into the feathery gray of the mountain-sage and seeming to carry sunshine up the hill, though it was all in shadow. Phœbe Ellen rode silently, and he was glad of that. Her mood of sullen patience was better than anything she was capable of in the way of speech.

All at once a whirring sound seemed to pass through the clatter of the wagon—a sort of acoustic blur, something deadening, benumbing—a sort of aerial paralysis. Was it a sound, or only a motion at a distance? It might have been an expansion or contraction of the air itself, a stir through infinite spaces; a hush, maybe, dropped from the serene blue zenith, or rising from unimaginable depths. The horses slackened their speed of their own accord, the mustang laid back his ears and flung out with a startled irregularity. For an instant—which was too long—the world seemed listening, breathless, intent on some horror to be let loose in the wake of this audible hush. And the hush itself—had a meteor crossed the sky unseen? Ordinary sounds made themselves heard—the ripple of the river, persistent, monotonous, horrible; then other sounds, louder and more horrible—the sound of solids straining apart, mysterious flutterings all about, as if the blind forces of Nature were stirring to anger.

"Wot is it?" whispered Phœbe Ellen, vaguely horrified, as one who receives a warning of death.

The solid earth quivered, a dull rumble broke the silence of the hills.

Sam Tinker knew what it all meant. He had been through it before.

"It's the landslide," he answered, with an awful calm.

Phœbe Ellen echoed his word, not understanding it. She was like one who has suddenly become deaf.

"The landslide?"

He nodded.

"It's started," he declared. His features were white, his lips were drawn thin against his teeth. "God A'mighty couldn't stop it now!"

"Wot a queer noise!" said Phœbe Ellen. It was evident that she still did not understand.

But the knowledge of their situation grew into her face in set lines which made her look as if she were screaming. Her first thought was of herself. She had not yet looked back towards her sister.

"But ain't we acrosst it?" she managed to gasp.   Her voice sounded as if a man's hand were at her throat.

"We?   Wot o' that?   But yer sister—"

He had turned in his seat, and was staring behind him with bursting eyes.

"Great God!   Look!"

She cared for what was happening behind her—she realized as the less of two horrors that some dreadful calamity had befallen her sister, but a still more dreadful fate was staring herself and Sam in the face.

"The horses!" she gasped, clutching his arm in her fear.   "They're pitchin' us over the mountain-side!"

Sam had forgotten the team in the horror of watching what was taking place behind him.   He turned, tightening the reins mechanically in a grip of iron.   The horses had dragged the wagon out of the road, and were rearing and plunging.   Another lurch, and they would all be hurled down the mountain-side together.

"Jump!" he cried.   "I kin hold 'em a minute, 'n' then they'll have to take keer o' theirselves.   The mustang's gone clean mad.   Jump!   We mus' go back to Phœbe Ellen!"

She gathered her skirts about her and cleared the wheel at a bound.   And even as she did so, by some dual action of the mind which is as mysterious as it is common, she felt a foolish anger that he should confuse her identity with her sister's—as if she had not given him sufficient reason to know her!   "I didn't reckon he was thick-headed," she had time to think before she touched the ground.   "But he is.   That 'll be a p'int agin 'im if I ever want to come down on 'im heavy."   And then she was standing by the road-side, conscious of nothing but that the world was full of horrors and that the climax had not yet come, and that she had no means of preventing it.

Meanwhile Sam had also leaped out, and, with a dexterous pull—the strength of steel operated by the quickness

of lightning—had got the horses once more into the road;
then he flung the reins over the dashboard, and left the
frightened brutes to rush as madly as they pleased towards
the barn.

All this had taken but a moment—a moment charged
with life and death. Then Sam was dashing full run up
the hill. He had breath and strength enough—Perseus
rushing to the rescue of Andromeda had not more of the
vigor of manhood in him — but it seemed to him that he
was struggling in a nightmare, beating the air vainly
with hands and feet, and panting in the agony of being
unable to move.

The rumbling in the air had grown to a roar—a roar
with potential volumes of sound behind it which might
crack the hills. The noise seemed to strike into the
ground and set it into sympathetic vibration; it was as
if the earth had been stricken with ague and sat shiv-
ering.

Sam's eyes were riveted upon the landslide, and he noticed the noises about him only as an accompaniment of
the horror taking place there. It was all before him—a
foot-hill in motion, a world falling back into chaos. Imagine a mountain-side torn off like a piece of rotten cloth,
and flung down by forces which are at once the preservers
and destroyers of the universe!

As yet there was little dust, and though things were
distinctly visible among the late afternoon shadows, Sam
saw them as if they stood out in the glare of the sun, or
as if they were illuminated by a light within them. The
rocks and trees beyond the moving expanse seemed to be
climbing uphill; there were queer, dizzying effects in
everything, as if the world were drunk and reeling.

Nothing irregular or irruptive disturbed the movement
of the downpouring mass, no tossing of cross-currents, no
upbreaking against obstructions, no heaving where opposing forces met; but a steady downrush, smooth and rapid,

like water pouring over a dam. Its smooth obedience to gravity must have seemed beautiful to Him who created force and gave it its power to upbuild or destroy. Nothing could heighten its speed but the energy which had set it in motion ; nothing could stop it but the same energy opposed in the solid earth on its own level. But with all its leaden compliance with the power which inspired it, it possessed the most resistless fury of all — the fury of inert things when they once get under way.

"She ain't in the wust o' it," thought Sam, still rushing upward. "She must 'a' been 'most acrosst." And, indeed, Anny had nearly passed the dangerous tract when it began to move. She had been caught in the hither edge, and the cataract of loosened soil was bearing her downward not rapidly, but with an uncertain, half-rotary movement, as a straw is whirled along the margin of a brook. The movement was at once confusing and terrifying ; and though slow, it was too strong to permit the three steps crosswise which would have led her to safety. That the swiftest current was beyond her was evident from the fact that she was still standing, though she remained upright with difficulty.

"They's a chance fer 'er," thought Sam, "if the slide makes a curve so 's to fling 'er out on the solid ground. But even then the shock might kill 'er."

Seeing that she would probably be carried below the point he was aiming at, he now shaped his course so as to come up with her lower down. The dust was billowing up the mountain-side as before a strong wind, but as yet the cloud had not reached them, and he could see her struggling to retain her foothold and remaining upright on the whirling ground as by a miracle. At the point towards which he was running there was a sort of eddy in the downstreaming mass, close by a group of mingled rocks and pines. He reached the spot just as she was a few feet above him. "If she passes me I'll fling myself in arter 'er, 'n' we'll both go down together," was his desperate thought.

Suddenly she caught sight of him. If she had called out before, the noise had drowned her voice, but now she flung out her arms towards him and uttered a cry. He heard it ringing out as if above the ruins of the world. Then a swirling eddy seized her. She tottered, struggled, and with her eyes still upon him and her arms extended, she fell, and he could distinguish nothing more; for the cloud of dust at this moment reached them—a breaking surge of neither earth nor air, but both, which blinded and suffocated and destroyed.

Had the broken soil near the rocks poured over and engulfed her—buried her alive? Would he not even be able to guess where she had fallen? If he could but find some trace of her—the hem of her garment, the flutter of a lock of hair, he might dig her out with his hands and restore her yet. He leaped up the few steps remaining between him and the spot where she had disappeared, while the adobe flood went pouring smoothly, thunderously past, until he heard it strike the valley with a crash as if two planets had come together in full career.

Close to the group of rocks Sam found her, lying face upward upon the ground, her arms flung out as if they had been wrenched by violent hands. She had fallen in the direction of the rocks, and the edge of the torrent had dragged her feet downward while a sort of side-ripple had buried her to her waist. Her face was uncovered, and he noticed, in spite of the dust, how white she looked against the moist gray of the upturned ground. She lay quite motionless; her eyes were half open in the glassy, unseeing stare of the dead.

The dog, which had been in advance of her, had come back, and now began to sniff about her clothing. Sam drove him off with a thrill of horror; there was something in the animal's approach that was like an assurance of death. He lifted and dragged the body back among the pines; the dirt fell away from her clothes in dusty flakes. Her weight was nothing to his strength, but he felt it with the dread of one who is alert to one particular kind of fear. Under the pines he bent over her, placing his ear to her heart. He could hear nothing but the blood in his own temples pulsating stormily. He straightened himself, flinging back his head and suppressing a cry in the effort to be calm. He bent again and laid his hand upon her heart, but it was quite still. He listened again, and the blood in his temples seemed to listen too; but there was no sound, no movement. She lay so horribly helpless that it seemed a proof of the worst.

Phœbe Ellen came panting up the hill. He did not see her till her face burst through the cloud which still surrounded them and thrust itself close to his. Even then he did not see her wholly, only the convulsed, peering face in a yellow blur which hid her body. It was like a meeting of lost souls in the nether world.

"She's dead," was his answer to the question her horrified silence asked of him.

CHAPTER VII

PHŒBE ELLEN'S wide eyes passed from Sam's face to her sister's. She was gasping, and it took some time for her to stop enough breath in her throat to make an audible sound.

"I don't b'lieve it!" she finally managed to say. But her voice cracked in the effort of speech, and she had to struggle anew before she could go on. "It's only a faintin'-fit. Lemme see."

She knelt down by the body on the opposite side from Sam and unloosed Anny's dress. Then she bent over, laying her ear close to the heart.

"It don't beat," she whispered, after a moment of strained listening.

"No," he answered, in a dull voice.

"*Is* she dead?" Phœbe Ellen's tone was piteous. She had settled back and was clasping both arms around her knee, while she awaited his answer. But no answer came. He turned away in silence. Was he crying? She could not tell.

Then they found themselves staring at each other across the body, helpless before the fact they could not fully realize. And Phœbe Ellen began to rock herself to and fro in a dreary, rhythmic way, quite meaningless, except as it gave color to this indefinite horror. She did not weep, she did not cry out. It was too soon for that, and probably it was not her way. But presently, as she swayed back and forth, she began to speak, at first brokenly, then with a dreary monotony of utterance whose very incongruity seemed to voice the doom of death.

"How queer, how queer 't she should be dead! How queer 't she should be layin' 'ere with 'er head on my lap 'n' 'er eyes wide open 'n' keep so still when I try to wake 'er up! Why, I've seen folks 't might a-died 'n' I'd never a-thort o' it a second time—I've heerd o' sech, 'n' 'peared like it was the reg'lar thing. But *her*—why, she was that full o' life—ye seen 'er, don't ye 'member how pink 'er cheeks was, 'n' how 'er eyes was allus shinin'? Ye seen 'er, ye know how she looked. It seems so horrid queer. Wot did she git out o' the waggin fer, anyway? Oh, them posies on the hill-side—it was Dan's grave she was thinkin' of. 'N' now we'll have to bury 'er up there 'longside o' 'im, 'n' make the stone-pile big 'nough fer two. 'N' she'd looked forrard so joyful to livin' out 'ere on the Rio Grande. She'd took a notion to the very name —I've heerd 'er say how it sounded like music. 'N' to die jes' 's she gits 'ere—"

Sam had been facing her with folded arms. She saw him dash his big fist across his eyes. "Where's God to let sech things go on?" he cried out. There was more in his words than rebellion against Heaven; it was the cry of a personal loss, the wail of a hope which had perished at its birth. Phœbe Ellen did not try to understand the agony which his voice expressed; she was too busy with her own grief to notice whether the grief of another was greater or less. She had loved Anny in her own hard, masterful way, and her sorrow was genuine.

"She mus' be kerried down," she finally said.

"*Kerried* down!" He repeated the words with the emphasis of torment. But he added, in a lower tone, "Yes, kerried down."

"Kin we manage it—you 'n' me?" she asked.

"Why ain't Leatherhead 'ere?" he demanded, in return. "He could help."

"She mus' be got down somehow," declared Phœbe Ellen. "I kin kerry 'er feet."

Sam lifted the prostrate form, resting the limp head against his shoulder. The staring eyes were close to his face; the tangled hair swept his shoulder. "Pore little gal!" he kept repeating under his breath. Her left arm dangled helplessly. "Lay it over 'er breast," he said to Phœbe Ellen, who obeyed. It seemed to him the dangling movement might hurt her as they descended the hill.

Half-way down they met Leatherhead puffing up-grade to meet them. He had a round, futile face with high cheek-bones and little eyes like buttons that showed the white all around the iris. His ordinary look was one of useless questioning—of helpless surprise, which neither grew nor diminished, neither asked satisfaction nor found it. But now fright put a momentary meaning into his face.

"Tripe!" he began. "She's hurt. Oh, say, *is* she hurt? 'D the lan'slide run over 'er? She looks bad. *Don't* she look bad? Wot if she's croaked? Ye don't reckon she *has* croaked? She *looks* like she had. Oh, Lord! wot if she has? *That* 'ud be a go!"

"She's dead," declared Phœbe Ellen, and Sam nodded in confirmation.

Leatherhead drew down the corners of his mouth far into his chin.

"Oh, tripe!" he began again. That was his inevitable word for joy or sorrow, hope or dread. "Oh, my size! Dead? No! Who'd a-b'lieved it? 'N' all to wunst like that! Great my!"

These exclamatory futilities overcame Sam with a rush of anger. It was an offence to listen to them. Leatherhead made a movement to assist him with his burden, but a glare warned him back.

"I'll 'tend to 'er," said Sam, fiercely. It was as if he were declaring her his in spite of death. And he bore the body alone, Phœbe Ellen struggling along at his side and awkwardly trying to support the dangling feet.

Leatherhead and the dog brought up the rear of the little procession, one about as intelligently sympathetic as the other. Leatherhead began an exclamatory remonstrance and explanation.

"Oh, well, tripe! Wot's the use o' gittin' mad? Wot's the use o' tromplin' all over a feller's collar 'n' dislocatin' his frame jes' 'cause ye want to kerry a dead gal down the mountain-side all by yerself? *I* don't want to tech 'er! Well, I don't keer—go it yer own way; wot's the odds? I ain't done nothin', 'n' I don't mean to. There I was—tripe! ye seen me yerself to the door, a-wavin' 'n' a-waggin'; I'd been lookin' fer a good hour afore ye showed up, 'n' then—there ye was! So I run back to see to supper—say, them trout I ketched a-purpose?—I'd jes' got 'em rolled in flour, 'n' was puttin' 'em onto the griddle when—tripe! there went the lan'slide! I knowed in a minute wot 'twas. I run to the winder full tilt, but I couldn't see things clear. Only the mountain was a-stirrin'—it was a-stirrin', I could see that. But say, in a minute I seen the hosses flyin' down the road? My shape! the way that buckboard struck the barn! But the trunk was in, 'n' nothin' wa'n't busted 't I could see. 'Well,' says I to myself, 'hell's allus up to suthin' in Collyrado!' But 'twouldn't a-made no differ if the hull outfit 'd been smashed. I wouldn't a-seen it. I fergot the trout—they're burnin' up this minute. Tripe! Dead! But which one is she? The one 't owns the ranch?"

Sam shook his head. Leatherhead's drivelling had grated on him at first, but now he was strangely passive.

"No," he answered. "It's the other—Phœbe Ellen."

"Oh, well, if the heiress 's left—" Leatherhead began once more. But no one was listening. Phœbe Ellen had opened her mouth to assert her individuality once for all —it seemed so stupid that Anny should be mistaken for her—but she felt sick and faint, and the idea of explanation was distasteful. "By-'n'-by," she said to herself.

She could not talk just now. Anny was dead—she could think of nothing but that.

She took no notice of the buildings as she approached, nor of the room into which her sister was carried. Leatherhead was standing about on one leg—his ineffectual face with its feeble, surprised eyes seemed staring from every corner—and Sam commanded him to bring some hot water and brandy.

"We mus' try to bring 'er to," Sam said, with something of his old decision. "It may be only a long faint. I've knowed cases where they was brought to their senses arter hours."

Leatherhead looked offended.

"Ye said she was dead!" was his wide-eyed expostulation.

"Git wot I tell ye!" was Sam's savage answer.

And Leatherhead disappeared, gazing back with his look of futile questioning.

The body was laid upon a bed near a window. A dull light came into the room—a twilight which seemed funereal in its sombre grayness. Leatherhead toddled in and out with inadequate bustle, casting wild glances of inquiry at nothing in particular, and bursting into incoherent ejaculations without notice and subsiding without cause. And presently, through a sort of sick blur, Phœbe Ellen saw Sam with a bottle and spoon trying to force some liquid between Anny's teeth.

"Wot is it?" she asked, vaguely. "Wot's happened now? Ain't she dead?"

But he was too busy to answer. He went on trying to pry the set jaws apart, spilling the brandy so that it ran down the girl's chin and into the neck of her dress, but persisting to the uttermost, as was his wont. It was ghastly to hear the spoon rattle against her teeth. Phœbe Ellen rose with a suppressed shriek.

"Wot be ye givin' 'er?" she cried, clutching his arm. "Let 'er be. She's dead. Wot's the use?"

He looked at her in angry surprise, but his eyes became pitiful as he saw how distraught she was.

"We mus' try to do suthin'," he answered, mildly.

She shook her head drearily.

"Wot's the use ?" she repeated.

"We'll be better sat'sfied in our minds arterwards," he said, in reply.

He poured some brandy into a tea-cup and handed it to her.

"Drink it," he commanded. "It 'll rouse ye up. I want ye to take off 'er shoes 'n' stockin's, 'n' put 'er feet into hot water. Then ye kin help by rubbin' 'er wrists 'n' temples."

The strong drink revived her, and the world came back with a rush.

"Yes, yes," she cried, "we mus' do suthin'—we mus' keep on tryin'." She was obeying Sam's commands with eager haste, and already Anny's feet were in the steaming water which Leatherhead had brought. The effort to do something brought her confidence and hope. "Mebbe it's only a bad faint. Lord ! if we could bring 'er round —gimme some brandy in the cup, quick ! I kin rub ! If it's only a matter o' workin' over 'er, we'll fetch 'er to."

They worked like mad, but without result. Sam managed to get some brandy between the clinched teeth, but it was not swallowed.

"Queer," muttered Phœbe Ellen. "She don't git cold. 'D ye notice that ?"

Sam's eyes lighted up with new hope.

"It's true !" he cried, almost jubilantly. "She's 's warm 's when we brung 'er in." He lifted one of the limp hands. There was no sign of vitality in it, but it was warm and flexible.

"Rub harder !" he cried, excitedly. "If she was dead it 'ud show in 'er fingers by this ! Harder, harder !" And he poured in more brandy, while Phœbe Ellen fell to work with renewed energy.

Presently she paused and laid her ear for the hundredth time over the patient's heart. Her cheek touched the soft white flesh, so that she could make sure of detecting any disturbance within.

"Does it beat?" asked Sam, pausing anxiously.

"No, but she's so warm. Ain't she warmer 'n wot she was? She can't be dead. But if she ain't, why don't 'er heart go?"

"Try it ag'in," said Sam.

She listened once more, Sam bending forward, eager and expectant. All at once she lifted a startled face.

"Wot is it?" he asked, breathlessly.

"I d' know—but 'peared like—"

"Like ye heerd it beat?" He took up the word eagerly.

"I'm shore I heerd it—jes' one little faint flutter." Her face was drawn in tense lines, and she was listening again while Sam sat in strained silence, as if his own breathing might interfere with what she was listening for.

"I heerd it!" Phœbe Ellen finally whispered. Her words were half lost in an excited sibilance which sounded hard and dry. "I'm shore I heerd it. Oh, sis, sis!" She pressed her ear closer to Anny's heart. "There—ag'in! Faint—so faint. But she ain't dead—she ain't dead! Now it's goin' quicker—now it's all quiet ag'in. Work— work! We'll bring 'er back yit, I tell ye!"

And they worked as if their own lives depended on the result. The amount of brandy Sam Tinker poured into his patient would have turned a practising physician's eyes to saucers; but his methods, heroic though they were, finally met their reward in a renewal of the life which they might easily have extinguished. There was perceptible a distinct relaxation in the muscles of the jaws, and after Phœbe Ellen had several times reported a distinct revival of the pulsations of the heart and a speedy subsidence in the inactivity, Sam declared with joy that the patient had tried to swallow. And the next teaspoonful really was swallowed, and the next, and the next. The heart-beats became distinct and firm, the half-open eyes closed as if in slumber, and the breath at last came strong and regular.

"'Thank God!" said Sam, standing off and looking down at the patient with shining eyes.

And " Amen !" responded Phœbe Ellen, devoutly.

CHAPTER VIII

JUST here Leatherhead burst into the room.

"I been tryin' to git suthin' out o' the supper 't burnt up, but—well, I don't keer fer myself, but when it comes to the rest o' ye— Tripe! is she comin' to?"

"She's comin' to," assented Sam, with satisfaction.

Leatherhead widened his little eyes till the whites looked as if they were painted.

"My size! She'll want suthin' to eat, too, won't she? I made shore *she* was dead. I swear, I feel like I was no good in life. Well, she'll jest nachelly have to put up with wot she kin ketch, I'll tell 'er that right now!"

Phœbe Ellen's face relaxed. On the whole, she liked Leatherhead. He looked manageable, annexable. Besides, he was genuinely solicitous for her welfare and Anny's.

"Never mind," she said, kindly. "We'll have some bran-new trout to-morrer—they's plenty in the stream. A cup o' tea 's all sis 'll want, 'n' the way I feel now I don't reckon I could take much more."

"I kin give ye cold b'iled ham."

"Ham's good," said Phœbe Ellen.

"'N' I might warm over some green pease 't was left from dinner."

"Ye needn't mind. I ain't hungry. Bring in the tea— I don't feel like I wanted nothin' more—'n' the ham, if ye got it handy."

Leatherhead sighed with satisfaction.

"Ham? Tea? That's soon doctored. Some wimmin 'ud be howlin' fer ice-cream 'n' oyster soup 'n' cowcum'er pickles. But she—!" And with this implied compliment for Phœbe Ellen he left the room.

"I'm afeerd I got orfle upset," Phœbe Ellen remarked. "They was fer a while I didn't know whether I was on my head or my feet—wot with the lan'slide 'n' the hosses 'n' sis a-keelin' over. 'Twa'n't business-like. I'm 'shamed o' it."

"I was upset, too," said Sam, in a low voice, with his eyes on Anny. "But I ain't 'shamed o' it."

"Queer she don't open 'er eyes," said Phœbe Ellen, her glance following his.

"'Pears like 'twas time, don't it?" was his rejoinder.

"Give 'er 'nother nip o' brandy, hadn't ye better?"

Sam complied, but this time the patient rebelled; not consciously, but by a reflex tightening of the lips which showed that the body knew what was best for it, even if the mind did not.

"She breathes perfeckly reg'lar," said Sam.

"Perfeckly," assented Phœbe Ellen.

"But they's suthin' horrid in the way she don't sense nothin'."

"Give 'er time—give 'er time. I wonder if she broke any bones. Have ye looked at 'er head? I hain't."

Sam made a rapid examination. The girl's hair lay in a tangled mass along the pillow. He parted it here and there, touching it gently as if it were a sentient thing; and finally on the right side of the head he discovered a bruise and a slight gash.

"See!" he said, parting the hair flat against the scalp that Phœbe Ellen might have a better look at the injured spot.

"That must have cold bandages on it," she declared.

"Sometimes them things is deeper 'n they look—I've heerd o' a thump like that bein' ser'ous. Is they any way o' tellin'?"

"Not 't I know of."

“ I've heerd o’ the brain bein’ stopped by a sudden jar, like it was a clock, ’n’ not startin’ up ag’in, either, till arter it had been doctored. If it should be anything like that—”

Phœbe Ellen got up on her feet.

“ Cold water won’t do no hurt, nohow,” she declared, with energy. “ Where’s some rags ?”

“ I’ll fetch some,” said Sam.

“ ’N’ some water in a basin. A ole sheet ’ll be jes’ the thing,” she called after him as he reached the door. “ Don’t spile nothin’ new by tearin’ into it !”

While he was gone Leatherhead came in with her supper.

“ Tripe !” was his greeting. “ Say, it looks purty thin, don’t it—tea ’n’ cold ham ’n’ bread-’n’-butter ? Sam’s allus ’cusin’ me o’ not havin’ a lick o’ sense, ’n’ ’fore George ! I’m beginnin’ to b’lieve ’im. Why didn’t I ’tend to my bizness ’n’ look arter the supper stiddier flyin’ up there to stop a lan’slide a hour arter it had struck bottom ? But them trout—one o’ ’em I’d been fishin’ fer down there to a pool all summer. ’N’ to have ’im scorched to cinders like that, right along o’ the others, like he wa’n’t no better ’n they was—say, that’s reel riz bread, though—none o’ yer sallyratus, cowboy truck—I made it myself ! Sam says I beat anything at bread-makin’. But he says I’d make a blame fool o’ myself trailin’ aroun’ on the range with the cattle. But oh ! that’s wot I’d like the best—to be a cowboy, with a lariat ’n’ chaps ’n’ a gun.”

“ ’N’ yer head smashed by a buckin’ bronco,” finished Phœbe Ellen.

“ That’s wot Sam says,” confessed Leatherhead, becoming pensive.

“ I’ll eat the supper by-’n’-by,” said Phœbe Ellen. “ Set it down on the stand by the winder. Wot time is it ?”

“ Eight o’clock.”

“ Good lan’ ! eight o’clock ! I recken ’t mus’ be, though

I hadn't noticed how dark 'twas gittin'. Fetch a light, will ye? I'll drink the tea. It 'll do me good. I hope it's hot."

"Nothin' but a light, then?"

"D' ye use candles?"

"Mos'ly, though we've got one lamp. But the ile 's out."

"Fetch a lot o' candles, then. I may have to set up all night."

"Well, tripe! say, now, see 'ere, that 'minds me!—how is she? My shape! She's better, ain't she?"

"Yes, but she don't sense nothin' yit."

"Great beeswax! She don't sense nothin' yit? Say, she'll git 's bad 's wot I be if she keeps on! Sam says I don't *never* sense nothin'. But I kin make bread—can't I, now? Well, say—tripe! But ain't it kinder funny she don't come to? She's had time."

"It may be funny, but that don't make it none the less ser'ous. She got jammed up agin a rock 'n' her head's bad."

Leatherhead was subject to unaccountable moods of doubt. One of them assailed him now.

"Oh, say!" was its way of expressing itself. "Her head bad? Say!"

She nodded. He popped his eyes at her, and, as if that were not sufficient, thrust his long neck in her direction, too. "Looks like his soul was leavin' his body 'n' startin' fer me," thought Phœbe Ellen.

"My shape!" he murmured. "Her head's bad!" And with a series of surprised ejaculations he left the room.

Sam came in, and together he and Phœbe Ellen prepared and placed the bandages. He was very quick and skilful, considering how big his hands were.

"He kin do anything 't a man orter know how to do," she thought, with admiration. Once or twice his hand touched hers and gave her a sharp, penetrating thrill.

"That's a funny feelin'," she thought, with surprise. "I never felt nothin' like it afore. How queer it'ud be if I was to take one o' his hands in mine 'n' hold it!" But she did not attempt that. What if he should draw it away in anger? What if he should laugh at her? "He's nicer 'n I thort he was, anyway," she concluded, still watching Sam at his task. Then, with a thrill of joyous anticipation, "'N' I'm to live 'ere in the same house with 'im and see 'im every day!"

The patient would take no more brandy, but Sam and Phœbe Ellen rubbed her wrists and temples and applied all the other means of restoration that lay in their power. She reclined among her pillows with her eyes lightly closed, motionless except for the regular, stertorous breathing, and an occasional nervous flutter in the throat.

After a long time Sam spoke.

"I don't like the way she acts," he declared, anxiously. "She breathes all right, she looks all right, but they's suthin' wrong. She's hurt 'way inside. She orter open 'er eyes. I never knowed o' a faintin' fit 't lasted like this."

Phœbe Ellen looked from him to the patient and back again.

"Suthin' *is* wrong," she admitted. "I never seen nothin' like it, neither. 'Pears like she was dead, but kep' on breathin'. They's suthin' horrid 'bout it."

"If it's struck to 'er brain 'n' par'lyzed it—" He stopped suddenly, controlling some strong emotion. Then with an effort, "I've heerd o' sech, though I ain't never seen a case. If that's the trouble, she orter have a doctor."

"A doctor! Is they sech a thing in the kentry?"

"They's a Boston man down to Halstead's—that's four mile b'low. He's queer—Halstead says he's crazy, but I say he's 's sound in his upper story 's I be, though he's got wild ways. He's a reg'lar doctor, though he had to give up his practice 'count o' consumption. He's purty young, but he's powerful smart. We might git him."

Phœbe Ellen considered.

"Mebbe she'd be better if her clo'es was took off, 'n' she was put to bed decent 'n' comf'table. S'pose we try that fust. If that don't do, we'll see 'bout the doctor. 'N' I'll keep the bandages goin'."

Sam left the room, and Phœbe Ellen undressed her sister and got her into bed. But there was no marked change. A little more color grew into the unconscious face, and a more natural look about the mouth and eyes. But the lids did not unclose, and there was no sign of returning consciousness. Still the same regular, mechanical breathing, as if the functions of life had been given over to a machine while the mind slept.

"It's the queerest thing," muttered Phœbe Ellen, hovering about the bed.

"Any signs fer the better?" inquired Sam, entering and approaching. But he immediately answered his own question. "She's got more color, her face don't look so drawn. The color's a good sign 's long 's they ain't too much o' it." He lifted one limp hand and laid his fingers on the pulse. "No fever. Pulse reg'lar. Not too fast nor two slow. Queer! I never seen the like. 'N' she ain't showed no signs o' coming' to?"

Phœbe Ellen shook her head.

"She's kep' jes' so. I've changed the bandages every two-three minutes. They don't git no warmer 'n 's if they'd been on my own head or yourn. I don't onderstan' it. 'Pears like I'd ruther have bad signs 't I knowed how to deal with."

"They can't be no great danger 's long 's the fever don't set in. Kin I look at the bruise wunst more?"

Phœbe Ellen removed the bandage and he examined the wound with critical intentness.

"The cut ain't nothin'," he declared. "She'll git over

that in a few days. The trouble's deeper. The only thing
I kin think of is 't mebbe the skull's cracked 'n' 's press-
in' on the brain. I ain't no doctor—but I d' know wot
else to make o' it."

"That orter be ser'ous," said Phœbe Ellen, after a moment's thought.

"Mighty ser'ous, if I'm right," assented Sam.

"'N' we orter have the doctor right off?"

"I should say so."

"Leatherhead could go fer 'im?"

"Yes; or I could, either."

"Ye've had yer supper?"

"All I want."

"Wot time is it?"

"'Bout 'leven."

"So late? Hadn't we better wait 'n' see wot happens
by mornin'?"

Sam went gravely into his own thoughts for reasons pro
and con.

"Fer her sake, no," he finally decided. "She orter
be looked arter right off if it's 's bad 's I'm beginnin' to
think. These things ortn't to wait."

He had evidently not finished, and she did not inter-
rupt him during a second meditative pause.

"But the doctor," he went on. "I was thinkin' o' him.
He's a sick man, 'n' he goes to bed reg'lar at half-past
eight. If I was to rout 'im out this time o' night, I don't
b'lieve he'd come—I don't b'lieve he could. 'N' I don't
b'lieve he could do nothin' if he did. It ud break 'im all
up—his nerves is bad. Prob'ly he'd have to go to bed
afore he could 'tend to 'er, anyhow."

"Well?"

"I can't see wot harm ud come to her from a few hours'
waitin', considerin' the state she's in. They don't seem
to be nothin' 'larmin' 'bout 'er. She breathes like she
was asleep. If the fever comes up it 'll be time to be

skeerd. We kin watch 'er keerful durin' the night, 'n'
I'll ride over to Halstead's fust off in the mornin'. Hadn't
ye better go 'n' lay down yerself ? Ye look wore out. I
kin 'ten' to 'er."

"We'll look arter 'er together," said Phœbe Ellen.

CHAPTER IX

Sam brought some pillows from the bed in the next room and made Phœbe Ellen comfortable in the hard old wooden rocking-chair where she had been sitting. Then he wrapped her up in a blanket and told her to go to sleep.

"I'll look arter the little un," he said, assuringly.

"'N' if she gits wuss?"

"I'll wake ye, shore."

She watched him dreamily till her eyes began to close.

"He's a nice feller when I ain't tryin' to boss 'im," was her last hazy thought. "A fust-rate feller! I'll never try to put my thumb on top o' 'im agin."

And with that she fell asleep.

She awakened at intervals, and always found him at his post. Sometimes she asked a question or two, but mostly she looked vaguely about, saw that all was well, and silently closed her eyes once more.

So the night wore on. She was more weary than she knew, and often she awakened with a feverish start, gasping a little till she realized the strange room, the prostrate figure on the bed, and Sam Tinker cooling the bandages in the tin basin and replacing them with a deftness which seemed impossible to his big hands.

"Any change?" she once asked, after it had fully come over her where she was.

"No."

"No fever?"

"No."

"Still breathin' reg'lar?"

"Like a clock."

"'N' 'er color 's good ?"

"Jes' the same."

"Ain't ye gittin' tired ?"

"Me ?" The settled solicitude which his long vigil had stamped upon his big kind face gave place to a slow smile which was a sufficient answer.

"Hadn't ye better nap a bit 'n' let me watch ?"

"No ; take yer rest. Ye'll need all yer stren'th fer to-morrer."

She was still agitated by a vague desire for his comfort.

"Why don't ye smoke ?" she asked. "It 'ud rest ye."

"No ; we mus' keep the air pure fer *her*."

"But ye could take a nip o' brandy now 'n' then—"

"I've been a-doin' that," said Sam, his smile dawning once more as he pointed to a bottle and tumbler on the stand.

She would not have believed they could be so kind to each other—or, rather, she would not have believed that they could ever have been unkind to each other. That she should offer to relieve him at his vigil and that he should decline on the ground that she needed rest gave her a good, contented feeling such as she had hardly known since childhood. Didn't she hate him, after all ? Or was she too sleepy to know ? Or had the hate been only a dream ? Or was it only a dream that she was learning to think of him as gentle and kind ? Perhaps he, too, was sorry for what had happened during the day and was trying to make up. She was willing to make up—nay, eager ; she wanted to be good friends. Or perhaps it was his interest in Anny that made him so kind ? No matter. At least, he was good to her now, and in the future there would be time enough for disagreeable contingencies. It was well to sleep and leave everything in such strong, competent hands. Poor Anny! What an entrance upon the inheritance brother Dan had left her! What if she were to die, after all? "She's fit to die—she'd go to heaven," Phœbe Ellen thought. Heaven—yes; but there was the ranch. If Anny were to die the ranch would pass into the hands of the next of kin, of course. "'N' I'm the next o' kin," reflected Phœbe Ellen. Well, wot then? Would Sam Tinker care any more about her if she owned the place? Hardly. He had taken to Anny from the minute he saw her. Phœbe Ellen did not mind that much just now— she was too sleepy. "I wish 't he liked me best," she thought; "but it's his own bizness." But if Anny were to die—and then, as she dozed off, she remembered that he still believed she was Anny. "Then he still thinks I own the ranch," was her last definite thought. "No; he wouldn't think no more o' me if I reely owned it. Shall I tell 'im the truth? I'm so sleepy—I'm shore he'd think I was talkin' in my sleep. They'll be time 'nough in the mornin'." And she fell asleep and dreamed that she had been wandering a weary way though breakneck paths in the mountains, carrying something heavy; and all at once she discovered that it was the ranch Dan had left to Anny, and that she herself was Anny, or people thought so; but she did not explain, and went wandering on, determined to cling to her burden even if the weight of it killed her. "That was a funny dream," she woke up long enough to think. And after that she fell asleep without inquiring how Anny was, though she plainly saw Sam replacing the bandages, and wondered to herself whether there was any change for better or worse.

At five o'clock she was awakened by some unusual noise in the room. She opened her eyes with the impression that some one had been calling, "Anny! Miss Anny!"

"Was ye callin'—*her?*" she asked, in a breathless way, staring up at Sam, who was bending over her.

He smiled faintly.

"I was callin' *you*," he answered.

"Oh!" she murmured, drawing a long breath. "Things sound so queer when a body's jest wakin' up." She flung aside her blanket, but still did not rise. "How is she?"

"No change." He shook his head dubiously.

"Queer," she muttered. Then glancing around, "Is it mornin'?"

"Yes. 'N' I reckon I better be makin' fer the doctor. He'll have to ride slow."

"The doctor? Oh, I 'member." She rubbed her eyes.

"Ye won't be afeerd to stay with 'er?"

She arose hastily.

"Afeerd? No. Wot should I be afeerd of?"

Her tone was resentful. Did he imagine she had committed a crime against her sister that she should fear to be left alone with her? Her dream had not come true, even if he still believed her to be Anny. But a sense of guilt was upon her. It was as if the thought had made the deed.

Sam did not notice the repudiation of fear which she was so deeply conscious of.

"She looks more 'n ever like she done afore she got hurt," he went on. "The same pink in 'er cheeks, 'n' 'er lips open a little. It's orfle to watch 'er like that hour arter hour, knowin' ye can't wake 'er up."

His face looked worn and anxious. She realized that the strain of that night watch must have been considerable even for his strength, and a sense of gratitude made her prompt to relieve him and ready for duty.

"Ye orter a-let me help ye," she said. "It was selfish o' me to sleep so long."

"Oh, I didn't mean that," he hastened to answer. "I was glad to do suthin' fer the pore little thing."

Even this declaration of his real interest had no effect in rousing her jealousy. At least he had been kind to her in being kind to Anny—had intended to be so, in fact. She was content for the present with that. "It's bizness to be sat'fied with wot ye kin git," she thought. "Besides, mebbe I kin git more—arter a while."

"Ye're shore ye're wide awake?" he inquired, examining her with his slow smile.

Her answering look was pleasant and cordial.

"Yes; though I ain't got quite shook out yit. I reckon ye better git started 's soon 's ye kin. Where's the wash-dish? A little cold water on my face 'n' hands 'll soon set me agoin'. I'll go out 'n' git ye some breakfast, if ye'll show me which way the cook-stove is. I reckon they's coffee 'n' ham 'n' eggs—"

"I've had my breakfast—Leatherhead got it fer me; 'n' the hosses is saddled aroun' by the verandy, one fer me 'n' one fer the doctor to ride back on. Leatherhead 'll be in afore long to see wot ye want fer breakfast."

"La! It's like bein' a reel lady," remarked Phœbe Ellen.

"He tole me he was goin' down to the river to see if they was a trout or two 't was sufferin' to be ketched. There! He's comin' back—hear 'im?" She listened, and could distinguish a shrill, unreliable voice above the wailing of the pines, singing "Every day 'll be Sunday by-and-by." "He was orfle cut up 'bout his supper yistiddy," Sam added.

"I'm shore he needn't be." Phœbe Ellen was in a kindly mood this morning and full of acknowledgment. "I'm obleeged to 'im, 'n' to you, too, fer takin' thort o' me."

"Don't mention it," responded Sam, cordially. And with that he was gone.

She heard him mount his horse from the veranda, but the windows of the bedroom all faced in another direction and she could not see. But presently she distinguished him galloping away at the foot of the mountains among the pines. The led-horse had evidently been trained to that service, for he galloped neck and neck with Sam's, keeping loose the strap by which the giant held him.

"Prob'ly he trained it," she thought. "Dan useter write how he broke 'em in, even the wust o' 'em." She followed rider and horses as far as she could among the shadows. "I wonder wot the doctor 'll be like? 'N' wot 'll he have to say 'bout sis?"

She turned back into the room and approached the bed. Anny lay on her back in precisely the position she had occupied ever since respiration recommenced—perfectly passive, without other movement than the regular rise and fall of the chest. The pretty, womanly profile stood out clearly against the pillows, and, though the candle was burning low and the light outside was too feeble to be of much assistance in taking impressions, she could see the long lashes curving back where they seemed to touch the cheek, and two or three little wrinkles about the chin where the head was thrust downward and forward, not quite easily. Phœbe Ellen had often seen her asleep and looking just so when she had awakened early at home in Nebraska and had lain for a few moments idly gazing about before getting up. "She ain't agoin' to die," said she to herself. "She's agoin' to git well." But beneath the thought lay a horrible hope which had somehow fastened itself upon her during the night. "She'll git well," she repeated over and over. But it was the same as if she had said, "She'll die—I hope she'll die!"

The face was unchanged; and what had happened that might have altered it as Phœbe Ellen had half expected? Nothing, to be sure. The accident was nothing, of course; she would be entirely recovered in a few days—a fortnight at most. Was the change in Phœbe Ellen herself? Did she want her sister different, to correspond with a difference in her own soul? She did not stop to think, but kept her eyes riveted upon the pretty, unconscious face. The same flush, as of healthy sleep, the same soft curve of the chin, retreating to the still softer outline of the throat, where the collar of the night-dress hid it; the same egg-like roundness of the cheek, the same faint discolorations under the eyes, the same little curls, pushing, tendril-like, in front of the small ears and softening the meeting of hair and forehead. Phœbe Ellen remembered them all, yet she went over them in detail, as if she had never seen them before.

"She's a purty gal," she thought. "'N' her eyes is purty, too, when they're open. She's got daddy's eyes. Mine's like mother's. They're both dead, daddy 'n' mother. But sis 'n' me 's got their eyes."

She propped her elbow against the headboard, thrust her chin into her hand, and stood gazing down.

"Dan had daddy's eyes, too," her thoughts ran on. "Dan 'n' Anny was alike—that's why he willed the ranch to her 'n' left me out. He allus liked her best, even when we was little uns. He useter give her things, 'n' when I'd ast fer some, he'd say he wouldn't, 'cause he didn't like me. He was allus partial, Dan was. He'd do anything fer *her*. But he allus left me out."

She shifted her position from one foot to the other, but without taking her elbow down or her chin from her hand.

"My temper's like mother's, too. 'N' she wa'n't 's easy 's wot dad was, but she had lots o' vim 'n' go. I wouldn't change—not if I could. Change!" She drew herself up with a mental jerk. "Why should I want to change? I kin manage sis, 'n' even if she owns everything, she'll do jes' wot I tell 'er. I kin run this ranch jes' like I owned it. 'N' so Dan didn't git ahead o' me, arter all. Well, that's all right!"

She stood erect, with her eyes still fastened upon her sister. After a strangely intent examination of the placid features, she said, aloud :

"Yes, she's purty. We look alike—everybody says so. But somehow she's purty 'n' I ain't."

She removed the bandage, rinsed it out in cold water and replaced it.

"*He* thort she was purty—I could tell by the way he looked at 'er. 'N' he made shore I was the devil. Well, that's all right, too !"

Her face was not pleasant as she turned away and went to the window. She looked out absently down the valley, then up at the pine-clad foot-hills. The sun was not yet visible except on the eastern heights and along the farther side of the valley. Here and there, too, a transverse bar of light lay flat and shining across the bottoms where a gulch or pass faced the hidden sun ; elsewhere the lowlands lay in shadow—such cool, green shadows, so restful, so chaste, looking as if the dew clung to them, and might be brushed off by a stray breeze or the wing of a passing bird. Some scattered clouds swung mistily about the summits, billowing lightly as the wind touched them, but settling back as if too lazy either to sink or rise. The pines looked black and flat — as if the trees themselves had disappeared and their vertical shadows had grown into their place. The only sound was the noise of the river and the faint, harp-like symphony of the pines.

So fast the sun rose that Phœbe Ellen could almost see the zone of light widen down the eastern slopes. The ground was uneven up there, and as the light appeared the shadows of rocks and trees lay in a black tangle, and to follow them in detail made one half believe that the sun was shining from all directions at once. Phœbe Ellen opened her window and leaned out. The fragrance of mountain-sage with the dew upon it rushed into her face, wholesome and pungent and good to smell.

6

She drew in a long breath. "It 'll make me hungry," she thought. "I want to be hungry—I want to eat well 'n' be strong, so 't I kin keep my wits about me. Queer things is goin' to happen. I feel it in my bones. I'll need to have my wits about me."

Two or three cowboys who had evidently slept in one of the barns strolled with yawns and eye-rubbings in the direction of the kitchen.

"Leatherhead 's gittin' breakfast fer 'em," she thought. "It mus' be 'bout ready." And at that moment the cook's voice rose in song:

> " 'Oh, dig my grave both wide and deep,
> Wide and deep !
> Place tombstones at my head and feet,
> Head and feet !
> And on my breast carve a turtle-dove,
> To signify I died of love !' "

"Died o' love !" thought Phœbe Ellen, scornfully. Then, suddenly directing her attention outside the window once more:

"This is a purty place," she mused. "I like it—it's a heap better 'n I'm used to. *He* likes it, too. He wouldn't like me no more 'n he does, though, if I owned it. No; fer he thort I owned it—he thinks so still. Well, he don't keer fer me, 'n' he does fer sis—that's how 'tis. He was nice to me las' night 'n' this mornin', though. I have a idee he likes a soft, gentle temper in a gal. Could I ever turn soft 'n' gentle, I wonder ? Wot rot !" She shook herself as if to cast aside the thought. "This ain't bizness !" She drew back into the room, leaving the window open. Her eyes fell upon her sister. "Everything 's come her way," her thoughts ran on. "She's purty, she's rich, *he* keers fer 'er. Well, wot's the differ ? I've got all the brains 't was put into the fambly, 'n' I'll know how to use 'em, too, when the time comes !"

And she went back to the bed and changed the bandages once more.

Some one knocked.

"Come in!" she called, and Leatherhead's surprised face appeared at the door.

"Mornin'," was his greeting. His little round eyes sought the bed anxiously. "I made shore I wouldn't fergit my manners *this* time, so — tripe! ain't she no better?"

"Jes' the same," was Phœbe Ellen's answer.

"Great my!" he murmured, in feeble surprise. "I reckoned she'd be up 'n' all over the ranch this mornin'. Wot d' ye reckon's struck 'er?"

"Sam's gone fer the doctor. *He'll* know."

"Oh yes—well, o' course; though I wouldn't let that doctor look arter *me* agin, I kin tell ye that! Suthin' was wrong with my stummick two or three weeks ago, 'n' say! the way his med'cine went a-cavortin' aroun' in there!— well! I never was s'prised so deep down. But, my size! say, how long ye been up?"

"'Bout a hour."

"Well, tripe! if I'd 'a' knowed that I'd 'a' had yer breakfas' fer ye long afore this. A hour! Why didn't ye call me? A hour! 'Ll ye have it fetched in 'ere? 'D ye eat wot I fetched to ye las' night?"

"Ye kin see." Phœbe Ellen swept her hand in the direction of the demolished lunch.

"Well, say, now, jes' 'tween you 'n' I, how'd ye like the bread? Sam says I'm too big a fool to go out on the range, but he owns up I kin make bread. My ole dad useter say 't God sends the vittles 'n' the devil sends the cooks; but I want to tell ye 't God sends 'em both on this ranch—see?"

"I'll be out in a minute," said Phœbe Ellen. "'S it ready?"

He nodded, bulging his little eyes. "D' ye dare to

leave *her?*" He jerked his thumb in the direction of the bed.

"Oh no; I couldn't leave 'er, o' course. I reckoned ye might stay with 'er yerself. Ye wouldn't have to do nothin' but change the bandages wunst or twicet."

Leatherhead's jaw fell and a slow palor overspread his features.

"Me? Tripe! Change bandages? Sufferin' Moses! On a gal? That's where I draw the line! Bandages on a gal? Ye'll take yer breakfas' 'ere!"

And he disappeared behind a slam of the door.

He was back in a moment, bearing Phœbe Ellen's breakfast on a kneading-board for a tray, and after depositing it on the stand by the window he stood off and contemplated her in an agitated way.

"There! Tripe! I ain't mad nor nothin'—I don't want no spikes to chaw. But lookee 'ere, I swear to gum I couldn't change them bandages—I *couldn't*, ye know! If it was a man—well, that 'ud be all right. But a gal! I'm willin' to do wot I'm told, but tripe! in this country a feller's got to draw the line."

"Oh, never mind," said Phœbe Ellen, who was in a good-humor—and hungry. It was as if a guilty thought had determined her to do at least a superficial kindness. "Well, wot a trout this is, to be shore! This is suthin' like livin'. D' ye like to cook? I should think ye would, ye do it s' well." Leatherhead still lingered, and she could think of nothing but the breakfast to talk about.

"Like it? No. But I reckon it's better 'n nothin'. I'd a heap ruther be out on the range with the boys, racin' up the foot-hills lickety-split with a buckin' bronco under me 'n' a snortin' steer to the front. Say, that's life! But every time I mention it Sam sets down on me with a loud smile all over his face. I don't keer! The time 'll come yit. 'N' say! Don't say a word 'bout it to a livin' soul— but I've got a sombrero 'n' a cuert 'n' a lasso all stowed away in the loft over the kitchen; 'n' all I lack 's some shaps 'n' a gun—'n' won't I s'prise the nation? Oh no! They'll jes' say it's a or'nary every-day matter—mebbe they will! But o' course I was got fer a cook, 'n' they've allus done the square by me—Dan and Sam both—though Sam *does* sometimes act like he had the hull world by the tail. Well, tripe! Folks has dif'rent ways—that's how 'tis."

"These 'ere sody biscuit," remarked Phœbe Ellen, "is fit fer the Gov'nor of Nebrasky; I'll say that fer 'em. Ye'll have to show me how ye do it. They're better 'n *I* kin make."

"Tripe! D' ye mean it? Say! I'll show ye joyful. It's the way I put the short'nin' in—that's wot 'tis. When d' ye want to try?"

"When sis gits better, so 't I have time. 'N' then I mean to do the cookin' myself. 'N' that 'll let ye out on the range."

Leatherhead really turned pale with joy for a moment. Then his face fell.

"Oh, say!" he objected. "It's Irish to give a feller the Josh like that!"

"No Joshin'," declared Phœbe Ellen, opening another biscuit. She could not have told why she wanted to be kind to Leatherhead. Perhaps a sense of inward guilt made her long for outward approval.

"Tripe!" began the roustabout, flinging his arms and feet about in noisy ecstasy. "Sam says I couldn't ride a saw-hoss, he does; but say! when I git my shaps 'n' sombrero on, if I don't show 'im! But it's a sure thing— hey? My shape! Well, see 'ere! If ye let me out on the range—"

"I hear hosses," interrupted Phœbe Ellen.

Leatherhead listened.

"So d' I, 'n' I bet that 'ere consumptive doctor 'll feel faint arter poundin' the saddle with that skeleton o' his'n all the way from Halstead's. Say, I can't stay 'n' look on while he 'xamines 'er!   But ye'll keep yer word 'bout the cookin' jes' the same, won't ye?   I hate to see a doctor pawin' over a patient; 'n' a gal, too—that's where ye have me queer.   But 'twon't make no dif'rence with the cookin', hey?"

Phœbe Ellen assured him that his presence at the examination was unnecessary.

"Mebbe the doctor 'ud like a cup o' coffee," she suggested.

"Tripe!   That's so," was Leatherhead's way of assenting.   And he banged out of the room.

CHAPTER X

PHŒBE ELLEN waited at the window, looking away absently at the pines. They stood stiffly out against the uneven slope of the mountain, and caught sharp gray highlights along the upper side of their branches where the needles reached up in prickly irregularity. Here and there gorgeous vetches shook out their barbarous colors in the sunshine and the yucca lifted its slender pyramid of waxen bells. The river wound away in the distance, sending a silvery flash from among its willows. The familiar sounds about the barns came as if from a distance; the roosters might have been crowing from the mountain-tops; the lowing of a heifer might have come from beyond the horizon.

"It's beautiful," she thought, her eyes following the river and the foot-hills. Then, after a moment, " But it b'longs to *her*."

She tapped her foot impatiently on the bare floor.

" O' course I'll run it—*she* never could. But it 'll *b'long* to 'er."

She turned to the bed with an unconscious scowl.

" Everything b'longs to 'er. Why does the idee haunt me so ?"

She took a turn up and down the room.

" Even *he* b'longs to 'er. That's plain 'nough to be seen. The way he looks at 'er, the way he hangs over 'er, the way he touches her hair when he changes the bandages—it ain't a thing 't kin be mistook. 'N' I—well, if they was to marry, where'd I be ? I wouldn't even be 'lowed to run the ranch. It ud be handed over to *him*."

She approached the bed, and gazed down at its occupant.

"If she was to die—"

She steadied herself against the head-board, and gazed deliberately.

"If she was to die—"

She had uttered the words aloud, and found herself clapping her hands to her mouth and staring about with guilty fear. But no one was visible—no one had heard. Then her thoughts began to justify themselves in a frantic mental protest.

"They ain't no sin in the idee o' 'er dyin'. I made shore yistiddy 't she was dead—so 'd everybody. 'Tain't no sin to think o' 'er bein' dead. 'N' it ud be better fer me if she *was* dead—it would, it would! I've got a right to think o' that. Fer then the ranch ud be mine—the ranch 'n' everything on it — the cattle 'n' crops 'n' the management. Nothin' could alter that. Whether Sam Tinker got so he keered fer me or not, nothin' could alter that."

She clasped her hands at arm's-length, then wrenched them apart.

"If we hadn't fussed over 'er so long—if she'd 'a' died—if I'd 'a' let 'er die stiddier workin' over 'er like I done, 'n' urgin' Sam to work, too—I'd be the owner o' the Thompson ranch this mornin', stiddier stan'in' 'ere with the prospeck o' playin' second fiddle all my days!"

Her features tightened and paled, her lips flattened against her teeth in unconscious expression of a wicked longing.

Then a dreadful possibility came into her mind. "I could kill her," she thought. But she thrust the idea back so quickly that it almost seemed as if it never had occurred to her.

"I won't—I won't think o' it!" her soul cried out in terror. "I don't want nothin' on earth bad 'nough to pay that price fer it ! I'd sooner have nothin' all the days o' my life 'n do sech a thing !"

She went back to the window, and stood there pressing her cheek against the casing.

"But it could be done." The thought finished itself as inevitably as she finished her breath after drawing it in. "'N' nobody 'd ever know."

She wrenched herself back into her ordinary course of thought as one wrenches himself awake from a nightmare.

"It takes that doctor a long time to finish a cup o' coffee." She uttered the words aloud, the more effectually to divert her mind from its horrid vagaries. "But mebbe he took a biscuit, too. 'N' a trout. I wonder if Leatherhead ketched more 'n one trout. Mine was powerful good—I hope if the doctor's got one it's 's good 's wot mine was."

She busied herself feverishly with irrelevant details of her imagination lest she should look guilty when Sam and the stranger came in.

"I reckon he's a thin man. I wonder why I reckon he's thin. Oh yes, I 'member—he's a consumptive, 'n' consumptives is allus thin. Like 's not he's got sharp eyes. I hate little sharp eyes 't pry into everything. He'll jes' look at sis, though—he won't take no notice o' me. Why should he ? I ain't done nothin' to be 'cused of. She's his patient—he ain't got nothin' to do with me. But if Sam was to interduce me as the heiress, he'd look at me then, shore ; 'n' I couldn't 'splain it here—it ud look like I'd been deceivin'. 'N' I hain't." The assurance was genuine, and she seized upon it with an eagerness which was almost fierce. "I hain't tried to cheat nobody 'bout who I be. Somehow they got it wrong from the start—Pinky, 'n' Sam, 'n' all o' em—'n' I hain't had no chance to set it right. That ain't my fault. But I couldn't 'splain afore the doctor. 'N' wot ud Sam think if

I kep' still 'n' 'splained arterwards? Oh, I reckon I could git out o' it somehow. I might say I hadn't noticed—but that ud be rather thin. Or the truth—why wouldn't the truth do better? It ud sound more sensible." She stiffened herself, pushing away from the wall. "If she was to die—"

Still that dreadful, recurring thought!

"If she was to die, 'twouldn't make no differ, one way or the other. It ud let me out o' 'splainin' entirely, fer I could pass off fer her, 'n' nobody ud know. Ud I dare to do it? Dare! Where's the danger? Everybody 'ere thinks I'm my sister, 'n' who's to tell 'em dif'rent? Pinky thinks so, 'n' Sam, 'n' all o' em. 'N' I hain't no brother nor sister to show up 'n' expose me. 'N' nobody from Nebrasky 'll ever git 's fur from home 's this. It ud save a heap o' lawin' jes' to call myself Annie, too." Phœbe Ellen had the superstitious dread of an ignorant woman for the law. "I'm the next o' kin, anyway. It ud only be steppin' into my own afore the lawyers said I might. 'N' it ud save expenses. The lawyers ud take the hull thing, like 's not, if I waited fer my rights to come through them—they would if they could. 'N' mebbe the law in this State 's queer. Mebbe Cousin Susan ud come in fer a share, 'n' Uncle Parker. If sis was to die—"

She flung up her hands with a movement either of resentment towards her sister or horror towards herself.

"If she was to die, that ud settle the hull bizness ferever!"

She started guiltily as steps were heard on the uncarpeted floor of the next room.

"They're comin'!" she whispered to herself. "If she was to die nat'ral, it ud be better." She caught a glimpse of her face in a little square mirror on the wall, and it was with difficulty that she kept from crying out. Her cheeks were flushed, her eyes were gleaming. Her features were drawn in hard, wicked lines. "Good God!" she thought, with horror. "Be I a-murderin' my own sister in my mind? Wot's come over me all to wunst? Is it the devil?" She deliberately faced the image in the glass. "The doctor 'll know whether she's goin' to live or die," she concluded, the lines in her face hardening still more.

She turned away in haste and began to work about the bed, arranging the covering feverishly and beating the pillows into softness about the helpless head. The door opened and Sam came in. She faced him, flushed with her guilty thoughts.

"He don't notice," she pondered, thankfully.

His eyes had sought the bed with unconcealed anxiety.

"How is she?" he asked. And she answered, in a voice more steady than his:

"No change. Everything jes' the same."

In the doorway beyond Sam appeared a man of not more than twenty-eight, thin, of medium height, with heavy, straight black hair parted near the middle of his forehead and forming a sort of thatch about the temples. His nose was long and slightly hooked; one could not help noticing the thin, sensitive nostrils, which expanded with every inhalation as if the lungs worked with difficulty. There was a pronounced stoop in the shoulders, and the chest looked sunken and inadequate. His appearance was that of a hopeless invalid, every nerve of whose body was on the strain, and might be set quivering at a word or look.

"This 'ere 's Dr. Sedgwick," said Sam. "Dr. Sedgwick, this is Miss Thompson." Sam moved his big hands awkwardly, as if to point them out to each other. He was never at ease in any sort of formality.

The flush died out of Phœbe Ellen's face, and she made her bow in due form. Miss Thompson might mean either herself or Anny; so nothing of a compromising nature had transpired as yet.

"I'm turble anxious 'bout my sister," she began, more

volubly than was necessary. She found herself pulling at the corner of her apron, and dropped it hastily. This doctor had the most remarkable eyes! "I reckon Sam's told ye all 'bout 'er," she went on. "The accident, I mean." Why did he look at her so closely? She folded her arms at her wrists, and held them close lest her inward trembling should become visible. When she spoke again her voice sounded steady enough to her own ears, but it was pitched high. "She's been jes' like this ever sence we got 'er breath agoin'. 'N' sech a time 's we had —we made shore she was dead. 'N' when she begun to swoller the brandy—oh, but wasn't we thankful? But this—to stay like this s' long, it seems powerful queer!"

The doctor passed his eyes rapidly over the patient, laid his hand on her temple—such a thin, helpless, stealthy hand!—then felt her pulse.

"You won't mind my sitting down, I hope?" he inquired, looking back at Phœbe Ellen. "I'm short of breath, and not at all strong."

Sam hastened to bring a chair, and placed it at the head of the bed. The doctor seated himself without removing his eyes from Phœbe Ellen's face, and still retaining the hand of the patient in his.

"It is a sad home-coming for you, Miss Thompson," he said, in a voice whose huskiness seemed to originate in the lungs.

"I was dretful scared," Phœbe Ellen managed to say.

"Such an accident at such a time was particularly trying," he went on, between short, audible breaths. "And not to be able to do anything—you must have felt it keenly." The words were simple enough—rather inane, in fact—but his eyes charged them with a mysterious meaning.

"We done the best we knowed how," Phœbe Ellen articulated. She was clutching her wrists with both hands till the nails ached.

"I can understand the extent of your suffering," he said. Did he speak ironically? She felt the flush come back and burn hotly in her cheeks and brows.

"It's a dretful home-comin', as ye say," she stammered, unable to meet his eyes and lowering her own to his shirt-front. "What shall I do—what shall I do?" she began to repeat to herself, hysterically.

"She has always been well?" continued the doctor, holding Anny's wrist. The words were commonplace enough, but the look and tone which accompanied them seemed to take cognizance of all the wickedness her thoughts had revealed to her that morning.

"Yes," she answered. Why didn't Sam say something to help her? Or didn't he notice?

"Never ill in her life?"

"Never."

She felt her orbits narrowing before his as before a growing flame. She had never seen such eyes before—or was it that her own conscience exaggerated everything? Conscience! She had never before experienced anything like this. Besides, she had not done anything. She had *thought* wrong things, but what of that? One can't always be master of his thoughts. She had done nothing out of the way. The deed—which she could not think of as but an echo of the thought—had not yet been committed and never would be.

The doctor, still riveting his eyes upon her as if he were reading the hidden characters of her soul, passed his hand lightly up the patient's arm. The movement reminded her of the soft, tentative efforts of a cat to pick its way among wet grasses. She watched, fascinated, still unable to brave him by a direct look. The slim, stealthy hand reached Anny's shoulder; then the sensitive fingers moved up the neck, past the ear, touching the hair lightly on the way till they reached the bandage, and, as if guided by a vision of their own, began rapidly to undo the cloth. There was something horrible in it all—Phœbe Ellen could have screamed.

"Sha'n't I help ye?" she managed to gasp. "It ain't fixed on tight!"

"Don't trouble yourself," he answered, with a singular smile. "I can find my way."

Would he succeed in reading that dreadful thought which had come into her head this morning? She could feel a luminous shaft from his eyes slanting across the darkened recesses of her brain, and revealing — what? "He'll find it—he'll find it!" she thought, with horror. "Oh, what shall I do?"

His presence was becoming unbearable. She had sunk into a chair, but now she rose to her feet, pale as a ghost. He did not seem to notice anything unusual in her face or manner.

"You are the owner of one of the richest ranches in the State, Miss Thompson," he said. The husky, insinuating tones made the simple statement an accusation. She propped herself against the wall, half turning away, and feeling faint and sick from very helplessness. Sam had told him that she was the heiress, then; or, worse still, had he read the truth in the depths of her soul and was he trying to torture her? She opened her mouth to assert her true individuality once for all, but before she could utter a word the dreadful voice went on:

"One of the richest and loveliest ranches in Colorado. You are to be congratulated! If I were to have my choice among all the cattle ranges I have seen in the State, I should certainly give this the preference."

By this time his bloodless fingers had found the injured spot on Anny's head, and he was manipulating it gently, with his eyes still riveted to Phœbe Ellen's.

"Is they any inflammation?" Sam inquired.

The inquiry came as a godsend to Phœbe Ellen. In another moment she would have cried out and confessed everything. But at the sound of Sam's voice the doctor shifted his gaze to the patient, and she had a moment in which to recover.

"No," was his answer, delivered after a pause, during which his eyes and fingers were working in unison.

"I made shore they wa'n't," said Sam, with a breath of relief, "or I'd 'a' been arter ye las' night."

Phœbe Ellen felt her strength returning. If he had found her out, at least there was to be no exposure at present. The tension of her mind being thus suddenly relaxed, she was left gasping. She felt as if she must go away out of that man's sight, if only for a moment. The strain of utter helplessness made her weak and tremulous. She could never fully recover in his presence.

"If ye don't need me, I reckon I better go out fer a little," she said. "I—I feel sorter faint. 'N' I feel like I couldn't stan' it to see the 'samination go on. If ye need me, I'll come back."

And she fled from the room as if followed by missiles. That man! Was he the Evil One?

"Somehow he's the master o' me," she thought, closing the door harshly and hanging to the knob as if she expected to feel him wrenching it from her grasp on the other side. "Does he know? He *can't* know!"

"She's nervous," she heard Sam saying in explanation to the doctor. "I made shore she wa'n't the kind to git so knocked out. She don't look it."

"No?" the doctor's thin voice questioned, vaguely.

"Ye orter 'a' seen 'er las' night. She stood up to it like a barn door, she did. Nothin' fazed 'er. She looked like she was ekal to anything."

"She seems to me to be keyed rather high," remarked the doctor. "You never can tell what these high-strung women will do when brought to the pinch."

The words seemed to carry with them a knowledge of

her guilty plans and hopes. Did he know that she was listening, and did he intend that she should hear?

"He'll git the truth out o' me yit, if he hain't already," was her last agonized thought as she turned from the door. "''N' then he'll tell it to Sam 'n' everybody!"

CHAPTER XI

SHE sped noiselessly across the room and out upon the veranda. The wind refreshed her, blowing in aromatic gusts from the piny heights all about. She opened her mouth the better to inhale it; she turned her face towards it, to feel its touch more definitely cool on cheek and forehead. She shivered as a thrill of reviving strength passed through her—an ecstatic shiver, which somehow assured her of herself. Half a dozen chipmunks were visible, some peering out from their hiding-places with shy, wild eyes, others staring with a saucy challenge of her right to pass. One chattered a shrill protest as she moved in his direction, but scurried off under the shadow of his violently agitated tail as she gave no sign of heeding his objection; another leaped headlong down a group of rocks as if to show her the superiority of squirrel athletics over those of men; another stood immobile on his hindlegs, with his forefeet crossed devoutly, and his queer, bright face half bowed. Phœbe Ellen went down the veranda steps and the animals scattered in all directions, but paused at a little distance to peer out at her from their hiding-places among the rocks and question her intentions with sharp, impotent barkings. She went up the hill a little way, over a carpet of pine-needles, which felt soft and elastic, and yielded a pleasant perfume of its own under her tread. The soft gray of the mountain-sage was all dewy; can you imagine what a mist would be like, stuck thick with pendent diamonds? That would pass for mountain-sage with the dew on it, but would seem a feeble substitute to one who is acquainted with the real thing. Where the pines were sparse and the sun fell warm, purple penstemons brightened the slope; and the Mariposa lily—which God must love especially, it is so beautiful—looked as if it had been dropped from above instead of having pushed its way up through the hard, dry soil.

Usually Phœbe Ellen noticed little of these things, but this morning it was inevitable that something of the peace and beauty of the world should steal into her heart by contrast with her recent agitation, and bring it in a measure into harmony with the tender stoicism of her surroundings. It was as if the flowers and trees said, "The world is beautiful; there is no place for ugliness in the good, bright world." The birds uttered optimistic noises; the water seemed to take nothing into account but the joy of its own movement and music. She did not understand it, but she grew calm; and to natures like hers a return of calmness means a return of self-assurance.

"Wot a fool I was!" she thought. "I wonder wot got a hold o' me, anyhow? Was I afeerd o' 'im? Bah! I could face the devil if I had bizness with 'im—I've allus prided myself o' that; 'n' to throw up the sponge at sight o' a little consumptive doctor from Boston! It was queer, though, the way he looked at me. But, la! the way I took it wa'n't bizness-like nohow. They ain't nothin' in life but bizness—wot's the use o' makin' out he was tryin' to read wot was goin' on inside o' me? It was his way o' findin' out wot was the matter o' sis—he was 'tendin' to his bizness a heap-sight better 'n I was. But I'll show 'im when I go back 't I kin 'tend to bizness, too. I was nervous—think o' me bein' nervous! But he didn't s'pect nothin'. How could he? I've heerd o' folks bein' hypnoozed, but I don't take no stock in it—they ain't no sech thing; but if he's tryin' it on — well, I'll show 'im! 'N' if he did read wot I was thinkin' of, how could he prove it? Oh, Lord, yes, I was wrong to think o' the dreadful thing I did — killin' yer own sister ain't good sense—it ain't bizness-like, fer ye're likely to git ketched at it; but that's over." She shuddered slightly. "I'll never go back to that, I'll never think o' it agin. I must 'a' been crazy to cal'late on that way o' gittin' the ranch into my han's. But if they was some other way—if she was to die a nat'ral death, 'n' I don't see why she shouldn't, bein' how she hangs on so 'thout eatin' or drinkin' or comin' to 'erself—then the hull bizness 'ud be mine, 'n' no harm done to nobody 'n' lots o' good to myself. 'N' wot 'ud be the differ if I'd let 'em keep right on callin' me Anny? None, fer I'm the next o' kin; 'n' I know she ain't made no will, so I orter have the proputty; but the law's a queer, unjust thing, 'n' it might cut the ranch into little bits 'n' hunt up relations all over God's country 'n' Kansas besides, jes' to have some un to give my land to. No; if she dies I'll hold my tongue — that's my line. 'N' the doctor don't know—I don't b'lieve in mind-readin' 'n' sech. I was nervous, that's all; 'n' I feel strong 'nough to face 'im now. But if he brings Anny to her senses—"

She considered a moment, then shut her lips tight.

"I'll jes' have to plead 't I was too shook up to notice 't they was mistakin' me fer her. They can't prove 't I'm lyin' nohow, though they may s'pect me."

She started slowly back to the house. In the kitchen Leatherhead was singing in a high, flat voice, which spread strangely in the air and reached her ear like an echo gone crazy:

> "Oh, my darling, oh, my darling,
> Oh, my darling Clementine!
> Thou art lost and gone forever,
> Dreffle sorry, Clementine!"

Phœbe Ellen listened with a sense of strength completely restored. The words and music were atrocious, but the state of mind which prompted the singer was healthy and human. And that was what she needed.

Ever since awakening this morning she had felt weak, flaccid of will, altogether unlike herself, and had been wandering about in an atmosphere of superstitious dread which stifled her, but from which she could not get away. She needed to have it impressed upon her that the world was going on in its old course, that folly was rampant the same as hitherto, and that the dreadful thought of murder which had come into her head, together with the possibility of mind-reading on the part of the doctor, were nightmares from which it was possible fully to awake. There was exhilaration in the assurance that these dream-fancies were not realities, and that there was still healthy absurdity in the world.

She ascended the veranda with a firm step, carrying her head well up. There was self-assertion in the swing of her shoulders and in the force with which she brought her feet down. She had never felt her will-power more vigorously active, more able to assert and maintain her large sense of personal claims. She did not pause to listen at Anny's door before knocking, as she would certainly have done had she still been in the state of feeble volition in which she had left the house. She knocked at once and stood with her hand on the knob, ready to enter without flush of cheek or droop of eyelid on receiving the signal that they were ready for her.

"Come," Sam's voice called out, and she entered with head erect and eyes wide open on the group which presented itself by the bed. She liked the sound of her heels beating the uncarpeted floor with a sharp, incisive rhythm, like the audible voice of her newly aroused will. She liked the sense of dilation in her nostrils, through which the breath flowed steadily to her lungs, filling them as with an assurance that her voice would not fail her when she had occasion to speak.

The doctor had finished his examination. The bandages had been restored to their proper place and deftly fastened with a pin which took the dull glitter of a half-light in the semi-dusk of the room. He was sitting where she had left him, but turned sidewise in an attitude of idle ease, his right elbow propped against the back of his chair and his cheek in his palm.

He lifted his eyes and fixed them upon her with that deliberate intentness which had so shaken her at their first meeting. But there was a stronger confidence in his glance than before—the fatal certainty of diving further into her thoughts and bringing up handfuls of mud from the very bottom in proof of his exploit. She recognized his self-assurance in a flash, and for an instant the same thrill of fear passed through her—the same sense of helplessness as before something supernatural, the same disposition to wring her hands and cry out, "What shall I do?" while she let him have his way. She felt as if she were about to be searched, probed, turned inside-out for his inspection; but even in this state of momentary yielding she felt her will rising as it were in the distance with a strong, voluminous rush which seemed to carry a roar with it. It touched her, lifted her, bore her out of his reach, swung her in exultant freedom, poised, triumphant, mistress of herself. She wanted to laugh out, but even here her self-control was manifest, for she restrained the impulse and gave him stare for stare.

"Well?" she asked, in a tone of cool inquiry.

A shade of perplexity came into his face, and his glance became less penetrating, stopping at her eyes.

"Your walk has done you good," he remarked.

His look seemed trying to feel its way once more into her mind; but whereas he had at first found her weak and unprepared, she now knew her danger and was on her guard. Her will rose like a stone wall between him and what she had to conceal. She felt it with a triumphant scorn which still wanted to manifest itself in a laugh.

But again she suppressed the inclination and stood looking down at him with masterful gravity.

"I 'ain't been sick," she answered. She felt an irresistible joy in the evenness of her tones. "Wot have ye made out 'bout my sister?"

He shifted his position slightly.

"You were pale—pale when you left the room," he declared. "You looked as if you, too, were about to be ill. But now—" ·

"I feel ekal to anything now," she retorted, still gravely defiant. "Wot 'bout my sister?"

He leaned forward, fetching his thin hands together between his knees and wringing the fingers hard.

"Equal to anything?" he faltered.

"To anything," she repeated, grimly. "To the devil hisself. Wot 'bout my sister?"

"Ah!" said Dr. Sedgwick, removing his eyes from her face, and again she wanted to laugh. What a fool she had been to fear him earlier in the morning!

Sam was looking at her. "Why won't he tell me 'bout my sister?" she asked him. "D' *you* know? Tell me wot he thinks."

But Sam turned away.

"*He'll* do it," he answered. "I can't." She saw that he was wiping his eyes on the back of his huge hand.

"Wot's the matter?" she demanded, sharply. Was Anny dead? No. She could see the steady rise and fall of the chest, the flutter of the breath in the white throat.

"Wot's the matter?" she repeated, turning to the doctor. "Is—is she goin' to die?"

"I haven't made out much," he answered, without looking at her. "Her brain has been injured, but it is impossible to say how seriously."

"She'll live, though?"

The question came with bated breath, but even in her suspense Phœbe Ellen was sufficiently mistress of herself to interpret her anxiety from the doctor's point of view.

"I see no reason why she shouldn't live to be an old woman."

Her long-drawn breath—not a breath of relief—brought the doctor's eyes back to hers. But she was completely on her guard and met them boldly.

"Then wot's the mystery? Wot's the matter with Sam? Why d' ye go beatin' roun' the bush like they was suthin' to be kep' from me?"

"Nothing is to be kept from you. There can be no doubt that your sister's skull is fractured and that a considerable tract of brain is pressed upon by the injured bone."

"'That's wot Sam made shore of," commented Phœbe Ellen, jerking her head in the cowboy's direction.

The doctor nodded gravely.

"'N' that's all ye made out?" Phœbe Ellen's restored self-confidence was manifesting itself in a slight lifting of her chin.

"All," he answered.

"'N' you a doctor!" Her thin lips curled. "I'll go to Sam fust, nex' time."

Certainly she was paying him out for the agitation he had caused her at their first meeting. She enjoyed the look of baffled scrutiny which he darted upon her and the tone of deprecation in which he began:

"These cases are all extremely obscure, and their results highly problematic. In the present instance—"

She interrupted him sharply:

"Wot be ye goin' to do? Let 'er lay there 'n' die?"

He was evidently nettled, and his eyes wandered over her face without fastening themselves upon any particular feature.

"There's nothing to be done—"

"'N' ye can't give 'er nothin' to bring 'er to?"

“Nothing.”

“Bah !” She turned away with a fling of her shoulder in his direction. “I wouldn’t let ye doctor a sick cat fer *me!* Wot be ye a doctor fer, anyhow ?”

A flush of irritation settled on his high cheek-bones.

“Nature must take her course,” he said, in a hoarse, tremulous voice. “Everything has been done that is possible. Keep up the bandages—”

“That’s wot Sam advised,” she remarked.

“Use plenty of cold water—”

“Any fool could tell that ! Keep up the bandages, use plenty o’ cold water, ’n’ let ’er lay there till ’er breath stops !”

After she had finished the fear crossed her mind that he might turn to her and ask, “Is that what you want— that her breath should stop ?” But the flush under his eyes increased and his voice became more deprecative as he said :

“She won’t die—I can assure you of that. She will wake up by-and-by—”

“By-’n’-by ?”

“In a day or two—”

“Good Lord !”

“Maybe longer.”

“But—but she’ll starve !”

“No, she’ll eat, though she’ll not be conscious of it any more than she is at this moment conscious of breathing. Leatherhead is preparing some beef-tea for her now. And you are to bathe her twice a day in brandy.”

Phœbe Ellen’s breath came hard between her teeth.

“Then she’ll come to herself—”

“I didn’t say that.”

“How ! Ye said she’d wake up, didn’t ye ?”

“Yes. But that is a very different thing.”

She had closed her mouth tight now, and her nostrils swelled as the breath rushed through.

"I don't understand," she said, fixing her eyes on his as if to dare him to say his worst.

The doctor paused an instant before he explained.

"Your sister will probably never be in her right mind again."

CHAPTER XII

PHŒBE ELLEN sank into a chair as if felled by a blow. Since the accident she had measured many probabilities, outlined many catastrophes, imagined many complications, but never anything like this. She had based her schemes on the assurance that Anny would die, or, if she got well, could be hoodwinked into the belief that no exchange of identities had been intended; but that there might be a mean between the extremes of dying and getting well—that the girl might live, but remain an idiot the rest of her life—was as remote from Phœbe Ellen's calculations as the question of her own possible insanity; and the revelation left her, as it were, among the ruins of her plans. All the logic of her wickedness seemed to go for naught, and for a moment it seemed as if she had been discovered, as if she would have to explain. The arithmetic of contingencies was difficult for her at all times, and now she could not think what this new emergency might mean to her future. With all her plottings she was at bottom strangely simple and sincere—one of those natures whose depths are like little pools over which a current from the shallows flows and affords hardly more opportunity for concealment than the shallows themselves.

"I—I don't think I onderstan'," she faltered, in a tremulous voice. "Ye said—"

The dreadful, mesmeric eyes wavered and shifted in her direction ; they fixed themselves upon her consciousness and burned in. Imagine two flames with a will and purpose of their own, eager to take advantage of one's weakness, greedy for insight !

"I said that your sister would probably never be in her right mind again," he repeated, distinctly.

"Great God!" was her involuntary ejaculation.

The cry was not so much one of horror for her sister's calamity as of personal dread for this man, who was determined to wrest her secret from her by the aid of the devil himself if need were. She closed her eyes against his with the instinct of a hunted thing for concealment.

But she felt that she must say something, and like one in a dream she made the effort.

"Not in her right mind?" The question had a dazed sound, and she still kept her lids closed.

Only for a moment. Then again the weird power of the doctor's eyes came like a threat across her consciousness—a power like prying and thrusting and digging in forbidden places. The secretive corners of Phœbe Ellen's mind were always open to inspection except when her will, with a tremendous effort, drew a veil over her thoughts and held it close at all four corners in hysterical dread of revealing what was stowed away behind it. Now she felt his eyes, like search-lights, exploring the very recesses of her soul. At present they sent only random flashes here and there—tentative, bright circles falling upon thoughts which it mattered little if she revealed, and resting there only long enough to determine that they were not what he wanted to find. But the horrid illumination was drawing nearer and nearer to the guilty hopes which she had packed away in her thoughts since yesterday, and which it would be death to have his gaze touch even in outline. Nearer and nearer; she felt it with a helplessness which might have manifested itself in a shriek; in a moment it would lay all her guilty secret bare. Then with a nervous shiver which made her feel as if cold iron had touched her, she remembered that Sam was in the room, that possibly he could help her. She roused herself with a nightmare effort, half unclosing her eyes and wrenching them in his direction.

·· Sam—Sam !" she articulated, in a suffocating voice.

In an instant the cowboy was at her side.

"Why, ye're sick," he said, taking both her hands in his.

The touch revived her.

"Don't leave me !" she pleaded, hysterically.

" No," he assured her.

She caught her breath and laughed brokenly.

"Wot a fool I be !" she managed to say. " But I'll be better in a minute." She clutched his hands more tightly. " He tole ye that afore I come in ?" she asked, as if requiring his evidence before being convinced of what the doctor had said.

" 'Bout—'bout how she'll wake up ?"

She nodded.

" Yes," said Sam.

" 'N' ye b'lieve 'im ?"

In the effort of questioning, her strength was coming back. The doctor's eyes were upon her still, crossing her own and blinding her, but their illuminated circle was narrowing, their glare was shrinking to a phosphorescent glow which she would presently be able to face and defy. The thought seemed to mark a sort of ebb-tide in his power, while her own strength rose higher and higher.

" B'lieve 'im ?" Sam repeated, in a choked voice. " How kin I help it ? He knows."

" Wot be ye cryin' 'bout ?" she asked. Then with a sudden remembrance, " Queer 't I couldn't think, wa'n't it ? My pore sister ! A fool ? It's silly to talk like that !"

" He knows," repeated Sam, jerking his head in the doctor's direction.

By this time she had regained control of her will, so that she was able to calculate the effect of her next speech.

" The doctors kin guess, but only God A'mighty knows,"

she said, and her voice had grown stronger. Then she spoke quite naturally. "Not in 'er right mind ? Sis not in 'er right mind ? Sam, Sam, that's a fearful thing !"

Sam had to gulp down something before he was able to speak.

"Pore little gal !" he said, in a voice that stuck in his throat. "Pore, pore little gal !"

Phœbe Ellen looked the doctor over from head to foot with her old defiance.

"Know ? *He* know ? He don't know nothin'. I wouldn't take 'is word 'bout a sick cat 't b'longed to my wust enemy." Her lip curled with scorn even while she began a new set of calculations on the basis of Anny's idiocy. "If she should turn out a shore-'nough fool, I might keep the ranch in 'er name jes' like she was dead 'n' nobody 'd ever know the differ," she was thinking.

Then she heard Sam speaking again. His voice was clearer, but he kept his face averted.

"We'll have to take 'is word," he said, hollowly, "anyways, till we kin see fer ourselves. Wot do we know, either ? We don't even know 't we don't know. 'N' the little gal—God help 'er, I say—so there !"

Phœbe Ellen said nothing for a long moment, during which she was preparing to face the doctor once more. She could not measure him except when she was staring straight at him, and she dreaded that he might beat down her eyes with the complete self-confidence of his own. Out of his direct range of vision she was not altogether mistress of herself, but in spite of her fear she was conscious of a potential mastery in her rising will which would crush him utterly. Then with a sudden sideward sweep of her thin shoulders, as full of self-assertion as her highest ambition could have pictured, she faced him with wide-eyed defiance, and her voice came from full lungs as she said :

"Ye mustn't mind wot I say, doctor." Her words were

so widely at variance with her manner that Dr. Sedgwick stared at her helplessly, then dropped his glance to his hands, which he began to twist together in his peculiar nervous way. Phœbe Ellen understood her advantage and went on exultingly : "I'm put out, nat'rally, 'n' don't jes' sense wot I'm doin'. But ye can't tell fer shore jes' yit how sis 'll turn out ?"

He looked back at her, and she waited for his answer without flinching, presenting a fixed, dreadless face to his examination. It was strange how slight she felt his mental aggression when she had her wits about her and faced him with her will alert. What a fool she had been, not to be prepared for anything in the way of news about Anny's case ; to be taken off guard and to let her surprise give him an advantage over her which would encourage him to future efforts. She saw that she had baffled him now and that he was conscious of defeat. The assurance gave her a thrill of triumphant joy which was intensified by a growing confidence in her ability to guard against future surprise. This man suspected her of something— had read the fact of her guilt, though the vagueness of its outlines had baffled him and he had been obliged to desist with nothing more detailed than a general assumption.

"Ye can't tell fer shore, then ?" she repeated.

"Not till she awakens," was the answer.

And her retort was ready on her lips :

"Wot good o' tellin' us *then?* We kin see fer our- selves !"

But he hardly seemed to notice. He looked broken and utterly weary, as if he had been tried beyond his strength. He had a habit of allowing his eyes to wander restlessly from one object to another when they were not dilated in that compelling gaze upon some one whom he expected to feel their power. Now he was examining a knot-hole in the floor, a fly on the window, the grain of the wood in the foot of the bed.

"She'll prob'ly come to with 'er mind all gone?" Phœbe Ellen continued.

He dragged his eyes wearily back to hers, but they made no attempt at intrusion now. They looked too dull and listless to see what was directly before them.

"I can't say that," he answered, in a worn, husky voice. "I only say she will probably never be herself again."

"But the 'mount o' change?"

"I can't tell that."

She was gazing at him with a good imitation of his former unwinking stare—she would have given the world to be able to produce on him the same effect he had produced on her in her moment of weakness—but under her scrutiny he displayed no more than his ordinary nervousness. He was never altogether quiet. Sudden jerkings of his shoulders and hands, spasmodic shufflings of his feet and reflex twitchings of his mouth were a habit, or, rather, a disease with him.

"Then all we kin do 's to wait," said Phœbe Ellen.

"Yes," was the dull answer.

She considered rapidly. And even while she felt more than ever convinced of the feasibility of usurping her sister's name and place should the girl wake up without a knowledge of her own identity, her habitual solicitude told her that it would be safer to have a doctor on hand to tell her and Sam what to do. Besides, if she were to ask him to stay, it would show how little she feared him, and above all things she wished him to understand that. Yet if he were to remain in the house he might come upon her in an unguarded moment and wrest her secret from her in spite of herself. But she went on questioning him, and as she did so her mind dwelt in a semi-conscious but perfectly clear way upon the pros and cons of the situation.

"She might wake up ravin'?" she inquired.

His answer came more wearily than before.

"She might."

"Pore sis !" thought Phœbe Ellen. "They orter be a doctor 'ere to look arter 'er." Then aloud, "Is it likely she will ?"

"I can't say."

"Is that mos'ly the way sech cases does ?"

"No."

"They mos'ly wake up quiet, hey ?"

"Yes."

"Quiet 'n' queer ?"

"Yes," with the faintest shadow of a smile. "Quiet and queer."

By this time she had decided her semi-conscious argument in the affirmative.

"'Ud ye mind stayin' with us till we see which turn 'er trouble takes ?" she asked.

"I thought of asking you to let me do that. I shall be interested to see how she comes on. Only—"

He turned his eyes upon her once more, and, weary as they were, she detected the spark which might widen to a search-light again, but she met and quenched it as by water.

"Only wot ?" she asked, with perfect composure.

"I didn't know that you would care to have me around."

Phœbe Ellen smiled.

"Queer ye should 'a' thort o' that," she remarked.

"Hadn't *you* thought of it ?" he asked, trying to flash his eyes into hers.

She laughed lightly.

"I shall be tickled to death o' my own 'count," she declared. "'Though when I ast ye I was thinkin' o' my sister."

The answer was a work of art, and as such Phœbe Ellen admired it almost as much as she did its creator. "I'm ahead," she thought, triumphantly, "'n' I'll stay there.

All I got to do 's to keep my five senses 'bout me. No more jabbin' o' them eyes aroun' in *my* insides. I've got the whip-hand 'n' I mean to keep it."

And aloud she said, "We'll make ye 's comf'table 's wot we kin. They's a room 'n' bed, ain't they, Sam ?"

"The best room 'n' bed," said the latter.

"I'll stay," declared Dr. Sedgwick.

"We kin send Leatherhead over to Halstead's fer anything ye want."

"Thanks. I'll see him about that by-and-by. Just now I feel that I must rest a little."

At this moment Leatherhead entered with a bowl of something that steamed.

"Oh, the beef-tea," said Phœbe Ellen. "I'd fergot that."

"Tripe !" interrupted the cook, rolling his vaguely surprised glance from one member of the group to another. "Ye don't mean ye're goin' to turn that into 'er while she's 'sleep !"

"Wait and see, if you like," said the doctor, with his uncanny smile.

But Leatherhead thrust the steaming bowl into his hand and made a dash for the door.

"Tripe ! See a gal loaded up with beef-tea while she's 'sleep ? See—a—gal—loaded—say !"

And with that he vanished.

"We are more sensible," said Phœbe Ellen, turning to the doctor with a smile as enigmatic as his own.

"Oh, we hide our feelings," he interpreted her.

"That's wot I meant," she retorted, with a flash.

The doctor drew his chair to the bedside within reaching distance of the patient's mouth. Sam and Phœbe Ellen drew near.

"We want to see how it's done," she explained. "It's suthin' new, this sort o' feedin' a person while they're asleep. 'N' mebbe we'll have to do it ourselves. But ain't ye too tired ?"

"I'd better show you how it's done, though there is really no mystery about it."

"All good roads 'n' down hill?" She stood above him altogether at ease, yet every sense on the alert lest at an unguarded moment he should attempt that mysterious intrusion, of which she stood so abjectly in dread.

He repeated the words after her: "All good roads and down hill." Then he tested the heat of the tea by touching the spoon to the palm of his hand. "That is about right," he said.

He brought the spoon to Anny's mouth as a mother feeds a baby—with the food at the point, so that it readily came into contact with the lips and tongue. The mouth contracted a little, drew in a bit of the liquid, and the tongue rolled it awkwardly about as if tasting it. Then it was swallowed.

"Queer," muttered Phœbe Ellen, from behind the doctor's chair.

He looked up at her, but he found her on guard over her emotions.

"There really is no mystery about it," he repeated, turning again to his patient.

"Oh, ye treat 'er dif'rent from wot ye do well folks, then," said Phœbe Ellen, just to show how completely she was mistress of the situation.

The doctor paused with the spoon half-way to the patient's mouth.

"I have a mysterious way of treating well people, then?"

"Ye *think* ye have," she retorted, with a short laugh.

"My means sometimes succeed in the end," he remarked, administering the tea, which the patient took with a mechanical relish such as puckers a week-old baby's mouth when a bit of sugar is dropped upon its tongue.

"That 'pends on who ye try 'em on," she replied.

"Well people's heads ain't cracked, 'n' they know their own int'rests from a side o' sole-leather."

"There!" said the doctor, rising and placing the bowl in her hands. "I'm worn out and will have to lie down for an hour. You see how to go on feeding her—I'll leave it for you to finish up. There's nothing further, except to keep on changing the bandages every few minutes, and feed her once in every three or four hours."

"How shall I know when she's got 'nough?" asked Phœbe Ellen, assuming the bowl and spoon, and taking her place at the bedside.

"She'll stop taking it."

"Oh! 'N' shall I give 'er anything to drink?"

"You can try her with water in a spoon. Give her all she will take."

"Ye *do* look ruther tired," remarked Phœbe Ellen, with a burst of concessive kindness.

"Thanks," he answered, dryly.

"Ye overestimate yer stren'th, I shouldn't wonder," she continued, becoming perverse again and speaking in a tone whose significance he could not mistake. She was master now, and her voice rang high and triumphant. "Ye orter be keerful o' that. It allus gits folks into trouble."

He did not try to oppose her, but left the room, preceded by Sam, who was to show him to his chamber.

"'Pears like he's purty well done out," remarked the latter on his return. "Wot d' ye think o' him, anyhow?"

His question was intended to be answered in a professional way, but, woman-like, Phœbe Ellen made it a personal matter.

"I hate 'im!" she answered, and went on feeding out her tea.

CHAPTER XIII

Finally the invalid's lips drew themselves up in an obstinate pucker when the spoon was presented, and Phœbe Ellen knew that her task was done.

Sam had been watching her over her shoulder.

"It sorter sends a shiver through a feller," he said. "It's 'most like ye was to feed a corpse 'n' it was to take to swollerin'." He turned away and walked the length of the room.

"I can't b'lieve all he says 'bout the way she's likely to wake up," declared Phœbe Ellen. "He ain't old 'nough to 've had much 'sperience. Wot kind o' feller is he, anyhow?"

"He seems to know a heap o' things, one way 'n' 'nother," responded Sam. "The way he brought Lafe Henderson aroun' arter the shootin' up to Ferguson's showed he knows wot he's up to."

"Ye reckon he's to be trusted, then?"

"I have that feelin'," he answered, sadly. "I wish 't I could misdoubt 'im. It's a orfle thing he's prophesyin' o' 'er. But I know he wouldn't say it 'thout he had groun's."

"I'm goin' to hope fer the best, anyway," declared Phœbe Ellen. Somehow she found it a rather cheerful business to hope for the best when the doctor had decided for the worst. "No man kin know wot's comin' for shore. The skull might be cracked 'n' not press the least speck on the inside. I've seen cracked eggs that way."

He shook his head.

"Eggs ain't brains. *He* knows. The Doc knows," he repeated.

It was a pleasure for her to talk over the case with him in this friendly way, and she almost forgot in his proximity that it was her own sister whose misfortune she was discussing. He seemed so cast down, so anxious about the girl's dreadful fate, that it satisfied a need of hers to console him and make him look on the bright side. Besides, his gloomy confidence in the doctor's judgment gave her a thrill of assurance, as if Providence were taking her part. Sam still believed her to be the heiress, and she might be so in fact if her sister were never to recover her senses. Everything looked favorable; however, there was one matter that must be looked after. She must take care not to compromise herself by a declaration of her usurped individuality till Anny awoke and it could be definitely ascertained how much she remembered of her past. As for her tacit admission that she was the heiress, she could always explain that by the agitation of the moment, when she had been incapable of noticing anything. Silence is never conclusively condemnatory, and she had done nothing more criminal than to hold her peace. She could manage it easily enough. The thing for her to be careful of during the remaining term of Anny's unconsciousness was to keep from being addressed by her sister's name; or, if so addressed, to overlook the fact so as to carry no consequences into the future. And even while she thought about it, a plan was forming itself in her brain by which it would be wellnigh impossible to commit herself in her sister's name. She was too self-confident to be troubled by the possibility that her plan itself might occasion suspicion; but her ingenuity was precisely of the sort to overlook details to which a less simple nature would have attached a proper value from the first.

"Oh, I didn't go to say he wa'n't ekal to his bizness,"

she said, *apropos* of Sam's last speech. "It's only nat'ral to want to b'lieve the best o' a feller's own sister. That's all I meant."

"I kin onderstan' that," he answered. "But it's all right to be prepared for the wust."

"Yes, but a feller kin do that 'n' be hopeful, too. Well, they ain't nothing fer us to do now but to wait."

"It seems kind o' dreary, don't it?"

"Three or four days? It seems a age! Ho w'll we ever git through it?"

"I'm glad we got to stan' it stiddier o' *her*," he said, after a little pause.

Phœbe Ellen adopted the sentiment readily.

"So be I. She don't know—she don't sense nothin'. It's us 't has to do the sufferin'. 'N' yit—pore sis!"

Her willingness to suffer instead of Anny must have rung false, for without being offended he changed the subject.

"'Pears like it's kinder queer how ye 'n' yer sister never calls each other by yer Christian-names. I noticed yer never doin' it wunst on the way over. 'N' sence we got 'ere ye ain't called 'er by 'er fust name a single time."

For an instant her heart fluttered in doubt and dread. Then she felt the dangerous ground grow firm under her feet as she saw her way across it to the outworking of a part of her plan.

"Oh, it's the way we was brung up," she replied, in easy explanation. This was true enough, and probably he himself had divined it. But her next statement went further. "'Pears like the habit o' never usin' our names to each other 's give us a kind o' horror o' 'em, sometimes. Back East there in Nebrasky, where we come from, we was never called by our fust names—I was Miss Thompson, 'n' so was sis. We growed used to it, 'n' I like it better. Ye made up yer mind some time ago 't I was a crank, I reckon?" She smiled at him, and he thought he had never before seen her look so pretty, so like her sister.

He was obliged to admit that she was not mistaken in his estimate of her peculiarities.

"It's the way folks does in Nebrasky, to call each other by their fust names arter they git 'quainted," she continued.

"So 'tis out West 'ere," said Sam.

"That's wot I reckoned. Well, now, I don't like it. I own I don't like it. It's too Western 'n' f'milyer — that's wot 'tis. I like to be Miss Thompson 'n' nothin' else. I may be funny—I reckon I be, but I can't help it. It goes agin me turble to be called by my Christian‑name—it allus did."

"Have I called ye that?" inquired Sam.

"No. Nobody hain't yit, 'n' I don't want 'em to. That's wot I'm talkin' 'bout."

"I'll 'member," he said. Evidently it was of no consequence to him what she preferred to be called.

"Thankee. 'N' say! 'Ud ye mind tellin' the doctor? I hate 'im, anyway, 'n' it 'ud clean set me on needles 'n' pins to have 'im go agin me like that. 'N' while he's here in the house, right under my face 'n' nose, so to speak, I'd like to git 'long with 'im 'thout rowin'."

"I'll tell 'im, though I don't reckon he'd call ye by yer fust name, nohow. Boston folks ain't up to sech-like."

"'N' I'll see to Leatherhead. The other boys 'll do like they hear you 'n' Leatherhead do, anyhow. Well, I'll be 'bleeged to ye fer tellin' the doctor. I want to git along peaceable 'n' harmonious."

Thus she provided, for at least a few days, against being called by the name which might compromise her. Against anything further she must take her chances. But she would have her wits constantly about her; and, with her will to back and direct them, she felt more than a match for mere chance happenings.

"Seems kinder queer the hatred ye take to people at fust sight," remarked Sam, in his slow way.

Phœbe Ellen smiled, and again she was like her sister.

"Now ye're thinkin' o' the way I treated *you*," she said.

He could not deny the soft impeachment.

"Oh, I've got over that," she declared.

He smiled in faint gratification.

"I'm glad o' that," he said. "I like to git along smooth 'n' easy. Life's too short fer the other thing."

"Ye kin do the other thing, though, I notice, when folks tries to run over ye."

"Yes," he admitted.

"Well, we ain't agoin' to fight no more. I was wrong, all wrong — one o' my queer spells took me. I told ye I had my crazy p'ints. Wot'ud the doctor do if I was to fly at 'im like that? Things orter go smooth between him 'n' me fer sis's sake."

"Yes." Sam saw the force of the last observation, and Phœbe Ellen noticed the light of conviction that settled in his slow, ruminant eyes. "I'll speak to 'im when he comes out."

"He's a orfle funny duck," remarked Phœbe Ellen, just to hear what Sam would say.

"Well, I d' know 's wot anybody 'd go agin yer jedgment there. He *is* a funny duck. They tell wild stories 'bout 'im over there to Halstead's."

"Wild stories?" she repeated. "That may mean anything."

"It means in his case 't he has the piercin'est way o' lookin' at people 't ever I seen. They say over there—"

"Oh, ye can't tell me nothin' 'bout the way he looks at people," interrupted Phœbe Ellen. "He tried it on me."

"I noticed. But he didn't seem to make out much."

She sniffed loftily, as much as to say, "Trust me fer that!" Then aloud :

“Wot d’ ye reckon he was trying to make out, any-how?”

“I d’ know in *your* case, but they say over there to Halstead’s ’t he’s allus ’sperimentin’ on some un like that, tryin’ to git on to wot they’re thinkin’. He stares at ye till he makes ye feel weak ’n’ queer, then he kin find out anything he likes. They say he reely kin.”

“I don’t b’lieve a word o’ it!” declared Phœbe Ellen.

“Mind-readin’, he calls it. ’N’ hypnoozin’. I d’ know jes’ wot ’tis, fer I ain’t up to sech; but I know he’s done some funny things with the folks over to Halstead’s. They’re full o’ it. They’re afeerd o’ him, though in spite o’ everything he ’ain’t never harmed nobody. He jes’ looks into folks till he finds out wot he wants, then he lets ’em go. ’Pears like it’s his way o’ havin’ fun.”

“He’d better not try it on *me* agin,” threatened Phœbe Ellen.

“Wot ’ll ye do?”

“I’ll show ’im he’s got a holt o’ *one* woomarn ’t he can’t make a fool of. La! it’s easy ’nough to git the start o’ him!”

“Be ye shore ye did?”

The question gave her a little chill, but she answered promptly:

“Course I be! I knowed wot he was tryin’ to do fust off, ’n’ I jes’ shet my mind up agin ’im.”

“I ain’t shore *I* could do it,” said Sam.

“Well, *I* ain’t afeerd o’ ’im,” she asserted, more boldly than ever. “It ’ud be queer if the hypnoozer found his-self hypnoozed one o’ these fine days, wouldn’t it now? Well, all I say is, let ’im look out. I’m likely to fly off the handle ’n’ stick in the wall! But say! Hadn’t ye better go ’n’ lay down a bit? Ye didn’t get a bit o’ sleep las’ night.”

“I was thinkin’ o’ that,” he answered. “If I’m to set up with ’er agin to-night, I might ’s well keep fresh fer the bizness. I reckon I better take the night watch right 'long till she comes to. 'N' I'll lay out to sleep durin' the day."

On his way to the barn, where he purposed taking a nap on the hay—Sam always slept where there was plenty of air stirring—he ran across the doctor, who was pacing restlessly up and down among the pines.

"Hello! ye didn't lay down long, arter all, did ye?" Sam called out. "Anything happen to stir ye out?"

"I never lie down long at a time," answered the doctor, pausing in the sun and working his clinched fingers together behind his back. "Not even at night. My legs begin to jerk, and I have to get up and move about. And my toe-joints grind together. Great God! Did you ever have that feeling in your toes, Sam?"

His eyes widened on the cowboy as if to give him a glimpse of horrors.

"Never," said Sam, unaffected except to the extent of considering it queer.

"Pray God you never may," the doctor went on. "There's no torture of the damned that equals it. To be on the point of falling asleep—to feel one's self sinking dreamily and peacefully away, then—wrench! grind! rasp! All the horrors of hell are in that feeling. Well! what are they doing back there?"

He jerked his thumb in the direction of the home ranch.

"She breathes jes' the same. They was gittin' some more tea ready fer 'er when I left."

The doctor glanced at his watch.

"It's time," he said. "She's prompt—your Miss Anny. How do you think you are going to like her?"

"Oh, that reminds me—she objecks to bein' called by 'er fust name. She wants to be called jes' Miss Thompson."

The doctor was silent during a pause of puzzled inquiry.

"Have you been calling her anything else?" he asked.

"Oh no," was Sam's answer.

There was another little pause, after which the doctor frowned.

"Oh, she was merely warning you beforehand? That was kind of her." The tone was sarcastic.

"I d' know 's t'was meant for me more 'n other folks," declared Sam.

"Did she mention names?"

"Yes, she did."

"For instance—"

"Yourn."

"That *was* kind of her," murmured the doctor.

"I d' know 's 'twas meant to be noways as kind 's ye 'pear to think. *She* didn't pertend to be up to the kind act. She jes' put it at me in the light o' a freak."

"Oh! a freak?"

"She said 'twas jes' 'er way. She liked it better."

Now the doctor's pause was filled with a wide scrutiny of Sam's large, simple features.

"She asked you in so many words to speak to me about it?"

"Yes."

"Not to call her anything but Miss Thompson?"

"Yes."

"And she gave no reason?"

"No."

"Did she seem to think I might call her by her first name?"

"I took it so."

"Queer, isn't it?" The doctor unclinched his hands from behind and folded his arms on his breast.

"Oh, we all have our queernesses," said Sam, philosophically.

"Very queer," repeated the doctor, biting his thumb-nail nervously as he walked away.

When Leatherhead brought in the tea Phœbe Ellen made the same request of him that Sam had made of the doctor.

"Call ye Miss Thompson, 'n' nothin' else?" he repeated, dropping his jaw and bulging his eyes in the meaningless astonishment which was the ultimate expression of his individuality. "Hang it, ain't that comin' it ruther high 'n' mighty fer the range kentry? O' course, back East there in Nebrasky, where they put on style, everything goes; but out 'ere— Miss Thompson! Say, we allus call 'em by their fust names arter we git to know 'em, 'n' sometimes we tack 'nother name on, too, jes' for a flier. There's Rawhide Sal over to Halstead's, 'n' Freckled Mariar over to Ferguson's, 'n' Slungshot Susan over to—"

"Never mind!" interrupted Phœbe Ellen, sternly. "Ye'll 'member wot I say?"

And thus the matter was settled with Leatherhead; and Phœbe Ellen once more went conscientiously to work feeding out the tea.

"I managed that purty well," she said to herself, approvingly. "'N' if Sam 'n' the doctor 'n' Leatherhead don't call me Anny, nobody will. So that's all fixed."

But in the midst of her self-gratulation a dreadful thought presented itself.

"Wot if sis was to wake up in 'er right mind *now?*"

The possibility made her gasp for breath.

"I couldn't excuse myself fer *this,* nohow. I'd jes' have to own up, 'n' take consequences. That'ud be horrid. But if she *should* come to in 'er right mind—"

The rest of the sentence came like the echo of a hammer's stroke.

"I might have a dose ready fer 'er, to be on the safe side!"

She cast aside the thought as best she could, and tried to think of something else.

"That's jes' like me; I never kin see a inch afore my

nose in broad daylight, nohow. Why didn't I keep my mouth shet 'n' run chances ? Wot a fix ! But she won't be 'erself—the doctor says she won't. I'll be good to 'er ; I'll give 'er jes' wot the doctor orders, *'n' nothin' more.* I kin 'ford to take good keer o' 'er ; she won't never be able to harm me. 'N' wot if Leatherhead should fergit 'n' call me Miss Anny, arter all my cautionin'; 'n' wot if that doctor should turn contrairy 'n' do the same, jes' 'cause I ast 'im not to ? I'd have to make a row, o' course, 'n' that ud fix it more 'n ever in their minds 't I'd been passin' under Anny's name. Well, I *am* a shore 'nough fool ! But she won't come to in 'er proper senses ; I know she won't !"

She looked down at her sister with hard examination.

"I won't pizen 'er, though — I swear to God I won't ! She's my sister—I mustn't lose sight o' that. Well, I got to make the best o' my folly ; but wot folly, to be shore ! Arter all, the chief thing to dread is 't she'll wake up in 'er right mind."

And in her anxiety she lost sight of the depravity evidenced by that dread. But she was not altogether cast down. We seldom are appalled by the probable consequences of our stupidity. And Phœbe Ellen had great confidence in what she called her " wits."

CHAPTER XIV

WHEN she and the doctor next met, a little before noon, they greeted each other with civility, and discussed the condition of the patient with all the outward signs of respect and confidence. The doctor looked at her only momentarily, and, as far as appearances went, for assistance in understanding more completely what she had to say; and there was no betrayal of antagonism in her answering glance. If there was indeed a feeling of opposition in her, she merged it so thoroughly into her very natural solicitude for her sister that it was undetectable in its diluted state. She was eagerly, anxiously helpful. Possibly her very alertness to danger gave her a more natural, because a more womanly, air; the womanliness resulting inevitably from any change not violently for the worse. But she was not her natural self; Sam noticed it, with a lively sense of improvement in her which his hopeful nature tried to think of as permanent. She spoke in a tone of subdued shrillness which in another woman would have been threatening, but in her was almost dove-like. She did not wag her head so much as Sam believed was her habit; her chin had a less forward slant; she stood less frequently with her arms akimbo; she showed a facility in smiling which reminded him more and more agreeably of her sister. These changes were all good to see, and if Sam did not develop an actual liking for her, he at least began to think of her as a tolerable sort of young woman, and to remember her conduct at the depot as one phase of that mysterious phenomenon called "nerves," by which men try in a word to explain the unexplainable in woman.

The doctor remained with the patient while Phœbe Ellen and Sam took dinner together. Throughout the meal she was uninterruptedly pleasant and conciliating. She complimented the cowboy on his way of managing the estate—she had actually found nothing that she would care to change, though she had a secret belief that she could, if she chose to give time to it—and listened to his statement of her bank account—Anny's bank account!—with but a slight intensification of the applause she bestowed upon the care he had taken in training the pea-vines to their present state of productiveness.

The doctor frequently came into the sick-room in the course of the afternoon, but he never remained long. He entered, made a few inquiries, noted the patient's pulse, removed the bandage and examined the wound, remarked that she was getting on as well as could be expected, and then went out. Sometimes he lay down for a few minutes in the room which had been prepared for him; sometimes he sprawled in the most fatiguing postures across a chair on the veranda; sometimes he spread himself out on the mountain-side in the sun, and lay kicking and twisting about, making hillocks of the carefully packed pine-needles.

After supper, while they were making their arrangements for the night, Dr. Sedgwick suggested several things for the comfort of both watchers and patient. He seemed kindly disposed, and there was nothing in look or glance to indicate a desire to poach on Phœbe Ellen's mental preserves. He engaged in some general conversation with her, went into the defects of ranch-life from a Boston point of view, and expatiated on the effect of the Colorado climate on pulmonary troubles. He even displayed a saturnine humor now and then which made her laugh: as when he remarked that he, as a consumptive, would rather make more desolate the most arid half-acre in Colorado than decorate the prettiest cemetery in New England. But she suspected him always, and never for a moment was off her guard. His eyes seldom met hers, and that fact in itself made her suspicious. He was lulling her into a sense of security, and when he found her absent-minded or on the point of yielding to some passing emotion he would enter her mind and take possession, just as he had done this morning, only more completely—explore its nooks and corners to the uttermost, pull out and examine its disgraceful possessions and publish their value and import to the world. She had a horrid conviction that if he were to gain the mastery over her again, it would be forever. Once in there after what had already occurred, she could never thrust him out; she would remain the creature of his will, unresisting, passive, disgraced by his knowledge of her soul.

The night passed without change in the patient's condition. Sam had slept sufficiently during the day to take up his post once more without fatigue, and Phœbe Ellen, desiring at least a formal share of his watch, arranged a bed for herself on an old lounge which was brought in from some obscure corner of the house and fitted up with comforts and pillows for the occasion. She awoke several times in the night, but always found Sam at his post, attentive, thoughtful, strong in the strenuous tenderness of kindly manhood which was so eminently his possession. She felt his presence in the room with the utter confidence which is so precious to woman in her relations with man.

The forenoon of the second day came and went. Still nothing unusual between Phœbe Ellen and the doctor. But her problem was assuming proportions of which she had never dreamed. At first it had been simple enough—to look after her sister, and, if the latter never came to her right mind, assume her name and estate in such manner as would best serve her own interests ; but now her chief care had become to avert the suspicions of a mind-reader, at whose ultimate power she could only guess. Everything but the mind-reader could take care of itself. And, realizing this fact, she found herself facing him with a steadiness of nerve which, while it put upon her a strain beyond her strength, gave her a confidence in final triumph, and yielded her a satisfaction such as underlies all strong volition in natures accustomed to dominate. She developed a sort of inward vision by which she knew when his eyes were upon her ; she was aware of his movements when her back was towards him ; at times she almost penetrated his thoughts.

He had been careful to avoid the use of her Christian-name ; he addressed her merely as " you," and, when Sam was present, indicated whom he meant by fixing his eyes momentarily upon her. That was best ; certainly it was easiest for her. But she was prepared at any moment to have him address her as Miss Anny, and to resent it with all the energy of offended majesty. The more she thought of it, the more stupid it seemed to her to have prohibited the name at all ; she should have said nothing about it, for the chances against her would have been no stronger than at present, considering the doctor's peculiar disposition to search and pry. She had been silly, certainly ; but this conviction operated beneficently in her case, for it sharpened her intellect, if not her conscience ; she became nervously alert to the means of forestalling whatever should tell against her, but was never really sorry for what she had done except as it rendered her method of procedure more difficult.

But on the afternoon of the second day Phœbe Ellen noticed signs of reviving storm in the doctor's direction. He came to the room where she was sitting with Anny, and, after his customary examination of the patient, settled back in his chair with the evident intention of hav-

9

ing a talk. Settling back in his chair, in the doctor's case, meant that he hooked his armpit over the pommel, twisted his fingers together, spread his thin legs — the horrible thinness of a consumptive's legs has never been touched upon in literature — and proceeded to writhe. His talk began naturally enough, and passed easily from one subject to another, Phœbe Ellen following it, inwardly watchful and defiant. Suddenly, in the course of some indifferent remark, he called her "Miss Thompson" with an emphasis which meant mischief. Phœbe Ellen was open to signs and portents, and was not slow to scent danger. She did not glance up from her mending at once — she had found that she could pick up a bit of work to advantage during the five-minute intervals of nursing — but kept her eyes riveted to her needle, and went on steadily drawing the thread in and out. Then as he paused in his speech, and she had a chance for a rejoinder, she glanced easily in his direction, as one naturally does before taking the conversation upon one's self. Nevertheless she was inwardly disturbed, and half expected the hypnotic stare with which she was familiar. His eyes were upon her, to be sure, but with a half-amused, half-sarcastic look, as if he were wondering how she would take his emphatic compliance with her wishes. She was confident that no change crossed her features as their glances met; she went on with what she had started to say, finished it, and was delighted to see the look of sarcastic amusement fade from his face before she once more lowered her eyes to her work.

But the doctor was not to be discomfited by one failure. He pulled himself together and proceeded to other topics of conversation. But "Miss Thompson," uttered with sarcastic emphasis, came in at every third word. The constant iteration, the nagging tone, the knowledge that he was trying to make her lose her temper, irritated her beyond measure; she was accustomed to meet anything of the sort with loud-tongued defiance, and the effort to control herself brought an ominous thinness to her lips and a wrinkle to the corner of her mouth which indicated the tension under which she was laboring. She began to count, and found that the effort quieted her. "Be I takin' my stitches reg'lar, I wonder? If I kin keep my mind on that, it 'll help me." Thus she gathered herself firmly in, adjusting her thoughts, not by what he was saying, but by the regularity with which she purposed to draw her thread in and out in spite of all that he could say. The determination to do her work evenly somehow brought evenness and regularity into her thoughts; and thus she succeeded in keeping her temper, which was the chief thing she was aiming at.

Finally she was gratified to see the doctor draw a long breath as if he, too, had been exerting himself, and with a final glance, either of defeat or threat, he left the room, and Phœbe Ellen recovered herself at her leisure.

The third day came without alteration in Anny's condition. Phœbe Ellen's care for the sick girl suffered no diminution; the food was administered with the regularity of clock-work, the bandages were changed precisely as the doctor ordered, the mechanism of the sick-room moved on with as little friction as if the entire thought of the well woman were expended upon the comfort of the sick one. Yet in fact very little of Phœbe Ellen's solicitude was for her sister. "If I didn't 'tend to 'er right, that man 'ud be shore to find it out," she thought. "I kin guard *one* secret, I reckon, but I couldn't keep 'im out o' more 'n that." Her thoughts were always upon the doctor and the conditions he would impose upon their intercourse. She waited upon the invalid with her spine, so to speak; but her brain and soul were directed with all the energy they were capable of towards the task of complete self-control.

The doctor did not immediately try to annoy her again.

They met each other quietly—so quietly that their attitude might almost be called a pose—and seemed to have
no other thought between them than the welfare of the
patient. Phœbe Ellen accepted the truce with readiness,
but she watched it as keenly as if it had meant open hostility. She was glad of peace, but she was quite prepared
for war.

"He's tried Miss Thompson on me," she thought, "'n'
found that don't disturb me, but wot if he was to take to
callin' me Anny? He'll do it, I know; I feel it comin'.
'N' he'll try to do it onexpected, when he kin git the disadvantage o' me. I'll git mad *then*, I know—he's been
told aforehand that 'll make me mad, 'n' o' course it will.
'N' if I git mad, wot then? 'Ll he be so scart 't he'll fergit to try to find out my secret? I doubt it. Lord, wot
will happen then?"

The best plan she could think of was not to get angry
at all, but to simulate a rage she did not feel, and thus
give consistence to the rôle she had proposed to herself.
With this idea in mind she rehearsed the impending scene
as an actor might, flinging her pretended anger into words
and looks and gestures which she made to resemble as
nearly as possible her genuine anger of other days, as she
remembered it. She brooded over this denouement when
she was alone, became familiar with it, incorporated it
into the substance of her thought. And at last she felt
prepared.

And on the afternoon of the third day, the doctor, lurching about in his chair after his examination of the patient,
turned suddenly on her with the question:

"These days of waiting must wear on you dreadfully,
Miss Anny?" And although her face was turned in
another direction she felt his eyes upon her, opening
slowly and revealing vistas of unholy light.

She was wiping a glass when he addressed her, but she
was prepared. Her hand did not tremble; there was no

danger of dropping the glass and breaking it. She felt the muscles of her voice altogether under her control. The first words of the harangue she had prepared came to her as distinctly as if they had been written on the wall, and she knew that the others would follow. She felt the power in her to deliver that speech, and to deliver it well, and she opened her mouth for the purpose. But nothing of the sort happened. At that instant something like an inspiration came to her. To her own surprise, she turned on him with a smile of perfect good-nature, and, still rubbing her glass, said, in the easiest manner in the world :

"I knowed that was comin', doctor. I reckon ye feel better now ?"

He was nonplussed. She could have laughed out with joy at the whole transaction, it had gone off so smoothly, so utterly as a matter of course. In an inspired moment she had at least partly undone the stupidity of her request to be called only Miss Thompson, and had established herself on the old basis of trusting to luck. "Now if sis wakes up in 'er right mind, I kin swear I done the hull thing out o' contrariness, jes' to see the doctor try to make me mad," she said to herself. "Anyway, I'm still ahead. Every time I rattle 'im, the less shore he'll be o' hisself when he comes at me agin."

She set aside her glass and seated herself, facing him.

"Ye *do* feel better," she decided with ironical composure, after examining him. "I kin see it by the set o' yer hair."

"You don't seem to resent the use of your first name so violently as one might have expected," he remarked.

"Oh, I have my own little ways o' 'musin' myself," she answered, in a voice which implied that he had done precisely as she wished him to do.

"Amusing yourself ?" he repeated.

She pursed up her lips and nodded at the same time.

"Amusing yourself with *me?* How do you mean ?"

“Oh, I jes’ wanted to see how contrary ye could be. I made shore it ud be funny.”

The delicate muscles of his chin gave a spasmodic jerk.

“You find it funny ?”

“Dretful funny ! Why not ?”

“Queer !” she heard him mutter to himself.

She laughed provokingly.

“Ye find it only queer ?” she asked. “To me it’s so funny it’s fairly comic.”

But he did not answer, and after a moment’s silence she continued, following his mechanical glance towards the bed :

“She don’t seem to be comin’ to ’erself so very fast, does she ? We’re nearin’ the end o’ the third day. How much longer d’ ye give this sort o’ thing to go on ?”

“*I* give ? Talk to nature. I have nothing to do with it.”

“How long d’ ye reckon nater is goin’ to keep it up, then ?”

He rose, twisting his thin shoulders about in his loosely hanging coat and scowling.

“Your sister may not wake up for another day. I never said there was anything certain about the time.”

“Not later ’n to-morrer, then ?”

“I should say not.”

“We’re to call ye when the change begins ?”

“By all means.”

And as he left the room she heard him once more mutter under his breath the single word, “Queer !”

Again she laughed out in half-contemptuous enjoyment.

“I’m ahead o’ where I was when I made that silly wish to be called Miss Thompson, anyhow,” she thought, “fer now I’ve puzzled ’im. If he calls me Anny now I’ll jes’ grin, ’n’ then it ’ll be easy ’nough to say, if I have to, ’t the reason I kind o' half-way passed off as the heiress was jes' to git a bit o' 'musement out o' the doctor. That was the best way out o' the hull bizness—that way o' smilin' at 'im. Well, I've allus heerd as the devil takes keer o' his own, 'n' now they ain't a doubt about it in my mind—not a doubt!"

CHAPTER XV

SAM watched again that night. Phœbe Ellen made him promise to rouse her at the slightest change, but, truth to tell, it was chiefly on his own account that he hardly took his eyes from the bed during his long vigil. However, no change occurred, and at six o'clock next morning Phœbe Ellen awoke to the same state of affairs that had prevailed when she went to sleep.

"This 'ere's the fourth day," she said, after Sam had finished his account of the night's watch. "The doctor said she'd shorely rouse up on the fourth day."

Sam looked anxious.

"I sha'n't go to sleep agin till it's settled one way or 'nother," he declared.

After breakfast they sat down together near the sick-bed and talked. They could decide nothing, of course, but it did them good to rehearse their hopes and fears, and wonder about this and that. And in the midst of their wonderings and hopings the doctor came in.

"Ye see," said Phœbe Ellen, waving her hand towards the bed. "She's jes' the same."

"Yes," answered the doctor, "but she must not be left alone a minute during the day. She may open her eyes at any time. And some one must be on hand to look after her !"

"S'posin' she was to come to fer a minute 'n' then fall asleep agin ?" asked Sam.

Phœbe Ellen had never thought of that, and awaited the doctor's answer with interest.

"No harm would follow, probably, but it would be

well to attract her attention and keep her awake if possible—at least, for a while."

" 'N' if we should fail, she—"

"She would probably awaken later. But—"

"She might not?"

"She might sleep herself to death," was the doctor's answer.

"We mus' 'member that," said Sam to Phœbe Ellen.

The doctor left the room, and presently was visible on a rock a little way up the mountain-side, dangling his thin legs among some wild sunflowers. Phœbe Ellen sat down by the window and took up her mending, while Sam flung himself into a chair by the table in full view of the patient's face. His cartridge-belt, with the pistol thrust into it, lay at his side, where he had flung it the night before when he took up his watch. He did not feel like talking, and Phœbe Ellen respected his mood ; so he idly fingered the cartridge-belt, and wondered, with an anxiety which was softened by a dreamy languor consequent on his long vigil, what they would do to attract the sick girl's attention should they find it necessary when she awoke.

There was a little nickel-plated clock in the room, and its ticking multiplied itself in a loud, hollow resonance which made the silence heavy. Sometimes its noise grew hurried, as if time had been lost and must be made up; again it became leisurely, and seemed to stop and yawn between-whiles. The river was audible as a faint susurrus, which at times deepened to a monotone, but always returned to that singularly elemental sound so common in nature, which plainly says, "Sh—sh !" The pines, too, were vocal, and took the wind with a dreamy murmur which left the mind vacant to everything but the languid ecstasy of swaying boughs and slumberous shadows. Sometimes the river and the pines united their voices in a long, wailing cry, which rose in shrill crescendo, filled the sky with an aërial climax, and died away in a sound like that of a sublimated trolley-car. Sam was sleepy, in spite of his resolve to keep awake. The ticking of the clock went on with a somnolent regularity which no longer broke into hurry or weariness; its clucking persistence became strangely soothing; its monotony got into his eyes and breathing, and before he was aware of it he was in a state of semi-consciousness. His eyes closed—uncertainly at first, as if in reflex obedience to a memory of duty; then more and more heavily, till the lids no longer trembled, but lay quietly closed, not exactly in sleep, but in that intermediate state which is a pure physical enjoyment. Sam did not lose consciousness; he knew all about the busy figure at the window, the sick girl on the bed, his own personality propped up against the table on one unstable elbow, the cartridge-belt and pistol at his side; but it was all mingled together in a happy vagueness which was as enchanting as the condition of the lotus-eaters, who saw and felt and heard, but only as an accompaniment to the vacant enjoyment of utter rest.

A lurch of his elbow brought him erect in his seat and staring. He had a wild feeling that something had happened; he knew where he was, but somehow it all seemed new, made over after a new pattern. He did not turn his head, and it was by the merest accident that his unwinking gaze fastened itself upon the occupant of the bed. And he saw, with a thrill of horror, that the invalid's eyes were open in a wide stare, as if the lids had been drawn apart by the contracting chill of death in the muscles. He could not have uttered a word or made a movement to save his life. Waking thus suddenly and meeting that meaningless glare in the girl's sightless orbs, he felt his throat contracting in a nightmare struggle to cry out. But no sound came, and in an instant the effort passed, though not the horror of it, and he was able to withdraw his eyes, with a stifling inhalation, to the spot where Phœbe Ellen was sitting. The sight of her brought him in a measure to himself. She was sewing placidly, the morning sunshine making a strong yellow light in her hair. He had time to think that the patient had probably opened her eyes at the same moment as himself, for Phœbe Ellen was watchful, and would have noticed a moment or two after the event occurred.

"She ain't dead," he thought. "She can't be dead." Something in the effort of self-assurance brought him to his feet, still under the horrid spell of his awakening.

"She's dead!" he cried, in a hoarse voice, in direct contradiction of what he had just been telling himself. And he stood, pointing.

Phœbe Ellen's eyes followed the direction of the pointing finger.

"No," she answered. "She's waked up. Go fer the doctor. He's in his room."

The calm, business-like tone reassured him, and he was able to shake off his horror. He left the room, still not quite steadily, but with an awakening sense that the crisis had come.

Phœbe Ellen dropped her work and took three steps to the bedside. In doing so she passed between the patient and the light, but attracted no attention from the staring eyes.

"They can't be nothin' wrong with 'er," she thought, as she reached the sick girl's side. "She's a-breathin' the same 's ever."

She came close and bent down. There was no recognition in the sightless orbs—only a ghastly stare, fixed meaninglessly upon space.

"Sis!" she called.

There was no sign of intelligence.

"Sis!" she repeated in a louder voice.

The unwinking eyes remained fixed upon vacancy.

"Sis!" she cried. "Wake up! Wake up! Don't ye know me?"

But the same vacant apathy was her only response.

All at once a wild look came into Phœbe Ellen's face—a look which seemed thrust to the surface ·by some unholy thought. "If she was to fall asleep agin she might die. That wouldn't be my fault. If the doctor 'n' Sam was to wait long 'nough—could I manage it? I might try to wake 'er, ever so gently, so 't it would be the truth if I told 'em I tried. They ain't no harm in that, nohow."

She glanced fearfully about as if dreading a spy upon her actions. The door was closed tightly—she listened. Sam and the doctor were not yet approaching—she would be able to hear their footsteps on the uncarpeted floor of the next room long before they neared the door. She bent close to the invalid's ear, intending to whisper her name. "That 'll be 'nough to sat'sfy my conscience," she thought, with a guilty tremor at her heart. But the next instant her better nature predominated, and she found herself shaking Anny violently by the shoulder, and crying, in a shrill, sharp tone:

"Sis! Sis! Why don't ye wake up 'n' be yerself? It's me 't 's callin' ye. Don't ye know me?"

Was she mistaken? Did the helpless head turn a little in her direction? No — surely it could not be; the eyes were as lack-lustre as ever; there was the same look in all the features as if the soul had fled out of them and left only their familiar lines where life had been.

And now a great desire took possession of her to recall this wandering mind, to force it back into its old habitation and make it take up its accustomed line of thought. For a moment the good in her predominated altogether, and she forgot the difficulties she might be preparing for herself in helping her sister back to life.

"Sis!" she repeated, accompanying the word with another shake.

She stood erect, the better to observe any change which might occur. Surely the eyes had narrowed a little; they were trying to fix on something definite close at hand !

Had she understood ? Phœbe Ellen's heart fluttered guiltily. Then a sense of her own danger came back, and the possibility that Anny might wake up in her right mind filled her with dread. She had never realized till that moment how she had counted on the doctor's word, and how much it meant to her that she should enter into her sister's name and place in the world. Would it not have been better to make true the first murderous thought of the morning following the accident ?

But even with this horrid regret in her mind she went on trying to awaken the unconscious girl.

"Anny !" she called, uttering her sister's name for the first time. What if the doctor and Sam should hear ? She could not help it. A power stronger than herself was driving her on.

Now the staring eyes were certainly turned towards her.

"Ye know me ?"

There was no response to the question but another effort of readjustment in the staring orbs.

"Ye know me—yer sister Phœbe Ellen ?"

The effort seemed to continue, but she could not be sure. It occurred to her that she might accidentally have placed herself directly in the girl's sight, and that she had only imagined the attempt to follow her movements. She stood a little to one side.

"Anny !" she called, trying to attract her attention in that direction.

The eyes did not really move, though the lids fluttered, as if the muscles were trying to adjust themselves to movement. But there was no further result that Phœbe Ellen could be sure of.

"Is she goin' to stay awake, I wonder ? Why don't she do one thing or 'nother, anyway ? If she was to go to sleep agin afore the doctor come back — would I try to hender her? Course I would! Ain't she my own sister? But I wonder if she was reely tryin' to notice. She might 'a' been jes' tryin' to foller the noise, 'thout 'memberin' her name 't all, so *that* ain't no sign she's comin' to herself. I wouldn't mind much wot else she 'membered if she'd only fergit 'er name 'n' the ownership o' the ranch."

Then Sam's heavy steps were audible in the next room, mingled with the light, irregular, dragging sound of the doctor's. The door opened, and the cowboy entered first. He was quite himself now.

"She's still awake?" was his first question.

"Yes," answered Phœbe Ellen, bending over her sister so as to conceal her own face. "But I can't seem to make 'er see me. I been tryin'."

The doctor came up. Excitement gave a momentary steadiness to his nerves, and he looked almost manly.

"We must make her see us," he declared.

He brought his open palm close to the girl's eyes, thrusting it back and forth threateningly, but the dilated pupils stared straight ahead without shrinking.

"She made more show 'n that when I hollered at 'er," said Phœbe Ellen, always ready to disparage any movement of the doctor's.

He shook out a red shawl in the patient's range of vision, but without result.

"Her eyes is shorely a-gittin' duller," declared Phœbe Ellen. Her words expressed a secret hope, but her voice betrayed only anxiety.

"Is she blind—d' ye reckon she's waked up blind?" she asked, in a hushed voice.

And the doctor answered: "No. She isn't awake yet, that is all. We must rouse her in some way. If we had a bright light—"

"'Ud the candle do?"

"Let us try it," said the doctor.

The candle was brought and lighted. The doctor passed it to and fro before the patient's eyes so closely that the glare would have been unbearable to the ordinary vision. Once or twice a slight tremulousness of the lids was perceptible, and Sam declared he had caught a momentary frown between the brows; but both signs were too elusive to count in the scale of returning consciousness. The pupils remained open and staring, and the eyeballs did not turn. Then, even while they wondered at the insensibility of nerve which gave no sign of shrinking before that blaze of light, the patient moved her head slightly, not as if to avoid the glare, but wearily, as if to find an easier position for the muscles of her neck. After that she nestled her head slightly among the pillows, drew up her left arm, and let it fall upon her breast with a sighing breath. Then, with the peculiar *tasting* movement of the lips which is common with sleeping people who have been disturbed and who are settling themselves for another nap, she turned her head still farther to one side, and the eyes, still undisturbed by the proximity of the candle, closed heavily and slowly.

"Be ye goin' to let 'er go off agin?" asked Sam, anxiously. "Didn't ye say that was dang'rous?"

"It must be stopped," answered the doctor, with decision. "We must get her attention somehow."

"I hollered in 'er ear afore ye come in," said Phœbe Ellen. "But it didn't do no good. She was as deaf as the wall."

"I kin go ye one better 'n hollerin'," declared Sam, seizing his pistol and dragging it from its belt on the table.

Phœbe Ellen looked as if about to protest, but the doctor nodded approval.

"Wot if ye was to skeer 'er into fits?" Phœbe Ellen demanded. When she felt like protesting, she always did it.

"Fits is easy cured," declared Sam. "Shall I let her drive?"

"Yes," said the doctor.

"Then put yer hands to yer ears."

And Phœbe Ellen and the doctor obeyed.

Sam got as close to the bed as possible, aimed the pistol at the floor, and fired. The noise in the little room was terrific; for an instant it seemed as if they were standing inside an earthquake. Then the deafness which followed the shock filled the world with a great blank, into which they seemed to be dissolving. But presently they remembered what it was all about, and glanced towards the bed.

The patient was sitting up and rolling her eyes about. She was holding both hands to her ears in a sort of spasm, thus indicating that she had located the sound somewhere outside herself. But that she was unaware of anything more definite than a crash of the nerves, a shock which had left every muscle quivering, was evinced by the meaningless, void gaze which wandered about in search of what had aroused her, but was incapable of directing itself to any reasonable explanation. The only expression on her face was one of helpless terror, and that was pitiful beyond the power of words. The whole occurrence was like a child's first experience of pain, which confuses and terrifies, but has no meaning beyond a rending shock.

Phœbe Ellen seated herself on the side of the bed and put her arms around her sister.

"There, there, sis," she kept repeating, in a soothing voice. "There, there!"

She became so interested in pacifying the terrified creature that she forgot her own interest in the issue.

"There, there! Don't be skeert. It won't hurt ye— it wa'n't nothin' to take on about. Don't ye see? We done it a-purpose to rouse ye up. We won't do it no more."

The invalid did not look at her or seem to have any curiosity as to who was near; but that she noticed and was comforted was evident from her leaning in Phœbe Ellen's direction, as a frightened child might do when mutely craving protection. Phœbe Ellen put her arms more closely about her and held her thus, saying:

"Did it skeer ye, sis? Did it make ye mos' jump out o' yer five senses? Well, it was horrid, but we had to rouse ye up. There! Now ye feel better, don't ye? Now ye ain't so skeert? See, it's me 't 's with ye—look up. Don't ye know me?"

The words and tone were perfectly natural, for Phœbe Ellen was altogether in earnest. She had forgotten everything but that her sister was weak and ill and terrified and needed comfort and encouragement. There was no danger of the doctor just then, for her strong and simple emotion of pity excluded all consciousness of intrigue and wrong-doing, and had he chosen to read her thoughts, he would have found nothing of which she need be ashamed. He was, however, even more deeply occupied for the time being than she. The explosion of the gun in his vicinity had given his nerves a shock which, had he estimated its intensity beforehand, he would have avoided by flight. He felt shattered, unable to concentrate his thoughts upon anything, least of all upon an experiment in mind-reading whose outcome was at best problematic.

He sank into a chair and lay there gasping and quivering.

"Good Lord, Tinker!" he finally cried, still holding his hands to his ears. "What kind of a gun do you carry, anyway? It couldn't be anything less than a mountain howitzer!"

Sam did not answer or notice. His eyes were upon the patient, who had nestled closer and closer to Phœbe Ellen, until, as if vaguely assured of her safety, she began to wail in a strange, high key, like the cry of a little child when the

world first comes in contact with it and makes it suffer.
It was pitiful, but uncanny. Sam listened with a sense
of chill, as to something supernatural ; but even as he listened, the unused voice deepened, the wail shattered itself
into sobs, and the weeping of the woman was audible where
the wail of the child had been.

"That is horrible !" cried Sam, turning to the doctor
for an explanation. "What does it mean ?"

The consumptive had recovered sufficiently to speak,
though brokenly.

"It means that her crying is typical of everything in
her future ; that her mind is utterly gone ; that she has
become a child again—"

"That she won't never know nothin', ye mean ?"

"She will learn some things—some very simple things ;
but they will be like her crying — she will begin them as
a child, and sometimes, not always, will carry them to the
condition of that womanhood which she has lost. She
must begin everything over again, and the point she will
be able to attain can only be a matter of conjecture."

Phœbe Ellen uttered an involuntary cry of protest.

"You seem to care," he said, evidently remembering
something he had fancied he had read in her thoughts
days ago.

"Care ?" she cried, indignantly. "Ain't she my
sister ?"

"Queer !" she heard him mutter once more.

CHAPTER XVI

"Arter all, it's wot I expected," said Phœbe Ellen, after a pause. She began to remember that the doctor was her enemy, and that she had to look out for him; but after glancing him over, it became evident that she had nothing to fear. He was too shattered to exert his power, whatever its nature or object; his voice shook when he tried to speak, and the vacant stammer of weakness interrupted his words.

"We orter be thankful even fer *so* much," said Sam, in a low voice. "I'm glad to have 'er alive on any terms."

"It's better 'n I expected," Phœbe Ellen declared.

"Hang that gun of yours!" chattered the doctor. "It struck the house like a clap of thunder. The least you can do now is to help me to my room. Great heavens! Why not kill a man at once? I can't walk!"

"Shall I kerry ye?" asked Sam, as if it were a matter of every-day occurrence to carry full-grown men about the house. And without waiting for an answer he lifted the consumptive and settled him in one arm as if he had been a baby.

The doctor half grinned, but did not rebel.

"Thanks," he said. "If I had your strength I'd move the world. There's some brandy in my room that will set me up again. Heavens, what shoulders you have! If she wants to go to sleep after this," he had turned to Phœbe Ellen with his thin face in proximity to Sam's big neck, "you may let her. It will be a natural sleep, and she will awake from it naturally. I sha'n't see her again for some little time—I shall have enough to do to get over the effects of that infernal gun. What's the use of a man's carrying a whole Fourth of July around in a gun-barrel, anyway?"

"Ye're shore she'll never be 'erself agin?" Phœbe Ellen asked as the two men reached the door. The question came of itself, and a thrill of dread went through her before it had passed her lips lest the doctor should detect the eager hope behind it.

But he noticed nothing.

"Sure," he answered. And then Sam bore him from the room, a creature who seemed made up of nothing but staring eyes and dangling arms and legs.

Phœbe Ellen found herself alone with her sister, but with none of the elation she had expected to feel at the final settlement of all her doubts. She had expected to rise from that assurance serene and dominant, with a scope of established power which would embrace the entire future and make life delightful. But with her arms about the sick girl, and the sound of her subsiding sobs in her ears, she could feel nothing but a great pity for the ruined life upon which her own prosperity was to be built.

"Pore sis! pore sis!" she kept repeating with genuine sorrow. And in the same breath she was thinking, "I'm mistress o' the ranch now. Sam's the overseer. We'll run it together—us two!"

She would be good to Anny—poor Anny, who had lost so much and who would never be herself again. But the generous outrush of loving protection was never altogether unhindered in its course by another thought. "I'll have a heap better chance with Sam now. He liked sis—I know he did. But he'd never think o' marryin' a idiot."

At last Anny's sobs subsided into short, sharp catches of the breath in the throat; finally these, too, became less vehement, and only an agitated rising and falling of the breast remained of the sick girl's terror. Her eyes had not closed, and there was no symptom of sleep in the staring orbs ; neither was there sign of intelligent consciousness. The vital functions were all alive and active, but behind the physical awakening the intellect lay dead—shocked into inactivity, like some delicate piece of mechanism when dropped, though still unbroken.

"S'posin' I try to see if she knows anything," thought Phœbe Ellen. "She's shorely awake, 'n' I reckon she ain't tired. I'll see."

She held the girl off at arm's-length and looked at her.

"If I could make 'er see me, she might reco'nize me in spite o' the doctor," she thought. "'N' then where 'ud I be ?"

She brought her face into focus with the wide-open eyes, determined to make them see her. But they only stared, they did not notice.

Then she began to speak.

"Look at me, sis," she said. "No, not there !" The sightless eyes turned indifferently towards the wall or the ceiling as the head rolled helplessly about. Phœbe Ellen braced the flaccid neck against her arm, and steadied the head so that the eyes looked fully into hers. "There ! Can't ye see me now ?"

She might as well have talked to a stick or a stone, but the effort of speech steadied her own actions and made them logical. "If she kin be made to notice, I'm goin' to make 'er do it," she thought. "Pore sis ! I mus' learn 'er all I kin, fer she'll be less trouble. Besides, she'll be happier ; 'n' I *want* 'er to git back all she kin 'thout makin' it too warm fer *me*."

She tried a dozen different ways of attracting the girl's attention, and gradually, as she gazed into the unresponsive eyes, she caught a hint of life in the slumbering soul ; an atom of intelligence, manifesting itself, as it were, in a point of life far back in the brain, a spark flickering faintly out of the depths of vacancy. It grew to a speck, a luminous blur which the gazer could be sure of. It wavered, turned back, swayed aside, seemed all but lost. There was nothing clear and definite about it. But it was intelligent and responsive. It seemed in search of something.

"She sees me," said Phœbe Ellen to herself. "But she don't look like she knows me."

She moved a little to one side; the luminous speck followed her. She drew back; it followed her still.

"The doctor's right," she concluded. "She won't be a fool, but she's got to begin all over. That bright little spark in 'er eyes kin be made to grow. But how much? That's the question."

She varied her experiment in many ways, and was rejoiced as a mother is in watching a child's first efforts at attention; but even in the midst of her pleasure came the wickedly calculating thought: "The spark won't grow too big fer my convenience; I'm dead shore o' that, fer the doctor told me. But if it should—"

She glanced away from her sister and fetched a deep breath.

"If it should—I could find a way to stop it."

Again she fixed her eyes upon the sick girl with kindly interest.

"She'll soon foller things," she thought. "She don't tire nothin' like 's quick 's wot a baby does. 'N' I'll do my best to learn 'er—I reely will. The best won't be nothin' 't 'll tell agin me. It's a God's blessin' she *kin* learn. I reckon it won't be no great shakes, nohow. 'N' I'll do my dooty by 'er, wotever comes."

Satisfied with her experiments thus far, she determined to go further. She lifted one of the limp hands and held it up in the girl's range of vision. After a minute's vague search the wandering eyes found it, and examined it with the gravity of a child who has just discovered its fingers. Phœbe Ellen let the hand go, and it fell helplessly upon the bedclothes ; the eyes tried to follow it, but failed, and gazed about with a puzzled expression. The experiment was repeated two or three times, and finally the eyes followed the hand in its fall, and rested curiously upon it where it lay upon the bed-coverings. Two or three times more Phœbe Ellen lifted it and dropped it, with the result that the eyes were able to keep it in view, but each time with increasing quickness. Finally the invalid, instead of letting her hand fall, held it aloft when Phœbe Ellen released it, and the eyes examined it with sober curiosity while the fingers worked a little. Then a slow smile overspread the features, whose vacancy had given place to an inquiring seriousness—not a smile of appreciation nor one demanding sympathy, but a smile which vaguely recognized the first successful outworking of the individual will. It was very pitiful—that childish smile on the mature features of the woman.

All this time Phœbe Ellen had been sustaining her sister in an erect position by her right arm, but now she gradually withdrew that support, being careful to leave the sitting figure in balance. But her care was ineffectual, the form wavered and would have fallen had she not caught it once more and eased it down among the pillows.

"Pore thing !" she thought, with a great pity. "She's even got to learn to set alone !"

She had expected some demonstration of fear from the toppling sensation which must have been experienced by the invalid, but there came no stronger expression into the face than a vaguely puzzled look, which gradually settled into the level lines of content as the stable softness of the pillows became a thing to rely upon. Phœbe Ellen did not disturb her again.

"I mustn't tire 'er," she thought. "That's 'nough fer this time."

And she leaned forward, gazing with an almost motherly tenderness into the half-conscious, wide eyes. The look of content on the invalid's face deepened as Phœbe Ellen gazed, and took on something more spiritual than the animal satisfaction which had been visible when she first settled back among the pillows.

"Kin it be she's learnin' to keer fer me?" thought Phœbe Ellen, with a strange thrill. "If she should, I b'lieve I could like 'er better 'n I done when she was well. But it 'ud be queer—'most like she was my own child!"

With a sudden impulse of tenderness she lifted Anny's hand and laid the palm to her cheek, rubbing it softly about. Then she left the hand to itself. For a moment it remained there, then it stirred softly, moving back and forth. And Phœbe Ellen saw that she was smiling contentedly, and with a new expression in her eyes.

"She's learnin' to keer fer me!" she thought, with delight.

She bent over and kissed her on mouth and forehead—an act of demonstrative fondness of which she had not been guilty for years. Then she rose, rubbed her eyes, and moved aimlessly about the room.

"I'll be good to her!" she kept repeating to herself.

Presently she thought of feeding her, and went into the kitchen to have Leatherhead prepare some gruel. When she came back, Anny was still awake.

Then she fed her, and the gruel was devoured greedily.

"That's right," was Phœbe Ellen's approving comment. "'N' now it 'ud be best fer her to go to sleep." And she adjusted the limp head upon the pillow and left her. Then she went out into the kitchen to leave the empty gruel-bowl, and when she came back the invalid was fast asleep.

By-and-by Sam came in to inquire after the patient, and they two stood by the bedside and discussed the case in whispers.

"By-the-way," said Sam, when they had exhausted

their subject, "Pete Hawkins was over 'ere to-day, and he says Pinky's sick."

"Pinky? Oh yes. Pinky Rose?"

"Ye'd fergot 'im?" smiled Sam.

"Well, ye must own up I've been purty busy. Much sick ? I hope not."

"A bad cold. He wanted Pete to tell ye, so 't ye wouldn't think it queer he hadn't been over."

"Oh, *I* wouldn't think it queer. I wouldn't think nothin' 'bout it."

"Well, it's purty plain *he* was thinkin' 'bout it. He hopes to be over in a few days."

"Oh, well. O' course. I'll be glad to see 'im."

"Is she puttin' that on ?" wondered Sam. "Or is it simon-pure don't-care ?"

"'Tain't noways likely nobody 'll have to set up with 'er agin," said Phœbe Ellen, dismissing Pinky with a jerk of her head in Anny's direction. "She'll prob'ly go to sleep early in the evenin' 'n' rest like a child till mornin'."

After that, Sam went out to the barn to take his nap, and Phœbe Ellen sat down by the window for a period of self-communion.

"I wonder if he reckons I'm in love with Pinky Rose," she meditated. "If he does, he's mistook, that's all. To be shore, Pinky ain't so bad 's wot he might be ; a woomarn could manage 'im 'thout any trouble. Yes, he'd be a reg'lar lamb fer managin' ; 'n' that's the kind o' man I'd marry if I hadn't ruther have one 't could manage *me*. Well, they's plenty o' time to settle *that*."

She leaned against the window-frame, gazing out at the rocks and shadows.

"Things seems to be comin' jes' my way," she continued. "I've got everything I planned fer—the ranch 'n' everything, 'n' nobody to say a word agin it. Nobody but the doctor, 'n' he don't count; I'm ekal to forty consumptive doctors from Boston, 'n' *he* knows it. Nobody 'll ever guess the truth about the bizness. How queer to have a secret like that, 'thout the least chance o' its gittin' out! The only chance is through *him*—'n' sech a little chance! He'll go back to Halstead's now; 'n' when I see 'im, as I reckon I'll have to wunst in a while, I'll keep my wits about me, 'n' if I can't hold 'im down, my name *is* Anny Thompson fer shore! Somehow I don't feel sot up like I reckoned I'd be. I wonder how that is? Mebbe it's 'cause I'm so downright sorry fer sis 't I can't reely take in the meanin' o' the rest. Then, too, 'pears like it jes' come nat'ral fer me to own the ranch. Wot if I'd pizened 'er that mornin' when the idee come into my head?" She shivered at the thought. "Then I *would* 'a' had suthin' to think about. But now I 'ain't done nobody no harm. *She* couldn't see to things nohow, not if it was known 't everything b'longed to 'er. The bossin''ud fall on me jes' 's much 's it will now when everybody b'lieves the hull thing is mine. 'N' so everything 's all right, 'n' nobody 'll ever know. Queer, how Pinky took me fer Anny from the start. 'N' Sam, too. 'Pears like they was a kind o' Providence in it."

She stirred restlessly at the window and began to beat a tattoo on the pane.

"I don't feel like sewin' jes' yet. Wot shall I do? Say —wot a idiot I be, anyhow! Here I've been 'ere four days 'n' 'ain't been over the house yit, 'n' 'ain't got no more idee o' wot's in it beyend the kitchen 'n 's if it b'longed to the Queen o' Sheeby. That's jes' wot I'll do — I'll go 'n' take a look at the rooms while sis is sleepin'."

In the aspect of the house she found little either to praise or condemn. "It's 's good 's wot ye could expeck from a passel o' men keepin' house together," was her comment. Somewhere in the rear of the house, however, she heard a noise above her which attracted her attention. A trap-door was open in the ceiling, evidently leading to a garret. She placed one hand on the ladder, and stood gazing up and listening.

"Who's there?" she called, as she once more heard some one moving.

"Oh, it's Leatherhead," she concluded, recognizing the irregular, irresponsible tread.

A moment later he appeared at the trap-door.

"Oh, tripe!" he called down. "That you? Anything wanted?"

"Nothin'," was her answering call. "Wot ye doin' up there?"

"I was lookin' arter some o' the doctor's truck. Want to come up 'n' see? The ladder's safe 's Moffatt's Bank."

"Truck? Wot kind o' truck?" She was already ascending the ladder, and in a moment was peering into the garret on a level with Leatherhead's feet.

The place was dimly illuminated by four small dusty panes of glass at the far end. There was absolutely nothing to be seen but small heaps of weeds, which seemed to have been spread out here and there for the purpose of drying.

"Oh, that stuff," added Phœbe Ellen, after taking in the room and its contents. "Wot is it?"

"Oh, say!" objected Leatherhead. "*You* know wot that is. Everybody knows loco-weed."

"Never heerd o' it afore. Loco-weed?"

"Well, tripe! Never heerd o' loco-weed? It grows everywheres."

"Wot's it fer, anyhow?"

"Well, ye'd know if ye seen a steer 't happened to git a holt o' a wad o' it by mistake. To see 'im hump 'n' throw hisself, 'n' stop 'n' glare like he seen a ghost, then fling his heels in the air 'n' snort 'n' flourish his tail! Well! Loco-weed is wot sets the cattle crazy—that's wot. Jest a little while afore ye come—"

"No matter! Wot's the doctor dryin' it fer?"

"He's agoin' to send a lot o' it to Boston to a friend to find out wot's in it to make the cattle go crazy. He got me to gather it fer 'im—he says it grows ranker 'ere 'n _over to Halstead's."

"Find out wot's in it? How kin they do that?"

"Why," said Leatherhead, with an educational air, "it's the chemistry. That's wot he said—the chemistry. I tuck it he meant the colorin' o' the leaf, but anyways that's wot he said. To pay express on a lot o' weeds like that, clear to Boston—say! He give me a half a dollar, though, chemistry or no chemistry. 'N' that's suthin' a feller don't find rollin' up hill every day!"

Phœbe Ellen meditated.

"'Ud the stuff make folks crazy, too, d' ye know?"

"Folks? I never heerd, but I don't see why not. Is folks stronger 'n steers 't the same truck won't set 'em off their heads? Excuse me from havin' it tried on *me!*"

Phœbe Ellen went back to the room where Anny lay. She stood examining her sister for some time.

"That 'ud be better 'n pizen," she finally muttered, half aloud. "But wot makes me think o' sech things now? It's all settled—they ain't no danger any more. Good Lord, wot a sinner I'm gittin' to be!"

CHAPTER XVII

IT is usually believed that the consequences of evil-doing lie in the direction of the deed; that the moral state following a wicked act is retrograde, and that a bad action is the harbinger of worse. This is true up to the point of reaction; by which is meant the point at which wickedness sees no advantage in becoming more wicked, but rather in curtailing itself and assuming, in appearance at least, the qualities of its shining opposite. Some sinners never attain even to the semblance of virtue, because the devil appears to them in many shapes and offers them rewards beyond the attainment of even moderate respectability; and it is to the sinful persistence of this class that the proverb owes its force and value. But to the majority of mankind evil beyond evil assumes a threatening aspect, and we assume a virtue though we have it not, from very fear.

Something of this sort happened to Phœbe Ellen. The assurance of an established position at the ranch softened and sweetened her. Sam noticed the change, and, though he had been by no means predisposed in her favor, was obliged to admit that she was changing for the better. She was less assertive, less inclined to dominate, less insistent on rising to the emergency when the emergency was not there. She was gentler, more pliable. Her voice grew less strenuous in self-assertion; the habitual line of her mouth became horizontal, with a more frequent upward curve; her eyes looked less hard and defiant; in talking, she struggled into a more frequent comprehension of other people's views; and when she argued she insisted less on her own way than on the way that was right or expedient. She did little things for people which she had never thought of doing before. She scolded a good deal — that is, for an average woman, but for herself it was hardly more than the feeble survival of a habit, and no one minded. In Colorado it is tacitly admitted that everybody one meets is a "crank," and worse offences than mere words arrange themselves easily on that basis. But it was noticeable that Phœbe Ellen never scolded Sam. Leatherhead and the boys on the range had their opinions as to the cause of this partiality, and it must be admitted that their judgment was based on sound inductions. They had heard of Sam's victory at the depot — which coincided with their preconceived notion of the condition under which a high-spirited woman ought to fall in love. She sewed on his buttons, and had been seen brushing his sombrero for him. She gave him a smoky-topaz charm for his watch-chain — a trinket which had belonged to her dead brother; and in fact showed an open preference for him which placed the state of her affections altogether outside the realm of mere surmise. And it was noted with no less interest that there was nothing in Sam's treatment of her that would lead her to imagine him a victim of her wealth and softening charms.

It would be impossible to say how much of Phœbe Ellen's improved manner depended upon her regard for Sam; probably it was considerable; for the most business-like of women becomes gentle in proportion as her heart is engaged. But there was another element in the complex of mental and moral processes which lay at the root of the change, and that was conscience. Phœbe Ellen's conscience was of the passive sort which makes no trouble as long as it is let alone; it sought no occasion for remorse; it never stirred without being prodded, and then only in the direction of the prod. It was an easily satisfied conscience, and she had never known the time when she could not appease it by the performance of a good deed of about the same dimensions as a bad one. The only good deed possible, in view of the secret wrong she was doing her sister, was to take the best possible care of the invalid, and by a sort of reflection of this generosity upon those in the neighborhood, look to it that she should not be the aggressor in any difficulties which might arise. The transaction was purely a commercial one. Her conscience had permitted her to wrong her sister, and in return her conscience required her to treat her sister well — in which process were included all those who might be indirectly concerned in Anny's wrongs. It was as easy as a sum in arithmetic.

The doctor remained five days at the ranch, and then returned to Halstead's. There was nothing further for him to do, he said—everything now depended on Phœbe Ellen's nursing. He shook hands with her at parting, as any ordinary visitor might have done, and showed no inclination to return to his mind-reading experiments. If anything was to come of his power it would have to occur in the future. She gloated over the idea that she had completely mystified him and that he had no data for immediate action.

When he was gone she went immediately to the kitchen in search of Leatherhead.

"Did he take that truck with 'im?" she demanded, looking in from the threshold.

Leatherhead looked up from his scrubbing.

"Oh, tripe!" he said, rolling his eyes up at her in surprised questioning. "Truck? Say, wot truck?"

"Them weeds up garret."

"That loco?"

"Yes."

"He took wot he wanted with 'im under the seat o' the buckboard.   Ain't that all right?"

"Yes.   But why didn't he take it all?"

"More 'n he wanted," nodded Leatherhead.

"'N' the rest 's up there now?"

"Jesso."

"Wot be ye goin' to do with it?"

"Pitch it out arter I git through scrubbin'.   Ain't that right?"

"Yes, yes.   That's right.   Pitch the stuff out.   *I* don't want it layin' aroun'."

And she hurried away.   But on her way through the back of the house she passed the ladder leading into the loft and paused to look up.

"I might go 'n' see how much he left," she thought, with her foot on the lower round.

In a moment she was at the top, peering in.

"I wonder how it feels 'n' smells," was her next thought.   "It mus' be powerful funny stuff."

And before she was fairly aware of it, she was examining the curious plant by the light of the window.

She did not remain long, however.   "Wot if Leatherhead was to come 'n' find me 'ere?" she thought.   "'Ud he think I was slippin' some o' it into my apron to dope sis with if she should ever come to 'erself?   No; I'll go right down."

And she hurried from the spot.   But not so quickly but that, almost in spite of herself, she seized a bunch of the dried weed on the way to the trap-door and wrapped it up in her apron.

No one was in sight on the lower floor.   "I'll make some more ginger-snaps fer sis, to pay fer this," she thought.   "She was powerful tickled with the ones I give 'er yistiddy 'n' this mornin'.   I'll keep 'em on hand fer 'er, bein' she likes 'em so.   I don't b'lieve they're bad fer the stummick."

And she hurried down the ladder to the room where the sick girl was sitting up in bed.

"Where 'll I put the stuff?" was her next thought. "Oh, I know. I kin hide it in my valise 'n' lock it. Pore sis! Don't she look innercent a-settin' there? God forbid 't I should ever have to use the truck! I kin throw it away when I feel dead shore. I'll go 'n' git 'er a ginger-snap now; she likes to hold 'em in 'er hands 'n' mumble 'em, pore thing!"

After that the days settled down into the wholesome monotony of regular occupations. Pinky got over his cold sufficiently to come and see her, though his nose and eyes were a sight to behold; and, not being able to work, she insisted that he should remain two days, during which time she dosed him with hot lemonade and whiskey, much to his satisfaction. After that he came over regularly twice a week, and an established friendship grew up between them. Phœbe Ellen always received him familiarly, but she did not permit the immediate and unbounded intimacy which her first profuse invitations had promised. However, he accepted with equanimity the distance she placed between them. It was never so great but that he believed he could see across it. A girl like Phœbe Ellen was not to be won in a moment. She was worth waiting for—she and her property—and he was content to let her manage the affair to her own liking. It is not necessarily to be inferred that Pinky was a mercenary wretch who would not have looked at her a second time without the ranch as a substantial background to her charms. There are people in this world—in good society, too, I have heard—the dimensions of whose affections can be measured only by the length of a bank account; and without the application of such means of measurement it would probably never be suspected that they had affections at all. For all of which—inasmuch as it is love alone which makes the world bearable—we ought to be devoutly thankful to the bank account for adding appreciably to the sum of tender sentiment in the world, instead of condemning it for multiplying the deceitfulness of human relations. As for Pinky, he admired Phœbe Ellen tremendously—and her property in an equal degree with herself.

CHAPTER XVIII

One day Leatherhead came to the front of affairs. He claimed the fulfilment of Phœbe Ellen's promise to take the care of the kitchen upon herself and let him out on the range.

By this time it had become a habit of hers to talk over all her difficulties with Sam.

"I don't seem to see how I kin git along 'thout 'im," she said, anxiously, after reciting the circumstances. "'N' yit I've give 'im my promise, 'n' I can't go back on that. 'N' it's time I was livin' up to it if I'm goin' to. But sis takes sech a orfle lot o' my time—"

The giant turned slowly in her direction, as if to study her face.

"D' ye begrudge it to 'er?" he inquired.

"Begrudge it? Good land, no!"

He gave a lurch away from her, as if satisfied with his examination.

"She don't git no more o' yer time 'n she needs. That's where yer time b'longs, jes' now."

"Ye-es, I know. But I can't be with her 'n' in the kitchen at the same time."

"That's plain," was his form of assent.

"Then wot be I goin' to do?"

"*He* go out on the range!" said the cowboy, with a snort and a laugh.

"He *thinks* he kin, 'n' that's jes' 's bad till he tries it. I could do some o' the kitchen-work—I'd like to. He might help with the washin' 'n' ironin'—"

"'N' bakin'," put in Sam.

"Ye pin a orfle lot o' faith to Leatherhead's bread," smiled Phœbe Ellen. "'N' I own he beats me. But all the same I don't see but wot we've got to let 'im try cowboyin'—leastways fer a while. 'N' sis 'll have to go neglected."

"No, not that. She's got to be took keer of, wotever comes. Neglectin' *her* don't go."

"Well, wot then?"

"S'posin' we let 'im try cowboyin'," suggested Sam, with an enigmatic grin.

"Let 'im try it?"

"Jesso."

"But he'll like it! Ye don't reckon he wouldn't like it?"

"I kin settle *his* stummick fer 'im," said Sam, with a series of slow nods, "in less 'n a pair o' minutes. Leave it to me."

"Ye mean—"

"Ye know Reddy?"

"Reddy the Brick?"

"The wust bucker on the hull Rio Grande. Well, Leatherhead *don't* know 'im. That might be a advantage—see?"

"Ye don't mean ye're goin' to turn Leatherhead loose on Reddy?"

"No; I'm goin' to turn Reddy loose on Leatherhead."

"But the danger—they *is* danger?"

"The beast 'll jerk knots in 'im!"

"'N' if he was to die?"

"I'll see to that. He deserves a sound bumpin', the way he's been takin' on 'bout his cowboy fixin's. He's been collectin' lariats 'n' sombreros 'n' chaps 'n' cuerts, like he was goin' to perform in a circus with a pack o' gals gawpin' at 'im from the benches. I kin cure 'im 'n' keep 'im in the kitchen at the same time; only don't say a word."

And with that he left her.

Phœbe Ellen knew when the experiment came off, for Sam told her; but Leatherhead's appearance would have proclaimed the fact to the world had all other portents failed. She saw him in all the glory of his cowboy paraphernalia pass out at the front door, turn the corner, and disappear behind the barn. "All the boys 'll be there to laff at 'im, fer Sam's made a sort o' party o' it," she thought. "But I'm glad it's out o' sight o' the winders. I don't want to see the pore chap hurt."

She heard all about it afterwards from Sam and the others, but Leatherhead's own account was by far the most graphic. He looked forlorn enough on his return. He had lost his sombrero and cuert; his red silk neckerchief—the pride of his heart—was twisted with a knot behind, so that a triangle of it covered his breast like a bib; his lariat was trailing in the dust; his leather shirt was torn; his chaps were unbuckled and hung flapping from the waist; he carried his cartridge-belt and pistol in his hand, and there was blood about his nose, and dirt on every conceivable corner and line of his body.

Phœbe Ellen saw him coming, and ran out upon the veranda in some alarm to meet him. But a single glance assured her that he was more scared than hurt.

"Tell ye 'bout it?" he replied, in answer to her question, flinging himself upon the floor and thrusting his cartridge-belt and pistol from him as if the sight of them made him sick. "Oh, wait till I ketch my breath!"

Phœbe Ellen smiled.

"Ye couldn't make it go, then?" she asked.

He turned over on his side and eyed her gloomily.

"Wot d' ye mean by *it*?" he asked.

"The bronco, o' course."

He settled back with a groan.

"Make *it* go? Great gum! Ye orter 'a' seen it make *me* go! Was ye ever on top o' one o' them things?"

"No, never."

"It 'ud scare the soul out o' ye! 'N' don't ye do it 'thout ye've got four hull foot-hills to fasten his feet to. 'N' to think o' the way I went up there 'n' skipped into the saddle, 's airy 'n' light 's if I was made o' pure joy— 'n,' well! D' ye reckon all broncos is like that?"

He gave a lame kick at one of the ranch dogs that came sniffing about his feet.

"Was it so bad?"

"Bad? Well, say—tripe! I should admire to see anything wuss, *I* should! Bad? If ye had a private graveyard anywheres on the place I'd go 'n' crawl into it 'n' never say a word. Ye see, it was jes' like this: I got into the saddle 's fine 's silk, 'n' the critter stood like a ewe lamb till I swung my right leg over 'n' got both feet in the stirrups 'n' the reins taut in both han's; 'n' then— oh, tripe! wot happened? I d' know, I can't tell; but it happened, wotever 't was—it happened all to wunst, 'n' all over me!"

"It must 'a' been bad," said Phœbe Ellen, shutting down on her smile and speaking with sympathy.

"Well, sech grand 'n' lofty tumblin' *you* never seen, I kin take my dyin' oath o' that! I shot up into the air like a hull box o' giant-powder 'd gone off accidental under me. I did, 's shore 's I'm a child o' Sin. I went up, straight up, fer ten minutes, I know I did. I had time to think o' all my sins, 'n' wonder which mountain-top I was comin' down on. I was so high up I could see all over Halstead's ranch, 'n' count the cattle on the range. 'N' Joe was gittin' out the cracky 'n' riggin' the red cayuse into it, 'n' ole Mis' Halstead was waitin' by the pigpen to go somers, with 'er bunnit on. 'Ain't I never goin' to start down?' says I to myself. 'N' 'peared like it'ud be a kinder lonely life to stay up there ferever. But when I come down—oh, say, the air 'n' the lonesomeness was pure joy arter that! 'N' it was the queerest thing—

that dum beast had shifted so 's to git right under me, 'n' I landed fair 'n' square on top o' the very saddle I'd shot out of half a hour afore! It cracked my liver. 'N' there was all the boys a-laffin' at me—'n' Sam along o' the rest. I never thort the like o' that o' Sam. Oh, Lord, wot a smash they was when I struck! I made shore I was goin' 's far down into the airth 's wot I'd been above it, but somehow I stayed in the saddle. Well, I hadn't much more 'n struck till—tripe! if that bronco don't do bizness by lightnin'! Up I started agin, 'n' says I to myself, 'I've got a better start this time, 'n' I reckon I'm in fer a longer v'yage.' I felt the blood a-runnin' out o' my heart like a augur-hole 'd been bored in the bottom o' it. But I kep' on goin' up. 'N' when I come down, that hoss struck me like a pile-driver workin' wrong end up, 'n' back I went into the air agin, seein' stars 'n' wishin' I was dead. Talk about earthquakes! I had *them* all the way up to the stoppin'-place 'n' back agin, 'n' they was jes' fun. But the landin' on the saddle—oh, say! I d' know how long I was circussin' aroun' atween that bronco's back 'n' the sky—I don't want to know. The bare thort o' it wears me out. But sech a churnin' 's I got! Every rib in my body 's busted—I kin feel the broken ends raspin' together here in front."

He drew himself into a sitting position and braced himself with one hand against the floor.

"Gimme my dish-rag 'n' let me go back to the kitchen!" he cried, tragically. "That sort o' life 's good 'nough fer *me!*"

Phœbe Ellen suppressed her laughter.

"Don't take it to heart," she soothed. "Good lan', ye ain't the first human 't 's got into a scrape, 'n' ye won't be the last. They's fun in life yit!"

"But the boys—".

"I'll see to it 't they let ye 'lone 'bout it. Go 'n' lay down. I'll have Sam give ye a rubbin' with liniment, 'n' ye'll be fresh 's a rose by mornin'. Don't take it to heart. It 'll come all right !"

Leatherhead rose stiffly. He regarded her a moment in a sort of bursting silence, then cried out, explosively :

"I allus swore ye was a trump card, 'n' now I know it ! 'N' when I git over this, if I do a thing but stay aroun' the kitchen 'n' wait on ye 'n' drudge fer ye, my name's *mud !*"

And with that he fled into the house as fast as his dilapidated condition would permit.

"Well, *that's* settled," thought Phœbe Ellen, with satisfaction. "I'll help Leatherhead in the kitchen, o' course —I like kitchen-work ; but sis has got to come in fust. It's little 'nough I kin make o' the pore critter at best. But I've got a good thing out o' her, 'n' if my time 'n' keer kin be o' use to 'er she's goin' to have 'em. It's only fair."

CHAPTER XIX

So time went on till August. The gray slopes of mountain-sage had taken a golden tinge from their hanging ball-blossoms; the wild sunflowers sent thrills of vivid color along the uplands; and the magenta of vetches was washed in, like some dainty water-color, below the sombre bases of the foot-hills. The mountains were more deeply purple than they had been in June; at morning they seemed but a deeper fringe on the flaring purple garment of the sky; and at certain hours of the afternoon, under those lovely evanescent lights the secret of whose making the sky only knows, they looked translucent, as if warmed and lighted from within by shaded purple astrals.

The willows were as green as ever, a-droop over the brown and gold of the shadowed water; sociable little groups of primroses danced together as the breeze passed; the groves of aspen on the mountain-side had not yet turned to gold, but still met the advances of the wind with those ecstatic, supersensitive shudders which make them seem so emotional and human. They are like delicate consumptive girls whom a breath of air cannot touch without setting them a-shiver. The only change one noticed in the pines was that their melody had become more thoughtful, as if the idea of the coming winter oppressed them.

The oats had been harvested, and another crop, self-sown like the first, was well under way. Its tender verdure contrasted vividly with the misty gray of the mountain-sage above it, and the harsh, faded green of the potato-tops below. The corn was half grown by this time, and the musical clash of its long leaves made a pleasant accompaniment to the mingled murmur of the river and the pines. One who had time might climb to the summit of the foot-hills—it was not so steep as it looked—and lie down on a ready-made bed of pine-needles, with the world at his feet and the sky very near; and when he returned to the valley he would walk in awed silence, as if he had just clasped hands with God.

The monotony of life at the ranch was broken only by the visits of Pinky and the doctor. Phœbe Ellen had assumed control of the kitchen, but on baking-days and wash-days Leatherhead was in evidence; at other times he was busy about the stables and fields. She was a kind mistress, and all the boys appreciated her; vociferous, it is true, in a sort of purposeless self-assertion, but careful and attentive, and on the whole quite acceptable. She had a business head which not only grasped principles but details, and Sam himself had learned to yield her a measure of admiration which he would have believed it impossible to bestow upon a woman in command. The thing that struck him as remarkable in his own relations with her—he was not sure, however, that it held true in her relations with the other boys—was the fact that she never went "a-hennin' around"; she left him to do as he liked, and accepted the results of his management as the ultimate good thing, beyond which her imagination could picture nothing better.

Phœbe Ellen's chief problem was Pinky; an emotional problem, to be sure, and therefore, it might be thought, one that would be easy of solution; but hitherto Phœbe Ellen's problems had all concerned material things, and she had settled them with little or no regard for anything higher than a momentary advantage, so that the irritating complex which results from being obliged to look to the sensibilities as a basis of solution had never imposed itself upon the simple directness of her methods. But now there were many things to consider. She liked Pinky and knew that he liked her—a combination which, in her experience, possessed the interest of novelty, to say the least. She wanted Sam to see that people liked her, too. (It always enhances the value of an article to know that your neighbors are dying to possess it.) But Pinky really came over too often — three times a week was too often, considering that Sam was usually around. She couldn't tell him to stop, either: first, because she wanted him to come, and, secondly, because Sam would notice and begin to wonder why she was unable to retain her admirers. Not that Sam appeared to care about Pinky's visits; on the contrary, he cared too little altogether. If he had only shown that he noticed and resented them, she would have stopped them with all the joy in life. Or if he had paid the slightest attention to other women, she would have unfurled Pinky before his eyes, so to speak, and kept him floating on the breeze from morning till night. But Sam never seemed to know when women were around; that was what puzzled Phœbe Ellen. And Freckled Mariar and Snickerin' Sal and all the other rustic beauties of the region exerted their charms on him in vain. He cared for Anny, she knew, but in a pitying way that was beyond the reach of jealousy. His life was as open and simple as the day. He went to bed early, got up early, rode with the boys on the range in search of strayed cattle, looked after the harvests, mended the fences, petted the dogs, and smoked his pipe in utter content. Once in a while he went to Eden City, got drunk with Pete Hawkins and Pinky, and came home the next morning without the least attempt to conceal what he had done. He felt the need of an occasional "toot," and took it as simply and naturally as he took his breakfast.

The doctor came over about once a week. He looked more worn and haggard and nervous than ever. "He'll have to take mighty good keer o' hisself if he keeps on top o' the dirt six months longer," said Phœbe Ellen to Sam. The Bostonian was deeply interested in Anny, and kept watch of her progress with something as nearly like affection as could be expected from a nature as distracted as his. There were frequent conflicts between him and Phœbe Ellen, though nothing so pronounced as what had occurred when they first met. These were conflicts of the eyes always, worked out in silence on the lines of suspicion and menace. But he never again really got a glimpse into her thoughts. Once or twice he had stood on the horizon of her mind for a moment, but her will had always risen like a tempest and driven him back. Whenever he approached her she drew herself together for resistance. It often occurred to her that she would have had a much harder time of it had he been in perfect health and possessed the strength dependent thereupon.

The two months since the accident had passed quietly enough for every one except Anny. To her they amounted to years of growth and change. She had begun life like a little child, her mind a blank, her past experiences obliterated by that dreadful catastrophe, as pencil-marks are rubbed off from a slate when a damp sponge is dashed across them. The injury had gone deep—to the very core and centre of mental being. But she learned to sit alone, to hold things, and finally to walk. At first she moved about with difficulty, as a child does—seizing hold of near objects to steady herself, then taking a few tottering steps alone, with now and then a fall, at which she laughed or cried, according to her humor; but later she walked from place to place with the ease which comes of habit and practice. Yet there was a lack of elasticity in all her movements which only those could appreciate who had known her before the accident. She dragged one foot when she walked; there was an uncertainty in her way of reaching for things which the will alone had been unable to overcome. It was as if the source of life had become muddied; and though the power of movement remained, there was none of the old grace and joy to animate it. She could talk, but slowly and hesitatingly—often ramblingly, as if the meaning of words corresponded but vaguely to her ideas. Notions were a slow growth with her, and she expressed them elliptically, as children do. She sometimes tried to sing, but as often as not she lost the melody, and her voice trailed away into queer, unmusical noises, which her ear failed to differentiate from the tune she had in mind. She learned many useful household tasks, and seemed to take pleasure in performing them. She could wash the dishes and set them away on the shelves very neatly; she swept and dusted, she sewed a little, she helped about the washing and ironing; but always Phœbe Ellen was near, as the guiding head, for the afflicted girl could hold her attention to one thing but a little while at a time unless some one was at hand to admonish her. Sometimes while wiping the dishes she would wander away with a plate in her hand, and set it down in some unheard-of place, while she herself strolled about among the pines, humming discordantly to herself while she plucked flowers and berries from the mountainside. Phœbe Ellen learned to have her eyes open for these fits of abstraction, and when she found the poor creature's mind wandering at her tasks she would recall her, sometimes sharply, but never unkindly, and then Anny would go on with her work with a sort of vacant gladness, never with resentment or pique. It was very pitiful, but it was the best that could be done. The doctor had said the girl would do better to have something to take her attention, and there was nothing outside the common household tasks to answer the purpose.

Phœbe Ellen had been very constant and kind. It was good to see her patiently explaining a more rational choice of words than Anny made use of, and teaching her to make consecutive sentences. She never lost her temper; and if she sometimes brought her pupil sharply to time, it was distinctly for the pupil's own good. In these efforts to restore to the injured brain something of its former power, Sam was Phœbe Ellen's warm coadjutor. He spent all his spare time with the unfortunate, patiently trying to give her more definite conceptions of things. It was a task that he loved, that he would not have dispensed with for the world; but it was sad, too, and the great creature was frequently observed wiping his eyes, while his pupil looked on in grieved and gentle wonder; and sometimes he had to leave her till he regained command of himself. Unlike Phœbe Ellen, he was never known to speak sharply; but it was observable that her instructions were more effective than his, and that the girl's advancement was more largely attributable to Phœbe Ellen's kind but rigid discipline than to any other influence brought to bear.

And though Anny learned many things, became, in fact, a help about the place instead of the hinderance into which she might easily have degenerated, she was but the shadow of her former self. Her face had suffered a most pathetic change. The old color was still in the cheeks, the softly curved outline of throat and chin was just the same, the low, pretty forehead gleamed as whitely from its fringe of curls ; but the eyes, without whose kindling fires the other features remain inert matter and nothing more, had the hopeless, blank, lack-lustre look of the feeble-minded, and were lighted only now and then by a gleam of intelligence, which gave them for a moment something of their former brightness and meaning. There was an intellectual lack in every movement of the body, every outline of the features, in the very tinting of the skin. The mental woman was no longer in control, and the physical woman, thus left to herself, was pitiful and, in a manner, dreadful to look upon.

CHAPTER XX

On the second Sunday in August Pinky appeared as promptly as usual at the Thompson ranch. His boots were freshly oiled, he wore a gorgeous necktie, and that ultimate adjunct of elegance, as the word is understood among the mountaineers, a " clean biled shirt."

" Well, fer any sakes !" cried Phœbe Ellen, meeting him, as he dismounted, on the veranda and shaking hands. *Did* she leave her palm in his a little longer than usual ? Pinky wondered. And *did* she squeeze his fingers the least little bit in the world as she obliged him to let go ? He would have given a month's wages to know. But she was rattling on at a great rate. " If ye 'ain't got all yer war-paint on *this* time, fer shore ! Good lan' ! Look at that necktie ! Well, if ye don't look like ye was struck by lightnin', I miss my guess. I shouldn't wonder if yer hair was combed in a reg'lar cowlick, too. Well, here's fine doin's ! Wot's up, anyhow ?"

" Nothin' ain't up, as I knows on," answered Pinky, with his *rose-du-Barry* grin. " I jes' come over, same 's allus. Be ye all to hum ?"

" Spected to find us all to meetin', I reckon ?" she retorted.

" Well," he answered, with magenta deprecation, " I d' know 's wot I went 's fur 's that. But Sam 'n' sis—"

" Oh, they're a-koosterin' aroun' somers. He was tryin' to learn 'er 'er letters a bit ago. Put 'im out in the barn, won't ye ?" She jerked her thumb in the direction of the horse. " Ye know where."

" I reckon he kin stan' 'ere a while," replied Pinky,

tying his tacky little mustang to the veranda post. "I'll put 'im out into the corral by-'n'-by. That's good 'nough fer *him*."

"Want to go in? It's nicer out 'ere. Go 'n' fetch a cheer—there's a good chap. *I* know why ye come over," she added, as Pinky returned with a deal stool and took his place at her side. She was in unusually good spirits, and he noted the fact with the hopefulness which lovers will understand.

"Well, wot'ud I come fer?" he asked, grinning as he propped both elbows on his knees and fixed his cheeks in his palms.

"Ye spotted a hen-fun'ral," she cried, in a tone of accusation.

"Ye don't mean ye're agoin' fer to perform the las' sollum rites over the diseased corpse o' a barnyard fowl to-day?" he asked, in mock surprise.

"I do—I do! At one o'clock!"

"Well, I *have* struck it rich this time, 'n' no mistake!"

"'S if ye didn't know we had hen 's reg'lar 's Sunday come around!"

"Ye was threatenin' ole Topsy all the week, I 'member. Oh, say, it couldn't be Topsy, now?"

Phœbe Ellen nodded a grim affirmative.

"Topsy it is," she announced. "She would set—I couldn't break 'er 'thout breakin' 'er neck, 'n' so ye see wot she's come to. I tied 'er to the corral by one leg, I ducked 'er a dozen times in the river, I hoodooed 'er in fifty ways 't Sam 'n' Leatherhead wanted me to try; but 'twa'n't no go. She would cluck. 'N' so—"

"Off went 'er topknot, hey?"

"Off went 'er topknot this mornin'. I done the bloody deed myself, 'n' enjoyed it, though Leatherhead wanted to take the job off my han's. Sech a obstinit critter! She's layin' in state this minute in the dish-pan in the sink, if Leatherhead 'ain't put 'er into the stew-kittle."

"I reckon I mightn't look at 'er, mightn't I?"

"Not afore the reg'lar service at one o'clock. We're goin' to bile 'er—she's powerful old 'n' tough, that Topsy. Sam 'lows she was the oldes' two-legged critter on the place, barrin' hisself."

"Is Sam so old?"

"Well, old 'longside o' a hen, I take it," answered Phœbe Ellen. "But 's fur 's wot humans goes, 'pears like he 'ain't outlived his usefulness. The ranch still has need o' him."

"By the ranch ye mean yerself, I reckon?" Pinky asked.

"Oh, yes, it's all the same thing! Me 'n' the ranch is one. Kin ye think o' me 'thout the ranch, or the ranch 'thout me?"

Pinky fixed his pale eyes fully upon hers.

"I kin think o' ye anyways ye like, 'ceptin' 'thout me aroun' to look at ye."

"That's all very well," said Phœbe Ellen, with a toss of her head.

"Yes," assented Pinky, "that's all very well, but it might be better."

"Oh, I allus know wot ye're goin' to talk about when ye look like that!" declared Phœbe Ellen.

"Then I mustn't say it?"

"I sha'n't urge ye."

"If I was aroun' to look at ye all the time—"

"Shockin'!" objected Phœbe Ellen.

"'N' if ye was to be where ye could look at me all the time—"

"Scan'lous!"

"We'd both be better off," finished Pinky, with shame-faced deliberation.

"Ye're wantin' a job on the range, I take it, or ye'd never come aroun' me like that," said Phœbe Ellen, folding her hands primly at her belt and slanting her face towards him. "Ye orter speak to Sam. He mos'ly looks arter them things."

"Ye're allus puttin' me off," complained Pinky.

"I reckon a gal has a right to do as she likes, 'n' I like time. I'm shore I've been good to ye," remarked Phœbe Ellen, in a pious tone.

"Oh, good, yes! Ye've let me come over to Sunday dinner—"

"'N' twicet durin' the week," she corrected him.

"Well, wot o' that? We have dinners over to Eden City."

"Yes—sech 's they be. But they ain't 's good—ye know they ain't 's good 's mine, Pinky!"

"No, they ain't 's good 's yourn," he was obliged to admit. "Ye beat anything in the kitchen—I'll own right up to that."

"Well, then, why not keep right on comin' over to dinner, 'n' say no more 'bout it?"

"I wa'n't talkin' 'bout comin' to dinner, nohow," objected Pinky.

"*I* was. 'N' why not put the hull thing on a dinner basis? It'ud be a sensible way."

"Oh, Lord!" groaned Pinky.

"Got a pain?" inquired Phœbe Ellen, kindly.

"Ye don't keer nothin' fer me!"

"I don't like to see nothin' a-sufferin'. Shall I git the campfire? It's powerful upliftin' to the stummick."

"Ye don't—ye don't keer a tinker's darn fer me, 'n' I know it, too."

"Well, how d' ye know it, now?"

"Can't I see?"

"I never *said* sech a thing."

"But ye've acted it—ye're actin' it now. 'N' actions speaks louder 'n words, every time."

"No, I never said it, 'n' I never acted it, nuther. Fer I do keer fer ye. So there!"

Pinky's face lighted up like a red gas-globe when a match is held inside.

"D' ye mean it ?" he cried, eagerly.

"Course I mean it. I liked ye from the start. Don't ye 'member how fine we got on the fust day over there to the depot ?"

Pinky's face fell.

"I 'member," he answered, gloomily.

"Well, then !" crowed Phœbe Ellen.

"Oh, I 'member ! 'N' we've got on jes' the same way ever sence. 'N' that's all *that* means !"

"Some folks 'nd kick if they was hangin'," she remarked.

"Anybody 'ud kick 't had been hangin' from June to August," he retorted.

A change came into Phœbe Ellen's features—a mental change such as shows itself rather in a readjustment of the lines of the face than in a fluctuation in the color of the skin. She fixed her eyes upon his with a look which he had never seen there before.

"Ye ain't the only one 't 's been hangin'," she said.

"Oh, I know the meanin' o' that," Pinky cried. He did not dare to speak directly of Sam in connection with herself, but it was altogether like her to go on of her own accord. Her next words were more positive.

"*You* d' know how long I been hangin'. Gals don't wear their feelin's fer bows 'n' ruffles."

"I reckon that's a crack at me, ain't it ? But men don't try to hide their feelin's. They know they couldn't. They'd git away with 'em, every time."

"But all men ain't alike," she objected.

"They be in that way."

She reflected a long moment.

"I don't b'lieve it !" she finally declared.

"No ?"

"Lots o' 'em could love a gal 'n' never show it !"

“ Fer instance ?”

“ Sam could !”·

Pinky shifted uneasily in his seat before he turned his red face towards her in answer.

“ Mebbe he *could*,” he answered, gravely. “ But he *don’t*—I’m shore o’ that.”

“ How d’ *you* know ?” scoffed Phœbe Ellen. “ Much *you* know ’bout wot Sam thinks. There he is now with sis, comin’ down from the spring. They’ve been up there together fer a good hour.”

“ ’Pears like he sets a heap o’ store by ’er,” remarked Pinky.

“ Yes—’n’ she by him.”

They were silent, watching the two descend the hill. Sam shortened his gigantic stride to suit the short, irregular gait of his companion, though he did not try to keep step with her. She had an uncertain way of lifting her feet, and she stepped long or short, with aimless lurches sideward and forward.

“ I ain’t turned off, then ?” inquired Pinky, whose thoughts had returned to his own love-affair.

“ I don’t never turn off nobody ’ceptin’ fer bad corn-duck,” answered Phœbe Ellen.

“ Then I’m likely to stay on the rest o’ my life.”

“ It ’pends on yer stayin’ power.”

“ Oh, I got plenty o’ that !”

“ In wot way ?”

“ I’ll be good—right along,” grinned Pinky.

“ Oh, ye’re good ’nough. I never said ye wa’n’t good ’nough. ’Tain’t that.”

She seemed willing to open up the subject anew, and Pinky certainly had no objection.

“ Wot is it, then ?” he asked.

She tossed her head.

“ Why, ye see, there’s my own mind,” she suggested.

“ Oh, that’s a big matter,” said Pinky.

“ It is with a gal, when she don’t know it.”

“ When she don’t know it’s a big matter ?”

“ A gal’s mind is allus a big matter when she don’t on-derstan’ it,” said Phœbe Ellen, explicitly.

“ Then I kin keep right on hopin’ ?”

“ No harm kin come o’ that, ’s I kin see.”

“ Does it bother ye when I talk about it ?”

“ It might, if ye was to talk too much.”

“ I’ll be keerful,” Pinky promised.

And at that moment Sam and Anny came up.

CHAPTER XXI

THE girl came heavily across the veranda to Phœbe Ellen's side and sat down on the floor. She looked tired and wistful. There was a set wrinkle in her forehead, which had grown there since the accident. It would have been less sadly conspicuous had it seemed the result of thought.

"Why not git a cheer?" asked Phœbe Ellen. "Wouldn't ye ruther?"

The girl turned her face upward in mute questioning. Phœbe Ellen saw that she had asked two questions in succession—a complication which her sister was often unable to follow.

"Why don't ye git a cheer?" she repeated.

Evidently Anny understood, but she shook her head.

"Wouldn't ye ruther?"

"No," was the dull answer.

"Ye like the floor better?"

"Yes."

"Tell me why."

Anny considered.

"I'm tired," she finally said, with a long sigh.

"Too tired to think?"

She nodded.

"But the floor—ye kin tell me why ye like to set on the floor?"

Anny considered again.

"It's big," she presently answered. "I can't fall off."

Phœbe Ellen smiled as she smoothed her sister's hair.

"D' ye have a good time with Sam 'n' yer book?" she went on.

Anny looked at her, perplexed.

"Book?" she repeated.

"Yes. Don't ye 'member yer book? See! Sam's got it in his hand now."

"Oh," said the girl, after a look in Sam's direction.

"D' ye have a good time with Sam?" repeated Phœbe Ellen.

"Yes," was the answer, not quite so dully given, but always with a vocal vacancy which corresponded with the eyes. Sam, who had seated himself on the edge of the veranda, smiled at her, but his face was sad.

"Ye like to be with Sam?" continued Phœbe Ellen.

"Yes."

"'Cause he's good to ye?"

"Yes."

"Sam's allus good to ye?"

"Oh yes."

The voice was becoming more expressive.

"'N' yer book—ye like that, too?"

"No."

"It's too hard?"

"Hard—hard! It's too hard!" repeated the girl, like a parrot.

"Sometimes I make shore I better not pester 'er with it no longer," Sam put in.

"*I* wouldn't," declared Pinky.

"I can't see 't anything comes o' it but the pesterin'," Sam continued. "She can't l'arn. It jes' worries 'er."

"Jesso," acquiesced Pinky.

"Her 'n' me 's talked it over, though." Sam jerked his thumb in Phœbe Ellen's direction. "She 'lows it's better to keep the pore thing stirred up."

"She'll l'arn to hate the sight o' ye 'n' yer book," said Pinky.

Sam looked startled.

"God ferbid!" he ejaculated, with fervor. Then, facing Phœbe Ellen with the anxiety still in his face, "Wot d' ye think o' that?"

"O' her hatin' ye?"

She met his eyes with perfect coolness.

But Sam was not reassured.

"If I made shore she'd do that—"

"Ye'd kill yerself, I make no doubt."

"I'd never make 'er look inside o' the kivers o' a book agin, ye may be shore o' that."

"Rot!" snorted Phœbe Ellen. "She keers too much fer ye to let a few letters in a book upset the bizness. Don't ye, sis?"

But Anny had been unable to follow the conversation, and answered her sister's question only by a vague "How?"

"The docter says how as it's good fer 'er," continued Phœbe Ellen. "It keeps 'er a-tryin', 'n' that henders 'er from doatin'. I don't reckon it pesters 'er, either, 's much 's wot ye think. She jes' sorter feels bad 't she can't do wot ye want 'er to. Mebbe that's a good thing in itself; the docter says so. It keeps 'er agoin', anyway. 'N' she likes to try to please ye—I know that. Does Sam pester ye?" she asked, suddenly turning to Anny.

Still the same vacant voice in answer:

"No."

"Does the book pester ye?"

"Yes."

"But if Sam wasn't to l'arn ye from the book no more?"

Anny pondered.

"How?"

Phœbe Ellen repeated her question very distinctly.

"No book no more?" asked the girl, eagerly.

Phœbe Ellen nodded.

"I'd like that," enunciated the poor creature after a moment.

"But if ye couldn't have Sam, either ?"

"No Sam ?" Anny's eyes widened in distressed surprise.

"The book 'n' Sam allus go together—see ?"

The possibility of losing Sam had momentarily sharpened the girl's faculties.

"Not allus—not allus," she declared. "Sometimes—sometimes Sam leaves the book behind !"

"But if ye have Sam, ye mus' have the book, too."

Again the interval of pondering.

"How ?"

"No book, no Sam," replied Phœbe Ellen, pausing slightly after each word.

"Oh," said Anny, after a longer pause than usual.

"Sam can't be with ye 'nless ye l'arn the book," declared Phœbe Ellen.

Sam's big, kindly face was full of pathos as he interrupted :

"Don't make a bugbear o' me—don't make 'er hate me !"

"Hush !" commanded Phœbe Ellen.

Anny had crept closer to Sam along the floor until she could touch his hand.

"I'll l'arn," she said, turning her vacant, pathetic eyes upon him, and laying her cheek softly against his hand. "I'll l'arn—I'll l'arn !"

"That's a good gal," commended Phœbe Ellen. "Ye'd do anything fer Sam, wouldn't ye ?"

"I'll l'arn—I'll l'arn !" came the discordant refrain.

"She won't hate ye, don't ye see ?" asked Phœbe Ellen. "She'd do anything fer ye. 'N' I know it does 'er good to try. It's harder on *you* 'n anybody else."

"I kin stan' it, if it's reely good fer 'er," said Sam, in a low voice.

"It *is* good fer 'er. If we was to let 'er have 'er own way, she'd go back to where she started. We mus' keep

’er a-tryin’. That’s wot counts—the tryin’. ’Tain’t a question o’ wot she wants, but o’ wot’s good fer ’er.”

Sam knew she was right, and said so.

“But it’s so dreadful,” he added, turning away his face from the girl, who was still caressing his hand.

“I know—but ’tain’t a question o’ that, nuther. ’N’ if ’twas, it’ud be dreadfuller to see ’er go back to wot she was.”

“Yes,” Sam admitted. And he was glad in his heart that Phœbe Ellen was at hand to urge him on by her wisdom. Left to himself, he would have acted on sentiment altogether, and would have permitted the girl to do just as she liked, regardless of consequences.

“How fur ’d ye git to-day?” continued Phœbe Ellen, turning once more to her sister.

“How fur ?”

The girl turned her vacant eyes first upon her sister, then upon Sam.

“How fur—up the mountain ?”

“No—how fur in the book ?”

“Oh, the book !”

She fell a-musing, while the lines of her face took a downward turn.

“No further, no further, no further,” she intoned, in a dreary throat-voice.

“Jes’ to C ?” insisted Phœbe Ellen.

“No further, no further, no further,” chanted the girl.

“But ye ’membered A, didn’t ye ?”

“A ? Yes. I kin ’member that. A allus straddles.”

“’N’ B ? Ye knowed B ?”

“B ? Yes.”

“Was it hard ?”

“Yes. B’s hard, but I ’membered it.”

“’N’ C ?”

“No.” She shook her head drearily. “They grow harder ’n’ harder ’n’ harder. I couldn’t ’member C.”

"But think how good 'tis to 'member A 'n' B! See how fine 'twas not to fergit 'em! Ye're a-gittin' on fine."

Anny was still caressing Sam's hand, as a child might have done. She turned her wistful eyes once more upon him.

"Fine—hey?" she asked, wishing to be assured of his approbation.

"Yes, fine!" he asserted, his face serious with a great pitying tenderness.

"Shore?" she insisted.

"Yes, ye're a-gittin' on fine. It was fine—fine 't ye 'membered A 'n' B!"

Her dull, anxious face lightened.

"Ye're glad to please Sam, ain't ye?" asked Phœbe Ellen.

"Yes—glad, glad! I'm glad when Sam's glad. I love Sam—he's good to me."

"'N' when ye learn C, then Sam *will* be glad — hey, Sam?"

Sam choked a little as he gave his assurance in the affirmative.

"The C's so hard, I know. It's hard, hey?"

"Hard, hard!" repeated the girl, with a dreary head-shake.

"But ye'll keep on tryin'—hey?"

She answered nothing for a moment.

"Ye'll keep on tryin', jes' to please Sam, hey?"

The girl placed her cheek in the giant's big palm and held it there.

"I'll try," she said, smiling feebly. And then, "I'll try—I'll try—I'll try!" she chanted, in that discordant throat-tone, which had something horrible in it, as if it were the voice of a departed spirit coming back and speaking through a dead body.

"Pore thing!" said Pinky, involuntarily.

But Phœbe Ellen patted her head kindly.

"That's right," she said. "Sis likes ye when ye try."

The girl faced her with something like eagerness.

"'N' Sam ?" she asked.

"Sam likes ye, too—when ye try."

"Shore ?"

The wistful, vacant face was turned towards Sam now.

He nodded in answer — there was something in his throat that would not let him speak.

"I'll try—I'll try—I'll try !" croaked the girl. And Sam took the pathetic, clinging hand between his own and held it there softly.

CHAPTER XXII

PINKY did his best to inspire something of his own warmth into Phœbe Ellen, but it must be confessed that, as he himself expressed it, his progress was of the stationary sort. Permanently stationary, too; for she was jealous of advances. He had attained to a certain point in her affections—she really cared a great deal for him in her way, though her regard was subordinate to several considerations—but beyond that point he found it impossible to go. She never rebuked him in his love-making, except by a retort or a laughing toss of the head. Her actions seemed to say, " Make me love you if you can. I am quite willing." And in fact that was precisely Phœbe Ellen's state of mind.

She had not the slightest objection in the world to him *per se*. He was a good enough fellow and would make a good husband. She could manage him without difficulty, and under her direction he would become an efficient overseer of the ranch. He was honest, not too strongly addicted to sprees, and he got on easily with the boys. There were advantages in the amalgamation which were by no means lost on Phœbe Ellen's sound business sense. Indeed, she often blamed herself for not acting upon this business conviction without delay, by accepting Pinky as a husband and partner, and thus setting the whole affair at rest at once and forever.

She had no illusions about Pinky. Intellectually she recognized him as a little above the average cowboy. His sheepishness in her presence—she rather liked the idea of his never getting over that—was positive man-of-the-worldliness compared with some things of the sort she had seen. He was not handsome. She knew just how his face in profile hollowed in at the nose and came out abruptly in the chin—Sam called it an "ingrowin' face." She knew just how red he was, how mottled, how easily he turned purple, how frequently his beard was interrupted by great tracts barren of everything but freckles. She knew just how far his ears stood out and how unfinished they looked. "They 'ain't got no hem," was her way of putting it to herself—and how when he laughed he twisted his eyes into little crescent moons with the concave side down, and how his soft, straight, yellow hair stood out at unaccountable angles, no matter from what side one viewed him. But the fact remained that he was acceptable to her, and that he occupied a place in her thoughts prominent and permanent, if not absolute and all-pervading.

That kind of stationary courting is a discouraging thing. In a way it is worse than active opposition, for in the latter case a man has at least the advantage of a difficulty to be overcome, possibly a grievance to be righted; and either may bring out the stronger, manlier qualities of the will. It is worse than an open rejection, for it gives a lover no chance to fly out and lose his temper, and thus settle the affair on a comfortable basis of permanence. But Pinky had nothing to do but go on. It was rather awful, in a way, to go on under the conviction that she cared more for another man than for him. She had all but admitted the fact; but, on the whole, it was more to Pinky's taste to go on than to back out altogether. There was still hope; a bird may be captured as long as it remains in the bush, and the question as to its preferences in the matter of its captor is one of little consequence, after all. The important thing is to get it into one's hand.

They had many talks on the subject. These were largely repetitions, but some of them may be recorded.

“Ain’t I wuth waitin’ fer?” she demanded once when he had pressed her for some sort of decision.

“’Tain’t a question o’ wuth, nohow,” was his answer.

“Oh! Then ye’d think jes’ ’s much o’ me if I was good fer nothin’! I like that!”

“I’m willin’ to wait fer ye—I’ve told ye that afore. But I’m gittin’ to feel like *I* may not be waitin’ for ye, arter all.”

Phœbe Ellen pricked up her ears.

“*You* not waitin’ fer me?”

“How d’ I know but wot it’s *you* ’t ’s doin’ the waitin’?” he asked.

“Me waitin’? How d’ ye mean?”

“There I tech ye on the raw,” remarked Pinky.

“Wot be ye drivin’ at? *Me* waitin’! Well!”

Pinky understood her effort to appear unconscious, for, by a tacit understanding, they had both ignored her semi-confession on a former occasion. But he had resolved to be bold and make a stand.

“How d’ I know but wot it’s *you* ’t ’s waitin’ fer some other man?”

“Oh, well,” snapped Phœbe Ellen, making a great clatter among the pans with which she was busy (Leatherhead was down in the garden pulling turnips), “if ye want to be jealous, *I* hain’t no ’bjections.”

“I ain’t jealous,” protested Pinky.

“Have ye ever seen me makin’ up to any man?”

“Not out-’n’-out, ’s I knows on.”

She did not stop to take exceptions to his answer.

“Have ye ever seen any man makin’ up to me?”

“No.”

“Well, then,” triumphed Phœbe Ellen, setting away her pans and starting in on the pots and kettles.

She always silenced him, and she liked him none the less for that; but she always knew, as well as he did, that she was wrong and he was right in the whole affair. Perhaps that was one reason why she did not condemn him to silence altogether.

"Oh, I'm willin' to wait!" he reiterated at another time, returning to the ever-recurring subject, "but, say! Hain't I got a right to know for shore wot I'm waitin' fer?"

Her answers were usually rapped out without pause or preliminary, but now she was silent a moment.

"I've told ye a hundred times. Ye're a-waitin' fer a chance to marry me, if I kin make up my mind."

"Then yer mind's the only thing in the way?"

"It's a big obstickle, as I said afore," she remarked, gravely.

"Ef ye'd only say out-'n'-out wot the obstickle is," he sighed.

"Well, I reckon ye've been a-guessin', 'ain't ye?"

"Guessin' ain't knowin'. Why can't we come down to facts? I might help ye out o' the way with the obstickle, wotever 'tis. I might git some sort o' moral crowbar under it 'n' give it a roll clean out o' sight. 'Tain't nothin' agin me?"

He knew it was not, but he hoped her answer would lead to something definitely illuminating.

"Say!" he continued, as she remained silent, "I've a big notion to tell ye wot I've sometimes thort." And then he paused. Something in her looks made it imperative that he should not go on without her permission.

"Oh, ye do sometimes think," said she, with mock satisfaction.

"If ye wouldn't git mad—"

"I've got a dretful temper—ye know that yerself."

"Yes, I know. But that don't cut no figger. I've got a puttickler good temper, 'n' we kin strike a average."

"Oh, thankee. How noble!"

"I like a gal 't kin howl the shingles off the ruff."

"I like that!"

“But all this ain’t wot I started in to say I’d sometimes thort.”

“It ’ll do fer a sample.”

“No—the rest ’s better. Say, ye wouldn’t git *too* mad
if I was to tell ye out-’n’-out, would ye ?”

“Suthin’ ’bout the obstickle ?”

Pinky nodded.

“ I can’t promise,” she declared. “Ye’ll have to chance
it. Go ahead if ye like—but it’s all on yer own hook,
’member !”

“Well, I *will* take chances. A feller’s got to do suthin’.”

“Suthin’ in the line o’ takin’ the bull by the horns ?”

Was she giving him a tacit permission ? He thought
he saw signs of yielding in the drooping eyelids and in-
drawn chin.

“Wuss ’n that,” he declared. “Suthin’ in the line o’
takin’ a gal by the heartstrings.”

“This ’ere’s interestin’,” remarked Phœbe Ellen.
“ Well ?”

“ They’s other men about the ranch.”

Phœbe Ellen did not lift her eyes.

. “ While ye ’re at it, ye may ’s well make yerself plain,”
she said.

“ It might be they was some other man ’bout the place
’t *you* keerd fer—”

“Oh !”

“Didn’t ye half own up wunst ?”

“Oh !”

“ ’N’ it might be he didn’t keer fer *you !*”

There was a silence, during which Pinky’s heart went
through a series of contortions which it would be impossible to describe from the outside. Phœbe Ellen turned
first pale, then red.

“Half own up ? Never !” she cried. “Well, if I’m
any jedge, ye’ve gone fur enough for *one* day.” After a

13

sideward glance at her, Pinky made up his mind that she had delivered herself more in agitation than in anger.

"I'll stop, if ye say so," he hastened to say. "But, while we're at it, hadn't we better have it out?"

"Ye've hinted at the same thing afore—"

"'N' fer that very reason hadn't we better have it out now? Then they won't be no more hintin', 'n' we'll onderstan' each other."

"Not this time, not this time!" she cried. "Wot d' ye reckon a gal's made of? Injy-rubber, or iron, or *wot?* No, I've heerd 'nough fer *one* day."

"Ye're mad at me," deprecated Pinky.

"Yes," she assented.

"But ye'll git over it 'n' make up?"

"Humph!" was the only answer he could get from her.

The conversation ended there for that day, and Pinky left with the impression that Phœbe Ellen was really very angry with him, and that he had probably given her just cause. He furthermore resolved never to broach the subject again, but to let affairs take their own course without any further urging or interference on his part. By affairs taking their own course he meant Phœbe Ellen's taking her own course, and it was very seriously borne in upon him that he would never again question her will in any way, or suggest himself even remotely as a possible means of helping to solve the problem of her future.

Arriving at the ranch a few days later in this humble frame of mind, he was surprised that Phœbe Ellen should almost immediately open up the same subject of her own accord. It was Sunday again, and she was reading a Denver newspaper when he rode up and dismounted. But before he was fairly seated she flung the sheet aside, and, clasping her arms about her knee, faced him with a frankness which was almost eager.

"Say," began her introductory speech, "ye 'member wot we was talkin' 'bout when ye was over a-Wednesday?"

"I 'member. But I've dropped it. I ain't never agoin' to bother ye with it no more."

"Well, I hated it, o' course. But I'm glad ye made up yer mind to drop it. It shows you keer fer my feelin's."

"I keer fer the hull o' ye, feelin's 'n' all," Pinky asserted.

"That's all right! But I been thinkin' it over a good deal while I been busy roun' the house, ye know."

"I hope ye ain't mad at me no longer?"

"No, I ain't mad—I wa'n't reely mad at the time. I jes' hadn't time to git a good fair look at the matter aroun' the corners. 'N' I've made up my mind I hadn't no call to git mad, nohow. Ye said wot was right, 'n' ye come at me the right way with it."

Pinky heaved a long sigh.

"It's more 'n I orter expect, I swear," he said.

"Ye had the right to do wot ye did. When a feller keers fer a gal, 'n' they're good friends, he has a right to ask why she can't like 'im back agin. 'N' she orter tell 'im."

Pinky sighed again.

"If she *kin*, it 'll be a comfort to 'im," he said, meekly.

"Well, I kin—'n' I will. It's only fair 'n' bizness-like. I could 'a' told ye from the fust. I did want to, but somehow I couldn't—it was a lot o' gal-nonsense 't made me keep still. Gals do have the wildest notions 'bout love-'fairs, anyhow. If a gal's in love 'n' the feller don't 'spect it, she'd no more think o' *tellin'* 'im o' it 'n she would o' flyin' to the moon. Would she?"

"Could *you* do it?" questioned Pinky.

"Couldn't I? 'N' wouldn't I? 'N' didn't I? Well, I don't mean to say I told 'im in so many words; but they's ways, they's ways! It was when I found he kep' his eyes 'n' ears shet a-purpose 't I begun to haul in my horns. I didn't want the boys a-sayin' 't I'd throwed myself at a feller's head 'n' he never even reached out to ketch me."

"I can't blame ye," said Pinky, with candor. "That sort o' thing tells agin a gal."

"Suthin' kep' me from it, anyhow. 'N' I had suthin' o' the same feelin' when ye up 'n' at me with it o' Wednesday. But I've had time to think it over. Now see 'ere!"

"Yes," said Pinky, all attention.

"We're good frien's, ain't we?"

"O' course!"

"Well, we kin talk it over like frien's, then?"

"That's the very thing I've allus wanted."

"'N' we kin be sensible, 'n' jes' 'cause we've talked over the marryin' subjeck, it don't foller 't we've got to make fools o' ourselves?"

"No," assented Pinky.

"Well, that's wot I want — bizness fust 'n' pleasure arterwards. 'N' this is bizness. That's the right basis fer it—it's a bizness transaction. 'N' I'm willin' to answer all yer questions now."

"Then ye do keer fer a man 't don't keer fer you?"

"I do," answered Phœbe Ellen, boldly.

"'N' that man is—"

"Sam."

CHAPTER XXIII

THE silence which followed was not of long duration. It was broken by Phœbe Ellen.

"Here's cornfessions!" she cried, with a shrill laugh.

Pinky smoothed the back of his neck, and finished by rubbing his chin with his palm.

She fetched a breath of relief as from great depths.

"I feel better," she declared. "I didn't know it was weighin' on me so. 'Pears like a great chunk o' rock 'd been rolled off 'm me. If ye only had suthin' to own up 'bout yerself—ain't they a gal somers 't ye like better 'n wot ye do me? A gal 't don't keer fer ye, but 's clean in love with some other feller? *That* 'ud even things up."

"I'd own up if they was. But sech a gal ain't on airth."

"Then you've got to stan' on the nex' ledge above me. But I ain't to blame, Pinky—I'd 'a' helped it if I could. It's jest a piece o' that gal-foolishness I was tellin' ye 'bout. Why should I keer more fer one man 'n another? They've all got two legs 'n' two han's; they kin all talk; they kin all git mad 'n' shoot; they kin all git drunk 'n' feel funny. Wot's the differ atween 'em? It's all nonsense to pick out one 'n' doat on 'im. It ain't bizness."

"Ye've tried to help it?"

She nodded.

"I've set 'im 'longside o' every man I've seen; I've said to myself over 'n' over agin 't I'm a fool, 'n' 't I like Leatherhead 'n' Doc Sedgwick 'n' Stormy Bill 'n' Shootin' Ike jes' well 's wot I do Sam; but 'tain't no use. The feelin' jes' sticks 't I like Sam best. It's a queer world!"

She heaved a sigh. "It's a queer world where a gal can't do wot she likes with 'er own feelin's!"

"I kin see all that," said Pinky. "It'ud come to the same thing with me if I tried to think I keerd more fer some other gal 'n wot I do fer *you*."

"Well, that's a sorter bond, ain't it? We kin onderstan' each other. D' ye know, I'm ruther s'prised at us a-settin' 'ere 'n' a-talkin' it over like this. It speaks well fer us. Most folks couldn't do it. I'd 'a' tried it long ago if I'd 'a' knowed how 'twas comin' out."

"It shows we're sensible," suggested Pinky.

"I knowed I was all that, o' course — but *you*; well, there I looked fer suthin,' I didn't know jes' wot. But it helps ye up in my 'pinion wonderful. I don't b'lieve nothin' else could 'a' done it. If we was to marry, I feel shore we'd git along."

"Then why shouldn't we?" Pinky's voice was eager.

Phœbe Ellen considered.

"If we was married ye could look arter the boys 'n' the cattle on the range, 'n' go to the round-up in the spring 'n' see 't I got my own steers; ye could 'tend to the plantin' 'n' harvestin', 'n' ye could make out yer report to me like ye do to the railroad. It 'ud be a lovely 'rangement on both sides. We could be o' use to each other."

"Why shouldn't we do it, then?"

"A lovely 'rangement," she repeated. "Only—"

"Only?"

"Where'ud my feelin's be?"

Pinky's face fell.

"Yer feelin's seem to be layin' 'round so loose, like," he said, pathetically, "they're bound to be tromped on whichever way we turn."

"It's that gal-foolishness," said Phœbe Ellen, with something like a groan. "If I could git over that—"

"Ye'll git over it," Pinky assured her.

"Well, when I *do* git over it, I'll marry ye, Pinky. Ye're next arter Sam."

"That's suthin'," remarked Pinky, gratefully.

"It's a heap! 'N' when I git him disposed of—"

"Why not marry me fust 'n' dispose o' him arterwards?"

"'Ud ye be willin' to do that?"

"Wouldn't I?"

"How ye mus' love me!" remarked Phœbe Ellen, eying him with renewed approval.

"'Tain't no name fer it!" he declared, following up his advantage.

She considered a moment.

"Well, *I* wouldn't be willin' to go into a thing like that, nohow. A gal can't sarve God 'n' Mammon in marryin' no more 'n wot she kin in religion. I've got to git Sam off 'm my mind fust; 'n' arter that we'll see wot we'll see!"

"How d' ye 'pose to git 'im off? Couldn't ye do it quicker if ye was to send 'im away?" questioned Pinky.

"I've thort o' that, but wot'ud life 'ere be 'thout 'im?"

"Oh, Lord!" groaned Pinky.

"I'm tellin' ye the truth—I couldn't bear to stay 'ere myself if Sam was gone. Mebbe I'll git over it, but that's the way I feel now."

She waited for Pinky to say something, but as he remained silent she went on.

"We're bein' honest with each other to-day, like good friends orter be; now lookee 'ere! D' ye reckon ye kin stan' a bigger dose 'n ye've had yit from me?"

"Go ahead! I kin see aforehand wot it's likely to be."

She cleared her throat.

"I've told ye I don't want to send Sam off yit. But the reason why—"

"Ye ain't quite shore but wot ye kin git 'im to keer fer ye yit, if ye don't send 'im away? 'S that it?"

Phœbe Ellen nodded.

"Ye've said it better 'n I could," she said, with a long breath.

"I 'spected it," said Pinky, without emotion other than some inward increment of sheepishness which manifested itself by a rush of blood to his ears. Then after a little pause, "It's only nat'ral."

"It's nat'ral fer anybody to git wot they want if they kin do it," specified Phœbe Ellen. "That's the bizness way o' lookin' at it. 'N' we're talkin' bizness."

"Yes," assented Pinky, still undismayed.

"Now, see 'ere! I've been a-studyin' this thing over 'n' I've come to cornclusions. The p'int I want to make 's jes' this: Sam mus' have a chance—see?"

"A chance to keer fer ye, ye mean?"

"Jes' that."

"'Ain't he had it?"

She took no notice of the question, but continued in an off-hand way, which showed that she had considered her line of action beforehand.

"I want to give 'im a chance to like me. He ain't a feller 't kin be brought aroun' in a minute. I want to give 'im time; I want to give 'im till nex' June."

"That 'll be a year, all told, sence he knowed ye."

"Jes' so. 'N' he orter know me purty well by that time. I ain't afeerd o' his knowin' me *too* well. I've learned to hold in my temper, 'n' that was my bigges' fault. Oh, I ain't agoin' to hide my light under a bushel; 'n' a year orter be plenty o' time fer 'im to make out jes' how bright 'tis—see? Well, that's the way I've sized it up. I'll give Sam till nex' June—"

"'N' then?"

"'N' then, if he don't come to time, I'll send 'im away. That's the only thing to do, as I see it. Wot d' ye think o' the plan?"

"I don't b'lieve he'll ever keer fer ye," said Pinky, frankly.

"Neither do I," was her equally frank reply. "But I want to try 'im, jes' fer my own satisfaction."

"S'posin' ye didn't git over yer gal-foolishness even arter ye sent 'im off?" suggested Pinky.

"Ud ye refuse to marry me?" she inquired.

"No!"

"Then why not call it a bargain?" asked Phœbe Ellen, holding out her hand.

Pinky took the hand and shook it.

"It *is* a bargain," he said.

And with that their conversation came to an end for that day.

They renewed it soon after, however, though on somewhat different lines.

"Say," said Phœbe Ellen, apropos of nothing in particular, "I want to ask ye suthin'. I've had a idee in my mind ever sence I come to Collyraydo, 'n' I want to know wot ye think o' it. It's 'bout Sam."

"That's where all yer idees seems to b'long," Pinky remarked without resentment.

"Sam 'n' the everlastin' gal-foolishness I can't git red of. I wanted to ast ye if ye seen anything queer 'bout 'im the fust day he met us over there to the depot."

"Nothin', 'thout it was the way he sot down on ye."

"Well, that *was* queer; but I meant suthin' else. I meant 'bout sis. 'D ye see anything goin' on atween him 'n' sis?"

"I 'member thinkin' to myself he acted a little *gone* on 'er."

"Jes' so."

She folded her hands and settled back.

"That's wot I wanted to know. *I* noticed it, but I wanted to make shore I wa'n't mistook. Then the way he watched over 'er arter she got hurt—that told a big story too. 'N' he 'ain't been jest hisself sence. It all means jes' one thing."

"'T he's in love with yer sister," formulated Pinky.

She nodded.

" I'd have a better chance at 'im if he'd never seen 'er," she added.

" That's one fer me," put in Pinky.

" It's a dozen agin *me*, though. Whenever he looks at 'er, 'pears like he turns sorter sorrerful, like he 'member-ed how purty 'n' bright she was afore she was hurt. 'N' he's that patient 'n' kind—sometimes it gives me a queer feelin' inside jes' to see how good he is to 'er, 'n' how it breaks 'im up. He's allus lookin' arter 'er 'n' doin' little things to make 'er happy. He allus brings 'er candy when he goes over to Pete Hawkins's place. 'N' he never thinks o' me! If he was to look arter me like he does arter her—but there! Ye see the gal-foolishness is on top agin. He *never* looks arter me, 'ceptin' in the way o' bizness."

" Ye *never* 'll git yer feelin's fer 'im on a bizness basis," remarked Pinky.

" Anyway, it 'll take a long time. I'd give half the ranch if I could, 'n' then me 'n' you could git married 'n' live comf'table on the other half fer the rest o' our days. So ye kin see jes' where I stan'. My only chance with Sam 's to—"

" Wot ?" asked Pinky, as she hesitated.

" Git 'er out o' the way," said Phœbe Ellen, deliber-ately.

Pinky had been looking out towards the river, but now he faced her.

" Git 'er out o' the way?" His face was pale. " Git yer own sister out o' the way?"

She was neither looking at him nor thinking of him, and she heard only his last speech, uttered in a low voice.

" Ye mean—ye mean ye're goin' to *kill* 'er ?"

Pinky stood erect and tremulous.

It was Phœbe Ellen's turn to be startled now. She rose too, her face as white as death.

"Pinky!" was all she could say. And she fell back, covering her eyes with her hands.

"'D I hear ye wrong?" he asked, looking down at her.

She dropped her hands, but made no effort to look at him.

"Pinky, Pinky, I'll never forgive ye fer this!" she cried.

"I *did* hear wrong!" he cried, approaching her with a look of relief.

"Wrong? Wot d' ye think o' me? My own sister! 'N' foolish at that!" She rocked herself to and fro. Why could she not face him defiantly and give loud utterance to the sense of outrage which came of being so misinterpreted? The answer was ready in her own mind. She remembered too well the bloody thought that had occurred to her on the morning after the accident, and she could say nothing. She could not utter the words, "I never thought of such a thing." They came to her; she longed to repeat them in self-defence, but the effort of utterance would have choked her. She was innocent this time—but she had been guilty. And to be suspected of such a design—to hear such a voice outside her own conscience, to understand its real significance on the lips of another, and, above all, to be unable to deny what it implied—gave her a chill of horror which for a moment made her tongue useless.

"I'll go 'n' empty them weeds out o' my satchel afore I sleep this night," she promised herself, during the interval in which Pinky was moving towards her. And with the resolution came a further calculation, "I sha'n't never need 'em now, nohow. She's foolish—I won't never need to make 'er crazy besides. 'N' that's all 't loco does."

She lifted her eyes to his in a sort of doubting terror.

"I might 'a' used other words," she managed to say,

recovering herself sufficiently for speech. The sound of her voice assured her. It had not altogether the accent of a guilty woman. "But fer ye to think sech things o' me—"

"Ye'll tell me wot ye reely meant?" he finally asked.

"Ud ye help do sech a thing?" demanded Phœbe Ellen, fixing her hard, gray eyes upon his.

"I was lookin' aroun' fer my hat," was his answer. "'Peared like if that was wot ye wanted o' me I couldn't git back to Eden City too quick."

"'N' d' ye reckon I'm so much wuss 'n *you?*"

"I was wrong," said Pinky, humbly. "'N' now ye'll tell me jes' wot ye *did* mean, won't ye?"

She had complete control of her voice now.

"I only meant 't she mus' be sent away. I know a place back there in Nebrasky where she could be kep'. We could give it out 't she was goin' to be treated. Sam 'ud have to be made to b'lieve that she could come back any time arter nex' June."

Pinky's misinterpretation made him even more ready than he otherwise would have been to accept her explanation and to bring about the result she desired.

"I want ye to help me," she continued. "That's why I'm tellin' ye all this. I'll never marry ye, never, till I've had a fair show. I want a chance, Pinky—I want a chance! A chance fer my own happiness, I mean—a chance to marry the man I love. I never keerd fer a man like I do Sam; I never kin keer fer 'nother." She had forgotten her horror at Pinky's mistake, and the tears were burning hot behind her eyelids. "Gimme the chance I want—ye kin do it. They'd be good to 'er back there. That was all I meant."

Pinky took a moment to consider.

"Ye'll help me?" Phœbe Ellen asked, appealingly.

"How soon?"

"I'll tell ye when the time comes."

And with that she left the room, intending to fulfil the promise she had made to herself to burn up the loco-weed in her sachel without delay ; but Anny came limping in at that moment, dragging Sam by the hand.

"Wot if I should need it, arter all ?" she thought, a twinge of jealousy passing through her as she saw the two together.

And the deed was left undone.

CHAPTER XXIV

CERTAINLY Anny was improving. Phœbe Ellen noticed it from day to day; so did Sam; so did Leatherhead; and Pinky declared the improvement most marked.

One day she and Phœbe Ellen were in the kitchen doing up the after-dinner work. There was an unusual flush in her soft, rounded cheeks, and her eyes for the moment had almost recovered their former lustre.

"It's lonesome, it's lonesome," she said, in her queer, unmanageable voice. "Oh, it's lonesome when Sam's gone on the range."

She was wiping dishes by the kitchen window and Phœbe Ellen was busy about the sink.

"Ye mustn't think s' much o' Sam," said the latter, emptying out a panful of water, and pausing with her dishcloth in mid-air while the water gurgled down the pipe.

"Why?" questioned Anny, with an arrested look which seemed capable of full comprehension.

"Because it ain't nice."

"Not nice?"

"Gals ortn't to keer too much fer the men," was the answer.

"Why?" came the discordant iteration.

"'Cause 'tain't nice."

"Oh, why?"

"Well, now, you jes' take my word fer it. It ain't nice, 'n' that's all they is 'bout it. 'N' I know nice things when I see 'em."

"Not nice to like Sam?" The girl's face looked distressed.

"That's wot I said."

Anny's brows twisted themselves into a faint frown.

"*I* think it's nice," she declared.

Phœbe Ellen looked up surprised. She had never heard her sister speak so positively since the accident.

"It ain't nice jes' the same," she declared. "If he was to go 'way 'n' leave ye—well,'ud ye call that nice ?"

Anny was unable to detect the fallacy in her sister's reasoning, but the idea of Sam's going away started her off on a new track. After the first look of dread, a faint smile came into her pretty, vacant features.

"Oh, he won't go 'way," she answered, with confidence.

"Ye never kin tell. Men is powerful onsartain. Here to-day 'n' gone to-morrer. He might pack up 'n' leave in the night, fer all *we* know."

"Sam won't go," repeated Anny, in the same tone of confidence.

Phœbe Ellen made a dab at the sink with her rag and began to scrub vigorously. She wanted to accustom Anny to the idea of a separation from Sam, and she knew of no better way than to proceed as she had begun.

"I tell ye he's more likely to 'n not," she declared, holding her face low over her work.

"No—no," repeated Anny.

Suddenly Phœbe Ellen looked up.

"That's silly," she affirmed. "Ye're actin' silly now."

"Silly to make shore Sam keers fer me ?"

"Yes, 'n' not to take my word 't he may go 'way."

"He *says* he likes me," said Anny, simply.

"All the same he may take a fit 'n' go. 'N' then if ye keerd so much fer 'im, wot'ud ye do ?"

Anny set her plate down on the table, rolled her drying-towel into a ball in her hands, and stood for several minutes staring straight before her.

"I ain't seen 'er when she looked like she was thinkin'

so fast," said Phœbe Ellen to herself—"not sence she got hurt.   Wot 'll she fin'lly say, I wonder?"

Evidently the girl's thoughts had wandered far, for her first words seemed altogether irrelevant.

"The purty little yaller chicken wot the waggin run over wunst—ye 'member it?" she finally asked.

"Is she gittin' loonier 'n ever?" was Phœbe Ellen's first thought.   But aloud she said:

"Yes; I 'member."

"Wot 'd it do?   I can't think," said the girl, in a distressed voice.

"Do?   It laid still," said Phœbe Ellen.

"Suthin' more, suthin' more," cried Anny.   "It laid still, but it done suthin' more!"

"Why, it died.   Is that wot ye mean?"

"It died," repeated Anny, nodding her head slowly.

Phœbe Ellen opened her eyes.

"Ye mean ye'd die too, if Sam was to go?"

She kept on nodding in the same mechanical way as she picked up her dish, shook out her towel, and went to work again.

"I'd die," she kept repeating.   "If Sam was to go, I'd die, I'd die!"

Phœbe Ellen shivered.   Then, turning suddenly upon the girl:

"'Ud ye ruther go yerself?" she asked.

"Me?   Go?"

"'N' Sam stay 'ere.   Wot then?"

"I'd die, I'd die," chanted the girl, in a tone which split into discord and made a horrible sound in her throat.

Phœbe Ellen said nothing more just then, but later in the afternoon, when they were seated together on the veranda, she took up the subject once more.

"Ye 'member how purty the world looks when ye stan' high up on the mountain?"

"Yes," said Anny, rocking busily back and forth in her

chair. "I 'member—I 'member." She nodded her head several times, and then peeped out under the veranda eaves, where she could see the tops of the foot-hills.

"Sam took ye up there wunst," said Phœbe Ellen.

"It's purty, purty, purty up there!" intoned the girl, in her high, cracked voice. "Sam went with me, 'n' I had a fine, fine time!"

"Ye kin see 'way off, ever 'n' ever so fur."

"'Way off—'way off! Sam told me he'd been there."

"Wouldn't ye like to go there too, some day?"

"Some day?"

"Jes' to see how it looks clost to."

"Oh yes, where Sam was. He tole me 'bout it, 'way off—"

"Mebbe I'll let ye go, if ye're good."

"I'll be good!"

But the childish eagerness in the face gave way first to a look of vacancy, then of wistfulness.

"Sam kin go, too?" she asked.

"No; Sam 'll have to stay to hum 'n' work."

"Then I don't want to go!"

"But if ye had to go?"

"No, I won't have to go; I'll stay. Where Sam is, I want to be. It's lonesome, lonesome, lonesome, when Sam's gone on the range. He's been gone all day. 'Ll he never come back? Ain't it time fer 'im to be back now? Wot makes ye talk like this when he's gone?"

"It's a purty world out there. They's houses 'n' folks 'n' purty things in stores wot ye could buy with money. 'N' ye could take a long ride, fust on the buckboard 'n' then on the cars—"

"I should die—I should die 'thout Sam!"

"But if Sam couldn't go?"

"Then I couldn't, nuther. I want Sam. Sam's my sunshine—Sam's my star. I should die 'thout Sam, I know!"

14

The monotonous iteration wore on Phœbe Ellen.

"Well, we won't talk 'bout it no more," she said, crossly.

"'N' I won't have to go?"

"If I tell ye to, ye'll go—ye kin make shore o' that," she declared.

But Anny's face grew clouded as she realized she had displeased her sister.

"Sis is cross," she said, wistfully. "Why, why?"

"'Cause ye're a stubborn thing!" was the fierce answer.

And Anny tried to think what she had done to deserve such treatment, but vainly. However, she was too accustomed to puzzling over things to be troubled long by her inability to understand; and presently she wandered out on the mountain-side and sat down in the sun, where the chipmunks came frisking and chattering about her.

"I know wot they say, but I can't tell it," she used to declare. And often it seemed to Sam that the girl told the truth.

And as Phœbe Ellen sat on the porch with her mending she saw Sam whisk up to the barn on his scraggly little mustang and enter at the back door.

"I wonder if he's had his dinner," she pondered. "Prob'ly he has, over to Halstead's. If he ain't, I kin warm over them mashed pertaters 'n' give 'im some ham 'n' eggs."

Presently he emerged from the barn with his pipe in his mouth.

"If he ketches sight o' sis, he'll start straight torrards 'er unless he's hungry," she thought. And she watched to see what direction his steps would finally take.

And, sure enough, after a leisurely glance in all directions, his eye fell on Anny as she sat full in the sun on the mountain-side; and without a glance at Phœbe Ellen he turned to the left, skirted the corral, crossed the overflow from the spring, and swung upward among the pines with long strides.

"'That's allus the way," said Phœbe Ellen to herself. "Whenever he ain't busy 'n' she's alone, ye'll find 'em driftin' together 's shore 's two chips on a tub o' water. Wot kin he see in 'er now, I wonder? I know she was purty 'n' had nice ways when she was herself. She could talk interestin', too, 'n' I didn't blame 'im fer takin' to 'er the fust time they met. But now—I wonder if she'll 'member wot I've been sayin' to 'er 'bout goin' off 'n' leavin' 'im? I shouldn't be s'prised. She's been pickin' up wonderful lately, even in looks. Her mem'ry 's twicet 's good 's 'twas a month ago, only she can't l'arn books. She ain't got beyend C yit. But she kin foller wot ye say better, 'n' she kin tell 'er own thorts straighter. Well, wot if she does let 'im know? He might 's well be gittin' ready fer it. She's got to go."

And she picked up her mending and set to work with a grim look about her hard, thin mouth.

Sam seated himself on a rock around which the vetches grew thick among the mountain-sage, and some late blue-bells swayed lightly among heavy purple tufts of early asters.

"'N' how's the chipmunks to-day?" was his greeting as he drew up his big feet and clasped his hands between his knees. "Talkin' same 's ever?"

"Jes' the same," Anny intoned, smiling back at him. "Jes' the same 's ever!"

He blew a leisurely whiff of smoke into the air.

"Ye look oncommon smart to-day," he remarked, fixing his kind dark eyes upon her. "Oncommon smart, I swear!"

"Smart? Yes. So 's the chipmunks. The little un there with the stripes so plain up 'n' down his back 's been tellin' me 'bout the pine-nuts he's got stored up in a holler tree jest up the hill. Sech a lot o' 'em stored up in a cosey dark corner—he tole me 'cause he said he knowed I'd never go 'n' steal 'em away. 'N' the big un 't run away when ye come up—he ain't half 's brave 's wot he makes out!—he was jes' tellin' me how nothin' ever skeerd him now; he'd got used to folks 'n' stood still 'n' made faces at 'em when they come by!"

"'N' I skeerd 'im away, hey?"

"Yes. But when he run he looked over his shoulder 'n' promised to come back. He seen I needed 'im."

"Needed 'im?" inquired Sam between whiffs.

She nodded gravely.

"I was feelin' sorter blue, 'n' he seen it, 'n' said he'd stay 'n' comfort me. 'N' he did; 'n' he tole me to cheer up 'n' not keer. He said he'd had troubles, too, but they passed off. He said everything allus comes out right."

"Troubles?"

"He didn't have time to tell me all 'bout 'em, but he talked jes' 's sensible! He said—"

"But troubles; *you* hain't got no troubles, now," said Sam.

"I don't have many, do I?" The lines of the wistful, vacant face became set in a deprecative smile. "Somehow I don't feel things. I feel like I orter—I sorter 'member when I did; but I can't do it now. They ain't nobody but you 'n' sis wot I keer fer—reely."

"Ye do keer fer me?" asked Sam, softly. He removed his pipe and sat regarding her with a sort of reverence.

"Oh, ye know I do—I've told ye over 'n' over. But other things—somehow I don't keer. I ain't allus happy, but—I can't tell how 'tis! I don't cry much, nuther, not 's much 's wot I'd like to; but they's suthin'—suthin'—"

"Gone out o' ye, somehow?" suggested Sam.

She caught at the words eagerly.

"Gone out o' me—yes, gone out o' me; that's wot I meant. Gone out o' me—oh, like I ain't wot I was long ago."

“Afore ye got hurt ’n’ was sick ?”

Sam’s pipe had gone out now, and after noticing the fact in an absent way, he withdrew the stem from the bowl, as his custom was, and thrust them both into his pocket.

“Sometimes,” she said, dreamily—“sometimes I kin almos’ ’member—I strain my mind, ’n’ I kin almos’ ’member. But suthin’ allus stops me. It’s like—”

“Like what ?” he suggested, as she hesitated. And she went on with a catching of her breath.

“It’s like a cloud on the mountain—ye look ’n’ look, ’n’ ye can’t see the mountain, though ye allus know it’s there.”

Sam had never heard her talk so lucidly and connectedly.

“The cloud allus goes,” he said, gently, “ ’n’ the mountain comes out clear.”

She fetched another long breath, and this time there was something like a sob in it.

“If it ’ud only go so ’t I could look back to wot I was afore I got hurt that day! ’Ll it ever go so ’t I kin do that, d’ ye reckon ?”

“Ye’re a-gittin’ better right along,” he assured her.

“Shore ?”

“Doc says ye’re better every time he sees ye,” he declared.

“I like the Doc. He’s allus good to me. Do I act better ? I *feel* better !”

“Ever s’ much better—ever ’n’ ever s’ much better. If ye keep on, ye *will* git well, I feel shore o’ it !” His face had lighted up, and hers caught an answering glow.

“Mebbe — mebbe, by-’n’-by,” she cried, clasping her hands in a sort of spasm—“mebbe I’ll be myself agin. Oh, if I could—”

“Ye’re improvin’ right along,” he iterated.

“It’s a dretful thing not to know anything ’bout yerself but wot folks tells ye !”

She rose with a convulsive jerk, and faced him as if she were flinging aside a veil which obscured her sight. Then, all at once, instead of the burst of light he half expected to see in her eyes, a dazed look came into her face, a sort of film such as he had before seen grow into her features after her mind had been subjected to too severe a strain.

"Don't worry, don't worry 'bout it," he said, soothingly. "It 'll come right—it 'll come right."

Her eyes cleared a little, as if his voice had power to dispel the clouds which enveloped her.

"The chipmunks don't have *reel* troubles, do they?" she asked, as she seated herself at his feet. "Not reel troubles like mine. They don't worry. Why should I?"

"No, don't worry. Be 's glad 's ye kin. Only be glad —that's the best!"

"I'm happy when ye're with me." Her face had brightened once more. Then she remembered Phœbe Ellen's vague insinuations. "But sometimes when I'm alone with sis—"

"What's she been sayin' to ye?"

"Sech dretful things!"

"Things to make ye onhappy, hey?"

She nodded, and he could see that her throat was fluttering.

"Ye ain't agoin' away, be ye?" she broke out. "Tell me, ye ain't agoin' away?"

Sam opened his eyes very wide.

"She told ye I was?" he asked.

She nodded dumbly. Then, with an effort:

"She said ye *might*."

"No, no," he soothed her, "I ain't goin' away."

The piteous face brightened again, and the girl crept close and laid her cheek against his knee.

"I told 'er ye wouldn't," she declared. "I told 'er I knowed ye wouldn't leave me. I knowed ye keerd for me. I told 'er so."

His big hand fell softly upon her hair.

"No ; I won't leave ye," he repeated.

"Never ?"

"Never." He uttered the word solemnly. It was like a vow.

She lifted her shoulders in a long sigh of relief.

"I knowed ye wouldn't—I knowed ye wouldn't," she kept repeating to herself. Then, after a long, vacant stare at the mountains, as if her mind were wandering, she came once more to herself. "If she was to send me away, ye'd go with me, wouldn't ye ?" she asked, her old wistfulness returning.

"Yes," he assured her. "I'd go with ye, wherever she sent ye."

"She said I might go 'way, ye know."

"Yer sister ?"

She nodded vacantly.

"Her. Down there," she said, pointing.

Again Sam's eyes opened wide and his brows went up.

"Ye might be mistook 'bout 'er sayin' that," he said, quietly.

"Mistook ?" she repeated, with vague inquiry.

"Ye might 'a' thort she said it when she didn't." He was thinking how she heard the flowers and animals talk.

"No," she said, very seriously, and Sam knew that she spoke the truth. "She said 't mebbe I'd have to go 'way. I heerd 'er. She was stan'in' by the sink. She was cross."

Sam's brows came down as he meditated.

"Did she say ye'd have to go fer shore ?"

"No ; only mebbe."

"Did she say why ?"

"No ; only 't mebbe I'd have to go."

"Oh," said Sam, slowly, after his habitual pause. "I onderstan', I onderstan'." He reached down and took both Anny's hands in his. "Has it tired ye to talk s' much ?" he asked, tenderly. "Yer face looks worn out.

Don't worry, little un—don't worry. Sam 'll look arter ye. Sam 'll allus be roun' to see 't things goes right. 'N' if I leave, ye shall go with me ; 'n' if ye leave, I'll foller. Ye b'lieve me, don't ye ? Don't worry. Stay 'ere 'n' talk some more to the chipmunks—they're merry little chaps, 'n' 'll cheer ye up. Or if ye feel like it, lay down on the pine-needles 'n' go to sleep. I got some things to look arter down to the barn."

He bent with the light of love in his kind eyes and kissed the girl's forehead as reverently as the devotee might have kissed the brow of a pictured saint. Then he left her with a forward fling of his huge body, and landed at the bottom of the mountain in three strides.

CHAPTER XXV

PHŒBE ELLEN's kindness for Sam became more and more apparent as time went on, and the nods and winks of the cowboys became pronounced to the point of violence. As for Sam, he was conscious in a half-amused way that he was overwhelmingly approved of. He would have been more or less than human had he been blind to his mistress's side-glances or deaf to the softened tones in which she addressed him after addressing another. He had a sort of elephantine alertness to the bits of ribbon she stuck on in becoming places when no one but him was likely to be around, and, more than all, he had an eye to the occasions she found for being alone with him, too frequent for the discussion of the business of the ranch, and often running into personal themes altogether after the few introductory words on the condition of the cattle over Baldwin way, or the advisability of putting in alfalfa on the slope beyond the river where irrigation was impracticable.

Sam saw these things truly, but he gave them a mild interpretation. He was not a lady's man, and saw nothing in the average petticoat beyond the probable price of the goods it was made of. Had he stopped to analyze his feeling for Phœbe Ellen he would have found it to be something in the nature of the magnanimous tolerance of a healthy man for a hysterical woman whose spasms would probably never turn violent — at least, in his presence. That she cared enough for him to make a fight for him, or that he was in any way worth fighting for, never entered his head.

Even after his conversation with Anny on the mountain-side his eyes were not fully opened. Something was abroad which he did not understand—something which concerned himself, inasmuch as it concerned the afflicted girl in whom his interest centred more than in any other human being. The talk of her going away had a meaning—he could not tell just what. He could hardly believe that her statement had originated altogether in her imagination; he had never seen her so clear-headed, so nearly herself, since the accident. And yet in the same breath she had babbled about what the chipmunks said and a hundred things which were utterly without foundation in fact.

"If they's anything in it, I mus' know it," was his thought. "I'll hang roun' the ranch more 'n I've been doin', 'n' let the range look arter itself. Wot I've got to do 's to keep my eyes 'n' ears open, 'n' put things together 'n' onderstan' 'em."

While he was in this state of expectancy he got a real revelation. It came from Pinky, as the two were driving over from Eden City to the ranch.

Ever since Pinky had acquiesced in the arrangement to wait till next June for a definite answer to his suit, the depot-man had been in a state of agitation about one thing. He wanted to make sure of Sam's potential feelings for the heiress. He had no reason to believe that the giant cared for her on any other than the legitimate grounds of friendship. But he was far from satisfied. And yet, why should he not know the whole truth? There could be no possible objection on Sam's part to an open and frank avowal of sentiments. Pinky had little of the commodity about him which is ordinarily known as delicacy. His actions were largely business arrangements throughout, and it was with this understanding of his own motives that he proposed to probe Sam's feelings.

"Ye know the missus," he remarked, in as casual a way as he could assume. "*Her*—ye know; the missus of the ranch."

Sam gave him a sideward glance of surprise.

"Well, I should say," was his answer, after a deliberate study of Pinky's face.

Pinky twiddled his thumbs in rosy anxiety.

"Ye 'member the fust time ye met 'er over there to the depot?" he continued.

Sam grinned.

"I 'member," he answered, still with his eyes on his companion.

"Ye 'member how I made up to 'er, don't ye? How we kep' hollerin' to each other so kind o' 'fectionate arter ye started off—hollerin' till we couldn't hear each other no more?"

Sam's grin grew broader.

"I 'member," he repeated.

Pinky rubbed a meditative hand up and down his knee —an operation which seemed to send the blood to his head—and finished by smoothing the back of his freckled neck.

"I reckon they wa'n't no discountin' the meanin' o' it— leastways on my side," he remarked.

Sam's grin had hitched up the corners of his big mustache to a level with his nose.

"Oh, it was easy 'nough onderstan'in' *you*," he re-remarked.

"Well," said Pinky, his embarrassment subsiding a little as he found himself well under way, "I've kep' the same thing a-goin' ever sense—ye'll have to own up to that."

"That's right!" was Sam's affirmative response.

"'N' I'm a-goin' to keep it up. When I see a thing I want, whether it's a pipe or a stick o' chewin'-gum or a gal, I git it if I kin. They ain't none o' yer stan'-up-in-the-corner-'n'-holler-fer-buttermilk 'bout *me*. I go in to win with sech showin's 's I kin find. 'N' if I don't win— well, there I be !''

"No wuss off 'n wot ye was afore," commented Sam, relaxing his smile and giving a momentary attention to the off mustang, who was "sojering."

"Jesso. No wuss off 'n wot I was afore. That's the way I look at it—no wuss off 'n wot I was afore. Well, but *her*—that's harder."

"That's so," assented Sam. "Gals is queer. Ye never kin tell 'bout gals."

"A gal—well, that's so. Ye can't tell where ye're at with a gal, nohow. Ye make shore ye got 'er solid when —lo 'n' behold ! she's trickled through yer fingers, 'n' there ye stan' a-lookin' at 'em with nothin' left but—"

"Mud," interrupted Sam.

"Mud," assented Pinky, with a grave nod. "That's right—nothin' but mud. Somehow, I d' know how, but 'pears like it's a gal's way. 'D *you* onderstan' 'er that day over to the depot ?"

Sam's answer came after a pause.

"Reckon I did," he finally said.

Pinky meditated a moment, and then it became evident that he caught the hidden meaning of the words.

"*I* didn't—not till arterwards," he said.

Sam raised his eyebrows and grinned.

"I mean it," declared Pinky, quite seriously. "I onderstan' the hull darn bizness, I do !"

Sam's amusement was altogether in his eyes as he asked :

"Wot d' ye mean by the hull darn bizness, anyhow ?"

"Her 'n' me 's talked it all over—well, that don't count nohow, fer I knowed it afore. But—lookee 'ere ! She keerd fer ye at the start, she 's keerd fer ye all 'long, 'n' that 'ere performance over to the depot was her way o' tryin' to bring ye to time."

Sam turned to his horses, and the look of amusement died out of his eyes.

"Wot o' all that?" he inquired, touching up the mustang once more.

"Wot o' that? It means ye've got the inside track 'n' kin keep it 's long 's ye like—that's wot! It means 't I ain't nowheres." Pinky's tone was bitter.

"All this 'ere ain't my fun'ral," remarked Sam, after his habitual moment of deliberation. "Wot ye comin' at *me* with it fer? Why don't ye go to *her?*"

"I did, 'n' she owned up to it," declared Pinky. "We had to come to a settlement, 'n' she let the hull thing out. She likes me next arter wot she does you—she said so; but while they's a chance o' gittin' fust choice, I ain't nowheres, o' course. She's jes' like me 'bout gittin' wot she wants—she does it if she kin, 'n' I don't blame 'er. Well, that's all right. But 'tain't wot I started to say."

"I'm ready fer anything else," said Sam, touching up the off mustang again.

After a brief twisting in his seat first in one direction and then in the other, Pinky continued:

"Wot I want to know 's 'bout yerself. 'Ud ye mind tellin' me frank 'n' plain? It's all atween me 'n' you, 'n' I don't see wot harm it could do to let me know. 'N' it 'ud ease up on me like anything if I made shore ye didn't keer fer 'er. I know ye ain't never let on like ye was in love with 'er; but a feller can't allus tell. It's jest atween friends, ye know. 'Twouldn't go no farther."

Sam deliberated.

"N-no. I d' know 's wot I mind tellin' ye my state o' mind, if it 'll make ye easier. But fust I want to know one thing."

Pinky's red face screwed itself inquiringly in his direction. Sam's question came after a pause, which gave it weight.

"Is she goin' to make a fight fer me?"

Pinky looked startled.

Sam's question became a demand.

"Is she goin' to make a fight fer me if I don't want 'er ?"

"She didn't say nothin' 'bout fightin'," said Pinky, somewhat sullenly. Then, with a quick glance at Sam's set face : "Wot d' ye mean by fightin', anyhow ?"

"Ye needn't let on 't ye don't onderstan'. But I'll make myself plainer. Is she ready to put some other gal at a disadvantage—I'm namin' no names, mind—so 's to give 'erself a better chance? Is that wot she's up to ?"

Pinky's jaw dropped.

"Good Lord! 'S if she would! 'S if they *was* any other gal !" he cried. But there was a false note in his disclaimer.

"They *is* another gal," said Sam, quietly.

Pinky looked almost pale.

"The little un ?" he inquired, after a pause.

"'Tain't no credit to yer wits to know it arter all ye must 'a' seen. I'd jes' 's soon the hull world 'ud know it—I ain't 'shamed. 'N' the one hope o' my life is 't she'll git well ag'in — well 'nough so 't she'll know 'er own mind 'bout marryin' me, 'n' we can go afore a justice o' the peace 'n' have the knot tied 'thout my feelin' like I was takin' a mean advantage. Lookee 'ere! I may 's well be plain with ye. I know wot the missus is goin' to do."

He fixed Pinky's eye so fiercely that the young man turned away.

"She's goin' to send the pore little gal out o' the kentry, 'cause she knows I keer fer 'er."

Pinky's telltale color came back with a rush and the truth stood confessed.

"No matter how I know," cried Sam, in answer to the question in Pinky's face. "I *know*, 'n' that's 'nough. 'N' ye're in the scheme—I know that, too. Hey? Be ye goin' to deny it? Ye might 's well own up."

Pinky took time to recover partially from his crushed attitude, and then found courage to say :

"Well, it was her idee. She wanted me to help 'er, 'n' I didn't see how I could git out o' it. I don't see wot wrong they is in it. The gal 'ud be well took keer of. But o' course if yer mind's made up not to marry 'er—"

Sam flung his head back, and there was a light in his usually kind eyes which made Pinky quail.

"My mind 's my own !" he cried. "Wot I want to know 's this : be ye goin' to tell the missus wot we've been talkin' 'bout to-day ?"

Pinky's freckles stood out with startling distinctness upon his thin skin.

"If ye don't want me to, o' course I won't," he stammered.

"Then ye won't," said Sam, briefly.

"'Tain't nothin' 't she *has* to know," said Pinky, in vindication of his ready compliance.

Sam turned full upon him and laid his huge left hand upon his collar. Then, with a cold thrill, Pinky realized that the iron fingers were drawing together in the cloth of his coat.

"If ye tell "—Sam lifted his companion from the seat and gave him a little shake as a testimonial of what he could do in that line if he liked—"if ye do, I'll break every bone in yer body ! Ye hear *me!*"

Pinky shrank together under that grasp of iron.

"I won't tell," he promised, cowed like a whipped boy under the hand of his master. He was dreadfully frightened, but even so, he had not lost sight of the main point. He wanted a definite statement from Sam. "Then ye've made up yer mind ye won't marry 'er fer shore ?"

"Marry 'er !" roared Sam, facing him with blazing eyes. "I'd see 'er in hell fust !"

And he lashed his horses into a gallop.

"I've seen 'im mad, but never like that afore," thought

Pinky, shrinking as far as possible into his corner of the seat. "Shall I tell 'er he said he'd see 'er in hell afore he'd marry 'er? It might hurry up the weddin' fer me; but she'd be shore to let it out, somehow. It 'ud *have* to come out if she fired 'im or made more o' me 'n wot she's been doin'. No, I'll keep my mouth shet; I ain't ripe fer heaven jes' yit. But if I don't marry 'er nex' June all right, I'm a turkey!"

And the two men exchanged not another word during the journey.

CHAPTER XXVI

For several days Sam hardly knew what to do with Pinky's revelation. He felt ready for anything, but nothing seemed as yet ready for him. Events moved on at such a comfortable jog-trot that it was difficult to imagine a hitch anywhere in the mechanism of the world. The ranch people got up early, worked hard at tasks which on the morrow had to be done over again, glorified God in a few of their actions and shamed Him in many, and went to bed with an unformulated sense of having lived. Why not? They put in their time, and that is what life consists of, chiefly. They lived because they didn't die, and the wisest of us can hardly account for ourselves more completely.

But it was a season of unusual anxiety for Sam. He went about with a busy frown between his eyebrows which betokened a soul ill at ease. He lay awake at night—this fact inclined him at times to the belief that he was a sick man—trying to plan out what he should do. But he never came to any conclusion except that he must wait for some overt act on the part of the missus; he must be ready, must have himself in hand, so as as to act vigorously at a moment's notice—vigorously to the extent of violence, if the need should rise.

"I know the little un wouldn't want to go," he said to himself, "if she had 'er way 'bout it; I know she'd ruther stay 'ere where I be. 'N' I ain't a-goin' to stan' aroun' 'n' see 'er carted off like she was a bag o' meal or a sick calf, jes' 'cause she ain't got the will to stan' up fer 'erself. *I* kin stan' up fer both o' us, if they's need o' it;

16

'n' I'll do it, too, when the time comes, missus or no missus !"

He no longer went out on the range with the "boys," but remained about the ranch, watching, listening, peering. One could detect a spark in his kind, slow eyes which had not been there before. He followed Phœbe Ellen with an assiduity which she misunderstood—it was sad and funny to see how ready she was to misunderstand if the prospect of her happiness brightened thereby—and which he was obliged to modify for very shame. More than once he leaped from his bed at night with a reflex readiness for danger as some unusual sound broke the stillness, and stood with strained nerves listening for something to confirm his nightmare impression that the mistress was carrying the little 'un away by main force while the girl was calling him in shrill anguish; but always he could see from his window by the cold, glaring moon that it was only the horses lurching against the corral in some aimless midnight escapade, or the dogs returning from an onrush at some fancied enemy approaching from the shadows of the pines. And he would stand at the window for an hour or more, pondering and pondering, till his thoughts seemed made of metal and clanked as he turned them over and over in his mind. And when he went back to bed he carried with him as something threatening an impression of the mountains surging darkly up from the horizon, and of countless stars falling in a luminous drizzle down the dizzy precipice of the sky. Pinky had been in earnest—there could be no doubt about that. The little un was to be taken away, but how and when Sam could only surmise. Perhaps the mistress herself did not know, but Sam was sure that her mind was made up to the fact. And he kept his eye on Anny as if afraid she might be snatched away bodily in some unguarded moment when his back happened to be turned.

If she were only in her right mind, so that he could talk to her as to a grown woman and tell her of his love ! She loved him—yes, he knew that—as a child loves its big brother, nothing more. He could expect nothing else in her present state—indeed, anything else was impossible. But if she were to get well ? The bare idea made him catch his breath. And she was certainly improving— slowly, to be sure, but unmistakably improving. He noticed the change day by day with a sense of joyful possession in her increased power of speech and thought. Her very appearance was changing. She stepped more firmly and regularly ; she stumbled and fell less often ; her will was more apparent in the use of her hands, her tongue ; her eye was brighter ; her very outline looked more intelligent. She observed and reported more accurately. She discriminated with a finer perception of resemblance and contrast. Her voice was less harsh and strident, and expressed finer shades of feeling. She was even learning to reason.

"If she was to git well—"

Sam often began the thought, but his imagination never completed it except by a question-mark. He could not be so sure of her in her strength as in her helplessness. Now she needed him, but of what use could he be to her if she were to become the glorified vision of his first acquaintance ? Sam's love made him humble, and he could think of the possible change with no other feeling than doubt mixed with faint, pathetic hopefulness. She loved him—if not as a woman, at least as a child ; and if she were to get well he might lose even that, and he saw himself hovering mutely about the edge of her horizon, venturing only on an occasional look of awed wonder. Still, she had seemed to like him as they rode home from the depot on that never-to-be-forgotten day of the accident ; he had discovered in her manner, without being able to formulate it, the suffusive eagerness which is a woman's way of confessing that she is impressed and wishes to give an impression. Some of her remarks had been too shy for ordinary conversation, others had been too bold. She had smiled a good deal, sometimes tremulously, often with the effect of trying to appear serious; and her eye had a way of refusing to be fixed by his—of slipping beyond it to some remote point in the mountains, or settling upon the top button of his jacket, all of which pleased him in the remembrance and which he thought he understood. But if he had been mistaken? Women are so incomprehensible and so—nice!

"If she was to git well, *would* she marry me?" He always finished with the question. If not, how he would miss the childish trustfulness of the clouded intellect with which he was still so divinely dissatisfied! And if she should learn to care for him—well, what would that be like? Heaven, of course; what else? A heaven of insatiate joys which Sam, in the materialism of healthy manhood, would not exchange for all the glorified, winged, harp-playing angels of the Apocalypse.

One day, while he was brooding over these things, he had an inspiration.

"She's so much better, 'n' so much depends on whether she's likely to keep on improvin'," he reflected, "'t I'll jes' take 'er over to Halstead's 'n' see wot Doc Sedgwick thinks o' her. He ain't seen 'er sence she reely begun to pick up, 'n' I shouldn't wonder if he could tell if it's likely to go on. If 'tain't, I orter know it, 'cause then I won't build no hopes on 'er; 'n' if 'tis, I want to know it, 'cause then I'll keep a-picterin' o' 'er as Mrs. Sam Tinker. 'N' the Doc's so sorter weak he can't come over 'ere 'thout a heap o' trouble; he fainted dead away t'other day, Halstead tole me, arter a little climb behind the barn. 'Sides, he'd better see 'er when the missus ain't aroun'. They ain't no tellin' wot she might do."

Sam scratched his ear meditatively.

"But how to git 'er away?"

At first he was inclined to finesse, and he thought of a dozen pretexts under which he might carry off the girl and attain his object; but he disliked them. It was his nature to be "open and above-board," as the saying is, and anything short of that left him dissatisfied with himself. But at last an interview with old man Halstead gave him a chance which seemed more direct and natural, though even this was not all that he desired.

"Ole Halstead says they's one o' our steers got in among his'n, 'n' if I'll go over to-morrer he'll help me cut it out," he said one afternoon, when he and Phœbe Ellen were together.

She looked up from her mending, settling it with a jerk in the centre of her lap.

"Want breakfast airly?" she inquired.

"I reckon I'll have time 'nough if I git off a little arter eight," he answered. "Breakfast won't have to be hurried. But I was thinkin' o' suthin' else."

"Want one o' the boys to g'long? Lengthy Bill's good at that, ain't he? Or Skinny Joe? Or Sufferin' Peter?"

"Any one o' 'em 'ud do. But they's work fer all o' 'em up Corpse Gulch, 'n' I reckon I kin git along with wot help the ole man kin gimme. Wot I wanted was to hitch up the buckboard 'n' give the little un a day off. It 'ud do 'er a power o' good."

"Sis?" Phœbe Ellen took his request more quietly than he had expected—in his broodings he had dramatized her as refusing flatly—but he noticed a droop and a twitch at the corner of her thin mouth which he had learned to regard as a danger-signal. She readjusted her mending, tucking it in so that no smallest edge projected over her lap. "Wot could she do to help you?"

"Nothin' to help me, 's I knows on."

"Oh! ye wanted 'er comp'ny?"

"Jesso—I want 'er comp'ny. 'Sides that, a ride 'ud

do 'er good—don't ye reckon so ?—'n' the weather 's like summer."

Phœbe Ellen's nostrils expanded slightly.

"I've allus treated 'er well—ye know it," she declared. "Ye ain't got no reason to try to git 'er away from me."

"Git 'er away from ye — no! But it 'ud be a nice change fer 'er, 'n' she's so fond o' ridin'."

"With *you*—yes," muttered Phœbe Ellen.

Sam heard, but took no notice.

"'Sides," he went on, "Mis' Halstead 's ast me time 'n' agin to fetch 'er over to spen' the day. It 'ud do 'er good to git out 'n' stir 'roun' more 'n wot she does. It 'ud brighten 'er up 'n' give 'er idees."

Her eyes were fixed upon his with hard examination.

"Anything else ?" she asked. The words came so easily that somehow they seemed unnatural.

Sam met her look placidly. Something told him that he would have his own way if he owned up to the simple truth. That pleased him best, and he resolved to try it.

"Lately it's been comin' over me stronger 'n' stronger," he said, "'t the little un's gittin' better right straight along." He paused to see if she understood the full bearings of his speech, but detected nothing in her answering gaze but a look of attention which had been fixed involuntarily. "Ye've noticed it ?"

Her eyes drooped to her mending, but she made no attempt to resume her needle.

"Yes," she answered, in the same facile, subdued voice. "I've noticed it fer some time."

Sam took up the word more eagerly.

"I've been goin' to speak to ye 'bout it," he declared, leaning towards her in his interest, "but I kep' puttin' it off. 'Sides, I didn't know but wot I might be mistook. 'N' then—"

"Ye didn't know how *I'd* take it ?" There was something dreadful in the smooth bitterness of the words, but he would have been ashamed to notice.

"Now, wot I was thinkin' was this." He brought the index finger of his right hand to the thumb of his left as if beginning a long enumeration. "I'd like Doc Sedgwick to see· 'er. I'd like to know wot he thinks o' 'er. He can't come over here—leastways, the ride 'ud be bad fer 'im. So wot's the matter with takin' 'er over there ?" His enumeration stopped suddenly, and he sat erect with his palms spread on his knees.

Phœbe Ellen was fumbling with her work again.

"I'd rather he wouldn't come over, anyhow," she said, in a low voice. "I got trouble 'nough 'thout havin' *him* aroun'."

"I reckoned so—I 'membered yer hatred o' him. 'N' the little un could stay with 'im while I went to look arter the steer, 'n' he could make up his mind 'bout 'er. If she's goin' to git well—"

"She won't git well—she can't git well !" The words seemed choked from her by a grasp of iron.

Sam went on with undisturbed equanimity.

"That may be so, too; 'n' if 'tis, we want to know it. We want to know it either way, fer it means a heap to all o' us. It does to *me*." He intended the emphasis as a confession of his feelings—why should he not confess ?— and he saw that she so understood it.

"It means a heap to me, too," she supplemented, in a voice that sounded more smothered than before.

"She kin go, then ?"

For a moment she sat relaxed and silent, bending forward with her eyes upon the floor. Then he saw that the muscles of her lean figure were contracting, stiffening, hardening — was she making ready for a spring ? The thin gingham dress quivered, loosely sympathizing with the straining flesh and spirit. Then she flung her work from her with a stiff movement of both hands and came to her feet with a leap.

" Yes, take 'er 'n' go !" she cried, with something like a shriek. " Take 'er—take 'er 'n' go !" Her voice made a sort of clangor in the low room such as he would have believed impossible for a human throat. " But it's the las' time, Sam Tinker—d' ye hear ?"

And, flinging these words over her shoulder, she dashed from the room.

Sam remained silent for a little space, then he rose with a sober smile.

" Yes, I'll take 'er 'n' go," he said, with a series of slow nods. " But the las' time — that's a big word, Miss Thompson, 'n' we've yit to see 'bout that !"

CHAPTER XXVII

"Where's the little un?" wondered Sam, as he passed out upon the veranda. "How happy it 'll make 'er to be told we're goin' a-ridin' together to-morrer!"

He found her at the corral, where she stood thrusting her arm between the upper logs and scratching the nose of a sleepy-eyed bronco with whom she had long ago made friends. She looked pretty and bright and interested. "Almost like 'erself," thought Sam. "I'd like to have a picter o' her jes' so!"

And aloud he said:

"Still makin' frien's with Scrubby? I tell ye, he didn't look 's meek 's that when yer brother Dan 'n' I was breakin' 'im two year ago! But say! 'ud ye like to go a-ridin' with me to-morrer?"

He approached and leaned against the corral at her side. "In the buckboard," he added, looking down tenderly into her eyes.

Anny's face lighted up.

"A-ridin'? In the buckboard? 'Ll sis let me?"

"Yer sister says ye kin go."

"Ye ast 'er?"

"Yes."

"Jest us two?" She had withdrawn her arm from between the logs and was standing erect at arm's-length from Sam's side.

He nodded.

"Jest us two," he repeated, with his serious smile.

"'N' nobody else?"

"Nobody else—not a soul."

“ Not even sis ?”

“ No one but us two.”

“ She’ll stay to home—fer shore ?”

“ Fer shore.”

She made an awkward little dash at him and seized his hand.

“ How glad I be !” she cried. “ How glad—how glad !”

He took her hand in his and smoothed it softly.

“ We’ll have a day to ’member all our lives !” he said, with an enthusiasm almost as childish as her own.

They started earlier next morning than Sam expected —earlier, in fact, than was altogether agreeable. Phœbe Ellen had breakfast for them at daylight—it was a good breakfast, cooked in her very best style—and though she was somewhat more silent than usual, there was nothing in her manner directly indicative of resentment or pique. She saw Anny comfortably seated in the buggy, tucked the lap-robe lightly in, and gave a last caution to the afflicted girl not to let her hat blow off.

“ If it does, tell Sam ’bout it the fust thing,” continued the voice of admonition. “ It ’ud be jes’ like ye to ride ’long ’n’ never miss it fer miles, ’n’ *he’d* never notice. A man never does.”

Anny was silent, evidently impressing the lesson of carefulness on her mind.

“ I’ll keep watch o’ it,” she finally said, touching the brim with heavy, awkward fingers. With all her improvement of late, she was by no means normal in her movements. “ I don’t want to lose my purty hat. ’N’ if it blows off, I’ll holler.”

“ I’ll keep a eye on it, too,” promised Sam. And with that they drove away.

“ She took it well, arter all,” said he to himself, thinking of Phœbe Ellen as she had appeared during the morning.

The red dawn was burning dully in the east, and the

shadows lay heavy in the gulches—so heavy that under
the pendent cliffs of the Halstead road the night seemed
to have settled permanently in a black liquid which overflowed the rocks and trees and left nothing certain but
an outline of the hills and a patch of dull sky. The pines
looked hardly more substantial than an upgrowth of the
desolate shadows; even after the cold gray gleam of morning gave emphasis and purpose to the landscape, the rocks
had a spectral effect in the half-light, and the underbrush
looked remote and vague. Now the walls of the cliffs
closed in and made a twilight through which one half
expected gray phantoms to pass and disappear; now the
sky became a streak as cold and white as if the moon were
still shining; now it broadened as the hills fell apart, and
they could see the sunrise above stormy pines, and the
mountains rising silent and intent as if waiting for an
impression of the dawn. And the seething color in the
east grew redder and redder; it heaved, bubbled, broke
into fiery spray like red-hot lava shot from Tartarean
depths; it sent a pink reflection back from the gray west;
it dropped upon the rocks in red flakes and stuck there.
Pale clouds stirred faintly on peaks seen momentarily as
a transverse gulch gave a glimpse of the high horizon;
a tremor disturbed the gray trance of the mist as the
rising wind passed over it. At best the luminous change
of the sky was visible only by spells; the foot-hills were
always thrusting mighty intrusive shoulders in the way.
And when the eastern horizon forced its broken red line
upon the sight, it looked unreal and strange, like the
imaginings of a half-mad painter, with the mountains
beneath it plunging down into abysses of aerial gloom.

At last the red upheaval sent a reflected gleam into the
gulches, and a luminous tremor passed along the rocks.
The mists turned pink, the rocks grew into a garish
prominence, the pines looked as if a stage-light had been
thrown upon them. There was a chromatic climax, dur-

ing which the landscape appeared as through red glass; then the light paled, the landscape took a healthy natural hue, daylight filled the blue dome of the sky, and a sense of satisfaction came over the world after the breathless surprise of the dawning. The beauty and mystery of peak and gulch were fully revealed. The white range in the distance rose like a line of clouds from the sea; the black surge of pines on the cliff broke towards the road with a liquid roar, then sank back only to heave forward again with a sibilant rush. The birds awakened—not to sing, but to lend the excited flutter of their wings to the agitation of awakened Nature. A rabbit bobbed across the road and seated himself comfortably on his fluffy white tail to watch the wagon pass. Squirrels chattered; there was a crackling of distant underbrush as if a deer were making a cautious flight into the covert of cottonwoods.

"It's all so purty," said Anny, nestling close to Sam's side and tucking her hand under his big arm as a child might have done. "I like it—I like it! Oh, I'm glad I'm alive!"

Sam smiled down at her, his face bright with sympathy.

"It's good to be alive when we're happy," he said.

"I'm happy — happy!" chanted Anny. "I'm allus happy when I'm with you!"

"I'm happy too—jes' 's happy 's you be. The only trouble seems to be 't we can't allus keep it up."

"Can't keep up bein' happy?"

"*You*'re happy most o' the time, though. That's right. I like to see ye happy, no matter 'bout the rest o' us."

"I'm allus happy," she repeated—"allus happy when I'm with *you!*"

"Then ye'd like me aroun' all the time, hey?"

"I would that!" she declared.

"Well, I been aroun' a good deal lately, 'ain't I? More 'n I used to be?"

"More 'n ye used to be—yes.   But—"

"But wot ?"

"But not 'nough—not 'nough !"

"I'm afeerd ye're greedy," said Sam.

"Greedy ?"

"Yes ; greedy o' *me !*"

"Is it wicked to be greedy ?"

"Wot made ye think o' that ?"

"'Pears like I've heerd sis say how 'tis."

"'Tain't wicked to be greedy 'bout nice things," said Sam, with his kindest smile.

"Like pie 'n' cake 'n' doughnuts ?"

"Oh, *they* ain't nice !"

"Then wot *is* nice ?"

"Why, *I* be !   See ?"

Anny faced him soberly—she was still very slow at grasping a joke—but at last her face reflected his smile with an eager jubilance.

"Oh !   Then 'tain't wicked to be greedy o' *you ?*"

Sam's eyes sparkled his enjoyment of her quickness.

"Ye kin be jes' 's greedy o' me 's ye like !" he declared.

He thought she was going to attempt some retort, but whatever mental effort her stammering concealed, it finally settled into a simple but appreciative "Oh !"

"'N' ye'll go to heaven, too," said Sam.

"Oh !" she repeated, in the same tone.   Then her face brightened still more.   "I'm agoin' to be greedy right straight along now," she declared.

"Well," said Sam, contentedly.   And he pressed his huge arm against the hand that still nestled at his side.

Presently he said :

"Ye're lookin' 's bright 's a dollar this mornin', little un.   Ain't ye feelin' spryer 'n usu'l ?"

"I'm happy, happy, happy !" she answered.

"Ye'll have a nice day over to Halstead's.   The ole

lady 's been wantin' ye to visit 'er ever s' long.   I never see 'er but wot she speaks to me 'bout it."

"'That's nice, ain't it ?"

"''Ll ye be lonesome while I'm out on the range with the ole man ?"

"'To ketch that steer?   No, I won't be lonesome."

" Ye know the Doc 'll be there."

Anny nodded reflectively.

" I like the Doc," she said.   "He's allus good to me when he comes over to the ranch."

" Ye ain't afeerd o' him ?"

"Afeerd ?   Oh no !"

" Don't he skeer ye with his eyes ?"

Anny laughed.

" He allus looks at me like he keerd fer me," she answered.

"''N' ye'll talk to 'im if he seems to feel like it ?"

" Oh yes.   I'll talk to the Doc.   I allus do."

The sun was well up when they reached Halstead's, and the shadows lay black and tangled under the cottonwoods all about the old ranch-house.   It was a shady spot in an opening in the foot-hills, and beyond it the mountains rose, hung with vapors.   There was a small stream close at hand, and the sun made a troubled lustre on the clear water ; mountains and trees were broken in the hurrying current as it slipped among the stones with a sound which carried with it a sense of coolness and calm.

They were met at the gate by Mrs. Halstead—a hard-featured old woman with a big brown mole in her eyebrow and loose corrugations of colorless flesh under her chin which no effort of retrospective imagination could fill with youthful plumpness.   She had iron-gray hair, which was combed straight behind the ears from an uncompromising parting and fastened in a hard, glistening gray knob at the back of her head, which looked as if it had been screwed in.   The mountains mould grim features into the faces of their human companions, but the harshness of Mrs. Halstead's nose and chin was corrected by her eyes, which were gentle and thoughtful and loving.

"Well, this 'ere's a sight fer sore eyes!" was her greeting. "'Light—'light 'n come in." In the eagerness of her hospitality it seemed impossible for her to get her visitors quickly enough into the house. "Jes' tie the bronco to the gate-post, Sam — I'll send Hank out to look arter it. Come in—come in! I've been longin' fer weeks to git the little un over 'ere fer a day." She kissed Anny, removed her hat, smoothed her hair, and set her in the wooden rocker by the window. "I declare, I been feelin' like a biled owl all mornin'—I tole Hank afore I got up I knowed I was goin' to put in a blue day, 'n' hoped some o' the neighbors 'ud drop in. Well!"—she stood off and contemplated her visitors with folded arms—"this suits *me* half to death, *I* tell ye! How's all the folks over on the Rio Grande?"

Sam opened his mouth to reply, but before he could utter a word Anny spoke up brightly:

"Sis 's well, 'n' Leatherhead's well, 'n' Pinky's well, 'n' everybody's well over on the Rio Grande!"

Mrs. Halstead opened her eyes wide and then laughed.

"The little un 's wonderful peart this mornin', ain't she?" she asked. She took the girl's hand and patted it softly. "'Pears like I've noticed lately how she's pickin' up. I says to Hank t'other day, says I, 'She's a-gittin' right along,' says I, 'she's a-gittin' right along!' 'N' shore 'nough, now, ain't she? I'll leave it to anybody, ain't she? Land! she'll soon be 'erself altogether at this rate!"

Anny looked up eagerly.

"I *be* better," she declared. "Ain't I, Sam?"

"I'm shore o' it," was his answer.

"I *know* I be," resumed Anny, with more confidence. "I feel it 'ere," she touched her heart, "'n' 'ere," she laid her hand on her forehead. "Oh, I feel it all over! 'N' wot if I was to git well?"

Sam's face shone happily. He had been afraid that the excitement of the visit would confuse her, or that the journey would weary and stupefy her, and that she would be unable to show off to advantage before the doctor; but instead of that it had stimulated her, and she would be seen at her best.

"If the Doc could see 'er at this minute," he thought, "I know he'd say they was hopes fer 'er." And aloud he asked: "Where's the Doc, anyhow? I come over partly to see 'im—it's a errand. 'N' arter that I mus' try to hunt up that steer. Doc feelin' any better these days?"

"No better—no. Keeps on in jest about the same ole way. He's out in the hammick up beyend the corral, where the sun 's warm on the rocks. Ye know, I reckon."

Sam nodded.

"I'll leave the little un with you," he said, and strode away.

He found the doctor in the place indicated, spread out in a sort of ghastly ease with the sunshine flaming full in his face and eyes. His half-closed lids were dark, as if shaded in with charcoal; his cheek-bones took a singular high-light which made them doubly prominent. He had a heavy gray shawl wrapped about his legs, and under him was a woollen afghan of mingled cardinal and black, its edges showing vividly over the hammock. The cotton-woods about the spot, seared by autumn, made a faded aureole beyond him, and there was a certain brightness in the very shadows they flung along the gray soil. Above him a foot-hill heaved its solid mass of rocky drift, broken by black pines which sang dirges in the wind; and still higher up the precipitous sky lifted its breathless curve of blue. Two or three white peaks were discernible between sky and foot-hill.

"Hello, there!" was Sam's greeting, two yards away. "Well, to see the way ye be a-soakin' in the sun!"

"Good God!" cried Dr. Sedgwick, flinging up his arms as if he were falling. The shock of Sam's voice brought a wild light into his eyes, which remained for a moment in a steady glare, then flickered and died out. Then, recovering from his start: "Oh, it's you!" He sank back, panting. · "Heavens! did you spring straight up through the ground? Are there trap-doors in this infernal soil? Why can't you come up to a man like a Christian? Oh, these healthy cattle, who don't know whether they have nerves and lungs! You've scared the life out of me!"

"I—I forgot how sick ye was—I swear I did," apologized Sam. Then, with a rueful glance at the panting invalid: "Ye're right, I *be* a brute. I orter 'a' thort—it was my place."

"Oh, that's easily said, and more easily believed. You needn't be scared—you haven't killed me yet. You can come over some other day and finish up the job. I wish you would—and quickly, too! Isn't it strange that a man can't die, even when it's plain his time has come?" The momentary excitement died out of his face, the ghastliness became less pronounced, and his skin resumed its customary flabby lifelessness of hue. "To go on breathing and thinking after one is really dead—to eat and sleep and move about, and see things that really belong to a past world—it's a horrible life to live, a ghost's life, I tell you! To survive one's ambitions, one's friends, one's contemporaries, one's very passions — can you imagine what it is like? If I could only cough like other consumptives, it would help to finish me off. No ; you can't imagine what it is like. You are still alive!"

Sam said nothing. He stood with one arm akimbo and the other behind him, in the awkward attitude of pitying attention.

Suddenly the sick man broke into a short, bitter laugh.

16

"You came over to hear that, I suppose. Well, you've heard it, and what do you think of me? Sit down; you make me nervous standing there like an overgrown schoolboy that's been spanked." Sam's grin was immediately reflected on the doctor's pallid features. "That rock there at the foot of the cottonwood—if you'll take that I won't have to twist my neck when I talk. Are there any sharp places on it? No matter—you won't feel them. Sit down."

Sam did as he was bidden, still grinning.

The doctor punched his pillow with one skeleton fist, and brought his thin face higher into the sunlight. His skull hung in his yellow skin, half visible, as in a bag.

"I was hopin' to find ye better," Sam ventured. "I'm sorry ye ain't. I hate to see a human critter sufferin'."

"I'm sorry to force you to do what you hate. But it'll do you good—you great animals have things too much your own way. Well, I like to look at you, nevertheless, and think how I would feel and what I would do if I had your muscles, your digestion, your nerves, your blood. It's maddening, of course; but so is everything. And you are at least a change."

Sam glanced about him at the sky, the mountains, the trees, the interplay of sunshine and shadow, and a sense of sadness crept across his sympathy with the healthy joy of material things. He did not try to express the feeling, but perhaps there was a sense of wistfulness in his question.

"Don't the brandy brace ye up?" he asked.

"Oh, brace me up, yes. It keys me up high—above concert-pitch, I tell you. But afterwards—if there were no afterwards, I'd keep full of brandy from morning to night. But what's the use? It's as if—" He made a gesture descriptive of a vain, aimless flight from misery, then sunk deeper into the pillow. "Well, what of it? There is plenty of good material in the world. Is there a God? He can afford to be lavish of it!"

Sam smoothed his knee thoughtfully with one big brown hand.

"'Pears like ye ain't reely got so fur away from yer ambition 's wot ye talk," he remarked.

"Oh, are *you* getting subtle ?" asked the doctor.

"*I* should say," continued Sam, "how ye was jes' tryin' to make yerself think ye don't keer fer nothin', jes' 'cause it makes ye onhappy to keer fer things. 'N' *I* should say ye couldn't quite make it out."

"You *are* getting subtle !" put in the doctor.

"No 'fence, o' course," said Sam, in apology.

The sick man's eyes lit up with a momentary smile.

"It's the last thing I'd have thought of *you*," he remarked.

"Well, let it go fer wotever it's wuth. The name o' it don't cut no ice. But if ye was to git a chance to show off yer skill on a good subjeck, now—a fust-rate subjeck 't'ud do ye credit—well, *I* bet yer ambition 'ud show itself, 'n' quick, too."

"You're becoming a mind-reader like myself," he said, half bitterly.

"No ; but I've brought the little un over fer ye to look at. 'N' if that don't int'rest ye, nothin' will. She's to be yer patient fer to-day—see ? I been 'tendin' a long time to have ye see 'er, but things allus come up to interfere. 'Pears like she's a heap better—we all think so ; 'n' I want to know fer shore. Ud ye mind talkin' to 'er a spell ? I'm goin' out on the range fer a steer."

"You seem rather interested in that girl," the doctor suggested, after a moment.

"I'd marry 'er to-morrer, *if* she'd have me."

"*And* if—"

"*And* if she was in 'er right mind."

"Ah !" said the doctor, smiling more broadly after a little pause. "Yes, bring her out. I'll examine her."

CHAPTER XXVIII

Sam captured his steer, corralled it, and was back to the ranch at one o'clock. He found the doctor propped up among heaps of chintz cushions in an easy-chair on the veranda.

"Well?" he inquired, anxiously, on coming face to face with the man of science.

The doctor looked worn and broken, but his face told a story of discovery. There was an idea in his look, his gestures, his attitude. Something had transformed him. He looked like a disembodied spirit with eyes of flame.

"I've examined her," he said, trying unsuccessfully to keep his lips from quivering.

"Well?" repeated Sam.

The doctor seemed to readjust himself inwardly.

"I've had a long talk with her—a long talk."

Again came Sam's anxiously patient query, "Well?"

"She's better," the doctor said.

Sam fetched an exhalation like a puff from an escape-pipe.

"I knowed it!" he cried. And then, with an eager lurch in the doctor's direction, "She'll git well!"

The doctor's voice trembled as he took up the word in his own way.

"Very much better. Better by far than I ever hoped she would be. But—"

Sam steadied himself against a veranda post, breathing hard.

"They's a *but* in the case, then?" he asked.

The doctor settled into the chair on the small of his back.

"A *but?* A very big *but,* I can tell you ! The biggest kind of a *but.* In a word—"

"She can't git well ?" cut in Sam, breathlessly.

"You've said it—she can't get well. She may improve still further—it's likely she will; she may learn to perceive more accurately, to memorize tolerably well, to reason a very little ; she may become so nearly herself that a stranger would see nothing peculiar about her. She may do all this—I hope and believe she will ; but she can't get well ! I examined her carefully—not by question only, but by actual manipulation of the injured spot. It used me up, and I've been taking brandy ever since—do you smell my breath ? You could skate on it !—but what matter ? The injury is of such a nature that she can never fully recover from its effects."

Sam pushed himself away from the post, turning so that the doctor could not see his face.

"Well, there's another hope gone a-glimmerin'," he said, in a tone which failed to conceal his real depth of feeling.

The doctor smoothed his cheek with a jerky hand, and ended by pinching the withered skin on his jaw in an excited way.

"I discovered something else," he said, in an altered voice.

Sam turned quickly.

"Suthin' else ?"

"I *believe* I have discovered something else," amended the doctor.

"Wot kin it be ? Anything in 'er favior ? Lord ! I do b'lieve it's suthin' in 'er favior !" Sam's face had lighted up.

"Yes, in her favor. But I can't tell you now—you have a right to hope—yes, and I have a right to tell you that you may. Only, I want time to think—I must have time to think. Wait—wait! Don't you see I'm all upset, in spite of the brandy? Great God! What if I should be the means of restoring that poor girl completely to her reason? Well, who would say *then* that Sedgwick the consumptive had lived for nothing—studied medicine for nothing? Restore her? That would be a feat which you with all your brute strength could never perform. Listen! But no; I swore I'd take two days to think it over, and I will. I want to be calm, careful, judicious. I must take time. Come over day after to-morrow and I'll give you my conclusion. Not before—no! Do you want to kill me by forcing me to speak before I'm ready? How would that benefit her? They've called you twice to dinner. Day after to-morrow, and till then say nothing to any-body. No, I sha'n't eat anything. There's Mrs. Hal-stead again—go!"

Sam went in, but for the first time in his life he had no appetite. He ate, not because he cared for what was set before him—he was really unable to distinguish one dish from another—but for fear his hosts and Anny would no-tice and make comment if he abstained. The chicken stew, which good Mrs. Haldstead had so carefully pre-pared for the occasion, might have been corned beef for all he knew. Even the hot waffles for dessert went down without a titillation, and he was glad when the meal was over and he was at liberty to wander out into the open air.

He hunted for the doctor, but that mysterious indi-vidual was nowhere to be found.

"I won't go home 'thout seein' 'im," he muttered, un-der his breath. "He's got to tell me wot struck 'im so hard. I can't live till day arter to-morrer on a crumb like that."

But the doctor had gone to bed ill and could see no one.

"Tell him to go home and behave himself," was the harsh message old Mrs. Halstead brought back.

"Damn it!" muttered Sam, and turned away.

But swearing was of no use, and like a wise man Sam abstained after that first outbreak.

"Day arter to-morrer it is then," he said to himself as he went to tell Anny it was time to start for home.

He had not expected to leave so early, but he managed to find an excuse—ranch-life is a fertile source of prevarication; and at last, to his infinite relief, he found himself seated in the buckboard with Anny at his side and the reins in his hands. Mr. and Mrs. Halstead were at the gate shrieking good-byes interlarded with wild invitations to come again.

"I'll send one o' the boys over fer the steer to-morrer," were Sam's parting words. "Or if not, I'll be over myself the day arter."

"The corral b'longs to 'im 's long 's he needs it," was the old man's hospitable response. "He's welcome—welcome 's the flowers in May. 'N' be shore 'n' bring the little un agin. 'N' tell the missus we're longin' fer a sight o' her smilin' face. We're powerful stuck on the little un, wife 'n' me."

"I'll come," spoke up Anny, on her own account. "I've had sech a good time. 'N' the chicken stew was lovely!"

Sam backed the buckboard into the road, and a moment later his horse's nose was turned homeward.

"Ye've reely had a good time?" asked Sam, looking down at his companion.

The excitement of parting was dying out of Anny's face.

"Yes," she answered, listlessly.

"But it tired ye, hey?"

"Yes."

"Ye had a talk with the doctor?"

"Yes."

“ A long un ?”

“ Not too long.”

“ Wot ’d he say ?”

Anny considered.

“ Oh, lots o’ things,” she finally said.

“ Fer instance ?”

She brushed her hair wearily back from her eyes.

“ I can’t think.”

Sam was touched by the words and the look which accompanied them—it was so plain that she was tired out—but his anxiety was greater than his compassion.

“ O’ nothin’ ?   Can’t ye think o’ nothin’ ?”

She shook her head.

“ No.”

“ Try—try,” he urged.

She shut her eyes and presently clasped her fingers to her temples.   Then she lowered her right hand and clasped it around his big arm.   Presently she looked up wistfully.

“ There was suthin’—” she began, with a tentative, helpless look.

“ Yes, yes !” he cried, eagerly.

“ I didn’t know jes’ wot it meant—”

“ Yes, yes !”

“ I couldn’t think it out, but ’peared like I orter know—”

“ Try—try to ’member—”

“ So I said to myself, ‘ I’ll ’member that ’n’ ast Sam.’ ”

“ But wot he said—can’t ye bring it back ?”

There was a long pause.

“ It’s gone, ’n’ I can’t bring it back !” she finally sighed, drooping her cheek against his shoulder.

Sam’s face expressed his disappointment, and he did not notice that she had turned a little and was looking up at him.

“ Ye won’t scold me ?” she pleaded.   “ No—no !   Don’t scold me !   I’ll try to think !”

He put his arm around her reassuringly.

"It don't matter," he said, gently. "Don't worry. *I* don't mind."

"'N' ye like me jes' the same 's ever?"

"Jes' the same."

There was another wistful silence.

"Ye'd like me better, though, if I could think wot he said?"

"I'd like orfly to know. But don't worry. It's all right!"

She lowered her gaze and leaned her cheek against his shoulder in the childish way with which he was familiar.

"Keep very still," she said. "Ever 'n' ever so still. It almos' comes back. I want ye to like me. I'll try to bring it back."

They rode on in silence. Sam noticed nothing of the landscape through which they passed; his thoughts were intent on the doctor and his idea. What was it? What did it all mean? Was there really something to hope for? Or was it only a hallucination—one of a consumptive's many distempered dreams? The sun wandered farther and farther down the sky; the mists condensed into white, woolly rolls above the woods; the rocks and trees seemed to engage in mute conference with their shadows. Pines hung on the horizon like storm clouds; close at hand they looked human, tossing their arms in impatience of their uninterpreted grief. Finally their moaning grew into the silence till the mind failed to distinguish between the two, and called it only silence.

At last Anny spoke without moving. Her voice was so low that when she began Sam mistook it for a softer murmur from the pines.

"I kin tell ye now. The pines helped me to 'member it. 'N' I'm so glad!" She heaved a long sigh.

Sam bent his head sidewise towards her so as not to lose a word.

"I'm listenin'," he said.

"He was lookin' at me with all his eyes—ye know how?—till I had to shet mine, like, to keep 'im out. It was like suthin' was borin' into my head. It skeerd me. Ye know wot I mean?"

"I know—I know!"

"'N' all to wunst he says, like he was talkin' to himself, 'If I ever find it out by mind-readin',' " says he, 'I'll have to git it from 'er sister.' 'N' then he stopped lookin' at me, 'n' went to talkin' 'bout the birds 'n' squirrels. 'N' that's all—only I'm glad I 'membered."

Sam could make nothing of the speech, and his countenance expressed as much. But Anny failed to see his disappointment; she was very tired, and would not have understood had she noticed his perplexed look.

"I'm glad, too," he said, gently. He was not unmindful of the effort she had made to please him.

She nestled closer, like a contented child.

"Ye like me now?"

"Ever so much."

His glance met hers, straight as a sunbeam. How pretty she looked with the flush of weariness in her cheeks and the light of affection in her eyes! For a moment he forgot what she was—an afflicted creature whose recovery was at best problematical—and remembered only that he loved her. He had been silent so long—surely she would understand! But he was in no mood to weigh chances; the desire to tell her of his love overflowed and bore away all other feelings like a sudden tide.

"Don't look away!" he cried, suddenly, as she was about to turn her head. "Look up at me—look up at me allus like that!"

She turned her face obediently to his without lifting her head from his shoulder.

"Like ye? I love ye!" he said, in a hushed voice.

"Ye hurt me," she murmured. And he woke to the

consciousness that he was crushing her against his breast with all his strength.

"I love ye—I'd die fer ye !" he whispered.

She looked at him, as he could easily see, without understanding the difference between like and love.

"I'm glad," she said, simply. "I like ye, I love ye, too !"

Her direct, innocent gaze gave him a pang. A sudden shame overcame him. It was as if he had confessed a man's passion for a child.

"I do love ye, little un," he repeated, in a different tone.

And in this mood he bent and kissed her softly on the forehead.

"Go to sleep," he said, as if she were his little sister, helpless and tired. He adjusted his huge left arm about her, and supported her so that the movement of the wagon would disturb her less. "Ye're worn out altogether. Go to sleep !" And there was a suspicious moisture in his eyes as he turned to his horse.

And thus they rode on through the gulches while the sun sank lower and lower to the cliffs, and the mists, which had settled like a white sediment upon the black solid of the pines, turned roseate, and the early sunset got tangled in the trees and made a hazy, sprawling glory of the shadows. And Sam thought:

"If she was to git well—the Doc said she couldn't, but he said they was hope, too — she couldn't go to sleep leanin' agin me like this ! Why, it's like she was a little baby 'n' trusted me completely, knowin' I'd never let 'er come to harm. How stiddy 'n' reg'lar she breathes, pore little tired thing !"

On through the thickening shadows, while the spirit of the wind passed in among the mists and scattered them in red fragments along the rocks. Sam noticed nothing of the rustling cottonwoods or the moaning pines. His mind was busy with the future.

"I'll be on hand day arter to-morrer to see wot sort o' magget that man 's got in his head," he thought. "He wouldn't 'a' talked that way fer nothin'."

When they reached the home valley Sam awakened his companion by drawing her away from him and placing her erect in her seat.

"Wake up !" he cried, when he saw that her eyes were open. "We're home agin !"

Anny yawned.

"I'm glad ye like me," she said, taking up her thought where she had left it off on going to sleep.

"Yes, but ye mus'n't let the missus hear ye talk 'bout it," cautioned Sam.

"No," acquiesced Anny, now fully awake.

CHAPTER XXIX

Two days later Sam started immediately after breakfast for Halstead's. He gave no intimation of the real object of his journey to any one, merely saying to Phœbe Ellen that he was going to drive home the steer which he had corralled on his former visit.

He found the doctor in his room, stretched full length upon the bed.

"I expected you," was the invalid's greeting. "No, I'm no worse—I'm merely trying to keep still. I don't succeed very well—no. Somehow, even when my mind is quiet—which is rare—my body keeps on going. That is horrible—the strain one feels when his mind and body are at odds. I'm glad you came early. I have better control of myself in the morning. Don't I seem rather more restful than usual? I've been saving up for your visit—you remember how you surprised me the last time?—and I'd like to think my preparations are discoverable in some sort of result. I've been thinking—you know I told you I would—and I feel sure of myself. I didn't when I saw you last. I had got an idea—they've been so scarce since I came to Colorado!—and it upset me horribly. Yes, I can cure that girl—I fully believe I can. I'd like to try; the thought of it has been tingling in me ever since it got into my mind—it's a sort of poison in my blood. Think of it—if I could cure her! I—I! You don't seem to know what that means. To you I suppose it would mean the same as if another man cured her, but to me! Why do I set so much store by it? I'm sure I don't know. Call it a freak—a sick man's whim. But I want to do it.

I've never had a chance really to do anything in my profession—I lost my health just as I had finished my course in the hospital ; but I know I had ability—others thought so as well as myself. I have ability still if my health would let me exert it. Cure her ? I tell you I can. Or if not—"

"Well, wot then ?" asked Sam, as his companion hesitated. "If ye didn't cure 'er—"

"She might die."

Sam felt himself stiffening, then as suddenly relaxing.

"If I didn't cure her, I might kill her," stated the doctor, explicitly.

Sam's eyes asked for another statement more definite.

"I believe, though, there would be no intermediate ground," said the doctor, in answer to that look. "It would be either one thing or the other. I don't mean that it would be impossible for her to go on as she is ; she might do it—with another physician. But not with me. I know it. You see I speak plainly."

"Oh !" was Sam's only comment. .

The doctor eyed him curiously.

"You don't seem to take to the idea," he remarked, cracking his skeleton fingers.

Sam made no answer. His eyes wandered thoughtfully out to the foot-hills and the vacant sky. Finally he bent his glance once more upon the doctor and inquired :

"Wot sort o' med'cine 'ud ye have to give 'er, anyhow, if ye was to try this scheme ? Pizen ?"

"Medicine ? I should give her no medicine at all."

Sam's glance became more alert.

"Wot, then ?"

"She would have to undergo an operation."

"A operation ?" The word had a loose signification in Sam's vocabulary, and he could not have defined it to save his life. In general he connected it with crude amputations of arms, legs, or frozen ears.

The doctor understood his perplexity, and though his eyes burned more darkly than usual, he smiled.

"No, I sha'n't cut her head off," he said. "They cut off hands and feet to perform cures, but never heads. I'll vouch for the girl's head."

Sam did not notice the sarcasm.

"But—'er brains, doctor?" he asked. "Wot about 'er brains?"

"And I sha'n't scrape her brains out," grinned the strange man. "An operation isn't always so radical as that."

"Then *wot*'ud ye do?"

"Let me tell you. You see—"

"Tell me in the littlest words ye kin think of," stipulated Sam.

"I'll do it so that a child could understand. The simple fact is that the girl's skull was fractured in the accident on the landslide—"

"I allus made shore o' that," put in Sam.

"And a piece of bone is pressing upon the brain. You understand?"

Sam nodded.

"Now, have you ever seen a set of surgical instruments?"

"Knives 'n' saws 'n' sech?"

"Yes—and other things."

"I've seen 'em," said Sam.

"Well, there are special instruments for such cases as this girl's. A skilful surgeon can cut through the scalp, lay open the flesh, reach down into the fracture, lift the displaced bone carefully up—"

Sam's eyes were wide with interest.

"Yes—yes! 'N' they kin keep it there?"

"Yes, they can keep it there. I've seen it done—assisted in the operation—"

"But never reely done it?"

“No.   But I know just how.”

“’N’ the patient gits well ?”

“Exactly.   The patient gets well.”

Sam pondered a moment.

“But if the surgeon lacked skill—”

The doctor shut him off peremptorily.

“Then he oughtn’t to undertake the operation.”

His perfect frankness pleased Sam, and he went on :

“But if he was mistook in hisself ?”

“The friends ought to make sure of that, and then decline to let him operate.”

“I’m a friend o’ this patient,” remarked Sam.

“So am I.”

“I want the thing done that’s best fer ’er.”

“So do I.”

Sam shook his head and sighed.

“Ye don’t feel fer ’er like wot I do,” he declared. “Cut into ’er scalp ’n’ go to proddin’ aroun’ amongst ’er skull ?   Ye never could do it if ye keerd fer ’er like *I* do.”

“I didn’t mean that. You are doubtless the best friend she has in the world.”

“’N’ the missus—she’s ’er friend too,” said Sam.   The words came half tentatively, half defiantly.

“Um-m,” said the doctor.

“*She* wouldn’t never cornsent to it.”

“Why not ?”

“Sev’ral reasons.   Fust ’n’ foremost, she hates the sight o’ *you*.   She wouldn’t let ye tech the gal.”

“Oh, I know all that.   I know more about the cause of her hatred, too, than you suppose.   But that’s altogether beside the question.   Would she be glad to have her sister recover ?”

Sam flushed.

“I ain’t ast ’er,” he answered.

“Ask her and see.”

"Ye're shore she wouldn't?"

"Aren't *you?*"

Sam gave an evasive shrug.

"She would never consent," the doctor went on, "but not because she hates me. *I* know her reasons: so do you."

"We might 's well onderstan' each other," said Sam. "Let's see if yer idees tally with mine."

"She would never consent, because she loves *you*, Sam Tinker—that's why. Do you suppose I am blind? You forget that I am blessed—or cursed—with a double vision—"

"Ye're the devil!" said Sam.

"Thanks! We'll discuss that later. I realize that the missus won't consent—and I know other reasons than either of us has mentioned; but they will keep. Some day, if you need them, you shall have them. Now, the question is, should the girl's fate be decided by one whose judgment is as biassed as that of your mistress? If so, the girl will have to stay as she is, for all I can see. It doesn't seem fair, though."

"No, it don't," admitted Sam.

"Put yourself in the girl's place a moment, can you?"

"It 'pends on wot ye want me to do."

"Wouldn't you rather die in an operation than live on with her prospects before you?"

"She ain't so bad," evaded Sam. "She's gittin' better."

"But the question—wouldn't you, now? Answer truly."

Sam faced the situation as best he could.

"Oh, *I?* Yes, I would. But *her*—to *her*—"

"Hasn't she the same rights as you? Does she forfeit her rights because she isn't able to judge for herself? And because you have to decide for her, are you not, in fact, a coward to assume that she is different?"

17

The doctor had braced himself on one elbow, and was facing the cowboy with burning eyes. Sam afterwards remembered those eyes in dreams.

" The missus is the one to decide," he still evaded.

" She is *not* the one to decide. She is prejudiced. You yourself admitted the fact."

" We couldn't do it if she *didn't* cornsent, though," objected Sam.

The doctor nodded slowly.

" You have the power to persuade her," he said.

" Ye talk like ye made shore I was in fer the bizness."

" I am."

" But if I tell ye I ain't ?"

" You will be when you think it over."

" 'N' if I was to say I don't b'lieve ye're onto the job ?"

" Not equal to it, you mean ?"

" Jesso."

The doctor bit his thin lip and settled back.

" Then the affair would have to end just as it is," he said, in a hollow voice.

" The missus 'll tell ye that when ye come to ast 'er," said Sam.

" But I'm not going to ask her. You are to do that. You *will* do it—if I give you time."

" 'N' if ye was to be nervous 'n' jab yer tools a leetle too fur into the little un's head—"

The doctor finished the sentence calmly.

" She would die."

IIe twisted himself into a position from which he could look more directly into Sam's face.

" On the other hand, if the case were managed right she would get well. IIave you thought what that really means ?"

" I ain't thort o' nothin' else, lately. It might mean sev'ral things."

“For instance ?”

“That she wouldn’t have nothin’ to do with me,” was the gloomy answer.

“Nonsense ! She’d marry you the next day after she got her senses. Any girl would.”

“Oh, *you* want the *job*—that’s plain ’nough,” struck in Sam, who was utterly impervious to compliment.

“Granted. But not for the money there is in it. I’ll do it for nothing when you get the missus persuaded. I want the job, yes. Would you like to be asked in the next world what you had done in this, and be obliged to answer only, ‘ I had consumption ?’ ”

“Ain’t that ’nough ? Wouldn’t the angels think it was ’nough ?”

“ Oh, enough—there’s no denying that ; but not of the right kind. And leaving the next world out of the question—fact is, I never took much stock in it myself—I’d like to feel on my own account that I’d done something to justify the pains my people took with my education. This is my last chance. That’s why I’m anxious. Think it over—think it over. There’s as much good in the affair for you as for me. There’s no hurry. I sha’n’t die for a month or six weeks yet. And when you’ve made up your mind—”

“ It’s the missus’s mind that has to be made up.”

“ You can bring her around. And if you can’t—”

“ Wot then ?”

“ We’ll do it without her consent, if you’ll stand by me.”

“ Oh ! I’m to bear the hull brunt o’ the bizness, am I ? ’N’ if she ’s to die, I’m to be ’sponsible ?”

The doctor smiled grimly.

“ I shall be out of that part of it,” he declared.

“ *You* out o’ it when ye done it ? Ye’ll be in it, *I* tell ye—strickly in it !”

The strange man shook his head.

“I should soon follow her,” he said, without emotion.

Sam snorted.

“Ye ortn’t to hurry on *her* ’count. They ain’t no reason to think she’d be puttickler glad to see ye, under the circumstances. Well, we won’t talk ’bout it no more. We’ll let the little un stay jes’ like she is — that’s wot you ’n’ me ’ll do. *I* don’t want no sech weight on me. The little gal ’t I love so ! Let ’er stay like she is !”

The doctor stirred restlessly.

“And you won’t speak to the missus ?”

Sam shook his head.

The doctor gave him a stare which went through and through him. Then he smiled.

“You’ll change your mind by to-morrow,” he said, quietly. “It won’t let you sleep till you’ve settled it. Think it over, I tell you. You’ll never be sorry !”

Sam left him with that, and as he drove the steer home through the devious gulches his thoughts, in spite of all he could do, dwelt on the doctor’s plan, and followed it out to its ultimate possibilities. He could not get away from it ; it followed him like a distempered dream. He was like one who adds a column of figures over and over that won’t come right. Up and down he went with a mental forefinger, recalculating with painful persistence, going back to correct mistakes, looking ahead for possible difficulties, perplexed, shaken, dissatisfied. The steer could have escaped him a dozen times in the underbrush or among the rocks had it not been a mean-spirited, docile creature that had grown up in the neighborhood of the home ranch. As it was, Sam kept at the animal’s tail without difficulty, and arrived home with no greater misfortune than the increased perplexity of his thoughts.

“Ye got it ?” asked Phœbe Ellen, meeting him on the porch.

He came to himself with a start.

"Oh, ye was talkin' o' the steer?" he inquired. "Oh yes, I got the steer."

"Wot else *should* I be talkin' of?" she demanded, sharply.

"Nothin'," said Sam.

CHAPTER XXX

For three or four days after his interview with the doctor Sam moved about the ranch in a condition of complete mental collapse. The man of medicine had spoken truth when he said that the cowboy would be unable to sleep until he had settled the matter of the operation for good and all. He didn't sleep; neither did he settle the matter. He performed his duties like a man in a dream, but with a face so careworn and perplexed that Phœbe Ellen began to be worried about his health.

"Wot's the matter?" she asked him a dozen times. And—

"Nothin'," was his invariable answer, delivered so shortly as to sound like a monosyllable.

"Suthin' 's up," Phœbe Ellen concluded. But just what was a matter which her imagination strained at vainly.

Sam lost his appetite; he grew thin; he became irritable. Often he rose at night, and, wrapping his big fur overcoat about him, wandered down to the river and sat by the hour gazing into the water, where he could see his face staring up at him with the same lack-lustre vacancy that filled the moon in the river as it stared back at the moon in the sky. Sometimes he grew nervous at the idiotic vision and flung stones into the quiet water along the margin, rejoicing to see his features crack into faintly luminous fragments, and wishing that by some such simple process he could break the mental incapacity which the image shadowed forth. At times he almost believed in the doctor's ability to carry the operation through;

but always a doubt immediately afterwards seized him and shook all hope out of him. Often he was on the point of telling the missus and thrusting the responsibility of a decision upon her, and as often his conscience silenced him by the assurance of her inability to decide. He knew beforehand just what her decision would be. And she had no right to assume control of the girl's fate without other recommendation than her own prejudices.

"The Doc was right when he said I'd got to settle the hull matter myself," groaned Sam.

Then he would remember certain of Sedgwick's words.

"He said we could git 'long 'thout the missus's corn-sent if I'd stan' by 'im. But how? How kin *I* cornsent?" And then, as an afterthought, "How kin I refuse?"

Sometimes his thoughts ran in figures of speech.

"I'm like Abe Fadden that time when a rattler fastened on 'im 'n' stuck, 'n' he didn't dare to take holt o' the thing 'n' tear it loose. Lord! wot a dirty world, when a man has no mind o' his own!"

And the burden of it all was:

"I mus' make up my mind one way or 'nother—I've got to decide." But he never did.

"This can't go on ferever," he told himself, grimly. "They'll have me in the 'sylum to Pueblo in 'nother week."

But one day an inspiration occurred to him which promised at least a partial relief from the dizzying torment of conflicting thoughts.

"Why not ast the little un 'erself? She knows jes' how she is; she can't learn to read, but she kin onderstan' a heap o' common-sense; we've talked over how she got hurt on the lan'slide a dozen times. She might not take a sensible view—great God! wot *is* a sensible view? —but then agin she might. She's got a heap more jedgment 'n' 'er sister gives 'er credit fer. Anyway, she may say suthin' 't 'll help me out."

That very afternoon he found her alone by Dan's grave on the mountain-side. She made a desolate picture among the dry grass and weeds, the black pines above her, and a few autumnal clouds wandering helplessly about in the sky. She had flung herself forward against the low pile of stones, her arms stretched out and her hands clasped. Her face was hidden; her attitude was one of deep dejection, perhaps of tears.

He paused in doubt, wondering if it were possible to retreat without being discovered. If he turned, he would be sure to arouse her. In his perplexity he stood quite still, and his attention being concentrated upon the prostrate figure, he could see that she was weeping. There was an irregular, convulsive heaving of the shoulders which told him everything, although he heard nothing. How still the world was! And yet there was a muffled sound from the river, and the pines seemed trying to voice a soul's extreme desolation.

"I'll go back," he decided, and turned cautiously. "Pore little thing—pore little thing!"

But the dry twig of a fallen pine brushed his shoulder and snapped with a loud noise. Anny lifted her head abruptly.

"Sam!" she cried, when she saw who it was.

He turned, but made no movement in her direction. The silence seemed to deepen with a slow crescendo from the pines and an explicit sibilance from the river.

"I was goin'," he said, at last. "I didn't aim to break in on ye."

"I'm glad I heerd ye," said Anny, straightening herself a little away from the heap of stones.

He came forward and sat down at her side.

"Ye was cryin'," he said, taking her hand in his.

She was no more ashamed of her tears than a child would have been, and her eyes were still overflowing as she looked at him.

"Yes," she admitted.

"Wot about ?"

"I felt like it." Her voice trembled a little, but he heard it above the pines and the distinct river. "I felt like it 'ud do me good. 'N' so I flung myself down. 'N' the tears come, 'n' I didn't try to stop 'em. I'm glad I done it, too. I feel lots better. Ye don't like to have me cry ?"

"No. I don't see how it kin be good fer ye. 'Tain't good fer nobody to feel bad. I like to see ye chipper 'n' happy."

"This time it done me good," she insisted, gently, but with deference to his opinion.

"Anything happened to make ye feel bad ?"

"No."

"Missus 'ain't done nothin' ?"

"Oh no."

"Then wot started ye up ?"

She was silent, evidently collecting her thoughts.

"I come out a-walkin'—I wanted to git some o' the purty red leaves up there among the rocks. 'N' I was passin' Dan's grave kind o' slow like, 'n' all to wunst I felt like I wanted to stop a bit, so I sot down. 'N' I got to thinkin' 'bout 'im—'bout Dan, I mean, 'n' wot ye've tole me 'bout 'im dif'rent times, 'n' how good he was, 'n' how ye was frien's with 'im, 'n' all the rest. Then I got to thinkin' 'bout myself, 'n' how I couldn't 'member nothin' 'bout 'im, not even his looks, sence I got hurt. 'N' then it come over me—I d' know how—but 'peared like I seen all to wunst how dretful 'twas—how orfle ! I wanted to 'member 'im—I wanted to think o' 'im like I must 'a' done afore the lan'slide ; but I couldn't think o' a thing but wot I'd been tole by you 'n' sis, 'n' that seemed so kinder faint like. 'N' it come over me 't likely I wouldn't never be no better, but 'ud allus be queer, not like other folks ; people kind to me, but pityin' me, too ;

’n’ fer a minute I wished I was dead. It ’ud be so easy to lay still, ’way down under the ground along o’ Dan—mebbe I’d know ’im there jes’ like I used to! So I laid my face down on the stones ’n’ cried. ’N’ I’m better now.” She looked at him, smiling tremulously through her tears. “I don’t cry much. Most o’ the time I laff at the rabbits ’n’ squirrels ’n’ grasshoppers. But this time it done me sech good! I’m ’most willin’ to be queer the rest o’ my life now—if I kin have *you* allus ’round!”

“I’ll allus be ’round,” said Sam, almost solemnly.

“I reckon I couldn’t live nohow if ye was to leave me. Anyways, I don’t see how. Sis is good to me—so is the others. But—”

“I won’t leave ye,” promised Sam. “But—wot was ye goin’ to say? Ye ain’t quite corntent, even with me?”

She sighed heavily.

“How kin I be, when I think I used to be like other folks ’n’ when I think ·o’ wot I be now? I’ve lost so much—so much ’t I don’t know ’bout, too.” The pathos of the words brought the tears to Sam’s eyes. “It’s all been comin’ over me stronger ’n’ stronger o’ late. I’m gittin’ better, I know I be; but the better I git the more I long to be wot I was—the more plain I see wot I orter be this minute—wot I might be if it hadn’t been fer that dretful day. I try not to think o’ it—I try to think o’ the squirrels ’n’ the cattle ’n’ horses ’n’ trees, ’n’ how good *you* be to me; but it comes back to me, spite o’ everything. I say to myself, ‘Sam loves ye, Sam keers fer ye, ye little fool. Ain’t that ’nough?’ I say, ‘If harm comes, Sam’s near to look arter ye.’ But all the same I keep hankerin’ arter suthin’ I ’ain’t got; ye know wot I mean?”

“I know—I know.”

“I feel kind o’ lost like. Sometimes I don’t know where I be or wot I’m lookin’ at. I want suthin’ I ’ain’t got. I can’t somehow say it—”

“I onderstan’. I’ve thort o’ it often myself.”

"I orter be corntent with wot I've got, I know—"

"No, no, little un. It's right 'n' nat'ral 't it should trouble ye."

"'N' ye ain't mad at me?"

The question was a common one with her, and he loved it as an evidence of her childish affection.

"No!" he answered. Then with unpremeditated vehemence, "I'd give my own soul to bring back your health to ye—I would!" The earnestness of his emotion left his mouth tremulous, and he controlled himself with difficulty, but he presently went on. "'N' you—wot must it be to you?"

She crept closer to him, taking his hand in hers and stroking it gently.

"Ye'll never be corntent to live like this," he said.

"No." She laid her hand upon his and sat quite motionless. "How kin I be, sence I've learned to think? I *have* learned to think, Sam—not allus right, mebbe, but better 'n wot I used to—ever so much better. I 'member how it was. I'd start to say suthin' 'n' I couldn't see my way clear, 'n' I'd either stop, or end by sayin' suthin' else. But now a idee stays with me—I start to talk, 'n' it's like a light was kerried in front o' me—I go straight ahead."

"Sech things almos' make me b'lieve in God," thought Sam. "If I'd prayed fer 'em, I *would* b'lieve in Him." But he said nothing.

Anny went on, stroking his hand again.

"'N' yit, why shouldn't I be corntent? Wot do I lack? I've got everything, when ye come right down to it, 's long 's I've got you. I'm 'shamed o' myself—I feel guilty. But—tell me one thing, Sam. Tell me honest 'n' true." Her face was so serious that he felt his own features drawing into sober lines from sympathy.

"Wot is it?" he asked, gently.

The question came with childish directness.

"Wouldn't ye keer more for me—tell me the truth!—if I was like wot I used to be?"

Sam recoiled as if he had received a blow. But she did not wait for an answer.

"I want ye to like me all ye kin—I need it, it's the life o' me. 'N' if that 'ud make ye think more o' me, how kin I help wishin' 'n' longing for it? Oh, I do wish 'n' long for it! If only the lan'slide had been a minute earlier or later! Then—then—"

Sam had recovered by this time, and spoke soothingly.

"I shall allus love ye, no matter how ye be. Listen! I come out to say suthin' to ye—suthin' 't I've had on my mind fer days. Ye're well 'nough to onderstan' it—yer talk to-day proves ye're well 'nough. It's a hard question—the very question ye've been talkin' 'bout. I'm goin' to tell ye the hull thing,'n' leave ye to jedge for yerself."

She faced him with grave inquiry.

"I'll try to onderstan'," she said, simply.

"Ye 'member yer visit to the Halsteads' a few days ago?"

She nodded.

"'N' the Doc?"

"Yes."

"Ye 'member the long talk ye had with 'im out there among the rocks?"

"Yes."

"'N' how he took holt o' yer head 'n' 'samined it?"

"He allus does that."

"But didn't it take 'im longer this time?"

She considered gravely.

"I reckon it did," she finally answered.

"Well, they was a objeck in all that."

"A objeck?"

"I mean, he knowed wot he was 'bout. He was tryin' to find out suthin'."

"'Bout my head?"

He rushed on as if afraid his courage would fail him.

"I knowed ye was better—I'd been a-knowin' it fer ever so long—'n' I wanted 'im to see ye 'n' tell me wot he thort o' ye. I wanted to know if they was a chance o' yer gittin' well."

He knew that her chin fell after a fashion she had when surprised or frightened, but he kept his eyes turned away.

"He was tryin' ye all the time ye was there to see if they was hopes."

He heard a little gasp from her, but still he did not turn.

"'N' arter I come back from the range I had a long talk with 'im on the porch. Ye wasn't there, 'n' didn't know nothin' 'bout it. Ye was with Mis' Halstead in the kitchen."

He looked at her now, with a half-expectation of seeing her face alter and grow into the expression which he remembered as belonging to her before the accident. But her eyes were only widened with a painful interest, and her parted lips were tremulous with an eagerness which he had often seen there in her present state.

"He said they wa'n't no hopes o' yer gittin' back yer mem'ry, even if ye went on improvin'. That is—"

She caught breathlessly at the conditional phrase.

"Then they *is* hope?" she whispered.

"No—'n' yes."

The relaxed mouth closed, but the nostrils dilated at the same moment with the passage of her hurried breath.

"Oh!" she gasped, faintly. "Wot made ye tell me?"

"I felt bad, too—ye kin make shore I did. I'd laid out not to be disapp'inted, no matter wot was said, but I found I was mistook. I *was* disapp'inted. He said he didn't see no reason why ye shouldn't go on improvin', but ye'd never git well."

"Oh!" was her faint exhalation once more.

"But he tole me 'nother thing."

She did not change her attitude, but her eyes looked into his with a keener light.

"He said ye wouldn't git well *if ye was left to yer-self.*"

"He meant—"

"He said they was hope—"

She flung herself forward with a wild look.

"Hope?" she cried out.

He laid his hand reassuringly upon her shoulder.

"Hope—if we could make up our minds to try the course o' treatment he wants us to."

She sank back against the stones of the grave, but without removing her eyes from his.

"I'll do anything!" he heard her breathe.

"He spoke o' a operation—"

"Wot's that?"

She sat erect and looked alert again.

"It means he'd have to cut into yer head 'n' pry a bone up 'n' fix it so it 'ud stay there."

"That's horrid!" she murmured, after a moment.

He did not answer, and she looked at him impatiently.

"Well?" she asked.

"The chances is—"

"'T I'd git well?"

"He says so."

"But I might—"

"The operation might kill ye. He was fair in statin' the case. It's dang'rous, 'n' he said so."

Anny was silent.

"I been tryin' to think wot to do," Sam went on. "I've laid awake nights weighin' it. But I can't make up my mind. It's so mixed. If it was only myself—"

"If it was yerself? Wot then?"

"I'd take my chances with the operation."

"But bein' it's me—"

“The chances seem too slim.”

“But they ain’t no slimmer ’n wot they’d be for *you*.”

“I think more o’ you ’n wot I do o’ myself.”

“Oh !” was her only answer.

He drew closer to her, taking her hand.

“Shall I explain it over ag’in ?” he asked. “Be ye shore ye onderstan’ ? Shall I—”

“I onderstan’,” she answered, dully.

“’N’ wot d’ ye say ?” he urged. “Ye see wot the chances is ?”

“I ’ain’t had time to think,” she murmured.

“The odds is in yer favior ; he said that, ’n’ he put the hull thing straight ’n’ fair. I couldn’t see ’t he was tryin’ to hide anything. Ye’ve got a good constitution. He said ye could stan’ it ’thout doubt ’s fur ’s that goes. ’N’ if the operation was to go right—if he wasn’t to dig too deep—”

Anny’s eyes were full of unutterable pathos.

“I don’t want to die,” she said, in a low voice.

Sam’s heart gave a great leap.

“Die ? No—no !” he cried out.

She seemed to forget what her meditations had been a moment before.

“I’m afeerd to die. ’Ud they put me here by Dan ? ’N’ pile rocks over me ? Oh, it ’ud be cold ’n’ dretful !”

“Don’t talk so !” Sam pleaded. “Don’t think o’ it no more ! Let it go !”

“Ye said ye’d do it if it was you, though.”

“I didn’t go to urge ye, little un — I didn’t, reely. Don’t think o’ it no more !”

“I know ye’d ruther have me alive—I know ! Ye want we should keep in this good world together. That’s wot I want, too. But oh ! Sam, it ’ud be a better world if I was well, wouldn’t it ? Think o’ it ! Ye’d love me twicet ’s well—ye’d keer twicet ’s much ’bout bein’ with me ’n’ talkin’ to me !”

"I doubt it," said Sam.

"If I was to git well 'n' be like other folks—why, we'd still be in this good world together, only ever 'n' ever so much happier."

"It might change ye," he said, sadly.

"Change me? How?"

"Ye might not keer fer me then."

"I'd keer fer ye if I was dead!" she cried.

He carried her hand reverently to his lips.

"Don't try to make up yer mind all in a minute," he said. "They's time 'nough. The Doc ain't in no hurry. We kin talk it over to-morrer, or nex' day, or nex'. They's plenty o' time. Only keep it in mind, 'n' when ye want to talk 'bout it, we kin manage to git together."

She looked quieter after this, and said:

"I'll think it over. I kin see why ye can't make up yer mind. I mus' do it myself. 'N' I will."

"But they's one thing. The missus mustn't know. Wotever happens, we ain't ready fer 'er to know jes' yit. Ye'll 'member?"

"Yes."

"I'll go down to the barn 'n' see if Leatherhead's workin' on that saddle I give 'im to mend. 'Ud ye ruther stay 'ere?"

"Yes. I want to think."

Sam smoothed her hair back from her forehead, glanced towards the house to see if any one was looking, then kissed her and strode away.

CHAPTER XXXI

Sam wandered down to the barn.

"How sensible she was 'bout it!" he thought. "She's got 's good jedgment, when it comes to a pinch, 's half the folks 't never had their skulls cracked 'n' their brains squeezed together. 'Ll she make up 'er mind to let the Doc go ahead? I hope not! I'll ast 'er to marry me jes' 's she is—she's got sense 'nough to decide—'n' we'll let the past go. I wish 't I hadn't said a word to 'er 'bout the bizness. But I'm afeerd it's too late now."

He strayed restlessly about the barn, touching this thing and that with hands that felt nothing but the desire to be on the move. He stroked his favorite mare Judy in an absent way, which that exacting lady resented by impatient tossings of her head; he acquiesced almost eagerly in the horrible job Leatherhead had perpetrated upon the saddle, and finally flung himself down under the thatched roof upon the hay. It was warm and fragrant up there. The day was drawing to a close, and the loft was full of reflections of the red evening. Through a chink in the wall he could look out at the darkening foot-hills, above which the clouds of sunset canopied the world.

At supper no Anny was to be seen.

"She wa'n't a-feelin' good," was Phœbe Ellen's answer to his question. "So she went to 'er room, 'n' I tuck 'er some vittles afore I rung the bell fer ourselves. She didn't act like she was sick—only tired like."

But Sam looked anxious.

"No fever nor nothin'?" he asked.

18

"Nothin' 't I could see."

"Did she eat the grub?"

"Not jes' then. But she will, I make no doubt."

"I reckon ye'd tell me if she was sick?"

There was a pause, during which Sam had time to wonder how his question would be understood.

"Oh yes," was the answer, delivered with perfect civility.

And with that he was obliged to be content.

The next morning, as he was crossing the open space between the barn and the corral, Anny darted out from the shadow of a pine and was upon him before he was fully aware. She had evidently been waiting for him.

"Sam! Sam!" she cried, in a shrill voice, seizing his arm and shaking it.

He looked at her, and his heart sank.

"Ye're sick," he said.

She did not notice, but shook his arm more violently.

"Think fer me! Think fer me!" she cried out, like one in a rage.

He drew back, horrified.

"Pore little un!" he said, in a broken voice.

She began to beat her forehead with her left hand, while she clutched his arm more tightly with her right.

"How kin I think fer myself?" she demanded, in a shrill, hysterical voice. "It's *you* 't mus' tell me wot to do!"

He smiled with an effort, though he was sick at heart.

"Then we'll let the Doc go hang," he declared.

But either she would not or could not understand. She had the look of one frantic with pain, sick with the torment of racked nerves and distempered thoughts. Her eyes had a lack-lustre, moony expression, which broke now and then into sudden brightness. She did not try to answer, but all at once broke away from him with an inarticulate cry, and fled towards the house. He watched her speed across the veranda and disappear in the half-darkness beyond the open door, and a great horror came over him.

"Have I set 'er crazy with all the rest?" he wondered.

He hung about the house for hours, now stung to despair by the memory of her wild, convulsed face, now sinking into a state bordering on apathy as his torment became too great to bear; now hurrying out to the barn in an aimless spasm of movement, but always returning to the house in the hope that she would again appear.

"She's sick," was all he could get from the missus, who eyed him with a forbidding glance, in which he detected a mixture of exultation and threat. "She'll come down when she feels like it. Till then ye kin jes' nachelly let 'er alone."

He did not see her again till afternoon. Then he was almost as terrified as before at the change which had taken place in her. She met him with smiling calmness and took both his hands.

"I've been asleep," she explained. "Ye're s'prised, ain't ye? But it ain't so queer. I didn't shet my eyes all las' night. Nor till mos' noon. I'd been runnin' aroun' the room, flingin' myself fust into one cheer, then 'nother, then rollin' on the bed, then settin' flat on the floor, tryin' to think wot to do. Then all to wunst 'peared like suthin' cool 'n' quiet come over me—like the sound o' the river when I'm tired, only this come stronger; 'n' I wanted to lay down 'n' rest. Oh, I don't know how I felt as I laid there—like a sunny bank when the wind blows over it. 'N' I went to sleep, 'n' when I woke up I was jes' 's quiet 's I was when I shet my eyes; 'n' 'peared like the nap 'd settled everything fer me. I felt shore now o' wot I wanted to do—so calm 'n' sure—I knowed I'd never change my mind. 'I'll be myself fer Sam's sake,' says I. 'Or I'll die. I'd ruther die 'n not be like wot God made me.' 'N' so it's settled. Ye kin see the doctor."

Sam examined her placid face with something like awe.

" But if *I* objeck ?" he asked.

She smiled, with the same still light of assurance in her eyes.

"'Twon't do no good now. 'Sides, ye won't objeck, not reely. Ye don't want me to die—ye don't want me to take chances, that's all. The cure—ye know ye'd like to see me cured. 'N' I won't die. I'll live to be wot I was afore that horrid day. Die? No! When 'll ye see the Doc 'n' tell 'im ?"

Sam's heart shrank in foreboding.

" I wish to God I'd never told ye o' it !" he cried.

" No," she said, with her new, calm smile. " Ye done right. It's plain 's day to me."

" Ye're shore ye've made up yer mind ?"

" Shore," was the quiet answer.

"'N' won't change it ?"

" Never."

He half turned from her.

" Ye'll die, I know ye will !" he cried, with a sort of fury.

" No—no," she soothed, approaching him gently and stroking his sleeve. " No—no! I kin see how it 'll turn out. Oh, I kin see so plain !"

He flung himself away from her with a vast impatience of himself.

" I was a fool. I orter 'a' borne it as my own trouble 'n' not forced it on *you*."

"'Tain't a trouble no longer. It's a joy. Won't I be tryin' to make myself better fer yer sake ? Wot kin I do better 'n that ?"

" Live fer me !" he cried, with something like a sob.

But she only smiled.

" When 'll ye see the Doc ?" she repeated.

"Never!"

"Must I do it myself? Must I go through the operation alone? Ah, Sam, ye won't make me do that! Wot friend have I got to look to but you? Ye won't fail me now. Ye'll stay with me 'n' help me—I know ye will!"

"Drop the hull infernal plan—it's the devil's work!"

"Don't urge me—my mind's made up. I could never go back arter this—I've caught a glimpse o' wot I was 'n' wot I may be. I'd be a unhappy critter—I'd be allus broodin' over wot might 'a' been."

"Ye're good 'nough 's ye be," declared Sam. "If I love ye, wot more kin ye ask?"

She shook her head.

"Shall I have to go over 'n' see the Doc myself?"

"Wait—wait!" he groaned.

"Wait? My mind won't change. Why not see 'im this arternoon?"

"Great God! This arternoon!"

"To-morrer mornin', then. Not later. Why not do it right away? I won't be put off!"

"Ye may change yer mind by mornin'," he persisted.

She gave him a slow, keen glance of comprehension such as he had never seen in her eyes before.

"I'll wait till then," she said, and turned away.

He met her before breakfast, and his heart failed him as he found her in the same quiet mood.

"Ye'll go this mornin'," she began, not with a questioning accent, but in a tone of calm statement.

"Then ye ain't changed yer mind?" he breathed.

"No. I know wot I'm doin'. It's fer the best."

"If harm comes o' it—"

"I'll bear the blame."

"Ye can't, fer it 'll be mine. Oh, Lord! Why couldn't I 'a' held my tongue?"

"Ye done right," she said, with a seriousness which

had grown out of her new hopes and fears. "The rest is fer me to do. Ye'll go this mornin'?"

"Yes," he groaned.

And after breakfast he set out for Halstead's.

He found the doctor in his room, poring over a volume on brain surgery.

"You have decided?" was his greeting.

"*She's* decided," Sam answered, gloomily.

"She? The missus?"

"The little un. I 'ain't told the missus a word. But the little un—o' course *she* had to know. She was powerful sensible 'bout it. Ye orter 'a' seen 'er. I left the hull bizness with her."

The doctor fetched a long breath.

"She *is* sensible," he remarked. "Is she ready?"

"Ready 'n' eager."

"You'll speak to the missus next?"

"I reckon. Well, I'll tackle 'er afore dinner, if ye say so. 'Pears like I'm in fer it now. I don't 'prove o' the bizness, I want ye to onderstan' that."

"You will after it's over. Come and tell me the missus's decision as soon as you get it," said the doctor.

"'N' if she won't listen?"

"I've thought of all that."

"I like to think o' it, myself."

"Like to think of it? Why?"

"Fer then the bizness 'll drop."

"Will it?" The doctor's smile was enigmatical. "You remember what I said the other day?"

"That we could go on 'thout 'er?"

"Exactly."

"I've wondered wot ye meant. We might bring the little un over 'ere to Halstead's—"

"No. The operation will take place at her own home."

"Well, I'll be—"

"I've gone over the entire ground. I know what I'm talking about."

Sam was impressed by the doctor's confidence.

"Well, *I* don't, then ! But how d' ye 'pose to manage it ?"

"Come to me at once with her decision," said the strange man. And more than that Sam could not get from him.

CHAPTER XXXII

Sam stated the case with an abruptness which would have been brutal had he intended to produce a fainting-fit in a woman less steeled against surprises than Phœbe Ellen. As it was, she turned pale—it was a hard pallor, which might have been painted on iron—and her features drew together in rigid lines which he felt would look even more unpleasant when they relaxed. She had been out in the wind, and there was the stiffness of aggression in her scattered hair. Her apron was on crooked, and even without the import of Sam's announcement in her face she had an appearance of antagonism which came of the feeling that the world had taken sides against her.

But she understood him. For a moment she stood quite still, facing him with wide eyes, through which flashed quick changes of calculation and threat.

"She knows I'll marry the little un if the doctor cures 'er," thought Sam. "She's gittin' it all clear afore she says a word."

And indeed Phœbe Ellen's control of herself was a thing to be wondered at. Her under-jaw did not drop—he had expected it would, as was her habit when surprised; but her lips parted in the thin, hard line against her teeth, as he knew it of old, and her breath came in quick impulses from the top of her lungs. Her whole expression was one of quivering excitement, overmastered by a momentary self-control which might give way as soon as it became conscious of itself.

And the fact was that, apart from his message, Sam's appearance at that particular moment was unfortunate.

She had been in a state of domestic exasperation all the morning. Things had gone wrong ; the work had set itself against her ; she could not do anything just as she liked. Leatherhead had been obtuse, and she had given him more than one lick with the rough side of her tongue. After all this, she was in a mood for decisions. She had delivered several in the course of the morning, and they had all proved rash and ill-considered, but there was a promptness of perversity in her to-day which craved outlet and action, and which soared equally above reason and sentiment in the delight of self-assertion. In this mood any demand upon her generosity was dangerous both to the cause and the pleader of it.

"Oh ! A operation ?" she repeated, after Sam had blurted out what he had to say. Her features did not relax ; she still preserved her self-control, and Sam could not help noting that there was something fine in the pose of the lifted chin and the backward slant of the face as she half shut her eyes against his. "A operation by Doc Sedgwick ?"

Sam nodded.

"A operation by that corpse—that toadstool ? Well !"

The lines around her mouth grew deeper, and her breathing came from still higher in her lungs, so that her voice sounded thin though smooth.

"He mus' be improvin' in health," she went on, showing her teeth more broadly in a vixenish smile. "He— he mus' be gittin' frisky to — to ondertake a job like that !"

"I d' know 's he is," answered Sam, somewhat awed by her obvious struggle for self-control.

He expected her to laugh scornfully, but she did not.

"Weak 's ever ?" she asked, in the same thin voice, in which he could detect her heart-beats.

"He seems purty fur gone, that's a fact." And to himself Sam wondered, "Wot's she drivin' at, anyhow ?"

"Trembly, oncertain, shaky?" continued Phœbe Ellen.

And now he saw the point she was trying to make.

"Oh, he kin brace up on brandy," he said, in a tone of assurance.

"Ye b'lieve it?"

The question came quietly enough, but her lips were quivering. In another moment her rage would break forth. Would it take the form of shrieks or tears?

"Yes," he answered.

"He b'lieves it hisself?"

"Yes."

"Fools!"

She almost yielded to the rage which Nature intended the word to express, but she caught her temper and a long breath at the same moment and went on:

"He wanted ye to ast me to let 'im op'rate on 'er?"

"He b'lieves he could bring back 'er reason."

"She's got a sight more reason 'n *he* has, to think o' sech a thing." Her voice was still tolerably calm, though the convulsive movement of her mouth continued. "D' *you* want 'im to try it?" she demanded, suddenly.

His answer was ready, and he delivered it with a quietness that surprised himself.

"It 'ud make me the happiest man on top o' God's green airth if she was to git well. Ye know that."

Something like a paralytic stroke distorted her features from chin to forehead.

"Tell 'im," she cried, in a voice that would have been a scream had it not still betrayed the beating of her heart —"tell 'im I'll never let 'im tech 'er—I'll keep 'er under lock 'n' key fust! Tell 'im"—there came a ghastly, chattering grin into the twitching muscles of the mouth that made her next speech tragic—"tell 'im I wouldn't let 'im op'rate on a sick cat fer me! Tell 'im I wouldn't let 'im op'rate on a paper doll! D' ye hear?" She burst into a dry, rattling laugh which cracked in her throat and left her gasping. Then, before he had time to wonder what she would do next, she turned and flew from the room like an animal in a fit.

Sam fetched a grim sigh.

"*She* won't change 'er mind, nuther," he said to himself. "'N' I swear, I d' know but wot she's right. The little un's mind 's made up fer keeps, too, 'n' in the op'site d'rection—she's so calm 'n' sweet-like 'bout it 't ye'd make shore to see 'er 't she'd had the hull thing settled from the beginnin'. Well, this is a case fer the Doc to settle. Didn't he say he had some sort o' medicine fer sech a crisis ? Anyways, it's too much fer *me*. I'll go back to Halstead's 's fast as Judy kin take me, 'n' see wot *he's* got to offer."

He found the consumptive as he had left him, propped up on the same tumbled pillows and reading the same leather-bound volume on brain surgery.

"Well ?" he questioned, as Sam took his place before him. "Sit down, for God's sake ! You make me wild, using up your muscular energy as if it didn't amount to anything. There, that's better. And now—what's the good word ?"

"She won't cornsent," said the cowboy.

"You call that a good word ?"

"Anyways, it's got its good side."

"So has the devil, if you make yourself akin to him. So she refused ?"

"From the start."

"You pleaded with her ?"

"If ye'd 'a' seen 'er, yo wouldn't ast that ! I knowed fust off 't she wouldn't listen."

The doctor closed the volume, and let it slip between his knee and the arm of the chair. It was too heavy for him to lift and thrust upon the stand at his elbow.

"I thought it only right to give her a chance," he said.

"Ye've got suthin' 't ye reckon 'll bring 'er to terms ?"

The strange man smiled.

"I have."

"Better give it up—better give it up! They's 's much to be said agin the hull bizness 's fer it."

"Never!" The doctor's thin face took on a look of resolution. "I tell you, Sam, I can cure that girl, and I'm going to do it. I've been reading on the subject—I knew most of it before, but I wanted it fresh in my mind. It will be the last act of my life—I know that—but could I quit the world under happier circumstances ? We've already talked over the reason why the missus refuses ! It's because she's afraid you'll marry the girl if she gets well."

"Her head's level there," said Sam. "If the little un 'ud be willin'."

"There's another reason, too."

"'Cause she's got a spite at ye ?"

"Go back to the cause of her spite, and you'll have it." Sam scratched his head.

"I never heerd 'er say why she hated ye," he said.

"No ? Then I'll tell you—though not in words. Sam, look me straight in the eye."

The command was peculiar, and the tone uncanny. Sam obeyed.

"Ye come at a feller like the devil in a dream," he murmured, after gazing a moment.

"Hold your eyes on mine—hold them there in spite of something in them that tries to wrench them away. Hold them there in spite of what you know I am looking at inside you. It is the easiest way to tell you why the missus hates me."

Sam obeyed with a sort of dazed passivity. A mysterious influence was certainly at work upon him. He felt a desire—it was like fear—to close his eyes against the doctor's, and shut out the light which he saw rising from abysmal depths and concentrating itself before rushing into his own soul and illuminating it.

"Ah! you want to turn away," the strange man said, in a voice which sounded afar off. "Don't use your will against mine—only be passive and let me look in. It will facilitate the business. Do my eyes hurt yours? No matter. It is but for a moment. Do you feel the light pouring in upon your thoughts—sending sharp flashes here and there? Don't fear—why, you are actually pale! Think of a fellow like me frightening the blood from the face of one of your stamp. 'Let me look in—let me look in. You have nothing to be ashamed of—nothing to conceal—nothing that should trouble you if I find it out. Think of something—anything you like. Ah! That is right. You go back involuntarily to the most important event in your life. Shall I tell you about it? It happened at your ranch somewhere farther south—Las Animas, is it? Shall I go on?"

"Go on," murmured Sam, like one in a trance.

"Your mind goes back a long way—such a long way! —to the time when you first came to Colorado and took up your ranch from the government—ten years ago and more. And who is this? Smith? Yes, Bill Smith, old Bill Smith is the name I read there. He settled on the next ranch above—how many miles?—five miles above. He had a daughter Sarah—blue-eyed, brown-haired, and with cheeks as red as the wild roses that grew in the cañon above the cabin. You fell in love with her—it was natural at your age. And really she *was* pretty; at any rate, she looked beautiful to *you*. Lord! How you loved her, how you used to follow her about, hanging upon her words, gloating over her movements! So did Tim Sullivan —he had dark eyes and a black mustache, did Tim, and that decided the business. That's the way with women— if it isn't a mustache, it's something else of equal importance. Tim got her, and you are thankful to-day, for she leads him a life, there on the ranch adjoining yours. But it cut you up horribly at the time. You left the place—handed the ranch over to your father and mother and a younger brother, and you've never had the courage to go back. I didn't know you were so sentimental, Sam!"

"Fer God's sake, let my affairs alone!" breathed the cowboy, in terror.

But the doctor went on:

"You could go back there now — it wouldn't hurt much, now that the little un has driven Sarah altogether out. But she cut deep, that Sarah, didn't she, Sam? You wandered about for years — Arizona, Mexico, Honolulu—and finally settled here as Dan Thompson's right-hand man. There! Have I read enough?"

"Too much," muttered Sam. "Lemme go — lemme go!" He was like a weak man struggling in the grasp of a strong one.

The doctor removed his eyes and the cowboy breathed a sigh of relief.

"You may go," he said, with his enigmatic smile.

Sam sat for a full minute rubbing his eyes as if to get the ache of the doctor's glance out of them.

"It beats all," he finally murmured. "How in God's name 'd ye do it?"

"Don't ask—I don't understand it myself. It's a gift, a curse—what you like. Suffice it that I did it and can do it again. The chief point is that you admit I read what you were thinking about."

"Ye done it, shore." Sam was still rubbing his eyes.

"Does any one in this part of the world know the facts I have told you about?"

"No."

"Did you ever tell any one?"

"No one, livin' or dead."

"My object in it all was neither curiosity nor unkindness. I wanted you to believe what I tell you next."

"Oh, I kin b'lieve anything now. I've heerd o' yer doin's afore, but I never took no stock in it. I 'member the missus—"

"Yes, the missus! She told you I tried my power on her?"

"Yes. 'N' she said she shet ye off afore ye found out anything."

"She was too sure. You believe I *can* read people's minds, Sam?"

"It shorely beats the world!"

"Well, I saw into the missus's mind as I did into yours, only not so far. And I want to tell you what I found there."

Sam pricked up his ears.

"Suthin' to skeer 'er with?" he questioned, quickly. "Suthin' to make 'er cornsent to the operation?"

"My idea to a dot! I didn't suppose you could grasp the situation so readily. It's true, though, that she shut me off before I found out all I wanted to know. She has a will, that woman. Rather hysterical, to be sure, but effectual as far as keeping me out of her affairs is concerned. But I found out something."

"Suthin' to the purpose?"

"I think so. Nothing definite—"

"I'm afeerd gen'ral statements won't go," remarked Sam.

"I think they will in this case. Listen! The missus has done her sister some great wrong."

Sam puckered his mouth to whistle, but relaxed it immediately to ask:

"Her sister? A wrong? The little un?"

The doctor nodded.

"A great wrong? Wot d' ye mean by that?"

"I wish I knew! That's what exasperates me; she shut down on me like a trap before I could discover a thing beyond the fact that the little un had been wronged.

It was evident, too, that the missus had done the wrong and feared detection."

"That beats *me*," muttered Sam.

"You have every reason to believe me," said the doctor.

"Oh, I b'lieve ye," Sam hastened to say.

"I've shown you what I can do in the mind-reading line."

"Oh, *that's* all right!" Sam's eagerness might have been construed into a dread that the doctor would insist on trying his experiment again.

"Then your course is plain. You are to go to the missus and inform her that unless she consents to the operation, the wrong she has done her sister will be revealed."

"But how *kin* it be revealed if ye don't know wot 'tis?"

The doctor stirred impatiently.

"Don't be particular," he said, in a fretful tone. "Make her think you know all about it—that's all you have to do. She'll know what you mean when you threaten her with the wrong. And she'll come down."

"I ain't no great shakes at pertendin'," said Sam, in a tone of regret.

"Pretending is wicked, of course, except when the end justifies the means. But this time so much depends on it—"

"A wrong," said Sam, meditatively. "Wot kin it be? The little un don't know nothin' 'bout it—that's shore. It must 'a' happened afore she got hurt. The missus 's been good to 'er allus, fur 's I kin see. A wrong! Ye're shore?"

"Quite sure." The doctor's tone was conclusive.

Sam fetched a mighty sigh from his abysmal lungs.

"I wish 't I was red o' the hull bizness," he declared. "'N' I'd stop right 'ere if I didn't know the little un's mind was made up. But"—he sighed again—"I'll try—I'll try!"

CHAPTER XXXIII

Early the next morning Sam again made his appearance before the doctor.

"It didn't work," was his brief announcement. "All I could git out o' 'er was 't ye mus' be crazy 'n' she pitied ye. That was 'er fust 'n' last word."

And he waited anxiously to see how the news would affect his companion.

"Oh !" was the strange man's comment, while his eyes brightened dangerously. "She said I was crazy, did she ? She said she pitied me, hey ?" He leaned back in his chair, and Sam could see his chest heave. "You came over in the buckboard ?" he suddenly inquired.

"Yes."

"There's room for my trunk in behind ?"

"Yer trunk ?"

"Why not ? I am going back to the ranch with you as your guest to stay a long time. Aren't you pleased ? I swear you look only surprised ! Try to look delighted, now, if only for politeness' sake."

"But the missus—" Sam began.

The doctor set his thin lips.

"I shall incidentally see your mistress, of course. But you will be the chief object of my tender solicitude, and I shall expect a good deal of attention from you in return. And you'll begin by packing my trunk for me, like a good fellow. Are you ready ? First, the brandy-bottle—look well to that ; and just give me a nip at it to brace me up for the occasion. Ah, so ! Take a smile yourself, won't you ? That's what you call it, I think, out here. Ah, I

19

thought you would, and now we both feel better. Next, the bottles on the shelf by the looking-glass—yes, the whole drug-store of them. You don't know what a lot of stuff a man in my condition has to take in order to fight off the undertaker. And the case of instruments—I've been examining them lately, and they're in apple-pie order. That's right! Now fill in with the under-clothing you'll find in the top drawer of the bureau. Good! No need to lock it—the key isn't there, anyway. Help me on with my overcoat, and carry my cushions out to the buckboard. Great heavens! What makes you stare so? I'm not a ghost *yet*. Who ever heard of a ghost with my present executive power? Aren't you ready? Do come on!"

"But ain't ye goin' to tell me wot ye mean to do?"

"Not a word. I've got it all to do myself, and it will come out better if no one knows what I'm at. Oh, I can do it—no fear of that. I haven't felt so well since I was at Harvard—I could lick my weight in wild-cats, as old Halstead says. When it's done, I'll tell you. Not a word till then."

Phœbe Ellen was surprised at the coming of the doctor, but her self-control did not desert her. She received him with civility, if not with cordiality ; and the strange man, in spite of the weariness induced by his ride, could not keep a touch of sarcasm from his greeting.

" Sam insisted so strongly on my coming over," he explained, with his enigmatical smile. " And of course I knew I would be heartily welcomed by *you*. The fact is, I have been vegetating there at Halstead's, and I need a bit of a change. Thanks, my health is much improved of late. *I feel equal to anything*." He emphasized the words to suit himself.

Phœbe Ellen returned the doctor's smile in kind.

" We'll git along nicely together," she rejoined, with diamond-cut-diamond aggressiveness. " I feel jes' that way myself—*ekal to anything!*"

And her emphasis was as marked as his.

"She'll fight hard," was the doctor's mental comment.

He inquired about her sister, and she assured him that she was well, only that she had been keeping rather closely to her room of late. Not ill—no ; only more quiet and reserved than usual.

" Ah, that may be a good sign," said the doctor.

After seeing him and his belongings bestowed in the guest-chamber—a room whose claims to gentility were based on an ingrain carpet, three chromos, and a walnut centre-table with turned legs—Phœbe Ellen ran down to the kitchen.

" Leatherhead !" she called from the doorway.

The roustabout looked up from the kettle which he was scraping.

" Run up the Eden City road beyond the three pines 'n' watch there till Pinky comes along. I'll do yer work 'ere in the kitchen."

Leatherhead's look of aimless surprise grew into a moony vacancy of satisfaction as he comprehended.

Phœbe Ellen continued :

" I want ye to tell 'im when he comes to wait there fer me. Tell 'im suthin' 's happened. Now, off with ye !"

And she pushed him from the house.

In the course of an hour he was back. She had been watching for him, and met him just inside the kitchen door.

" Well ?" she inquired. " He's come ?"

"Come ? Well, I should say ! 'N' he's got on a new hat from Lagunitas—I tole 'im I wouldn't be seen to a dog-fight with it, 'n' he said I wa'n't nothin' but sloppy Dutch, nohow. Oh yes, he's come. Ye could 'a' knocked 'im over with a crowbar when I tole 'im suthin' 'd happened 'n' he mus' wait fer ye. Oh, be ye gone ? Well ! To leave a feller right in the middle o' a speech like that !"

And a moment later Leatherhead's voice was heard from the kitchen singing at its highest pitch :

"I owe five dollars to O'Grady,
   And he thinks he's got a mortgage on my life !"

Phœbe Ellen passed stealthily out through the wood-shed, then up the slope among the rocks. The sun shone brightly, and gave a fierce blackness to the shadows on the mountain-side. A south wind was blowing, and the music of the pines was the only sound that broke the autumnal silence of the hills.

A little beyond the spot where the road disappeared above the ridge she found Pinky with two horses and a buckboard.

"Come down — come down !" she cried. "I'm out o' breath 'n' can't climb up there on the seat beside ye. I've got a world o' things to say. Don't mind tyin' the beasts —they'll stan'."

Pinky seated himself at her side on the trunk of a fallen pine.

"Wot is it ?" he asked, anxiously.

"She mus' go to-night," said Phœbe Ellen, in a low voice.

"That's wot I come fer," he answered. "I got yer letter, 'n' I made ready like mad. Does Sam suspect ?"

"We could git along if we only had *him* to deal with. To Nebrasky. Ye onderstan' ? Ye're to take 'er to the address I'll give ye later on."

"I've fixed everything so 't I kin leave at midnight on the down train."

"Good ! But ye mus'n't come down to the house, nor let 'em know ye're anywheres near. Sam wouldn't s'peck nothin'—we could pull the wool over *his* eyes all right. But a dozen things has happened sence I seen ye. Ye know why I want 'er to go. I tole ye wunst."

"I ain't likely to fergit it," said Pinky.

"Oh, that—that wa'n't no reason, though I thought it was at the time. But now—Pinky, it's a matter o' life 'n' death !"

Pinky's eyes were alert but puzzled.

"Suthin' new ?" he asked, with increased anxiety.

"Yes. I didn't want to hurry things—I knowed it 'ud set Sam agin me; but now that don't tech me. She's got to go, 'n' quick, too. Sam 's forced me to it—him 'n' that doctor. They—they want a operation."

"A operation ?" Pinky's mouth was wide with wonder.

"Ye don't onderstan'—o' course not. But the Doc 's got a bran'-new maggot in his head. 'N' Sam's with 'im. They say sis could be cured by a operation. Sam come at me yistiddy like a airthquake—ye'd 'a' made shore the world was comin' to a end. That's why I sent fer ye to come right off. Suthin' had to be done."

"A operation," repeated Pinky, considering deeply. "Well, why not try it," he finally asked, "if the Doc makes shore he kin cure 'er ?"

Phœbe Ellen had her answer ready. She could not trust Pinky with the whole truth. He had unreservedly taken sides with her thus far, but she had an instinctive assurance that he would have nothing to do with the kidnapping if he understood the deception she had practised in the ownership of the ranch.

"Try it ?" she cried. "He'd kill 'er ! Don't I know ? He ain't no more fit to do a doctor's operation 'n a chatterin' corpse ! He'd kill 'er—'n' how 'd we all feel then ?"

"He'd kill 'er the fust thing," assented Pinky, after another spell of meditation.

"He would, fer shore. Our only chance is to git 'er out o' the way 's quick 's ever we kin, fer him 'n' Sam 's laid their heads together, 'n' they're bound to rule or ruin."

"I'm s'prised at Sam," said Pinky, with a grieved headshake.

"So be I. But the wust 's to foller. I tole Sam I'd never cornsent—I tole 'im plain 'n' solemn, 'n' a body 'd think that orter settle it. But it didn't. Wot d' ye reckon he's gone 'n' done ?"

"Can't 'magine," said Pinky, with another shake.

"He's gone 'n' brung the doctor over on a long visit. Don't I see through 'em ? They mean to do that operation some day when I don't happen to be on my guard. 'S if I wa'n't cap'ble o' managin' my own sister 't ain't able to look out fer 'erself ! No ; it ain't a question o' marryin' Sam now, Pinky. That's all over. All I want 's to keep 'im from murderin' my pore sister. I have a right to see to that."

"No doubt o' that," acquiesced Pinky.

"'N' if ye git 'er safe to Nebrasky—"

"Yes ?" interrupted Pinky, eagerly.

"I'll marry ye the day ye come back ! No—ye needn't kiss me—I don't feel like it. But I'll do wot I say. 'N' see 'ere. Git the team 'n' yerself out o' sight 'n' keep 'em there fer any sakes. That doctor 's the devil's own—he kin read ye like a open book. He's tired now, 'n' prob'ly he won't start in with his proddin' and pryin' afore to-morrer, 'n' by that time—"

"It 'll be too late," finished Pinky.

"It 'll be too late ! 'N' he kin go back to Halstead's 's soon 's he likes, 'n' die there ! 'N' as fer Sam—"

"Yes—Sam ?" questioned Pinky, more eagerly than before.

"I'll fire 'im off the place to-morrer !" was Phœbe Ellen's ultimatum.

And she rose to go back.

"Ye kin drive off somers amongst the rocks 'n' trees where they won't be apt to find ye, can't ye ? They's a open space up there beyend them rocks 't nobody's likely to go to. I'll bring ye suthin' to eat 'n' a pack o' Leatherhead's *Police Gazettes* to look at. They're interestin'—

mighty interestin'. Full o' blood 'n' pizenin', 'n' all sorts o' wicked things. I'm sorry—"

"Oh, that's all right," Pinky assured her. "I sha'n't be lonesome. I'll be thinkin' o' our weddin'-day, 'n' that 'll make the time pass."

"Oh, well," was Phœbe Ellen's somewhat absent acknowledgment as she started down the hill.

CHAPTER XXXIV

THE doctor was indeed tired—so tired that Sam carried him to his room and put him to bed as if he were a baby.

"I'll go to sleep presently," the sick man said. "I'll have to take something, though—don't you see how nervous I am? Not brandy—no, that doesn't suit the case. Take the things out of my trunk, won't you?—there's a good soul—and hand me the bottle with the dark liquid. Never mind the clothes—toss them into a corner anywhere. Did anything break? No? That's lucky. You must have packed them more carefully than I thought. No—not that bottle. That's dark, to be sure, but it isn't what I want. There was no use bringing that along, anyway; but I suppose it was with the others, and I didn't notice. It isn't medicine—at least, not *my* medicine. By the way, you might be interested to know what it is. Well, it's an antidote to loco poisoning."

"Loco poisonin'?"

"Of course you know the loco-weed that grows hereabouts?"

Sam nodded.

"Last fall I got Leatherhead to gather me a lot. I wanted to send it to Stafford. Stafford's a friend of mine in Boston—a chemist, keen for poisons, you know. Well, I was curious to have him get at the real principle of the loco-weed, and so I sent enough of it to set all Boston crazy — or, according to Hahnemann, enough to make them all sane. He went at it with all the joy in life, you may be sure, and frequently reported progress by letter.

Well, he has discovered that loco-mania is the result of anæmia of the brain; in other words, loco-weed drives the blood from the brain. So an animal that takes loco-weed into his system simply causes a rush of blood *from* the brain, and that makes him mad."

"Lord!" ejaculated Sam, wide-eyed.

"Stafford thinks the drug can be used to advantage in apoplexy, and I don't see why not. But I was going to tell you about the bottle there. It's Stafford's antidote. Antidote means cure, you know. Now, a few drops in water would cure a locoed steer in half an hour. And a man—did you ever hear of a locoed man, Sam?"

"They was a Mexican señorita down in Sonora when I was there 't dosed a feller to git revenge, 'n' he died a ravin' maniac."

"Three drops of that liquid in half a tumbler of water would have saved him," said the doctor, sententiously. "Stafford has tried the poison and the remedy on himself. A half an hour does the business. Ah! There is the sleeping-potion; would you mind pouring it out for me? A teaspoonful in water—thanks, I *ought* to have a pitcher of water in my room. I'll have to ask lots of such things of you, but you'll lose nothing by it in the end."

The draught was administered, and the doctor adjusted himself among the pillows while Sam tucked him snugly in. Then he darkened the room, placed the glass and pitcher on a chair at the head of the bed, and, his services being no longer required, he left the room.

"I 'ain't seen the little un to-day," he said to himself, as he crossed the open space between the house and the barn. "She's quiet, the missus said, but perfeckly well; 'n' the Doc said that might be a good sign. I don't want to see 'er to talk to 'er, fer I 'ain't got nothin' to say; but it 'ud be good to know she's up 'n' aroun'."

He involuntarily glanced up at Anny's window, and even as he looked the well-known figure appeared, lifting

the white cotton curtain for a glimpse of the world outside. She immediately saw him and waved her hand,
though she made no effort to stop him. He was glad of
that, for, as he had just told himself, he had nothing to
say. He answered her signal eagerly, but turned away at
once lest she should want to speak with him.

"'The thing's in the Doc's hands now," he thought,
"'n' I'm goin' to leave it there. When he's ready fer me
he'll tell me. I'm gittin' a power o' faith in the Doc. I'm
glad he's come over, arter all."

Sam went to bed that night with a quiet mind. He had
never before realized the load of responsibility he bore in
looking out for the little un's safety. Now that the responsibility was divided, he could sleep in peace.

"If anything happens, the Doc 'll know," was his last
thought as he closed his eyes.

He must have slept himself back into his old state of
watchful dread, for later on, when he was awakened by a
blow struck by something hard upon his door, he was out
of bed and had his trousers on while he was still calling,
"Who's there?"

Before the answer came he had time for a conclusion.

"It's come, it's come 's I knowed it would!" he thought,
setting his teeth. "Be they takin' the little un off, or
have they done it a'ready?"

"Don't shoot," pleaded the doctor's voice from beyond
the door. "It's I! Is the door unlocked?"

"Come in!" called Sam, jumping into his first boot
and reaching for his second.

The doctor entered with a comfort around him and
sank into a chair. He had a soap-dish in his hand,
which he had evidently brought with him as a knocker.

"She's gone!" he said, in a hollow voice.

The boot went on with a "chug," and in another moment Sam was inside his vest and jacket.

"She?" His voice sounded hoarse and strained.

"The little un. They've taken her—she's been gone an hour and a half."

Sam thrust his hat upon his head, and for the first time faced his visitor.

"How d' ye know all this?" he demanded. "Ye seen 'em—ye heerd 'em go?"

"I haven't been awake more than five minutes. I can't tell how it was, but as soon as I opened my eyes I knew she was gone. Oh, it's true. You needn't stare. The missus is here—she isn't yet asleep. And at this moment she is rejoicing that the deed is accomplished."

Sam drew out his huge silver watch and examined it by the moonlight.

"It's half a hour till the down train at midnight. Pinky's in this bizness, 'n' that train's wot he's aimin' at. Five minutes to saddle Judy—that's time 'n' to spare. It's seven mile from 'ere to the station. Judy kin make it! She's gone ten mile at the rate o' a mile in three minutes on mountain roads, 'n' she kin do it ag'in. Twenty-one minutes fer the journey—that leaves four minutes fer accidents. It's enough!"

He rushed from the room, and the doctor heard the echo of his big boots through the sitting-room and out upon the veranda. As for Sam, he had forgotten everything but the work which lay before him. But he was not blind, and as he dashed around the corner he saw a white-robed figure leaning from the window under the roof.

"Wot's the matter?" Phœbe Ellen's voice called out. And—

"Hell's broke loose!" was the cowboy's answer as he bounded towards the barn.

The barn door was bolted. He dashed his huge hand against the iron bar in a fury of haste. The bolt caught; he seized it, drew himself in at the shoulders, as was his custom before a mighty effort, then wrenched the entire complex of fastenings loose, screws and all, and flung them aside among the weeds. The hollow gloom of the barn yawned before him, crossed by bars of moonlight here and there from crack and window. He leaped into the dim, spacious quiet, stumbling a little, but regaining his footing with an effort, in which his head took no part. Judy's stall was directly in the moonlight—good. He bounded thither, pushed her aside so that the light fell full upon her, and slipped her halter loose. The saddle hung on a peg in the wall four feet from her heels. He had it in his hands, was shaking out the girth-straps, which had somehow become twisted—no, that would not do. He must separate them carefully—had the devil been about the place to upset things so ? Now ! The saddle came down on Judy's back with a slap which made her shiver and draw her four feet together. He reached for the cinch-strap—it had caught under the saddle on the other side, and his hand grasped only the air. With one stride he was at Judy's heels—had she known her business she might have settled her midnight journey then and there —with another he was at her side, lifting the saddle with his right hand, and fumbling underneath for the delinquent strap. He brought it out with a force that sent it spinning its length. Now he was back in his old place, the belly-band in his hand ; he drew the strap through the ring, and pulled it with all his might. It gave a slight noise of ripping, but he did not notice. Tighter and tighter—aye, hump yourself and groan, Miss Judy, you've a tidy bit of work cut out for you this night ! The bridle found its place more easily, in spite of Judy's clinched teeth ; Sam had but to slip a vicious forefinger into the back of her mouth, give it a twist, jam in the bit, and buckle the strap at the side of the head. Then—out into the moonlight, leaving the barn door flapping.

He leaped into the saddle without the aid of the stirrups, got his feet into place, shook the reins, spoke once in a voice which Judy understood, and with a bound like a rubber ball the animal was up and away.

Phœbe Ellen was still at her window. She shouted something either in deprecation or defiance, he could not tell which. One word rushed back at her — his answer: " Hell-cat !"—and he dashed on up the hill.

His eyes were upon the road ; he felt Judy's slim, firm back beneath him, her ribs against his knee ; the undulations of her body went through and through him, as if he were lifted and let down by the waves of the sea, and a sort of joy rushed into his blood—the fury of struggle against odds, the determination to win, the dashing of himself against circumstances with the resolve to beat them down or die. He could have laughed.

Up the hill to the three pines on the summit, where Pinky had concealed himself the day before; the saddle creaked—there was music in the sound ; his legs pressed the taut stirrups hard—there was assurance of victory in Judy's easy resistance to his weight. On the summit he took out his watch and examined it by the moonlight. A curse escaped him.

"That devilish belly-band ! Why didn't I take time to straighten it out afore I hung the saddle up ? We've got twenty-one minutes fer the race, ole gal. No time fer foolin' or fer accidents. Kin ye make it—be ye onto yer duty, my bird ?"

He glanced back over the valley just an instant ; then he was straining forward in the saddle once more, his knees clamping Judy's hard ribs, his eyes fixed upon the flying track. But he carried a picture of the river bottom with him as he rushed forward through the night. He could see the shadows lying black against the moonlit ground ; the house, transformed among the cottonwoods, looked like a big white swan among gigantic reeds ; the river shallows had a hard, frozen shimmer, and the moonbeams shook lightly over them as if they were drifted snow.

Now came the gradual down-grade from the summit, transfigured by the shadows of rocks and trees ; below, the white, hard road ; above, the immeasurable blue and the twinkling stars. A night bird fluttered across his path in scared silence, and disappeared. The sluggish mists on the mesa heaved inertly and settled back. The wind seemed to blacken the pines as it swayed them ; there were urgent impulses to effort in the very boulders, which seemed to lean forward and watch his flight. Here were the red sandstone rocks, worn into queer shapes by the storms of ages ; they flung momentary dizzy shadows across the road, which made Sam shut his eyes with a foolish, involuntary fear that they were solid and would cause the horse to stumble. Now he comes out on the hill above the cañon into which he must descend farther on. It is a huge crack in the world, black as seen from above, and mottled with blacker spots where rocks and trees spring from the bottom and sides. The creek can be heard like an approaching storm ; there is a sound as of thunder borne through watery depths of air.

"A mile," Sam counted, as he looked at his watch. " Ye've made it in jes' three minutes, ole gal !"

And he laughed aloud.

CHAPTER XXXV

Now he is in the bottom-lands by the stream.　He flies through darkened spaces which never felt the radiant inspiration of the sun ; he comes out in bald opens where even the sage-brush refuses to grow.　The wind sweeps strongly down from the pines ; its sounds hollow and faint and sentimental ; Sam hears it, and shudders and laughs. Here is the ford below a fallen pine where an Indian encampment used to be ; the bark is peeling off the huge trunk in longitudinal lines, leaving white gaps like rifts in the side of a ruined boat.　Judy splashes in, the spray flies up and catches the moon, the stars shatter themselves against each other in the disturbed current. Sam's thoughts are galloping as if to keep pace with the galloping steed ; he does not plan the future—he has no time for that ; only, will the little un still care for him when she gets her mind back ?　Or will she turn out like Sarah ?　Sarah ! Sam's eyes are moist as the comparison occurs to him, and his hopes grow dim as memories seen through tears. And on, on the horse and his rider go, steadily, rhythmically, as if borne by strong wings.

The road runs more deeply into the soft, loamy soil of the bottoms, and the hoof-beats become muffled and the mud flies ; then the ground hardens at the foot of the slimy caverns where green moss grows and petrifies on the walls ; and now he is out on the uplands once more, and below him spreads the calmness of a lake in whose depths earth and sky are reflected.　Gullies lead the eye upward into darkness ; the undulations of near trees have a dizzying effect ; now the pines make an impenetrable black roof; now he is out again under the echoless heaven and the plunging moon. The regular puff, puff of Judy's breath grows into his mental habit; it becomes a part of the landscape and his own desperation. Here is the barbed-wire corner of Mead's ranch, whose owner lives two miles away.

Sam looks at his watch.

"Three miles we've made in nine minutes," he says, with satisfaction. "That leaves four to make in twelve, ole gal. Keep it up as ye've begun, 'n' we'll have time to spare!"

They turn an angle of the canon, ascend a slope, and come out on a summit where the pines stand motionless in the half-light, as if in a translucent silvery liquid. Mists are forming along the stream below, like clouds exhaled from marshes. The sound of the water rises as from under a weight; the ghostly murmur of the pines has the effect of nuns singing between stone-walls, and trying to voice the wasting grief of their darkened lives. An owl hoots from the cliff. The night is full of sights and sounds of awe. The deaf earth seems listening, the blind rocks peering, the dumb sky trying to speak.

Up-grade again into the moonlight, down to water again and into the loamy bottoms. Again the creek is forded, again there is a stretch of muddy soil on the farther side. A splash—the water lets them pass with a tearing sound; the yielding loam deadens the flying hoof-beats, the ear gets a rest, and again the strain of flight seems momentarily relaxed.

"Good God!"

It is Sam's voice, though muffled with strong emotion. The two words rise distinctly above the creaking of the saddle and the hiss and puff of Judy's laboring breath. Something has given way under him—not Judy's back, Sam knows better than that. He throws his weight a little to the right—the saddle follows him; to the left, it shifts in that direction. Judy's wild eyes glare back at him in the moonlight; she slackens her speed a little; she knows there is something wrong.

"On, on!" Sam bellows, at the top of his lungs. And the animal leaps forward as if shot from a gun.

But the cinch-strap is broken—Sam realizes the truth. It is dangling against the horse's legs; the flying thong lashes her sides; it strikes his own foot, and stings even through the thick cowhide boot. Judy is disturbed. She gallops less evenly, she snorts a little, she glances behind her, not fearfully, but nervously, with the annoyance of an intelligent being whose purpose is crossed.

Sam rides thus a minute or so, still at full speed. The saddle slips from side to side. With all his efforts he cannot keep himself poised. A sudden turn in the road almost flings him off. He readjusts himself, balances, shakes his feet free from the stirrups. Judy quivers. She is alert, but she does not slacken her speed. He seizes her by the mane, leaps the pommel of the saddle, and lands on her shoulders, clinging to her neck. For an instant the saddle retains its place on the horse's back. Sam kicks back at it. Vainly. With a backward thrust of his body he pushes it loose, and it slips to the left—falls, but not clear of the horse. The broken strap catches her hind-leg and wraps around it like a snake. Her foot comes down upon the saddle with a clash and scrape. The strap still clings, Judy's onward impulse for an instant drags the saddle in the dirt. She stumbles—what chance is there to recover her footing, going at that mad gait? She falls and strikes the ground with a groan. But Sam is on top. With the cowboy's instinct of self-preservation he calculates the direction of the fall, flings his right leg free, and falls astride the prostrate beast. He doesn't stop to curse—there is no time. He drops the reins, gets his feet together on the saddle, stands up, bends over and unwinds the strap from the helpless fetlock.

20

The horse does not understand her freedom; she turns her long neck, panting, and faces him with a wild human glare in her eyes. Her nostrils quiver; she seems to breathe through her whole body.

"Up, Judy!" he cries. It is the first time in her life that the faithful beast has disobeyed. Now she cowers to the ground, frightened and inert. "Up—up!" She glares back at him, and her breath comes with a sobbing sound. It is no time for tenderness, though Sam would have exhibited it to the full under other conditions. He kicks the prostrate animal unmercifully in the ribs. She starts, draws her fore-feet under, struggles, finds herself free, and rises with a snort. Sam leads her a dozen paces, examining her gait. There is no visible limp.

"We'll make it yit!" he says to himself, with set teeth.

In an instant he is astride her again. He puts the spurs to her as if the devil were in him, and dashes bareback up the slope among the pines. Judy understands the need of making up lost time. Whatever speed there is in her shows itself now. It is useless to urge her. The spirit of her rider has passed into her flying legs; it is her own necessity as much as his to strain forward to the end of their journey. She lays back her ears—there is speed in the very tips of them—straightens her neck, reaches out for the ground with all fours as if it were a thing to be desired, grasps it, dashes it behind her as if, having attained it, she found it useless; and reaches out again with renewed effort, fiercer resolve. In a flash of moonlight Sam takes out his watch and examines it.

"Three mile to make in eight minutes!" he announces. And Judy knows that he is not satisfied with her yet.

Up hill and down they go, wheeling around rocky promontories, circling projecting pines, ascending, dropping, as a bird scales the sky. The stars flash into each other;

the moon looks blue. The wind rushes one way, they the other. It whitens the aspens behind them as foam whitens the waves in the wake of a boat. Sam hears nothing but the dash of the air against his ears, and the beat, beat, beat of the horse's hoofs; beat, beat, beat, as if his own heart were throbbing outside him. The pines reel past in a maniac dance; they clutch the blue moon, wrestle with her, hide her in their huge black arms, then toss her high into heaven again. The shadow of the horse in the white light, long-legged and distorted, projects itself against the rocks, disappears, heaves into sight in unexpected places, flattens, grows big, draws in like elastic, but always follows. Is it possible that Judy is going faster? Or is it only his own desperation, trying to realize what he most desires? At any rate, she is not giving out. Her breath comes with a hiss and goes with a puff that reassures him; he can believe it belongs to himself. The outward fling of the fore-feet comes regular and strong, and the answering crash as they strike the ground sends no uncertain quiver through the slim, firm back. Sam sits with his knees screwed into the animal's ribs, his hand on the bridle, not for guidance, but encouragement; he feels the beast's sympathy along the leathern thong, as if it were an electric wire; his lips are drawn, his nostrils wide, his teeth set, his eyes fixed. From the crown of his head to the sole of his foot he is the embodiment of a terrible purpose.

Now he is in Cogswell's cañon, with only the mesa between him and the valley where the station is. Suddenly a sound drifts in along the darkened air—a remote sound, spreading into shallow echoes among the rocks. It dies away, is repeated, again sinks into stillness.

"It's the midnight train!" Sam says, under his breath. And he dashes his spurs into the horse's bleeding sides.

She leaps like a boat shot from the crest to the trough of a wave. "Faster—faster!" he calls, leaning far forward. "Faster—faster!" After all his hard riding, will he be too late?

The wind strikes them hard on the top of the mesa overlooking Eden City. The train is not yet visible. Sam knows where it is—in the cañon a mile above. He must race with it—well; and "Faster—faster!" he still hisses into Judy's ear.

They cross the mesa like an electric shock. The moon finds them out and takes her place at their side. They race together—the galloping horse and the galloping moon. Sam is dizzy with the wild flight. The stars dash against his eyes like hailstones.

"No jimmyin', ole gal!" he says, to bring himself back to his senses.

They are down the mesa and out upon the level road. There is an audible quiver in the air—the train is not yet in sight, but it is approaching.

"We'll beat it!" Sam roars. And Judy responds with her heels.

The headlight of the engine flashes into sight from behind the rocky promontory above the depot. It thrusts a long cone of light towards him, big end first.

"Now—now! Take to yer wings, my bird!" he cries. "Ye've got 'em!" And Judy splits the air like an in-driven wedge.

The train slows up before halting. The breathless steed flies on. The station is close at hand. Sam can distinguish three waiting figures on the platform—two men and a woman: Pete Hawkins, Pinky, and the little un. He has hardly made them out in the moonlight before he dashes up to the platform like a cloud torn from a hurricane.

He strikes the ground—whether on his head or his feet he never knows.

"Sam!" cries the little un, rushing up to him and seizing his arm. "Sam—Sam!" and her voice dies in a hysterical whimper.

"All aboard!" roars the conductor, a car's-length up the platform.

Sam puts his arm around the girl, but does not look at her.

"Ye'll see to Judy, won't ye, Pete?" he asks. "I reckon I've killed 'er; but—it's wuth it, I swear!"

"All aboard!" the conductor roars again. And the engine coughs and wheezes.

Sam draws his companion towards the nearest car. And now Pinky, for the first time, ventures to make himself heard.

"Where—where be ye goin' with 'er?" he calls out, in an uncertain voice.

Sam turns on him with a vicious grin.

"Now ye're askin' fer information," he says, as he assists Anny up the platform and into the car.

CHAPTER XXXVI

Pinky watched the receding train with doubt in his eyes. He stood silent and awkward for a while, brushing up his pale hair behind and contorting his body into an oblique straddle.

"Well," he finally said to Pete Hawkins, "all I got to do's to hitch up ag'in 'n' go back to the ranch. I hate it like a dog."

"Queer doin's," was Pete's only answer — "mighty queer doin's." And he led Judy away to the stable for a rubbing-down.

Pinky found the mistress of the ranch up and dressed and waiting for him. She met him on the veranda with a lamp in her hand.

"He ketched ye!" was her greeting. And then, with a pucker of her hard, thin mouth, "I knowed he would."

"I couldn't help it," said Pinky, in a tone of exoneration.

"God A'mighty couldn't 'a' helped it," she declared, and a look of relief came laxly into Pinky's face. "Don't I know 'im? If he sets out to do a thing, he'll do it if the heavens fall."

"He come up jest as the train stopped. If he'd been two minutes later, I'd 'a' had 'im. Ever'thing was goin' smoothly, when up he comes like the devil shot through the solid groun', 'n' wot could I do? I couldn't knock 'im over 'n' drag 'er into the train."

She screwed her mouth still tighter.

"No. Had they started back when ye left?"

"Back? I should say not! They tuck the train together."

Phœbe Ellen's mouth relaxed so abruptly that it seemed as if her very teeth must be loosened.

"They tuck the train together? Wot for? Sam 'n' sis? But where was they goin'?"

"He wouldn't say a word. I ast 'im, 'n' he grinned like he was swollerin' vitriol, 'n' looked dang'rous. I've seen 'im like that afore. It allus means suthin'—suthin' 't ye don't expeck."

Phœbe Ellen had led the way into the house, and was sitting bolt upright in a chair. Now she drooped a little, as if in meditation, and rested her chin in her hand.

"I kin think wot it means," she finally said.

"Well, wot?"

"Can't *you?*"

"I been muddlin' my brains with it all the way over from the station, 'n' I can't even git a tail-hold o' it. Only, his idee seems to be to git 'er away from us. That's plain."

"Yes. But they's plenty o' ways o' gittin' 'er away from us. He's tuck the shorest way."

"How d' ye mean?"

"He means to hide 'er somers—like 's not down south there on that ranch o' his. He's got friends in Lagunitas, too; he might leave 'er with them. They's dozens o' ways 'n' places. But we mus' be ready fer 'im, that's all. While I been waitin' 'ere fer ye, I been thinkin'; in fact, I've put in the time hard. We've got to do suthin', you 'n' me; 'n' I'm ready fer anything. Say!"

There was something peculiar in her tone, and he gazed at her with alert inquiry.

"Wot now?" he asked.

She met his eyes unabashed.

"Ye still want to marry me?"

"Don't I?" Pinky's voice was eager.

She nodded several times with slow decision.

"I don't blame ye," she remarked. "It 'ud be a good

thing fer ye, 'n' I make no doubt ye keer fer me.   Well, we'll go 'n' be tied at daylight."

Pinky got upon his feet.

"D' ye mean it ?" he cried.

"Set down—set down 'n' keep yer hair on.   Ole man Halstead's a reg'lar ordained Methodis' preacher—used to preach back in Indiany somers.   He tole me so hisself. We'll have 'im do the job arter breakfas'.   He don't talk much 'bout it, 'cause he's kind o' out o' the gospel biz- ness, I reckon, 'n' sech things don't recommend a feller in Collyraydo, nohow.   But it's all right.   I'll answer fer that."

"So 'll I," was Pinky's suffusive rejoinder.   "But—"

She understood his objection before he uttered it and faced it boldly.

"Do I love Sam any more ?   Shucks !   I hate 'im. There !   Be ye satisfied ?   'N' I need ye, Pinky, to help me fight 'im—that's why I'm in sech a hurry for the wed- din'.   We'll see if a man kin run off with a idiot gal 'n' hide 'er away from 'er folks 'thout bein' brought to time fer it.   If we can't fix 'im in one way we kin in 'nother. 'N' as a las' resort, there's allus the law.   Be ye willin' to stan' up agin 'im, with me 'n' the ranch to back ye ?"

"Willin' ?"   Pinky's eagerness was too evident to re- quire a declarative sentence, and Phœbe Ellen accepted it in its interrogative form.

"Well," was her way of concluding the arrangement, "we kin git a couple o' hours' sleep yit afore breakfas', I reckon, 'n' we'll need it if Sam should take it into his head to come back to-morrer.   Ye kin have his room—ye know yer way.   Good-night !   Be ready when I holler fer ye in the mornin'."

After breakfast they set out without a word of explana- tion to any one, and on their return the mistress remarked to Leatherhead :

"I've ast Pinky to stay with us all day, 'n' 'pears like

he's inclined to be fav'rable. In fact, I shouldn't wonder if he'd stay sev'ral days. I've made a proposition to 'im to stay right along 'n' board with us 'n' let Pete Hawkins look arter the station altogether. To make a long story short, we've gone 'n' got married, 'n' nat'rally he'll stay 'ere right along where his wife is. So ye kin lay a plate fer 'im reg'lar when I don't set the table myself."

And Leatherhead departed in silence, for once in his life too completely surprised for utterance.

In the living-room they found the doctor. He had seated himself at the east window, where the bright autumnal sunshine made a yellow square on the floor and filled the room with a pleasant warmth. He was propped up on pillows, and each of his eyes had a bright, interested spot in it as he turned to examine the new-comers.

The point widened into a sphere as his glance met Phœbe Ellen's. She knew what that meant—she had seen that strange luminous expansion there before. But it affected her differently now. She did not fear it, she did not care for it; she wondered how she ever could have stood in awe of it. She felt new, independent, careless of supernatural pryings; she stood outside the pale of praise or blame. Her wedding had acted upon her as a process of cutting loose from old fears; it was the beginning of complete emancipation from old limitations and dominations; she felt herself expanding forcefully into infinite spaces of egotism, supreme, vociferous. A spirit of utter recklessness came over her—a longing to assert herself at any cost, to stand up in utter defiance, to face the adverse powers of earth and heaven, and coerce them with the authority of rampant irresponsibility. Let him read her thoughts if he chose—what could he do with the knowledge, after all? She could have clutched the zenith and torn it down about her ears and rejoiced at her own fall into chaos. Besides, what assurance had she that he could read her thoughts? Perhaps it had been only a nervous fear on her part. She would see, let it cost what it might.

Her eyes met his with a fierceness in which there was no effort at concealment. "Look!" her haughty glance said, "and I'll make it all plain and easy. Wot have I to fear from the like o' you ?"

Then, with her eyes still upon his, she formulated these words distinctly in her thoughts :

" Pinky 'n' I are married. Ole man Halstead done it a hour ago."

" Ah !" said the doctor, as if she had spoken aloud.

" Wot be ye goin' to do 'bout it ?" she added, mentally, as before.

He understood her, for he answered with a half-laugh:

" Nothing. Nothing at all. But it is very interesting —you can't think how interesting to a man of my peculiar prejudices. I knew Halstead was a regularly ordained parson, only I somehow always thought of him as obsolete—in no way connected with a living issue like this."

Pinky, to whom the doctor appeared to be answering a question which no one had asked, spoke up at this juncture.

" This is all-fired queer," he remarked from a distance.

" Shet up !" retorted his wife. " 'N' don't fool aroun' with wot ye don't onderstan'. This is my bizness, anyhow. I want to see wot he kin do."

She turned on the doctor with the reckless *abandon* of defiance.

" D' ye want to read further ?" she demanded, shrilly.

" Give me half a chance and I'll show you," was his answer.

She flung her head back with a gesture of triumphant upgiving to her scorn.

" Read, then !" she cried, not less shrilly, but in a tone that hardened as its defiance became hysterical. " Read, 'n' know it all, if ye like. I won't keep nothin' back. Wot do I keer ? Who'd b'lieve ye if ye told it all in a court o' jestice ? 'Ud Pinky b'lieve ye if ye was to tell 'im now ?"

" Husbands are proverbially obtuse where their wives' defects are concerned," answered the doctor, with his half-sneer.

She stiffened herself more inflexibly by clasping her hands back to back behind her. Then she thought out her words slowly and deliberately, not for utterance, but for the gratification of that mad spirit of defiance which had completely taken possession of her.

"I ain't the owner of this ranch." She felt his eyes perusing the words in her brain before she really thought them out. " It b'longs to my sister. I'm Phœbe Ellen— she's Anny. She was hurt in the lan'slide, 'n' I seen I could take 'er place, so I done it. I ain't sorry. The place b'longs to me 's much 's wot it does to her, only Dan was partial. I mean to keep wot I've got, too. D' ye reckon ye kin git it from me by tellin' ?"

"'Thanks," said the doctor, with his ghastly, sarcastic smile. "I read every word of it — you made it very plain. Get the ranch from you by telling? Will you blame me that already I've thought of it ? I have a queer mind in some ways ; it often leaps to conclusions."

" Pinky, go out in the kitchen 'n' stay with Leather-head ten minutes. I'll be through by then," commanded the bride.

Obedient to the demands of his new marital rôle, Pinky shuffled out of the room.

"He don't know," said Phœbe Ellen, jerking her head towards the closed door. "He never will."

" Won't he ?" inquired the doctor, in a voice that sounded exclamatory through the question.

She moved closer to him, her face stiffening into lines of vindictive triumph.

"'Take it to court, if that's wot ye mean ; I defy ye. Who'd b'lieve a crazy consumptive like *you*, anyhow ?

How'd ye git to court—tell me that ? Ye'd die afore ye could git to the station. 'N' I could bring witnesses 't ye've allus acted crazy. Take it to court! How kin ye harm me ? Bah ! I snap my fingers at ye !"

The doctor eyed her curiously.

"You've evidently thought it all out," he remarked.

"I have. 'N' ain't I right? 'Ud any court o' jestice in thé lan' take yer word fer sech a thing ?"

"No," he admitted.

"Well, then !" crowed Phœbe Ellen.

The doctor left her a full moment's enjoyment of her triumph before he said a word.

"You've considered the matter from all sides, I suppose." His tone was curious, and his idea, being merely a repetition of what he had said a moment before, arrested her attention as if he had discovered a flaw in her logic. But she snapped her fingers once more and tossed her head.

"From all sides," she asserted, with confidence. "I know where I stan' !"

"Sometimes I've almost thought, as I have studied your character during the past few months, that you might be capable, under the stress of strong feeling, of overlooking the essentials of a situation and fastening upon the irrelevant details." He watched her with that enigmatic smile of his, half sarcastic and half serious.

He saw her nostrils dilate as if she were catching her breath, but there was no other hint that he had touched her.

"Hasn't it sometimes occurred to yourself, now, that you might miscalculate in such a case ? I merely throw it out as a suggestion, you know ; but mightn't you have considered the matter from all sides but one—one little corner of a side, so to speak ? The wisest people sometimes overlook the very thing they are searching for."

Phœbe Ellen grew pale. This was the very mistake she

had all along felt capable of making, and against which she thought she had especially guarded.

"Shucks!" she scoffed, but there was an incipient tremor in her voice. "Ye can't skeer *me!*"

"Oh, well, I'll say nothing further about it, then. I merely suggested the possibility. Now, it has occurred to me—"

"Yes?" she demanded, as his voice trailed away in well-simulated meditation.

He did not notice her at once, but finally he roused himself and went on:

"As I was saying, it has occurred to me that I might easily send back to Nebraska for the proper identification of yourself and your sister—"

"Good Lord!" gasped Phœbe Ellen, sinking into a chair.

CHAPTER XXXVII

"You see?" smiled the doctor. "The simplest thing in the world. And the court wouldn't have to take the word of a crazy consumptive, either."

"I'm a fool!" muttered Phœbe Ellen, hoarsely.

"It's a case where vaulting ambition o'erleaped itself and fell on the other side, that is all. Don't feel badly about it. Wiser people have done the same thing, as I think I remarked before. Sam will be glad to know of it. I've no doubt he'll take action immediately. He is somewhat exasperated already, you know; and this will set him quite off."

"I'm a fool!" repeated Phœbe Ellen. She looked hard at her tormentor, who returned her gaze with the sarcasm of complete composure. "I'm allus seein' nothin' but the mood I happen to be in. I'm allus scratchin' my face jest at the minute I want to look purty."

"You've certainly done it this time," was the doctor's only consolation.

She seemed on the point of whimpering, then suddenly changed her mind.

"Why couldn't ye 'a' died afore las' night?" she cried out.

"Providence," smiled the doctor. "I begin to believe there really is such a thing. Yes, I am quite certain it was Providence. I have been reserved for a great moral work in my last days—in my last hours, if you like that better."

"I do," she interrupted, shrilly.

"Suit yourself—suit yourself," he said. "I shall be willing to die after I get this affair straightened out."

"Not afore?" she hinted, viciously.

"Oh, I shall not go before, I assure you," he smiled—"that is, unless you've got some poison around. Have you? I shouldn't wonder!"

She started guiltily as she remembered the dried loco-weed in her valise—she had not thought of it for weeks; and if the doctor's eyes had been upon her at that moment he would have found no difficulty in reading the truth. But as chance would have it, he was gazing absently at his slippered toes, and it was evident that the question was only one of those sarcasms to which he attached no importance beyond the utterance. She could see that he was in reality thinking of something else.

"Bah!" she said, in the shrill, bullying tone with which he was familiar. "Go on insultin' me—that's right, go straight ahead. If ye was a *man*—"

He looked up with a sarcastic, ventral laugh.

"There is compensation in all things, as Emerson long ago taught us Bostonians. He was a great man, that Emerson. My father knew him personally. Would it interest you if I were to reminisce a little?" He examined his victim with a smile which had a delicate gloating in it. "No? I see by your look that you are not interested in Emerson. Well, not to speak further of your folly in revealing your secret—it *was* folly, rank folly, even my natural charity is obliged to declare—but leaving all that out of account for the present, suppose we take a moment or two to regard the matter objectively, as it were. It may help us out."

"Us?"

"You, I mean. Ah! It is lovely to be exact. There was Dusenbury, my mathematics teacher at Harvard, one of the most accurate of men. You should have seen him! One day Hackett, my chum — I could tell you more stories about Hackett than you could shake a stick at, as the saying is—well, one day Hackett—"

Phœbe Ellen tapped her foot impatiently.

"Ye wanted to talk things over?" she reminded him.

He grinned.

"Oh yes, objectively. To be sure. I forgot. Objectively means in a sensible manner. I'm inclined to wander a little, you see. Probably it's a part of my disease—or a result. Yes, by all means let us regard the matter objectively. To begin with, you've got yourself into a boat. That is very evident. You agree?"

She made no attempt at denial.

"Well?" she questioned.

"You're in a boat," continued the doctor. "That's sure. Now, naturally the question suggests itself to you, How shall I get out? You say to yourself, not without agitation, as I can perceive, How shall I reach solid land again? Am I right in this also?"

"Well?" repeated Phœbe Ellen.

Suddenly the doctor tittered.

"Have you ever heard of Mrs. Micawber?" he asked.

"No sech person where I've ever lived."

His titter died in one of those ventral laughs which Phœbe Ellen detested.

"My method of reasoning reminded me irresistibly of her," he said, and then paused.

"Was that wot ye started to say?" demanded Phœbe Ellen.

"Pardon me. I was wandering again. You are right —you do well to call me back." Suddenly he opened his eyes full upon hers. "I can see a way out of your difficulty," he said.

"D' ye feel like dyin'? That's the only way!"

"There is another way," he replied, smilelessly now.

"Fer *me?*" She was leaning forward eagerly.

"For you."

"Not fer *her?*" she insisted.

"That may or may not be."

“Ye *be* jokin’. Wot good kin it do me if it leaves a chance fer her ?”

“At least I can see a chance for you ; and that is the principal thing for you to consider.”

“Yes,” she admitted, after a tremulous moment ; “that’s the principal thing.”

“You will understand, of course, that I am not helping you out on account of any love or admiration I bear you.”

“Oh, I onderstan’ that ! ’N’ I’d objeck to bein’ helped under them cornditions.”

“Good ! I have my own ends to serve—that is the long and short of it. They may be good, they may be bad, they may be a mixture of good and bad ; that is not your affair. But such as they are, I purpose to attain them before I die. If you attain your safety at the same time, well and good. I wash my hands of that responsibility.”

“I can’t make ye out,” said Phœbe Ellen at this point.

“You won’t altogether, even when I’ve finished. But I’ll explain all that’s necessary. You remember the operation that you wouldn’t consent to ?”

She nodded.

“That is the mainspring of the whole situation. Have you no imagination ? Can’t you see the rest ? I’ve set my heart on that operation, and I simply *won’t* die till it is accomplished.” He set his mouth in a ghastly grimness that had the hardness of stone. “Call it a mania, a sick man’s freak, a thirst for human blood—what you will. Ah, to feel the scalpel in my fingers once more, and the warm resistance of human flesh under it !” His eyes shone, there was a tingling eagerness in the tremor of his hands. “No matter : you don’t understand. Besides, I’d like the last effort of my life to be for good—so many of its early efforts were in the opposite direction ! Well, have I said enough ? One word more.” His teeth came together, and his bloodless lips parted around them in a grin which had the tenacious purpose of death in it. "I'll stay in this world and I'll keep your secret at my disposal till that operation is performed. You may as well make up your mind to that."

She looked sick and frightened, but she managed to articulate :

"'N' arter the operation ?"

"After that affairs will be in your own hands."

"I might 'a' kep' 'em there 'thout any say-so o' your'n if I hadn't turned fool 'n' defied ye. I could 'a' shet ye out o' my mind like I'd done a dozen times afore."

"True," he smiled back at her, with a renewed tightening of his lips against his teeth. "But the point you have to consider is, how to make the best of your own folly. It isn't an uncommon alternative. Regret, you may be sure, makes nothing either way."

She braced herself erect in her chair.

"Ye wanted me to cornsent to the operation ?" she demanded.

"Precisely my idea !"

"She ain't 'ere to be operated on. She's with Sam. How 'll ye git 'er back ?"

"I'll look out for that."

"'N' if I won't cornsent ?"

"I shall tell Sam the whole truth as soon as ever he returns."

"'N' if I do ?"

"I promise never to speak of the matter which you so inadvertently revealed to me."

She fixed a big, rigid wrinkle between her eyes in meditation.

"I reckon ye feel like they was a purty good chance o' curin' 'er," she finally said, in a tentative voice.

"There is certainly a chance."

"A purty good un ?"

“At least not a bad one.”

“Ye’ll do yer best fer ’er ?”

“On everybody’s account—yes.”

“Everybody’s !” she objected, bitterly.

“Except yours.” He made his amendment gravely.

“’N’ if ye cure ’er—”

“She will attend to the matter of her inheritance herself.”

Phœbe Ellen sank back with a groan.

“That ’ud leave me jes’ where I be,” she complained, more bitterly than before.

“Exactly,” was the doctor’s only answer.

“Then wot’s the use o’ me cornsentin’ in the fust place ?”

“Haven’t you grasped the point yet ? Because, as matters stand, your case is altogether hopeless. I shall tell Sam the whole business as soon as he comes back, or as soon thereafter as I may see fit. You understand what the outcome of that will be.”

“He wouldn’t give me the ghost o’ a show.”

The doctor nodded with cheerful assent.

“Whereas, if you permit the operation to take place, there is a chance that your sister will die. In that case, no one will ever know the truth, and your secret will be buried with me in my grave.”

“If ye hide the truth, ye’ll be ’s deep in the mud ’s I am in the mire,” sniffed Phœbe Ellen, wheeling to a vindication of herself in his complicity.

The doctor seemed not disinclined to take up that side of the question.

“Oh, I never pretended to be good,” he said. “I made friends with the devil when I was young, and have never had the slightest desire to break off the acquaintance. He’s really a very pleasant chap — not half so black as he’s painted. My only difficulty has been that, of late years, on account of my poor health, I’ve been unable to meet the old fellow on his own terms. One has to have an iron constitution really to get into the merits of the devil's companionship."

"Like 's not 't was yer friendship fer 'im 't broke down yer health," said Phœbe Ellen, still in a moral tone.

"Not a doubt of it," was the answer, delivered with ghastly cheerfulness. "Not a doubt. And if I had my life to live over again, and knew all the consequences, I declare seriously I should in no way do differently. I have lived as far as I had a chance—that might be put upon my tombstone, and it would indicate the truth. But to the affair in hand. What do you say? Have you made up your mind?"

"I don't see 's ye're grantin' much to me, nohow. If she don't git well, she can't manage the proputty, 'n' things 'ud have to stan' jes' like they be. If she dies, I'll be heir in spite o' everything."

"This is all on the supposition that the operation takes place."

"'N' if she gits her mind back, the hull thing comes out."

"Exactly. No one can help that."

"The only gain to me is, 't if she don't git well, or if she dies, nobody 'll know how I've been monkeyin' with the law."

"You have it to a dot."

"'Pears like ye might do better by me," she began, in a wheedling voice.

"As for instance?"

"Let the operation go!"

"And keep my mouth shut? You are modest!"

"If ye should kill 'er, I could have ye 'rested!" she threatened.

The doctor laughed with faint enjoyment of her perplexities.

"The operation is essential," was his only comment.

She looked at him a long moment, as if to assure herself of the fixedness of his purpose, then flung out her hands with a gesture of desperation.

"Oh, ye've got me!" she breathed. "Wot kin I do but cornsent? Yes, I cornsent. Do the operation when ye like. Wot a fool I was—wot a snortin', howlin' fool!"

"Thanks," said the doctor, with ambiguous politeness. "Sam will probably be back some time to-day, and I'll talk the operation over with him. Rely entirely on my discretion in the other matter. I have promised to keep silence, and I shall have the fact constantly in mind. Though the devil and I are friends, he has always found me a man of my word, and so will you. Would you mind leaving me to myself for an hour? My rest was disturbed last night, you know, and I think I could sleep a bit. Thanks. I really begin to feel the strain of events. *Au revoir!*"

And the doctor found himself alone.

CHAPTER XXXVIII

Sam came home a little after dinner, and, to the surprise of every one, he brought Anny with him.

"We had dinner with Pete Hawkins," he said, in answer to Leatherhead's inquiry. "He's got Judy in fine shape, cornsiderin'. I'm goin' to leave 'er with 'im a few days till she reely gits on 'er feet agin. He lent us his horses 'n' cracky to come over with, 'n' said to tell Pinky everything was all right to the depot. The little un's stood up to these 'ere doin's like a soger in the reg'lar army. Ain't she lookin' fine? Where's the missus?"

"The missus?" repeated Leatherhead, his eyes expanding and rolling. "The missus? Why, she seen ye comin', 'n' flew up-stairs like a cat in a fit, she did. Say, is it so 't she was tryin' to git the little un out o' the kentry? I'd like to know."

"It's so," was Sam's answer.

"Oh, tripe!" was Leatherhead's comment. Then, with a new access of excitement: "Say, suthin' 's happened sence ye was gone. Guess wot!"

Sam shook his head.

"Oh, guess!" pleaded Leatherhead. Then, with a gush: "Ye never could guess, I know."

But Sam still shook his head.

"She's married!" cried Leatherhead, brief for once in his life.

"She? Who?"

Leatherhead nodded and gulped.

"The missus, o' course, 'n' Pinky. He's out there in the kitchen now. Fust he goes to the winder 'n' looks out; then he comes back 'n' stares at the sink 'n' grins, 'n' shakes 'is head like it was clean empty. I left 'im gazin' at the wood-box 'n' rollin' 'is eyes like a dyin' duck in a thunder-storm."

A slow smile dawned on Sam's features.

"Wot a purty idee!" was all he said as he led Anny away.

"Ye kin go to my room," he said, as he parted from her. "Ye won't mind my leavin' ye a little while to speak to the doctor?"

"No," was the answer; "I ain't afeerd."

And they separated without further words.

Sam found the doctor propped up in his chair, hugging the square of noonday sunshine which struggled through the window. The strange man looked up with grave expectancy. He was more calm than usual, more steady, more forgetful of himself; his heels kept their place on the floor without effort, and there was little or no strain in the attitude of his hands upon the arms of his chair.

The two men faced each other, their eyes meeting in a long gaze. Sam had intended to speak and explain, but there was no need with that steady gaze overmastering his, feeling around the edges of his thoughts as if they were material things and could be identified by touch.

"Ah!" murmured the doctor, finally removing his gaze.

"Ye've got it all?" asked Sam, with a doubtful smile.

"Yes. It was unnecessary, though. But I'm glad of it."

"Unne'sary?"

"I've brought the missus to terms myself."

"You?"

"I!"

"'N' how 'd ye do it?"

"No matter. I promised not to tell. But she has consented to the operation."

"Well, I'll be darned!"

The doctor nodded slowly.

"At any time I see fit to mention," he added.

"Well, we've got 'er now, fer shore," remarked Sam, fetching a long breath. "You wunst 'n' me wunst. She can't git loose from both o' us."

"Your wife wishes it as much as ever?"

"More 'n ever."

"And when will she be ready?"

"To-morrer!"

The doctor smiled.

"Good! But I doubt that. She must diet two or three days in order to get her system into proper shape. She seems well?"

"Sound as a drum!"

"But you are to see to it that she eats no meat, no pastry of any sort, and drinks no tea nor coffee. She is in a quiet frame of mind?"

"Cool 's a cowcumber!"

"Keep her so. Possibly the operation may take place day after to-morrow—certainly not before. Bring her down after a while and let me see her myself. I want a good look at her."

"Well," said Sam. "'N' ye feel ekal to it yerself?"

"I haven't been so strong for months. And with the knife in my hand—I can feel it now! One thing comes over me strangely, though. Shall I tell you? It means no harm, not even to myself, but it's a queer thing—a new outcropping of my fate, so to speak. Have you ever felt that you were the victim of an idea, that you had an invisible antagonist somewhere who seized you at the moment of your triumph and put your head under his heel as if to prove that you were subject to his law?"

"Never thort o' sech a thing in all my life!"

"It is a horrible conception of one's relations with the universe, but it has come over me frequently. Time and

again in my life I have made an effort about something—
a mighty effort—only to find at the last moment that all
my struggling was useless. Just on the point of victory I
have failed utterly, or if I succeeded it was altogether by
accident and never by the means by which I had chosen
to prepare myself for success. It was so with my medical
studies—I was on the point of winning the highest honors,
when my health broke down. You see how it has been
with this operation; I have worked for it as I never
worked for the kingdom of heaven—as I never *could* work
for the kingdom of heaven—and at the last moment my
trouble is made unnecessary by the power your marriage
with the little un gives you over the situation. You see
how I mean? It is as if the evil genius of my life said,
'Struggle on your own account if you like, but you are in
my power. If you succeed at all, it is by the efforts of
others, and never by your own.' I have a queer feeling
about this operation, too. It will be successful—I know
it as by second-sight. But something—I cannot now see
what—will happen to take the knowledge of success away
from me. Perhaps I'll die before she recovers—you know
it may take her some time. I have a feeling that I will
go into the next world without the assurance of having
accomplished anything in this; that would suit my evil
genius too well. Do you follow me?"

Later in the afternoon, when Sam went to his room to
inquire how the little un was passing the time, he found
Phœbe Ellen already established there. She rose to meet
him, startled but defiant, while a quick flush appeared in
her thin, hard cheeks, and an angry gleam came at him
like a visible prod from her eyes.

"I wa'n't a-lookin' fer *you*," she began, with a warlike
toss of her head. "I come to see my sister."

"*I* come to see my wife," was Sam's retort. He seated
himself at the foot of the bed where Anny was lying, and
crossed his huge legs comfortably.

An electric shock seemed to pass through Phœbe Ellen.

"Yer wife ?" she screeched.

"'Ain't nobody told ye?" he inquired, with composure. "Then I reckon the Doc 'ain't opened his head yit. He's the only one 't knows."

" Married !"

Phœbe Ellen's voice grew muffled, but somehow lost none of its shrillness.

" We be," was the cool response. "We got to Lagunitas at daylight, took breakfas', hunted a squire at eight o'clock, had the bizness done in apple-pie order, 'n' started back at half-past."

She burst into a dry, whinnying laugh.

" Oh, she's got some un to look arter 'er now !" she choked. "She's got some un to look arter 'er now, fer shore !"

"She has," assented Sam. "'N' the fact 'll be made plainer to ye as they's need o' it. I'm glad ye come in this arternoon. It's time you 'n' me was gittin' at a onderstandin', arter wot happened las' night. Sech doin's can't go on where my wife's cornsarned—o' course ye onderstan' that ?"

" I onderstan' that, ye may be shore," retorted Phœbe Ellen, with spirit. "'N' I onderstan' more 'n that, too. I onderstan' 't I own this 'ere ranch, 'n' 't I inten' to run it. 'N' if outsiders makes up their minds they're goin' to stay 'ere 'n' live off 'm me 's long 's they see fit to do nothin', all I got to say is they'll git slipped up. That's wot *I* onderstan'. So ye kin jes' nachelly take yer wife 'n' shin out with 'er 's quick 's th' Lord 'll let ye. 'N' the sooner the quicker—so there !"

The same masterful look which she had first seen at the station came into Sam's face at this moment, though he grinned.

" We thort o' stayin' till arter the operation," he remarked.

“Oh, ye did, did ye?   Ye ’lowed ye’d stay till arter the operation !   Well, who invited ye ?”

“ We invited ourselves, ’n’ ’ere we stay till we git ready to go, though ye turn black in the face with orderin’ us out.   ’N’ if you turn *too* rusty, I’ll kidnap ye ’n’ Pinky both, ’n’ tote ye down to Lagunitas to have a interview with a lawyer I know down there.   ’Ud that please ye ?”

Phœbe Ellen sniffed, but she knew by certain unmistakable signs that Sam was quite capable of carrying out his threat.

“ I tole the Doc ye could stay till arter the operation,” she said, in a milder tone.   “ I never ’d ’low it from *your* say-so, though,” she flashed out again.   “ ’N’ arter the operation ’s over ?”

“ We’ll stay till my wife is perfeckly well ’n’ able to travel,” said Sam.   “ ’N’ we’ll have the best the house affords, or they’ll be scenery on the Thompson ranch !   The ranch is your’n—I own up to it.   But arter las’ night, *we* have some claims, my wife ’n’ me, ’n’ we mean to work ’em for all they’re wuth.   Was she botherin’ ye afore I come in?” he asked, in an altered tone, turning to Anny.

“ No,” was the quiet answer.   “ She jes’ come in a minute afore wot you did.   She said she was glad to see me.”

“ How purty o’ her !” said Sam, turning to his visitor. Phœbe Ellen bridled.

“ I reckon I got a right to be glad, arter she’s been run off with by a runnygate ’n’ nobody could tell whether I’d ever see ’er agin, ’n’ her not knowin’ how to take keer o’ herself.   I d’ know who ’s got a better right—’less it’s my sister ’erself !”

“ Yer sister ’d better be a cat in hell ’thout claws ’n to live in the same house with *you* ’thout some un to look arter ’er,” remarked Sam.

“ Oh, she’s got some un to look arter ’er *now*,” repeated Phœbe Ellen, viciously, for the third time.

"My only shame is," said Sam, "'t I feel like I'd took a advantage, her not bein' 'erself. I'm fair 'nough to see 't there's where ye've got a p'int agin me. But this I say : she ain't my wife 'cept in name till arter the operation 's over 'n' she's got 'er own mind back, 'n' kin make 'er own ch'ice. Till then she's my sister, only I have a husban's right to watch over 'er 'n' see 't she gits fair treatment. Arter that she kin git shet o' me if 'er mind comes back 'n' she feels like I'd been imposin' on 'er. It 'll be a easy thing."

"'N' if 'er mind don't come back ?"

"Then I'll take 'er away as my sister, 'n' I'll look arter 'er as sech the rest o' my life. Be shore I won't leave 'er to *you*."

"That's a relief," snorted Phœbe Ellen. "Ye kin make shore *I'll* never make a fight fer the priv'lege o' lookin' arter yer wives."

Sam took no notice of this retort, but reverted to the theme uppermost in his thoughts.

"The Doc says 't all the 'rangements fer the operation 's been pervided fer atween you 'n' him. He didn't tell how he managed it, but that's all right."

"Yes, it's all 'ranged."

"I wouldn't 'a' married the little un jes' yit—it's only right to say so—if I'd 'a' knowed he could 'a' got yer consent like this 'ere. I'd 'a' waited till arterward, when she could 'a' had a fairer show fer a husban'. But I ain't sorry. I can look arter things with a heap more sperrit 'n' carefulness 'n wot I could if I didn't have a husban's rights."

Phœbe Ellen tossed her head.

"Oh, a husban's rights !" she snapped. "Very purty —very fine ! But they's others besides you 'round this ranch 't 's got husban's rights sence ye left 'ere las' night at midnight !"

"Pore Pinky !" murmured Sam.

"*Pore* Pinky?" flashed Phœbe Ellen. "I like that!"
Sam's face relaxed into a broad grin.

"Leatherhead tole me 'bout it," he said. "Pore Pinky!
I hope he won't live long, 'n' 't he'll be happy if he kin!"

And with that their interview ended. But Phœbe Ellen did not fully realize what Sam's marriage meant until
that night she stumbled upon his huge body stretched in
a blanket before Anny's door. He was guarding his wife
against a second kidnapping. And the mistress of the
ranch passed on with rage in her heart.

Two days later, at eleven o'clock in the morning, Sam might have been seen in the doctor's room, lending such assistance as he could in the preparation of a table at the head of the bed.

"The light will be perfect in about an hour," said the man of science. "I've been watching it ever since I came, and I know just how it lies in the room at every hour of the day. The two windows are precisely what we want. Do I look excited?"

"No," answered Sam, after a deliberate examination of the sick man's features.

"*You* do," declared the doctor.

"Ye don't expeck me to go aroun' singin' like a Texas mockin'-bird," reproved Sam, "when my wife's on the p'int o' havin' 'er head cut open?"

"No. But you know how I look when I'm fluttered? You've seen me?"

"Plenty o' times."

"Feel my pulse."

Sam laid his fingers on the doctor's skinny wrist.

"Stiddy 's a clock," he announced, after a moment.

"The same thing can't be said of you, I warrant! I'm not tremulous—I don't appear weak?"

"Ye're like another man. I feel like I hadn't never reely seen ye afore."

The doctor laughed softly.

"You know how I brought it to pass?"

"Brandy," answered Sam.

"Right you are—brandy respectfully approached and

appealed to with a rational regard for its intelligent help-
fulness. There isn't one man in ten thousand that understands the real nature and significance of strong drink
—its essential benignity, the true kindness of its heart, so
to speak, its purpose and place in the creative plan. But
brandy and I understand each other. Our relations have
been prolonged and peculiar; we are good friends. It
has never gone back on me in all my life when I have approached it in the spirit of reverent appeal. There's
something besides brandy, though, that has strengthened
me to-day."

" Ye feel like this 'ere operation was goin' to be the
bigges' thing ye've ever done, I reckon," said Sam, who
had heard the doctor say as much.

" The biggest thing. The climax. The *ne plus ultra.*
My *raison d'être.* Do you understand ?"

The doctor seated himself in the arm-chair facing the
table. His instruments were spread orderly before him
upon a white cotton cloth ; at the back of the table stood
several bottles with such significant labels as chloroform,
ammonia, morphia, brandy. A row of half a dozen scalpels — rough - hafted, so that the hand of the operator
would not be likely to slip, in spite of blood—caught the
sunshine along their edges in keen flashes. There were
bistouries, too, closed in their handles like pocket-knives
or only partly open, as if their owner intended them not
for use but for company to the others. Needles, saws,
probes, directors, forceps, and other ghastly implements
of the profession were scattered about for the doctor's
gloating contemplation—possibly for the gratification of
a desire for completeness and detail which he was known
to possess in professional matters. The sunshine flashing
from them back to the ceiling made a tremulous glimmer
up there as if reflected from unquiet water. Sam's razor,
newly sharpened, had an important look among the other
instruments, opened from its haft at an angle. Besides

these things there were bandages, sponges, a basin of water, and several towels.

"It makes me feel young again," said the doctor, suddenly removing his eyes from the instruments to Sam's face. "It makes the blood flow, the pulse beat, the muscles stiffen! It gives me the spring, the poise, the zest of other days. And you, Sam—why, you look old and anxious; you actually do! *Are* you frightened? Look at you! You are as nervous as I ordinarily am—you can neither stand still nor sit down. If the sight of blood makes you faint—"

"It don't," was the positive answer. "I never felt faint in all my life."

"You never saw the blood of your sweetheart—your wife," suggested the doctor.

"Oh, don't worry 'bout *me*. I'll be all right," Sam declared. Then, to change the subject: "I reckon ye 'ain't fergot nothin'? It 'ud be awk'ard to have to go 'n' hunt fer anything arter ye got fairly under way."

"Forget? No. I haven't had anything for weeks to think of but this hour—I've planned for it, hoped for it, lived for it. I've arranged that table a hundred times in my thoughts—the scalpels here, the bottles there, everything just as you see it. I've dreamed of it at night—felt the tightened skin under my fingers, seen the first drop of blood follow the knife, cut lengthwise of the muscles where I could—and awakened to live it all over again in the dark, but rearranging everything by an inward light of my own. Forget anything? No, no!"

He pushed a saw aside, and it came in contact with another of its kind with a soft clash.

"Of course, I sha'n't use all these things—you understand that. But I wanted them in sight as a sort of inspiration. Oh, I sha'n't try to make the operation hard— I sha'n't keep on cutting after I've finished, just for the joy of cutting. I have distinctly in mind what I must do, and I sha'n't try any flourishes. Desault says that the simplicity of an operation is the measure of its perfection, and mine will be quite perfect — quite perfect. Is — is Mrs. Tinker as quiet in her mind as she was two hours ago ?"

It was the first time any one had called Anny by that name, and Sam noticed, though he was too full of other thoughts to speak of it.

" Jes' 's quiet," he answered.

" And you haven't told her the hour ?"

" Not a word. Ye said 'twouldn't be best till jes' afore she was led in."

" You'd make an excellent surgeon's assistant, Sam — though possibly a better soldier. She keeps up wonderfully. If she were in her right mind she'd be a hundred times as nervous—Lord ! you ought to see some of them in the hospitals. Are you afraid I'll fail at the last moment, Sam ? Tell me the truth—are you afraid I'll fail?"

Sam looked him over from head to foot.

" No," he answered, deliberately.

" Good ! You have grounds for your confidence. I shall succeed—but—but there's something beyond that I can't make out. Queer, isn't it, how everything in my life, even my gift of mind-reading, has amounted to nothing ? I used to despise it as something beneath my profession — a trait that would stamp me as a charlatan. Well, it's a fatality. You see how it turned out here when I tried to use it for your good—or no, you don't know. But it was by that means I brought the missus to give her consent to this business—no, I sha'n't tell you further, for I gave her my word. But you neutralized my efforts by marrying the girl—it's the way everything goes." He took out his watch, looked at it, and restored it to his pocket. " Fifteen minutes yet." There was a flush on his face that made his cheeks look fuller and younger. " Jove ! This is glorious." He began to pace slowly up

22

and down, his feet meeting the floor in a firm, steady tramp. "Why isn't it something more difficult?" He poured out some brandy into a glass, regulating the quantity by a scale on the side. "I tell you, I could cut a human heart in this mood, and restore it in perfect condition!"

Sam shuddered. He had never before witnessed an outburst of such professional fury.

"Ye'll make it go," he said, thinking of the outcome of the operation.

The doctor fetched a breath as from the bottom of his lungs.

"I haven't breathed like that before for four years," he declared. His eyes burned into Sam's. "Oh! It couldn't be that I am to get well again?" Then, as the absurdity of his question dawned upon him, he fetched another breath deeper than the first and laughed. "At least, I know what it is to *feel* well once more before I die!"

He shifted one or two of his instruments into more symmetrical order on the table, and their glittering reflections followed the changed position on the ceiling.

"The light is perfect," he declared. "These windows couldn't be better if they had been made on purpose." He glanced at his watch, smiled, and nodded at Sam. "You may bring her in. It is time." There was something beautiful, dignified, and noble in his aspect. Sam was almost awed.

The doctor stopped him with his hand on the door.

"See that her clothing is loose about her throat and waist," he said. "And don't look frightened, even if you feel so."

In a few moments Anny came in, followed by Sam. She was a little pale, but there were no signs of undue excitement in her eyes. Her hair was loosened, and hung in pretty shining masses all about her neck and shoulders.

As her eyes met the doctor's she smiled.

"No, I ain't skeert," she said, as if in answer to a question. "Why should I be? It 'll all come right."

"Good!" said the doctor, standing erect by the table. "You'll do nicely. It's half in the spirit in which one approaches these things. Sam, tell the missus we're ready. She wanted to wait outside the door, and I thought it wise that she should. We may need her."

Sam was gone but a moment, and, returning, closed the door.

"She's there," he announced, in a faint voice.

The doctor nodded approval.

"Lie down," he said to Anny. And, as the girl obeyed: "A little farther this way—the shadow of the head-board falls on that side. There, that is better. The light is all that one could wish. Now!"

He took a towel, squeezed it together, poured some chloroform over it, loosened it a little in his hand, then held it near the patient's nose.

"She takes it beautifully," he nodded to Sam. "Sometimes they struggle. Evidently her heart is in good condition."

When the patient was asleep and breathing satisfactorily, the doctor, after an instant's manipulation — Sam could not help noticing the quickness and lightness of his touch—began to cut away the hair close to the scalp. Sam understood, and had his razor ready; and in less time than it takes to tell it a good-sized portion of the skin showed white and smooth.

The doctor uttered not a word, and there was something awful in the firmness and poise of his movements. He stretched the shaven scalp carefully with his left hand by the opposing pressure and pull of two fingers, and Sam saw the flesh grow whiter as the blood underneath was forced out of the sphere of manipulation. The knives were within reach; the doctor selected one, and in the act his eyes looked lightning. He brought the instrument into position and bent over, taking care to keep his hand out of the light. Sam found himself catching his breath and letting it go with a faintly audible shudder. Would he cry out when the knife touched the flesh and brought the blood ?

He followed every movement with the fascination of expectant horror. The doctor's eyes revealed the light and heat in him as do the doors of a furnace suddenly opened. The knife descended with a tentative directness, making towards the desired point as by the homing instinct of a bird. It felt its way before it cut—not uncertainly, but cautiously; it seemed to be taking a long look ahead. Presently it found what it wanted—found it and touched it with the deliberation of a living soul determined to make sure. It was beautiful but terrible —a knife acting as if it possessed a mind and nervous system of its own, and were following out a line of intelligent action which it had learned through experience. Sam watched with a feeling of growing sickness—a sense of sinking, expanding, evaporating. His stomach seemed to turn over, as if a slow wave had rolled under it. There was a big oblong link of ghastly white around his mouth. His lips were dry and bloodless.

The knife drew itself deliberately to the left along a line which might have been made by a ruler; it gave out a softly rasping sound, as if a thumb-nail had been drawn across planed pine. Blood followed, oozing up in a raised line and lying there like a wet scarlet thread. Sam opened his mouth to cry out, shut it, and opened it again.

"I can't stan' this, Doc," he gasped, in a stifled voice.

The doctor paused without looking up. But his features were all visible. Even with that dreadful faintness heaving through him, Sam was awed by the beauty and terror of the strange man's eyes.

"Go to the farther window, out of the light," said he, intent upon his work. "I'll call if I need you."

Sam obeyed with difficulty, his knees manifesting a jack-knife propensity to double up. He leaned against the window-frame, for the moment unconscious of everything but the horrible uncertainty of semi-consciousness. He could not have raised the sash to save his life—he was as weak as a baby. His lungs struggled as if under a weight; his stomach heaved and rolled; his nostrils contracted and shut out his breath; his throat was too small; his tongue and palate were in the way.

But presently the faintness began to pass. He flung up the window and took in great gulps of air. There were queer sounds all about — sounds which his own mind made and echoed. The pines had little shadows close about them like puddles of black liquid; the shallows of the river looked as if whitened by a wind that struck them vertically; there was a pale level cloud above the mountains, and the blue heaven faded into it as a sunny sky merges into a sunny sea.

The memory of what was taking place behind him returned, and he began to wonder how the operation had progressed. Should he turn and see? Not yet! Anything but a recurrence of that horrid, aimless, unplaceable disturbance of the very source of life; he felt certain that he could never live through another such qualm.

"If I only had some water," he thought. "Could I git to the table back'ards, I wonder, 'n' git a drink out o' the basin? No; I might cut myself fumblin' aroun' amongst them knives. Oh, I'm better. I'll do perfeckly well now. Wot a bright day 'tis, 'n' how the dogs chase each other up 'n' down the river-bank! Where do they git the breath to do it with, I wonder?"

But suddenly he was brought to his senses by a cry—a hideous, animal cry, full of nightmare effort, part bellow, part bark, part shriek. He turned with a leap and saw

Anny half erect on the bed, her eyes open, sightless and staring, her mouth drawn and tense, her throat corrugated by the strain of that frightful effort of pain. The doctor stood over her, knife in hand, his body slanting backward, as if that inhuman sound had given him a push. Even as Sam looked the rigidity of Anny's figure relaxed, she wavered, sank back ; her jaw dropped, as he had seen in the case of people dying. A change came into the doctor's attitude, too ; the knife fell from his hand to the table, where it clashed edge against edge with the other instruments ; then he staggered back into his arm-chair and lay there with closed eyes.

"I've killed or cured her !" Sam heard him mutter. "Killed or cured her, by God !"

CHAPTER XL

PHŒBE ELLEN came in with a rush. Her eyes met Sam's in a question which he did not try to answer.

"Look arter the doctor," was all the explanation he had time to give. "I'll 'tend to *her*."

He applied all the restoratives at hand—water, brandy, ammonia; he rubbed her wrists, chafed her temples; he lowered her head over the side of the bed, holding it so that the weight would not wrench the muscles of the neck. His eyes were too intent on the pale, unconscious face to notice definitely what Phœbe Ellen was doing, but he knew that she was applying the same restoratives that he had used, and in the same way. Presently he was gratified to see that his patient began to breathe again. But her eyes did not unclose, and there was no sign of consciousness.

He laid her head gently back upon the pillow. The wound in the scalp was still bleeding with a slow persistence that made him shiver. He spunged it off—it looked horribly deep after the blood was washed away—drew the edges of the flap together, pressed them firmly down, and applied a bandage. Then for a moment he stood off to contemplate his work.

"Sam," he heard the doctor call, faintly, behind him.

For answer he approached the chair. He thought he detected a ghastly humor in the drawn mouth and fading eyes.

"You—you see?" the stricken man articulated, in a voice that rattled in his throat. "I knew—I wouldn't live—to see how it turned out." He lifted his dim, fatal eyes. "It's God's fault—not mine," he whispered.

And with those words he died.

"Call Leatherhead," said Sam. "Let 'em kerry 'im to my room. I'll stay 'ere with the little un."

Sam never once left his wife's side during the next two days. He did not even attend the doctor's funeral, but remained at the window, with one eye on the bed, so to speak, and the other fixed upon the mournful group on the mountain-side, standing uncovered in the clear autumn sunshine as old man Halstead read the service for the dead.

"Dan 'll be glad to have 'im layin' there beside 'im," Sam thought as he turned to the bedside once more. "He done his best fer the little un, however it turns out, 'n' Dan 'll know."

And he sat down at the head of the bed to watch.

"It's jes' like the sleep she fell into arter the accident," he thought for the hundredth time. "How 'll she wake from it, I wonder? Better or wuss, or jes' the same?"

Phœbe Ellen came in from the funeral with her hat on.

"'Pears like she's breathin' stronger," she said, after a momentary examination. "Had ye noticed?"

"I thort so myself," was Sam's reply.

She took off her hat and sat down on the opposite side of the bed. She appeared worn and anxious; but there were determination and prospective triumph in the hard curve of her mouth.

"She's gittin' to look older," thought Sam, giving her a long, examining glance. "'N' wickeder. She wa'n't like that when she fust come. Wot's she thinkin' of, I wonder?"

"Doc Sedgwick 's dead," was the thought that had given expression to Phœbe Ellen's face and occasioned Sam's curiosity. "He died 'thout tellin' wot he knowed —he kep' his word, 'spite o' knowin' how I hated 'im. 'N' now I got to fight it out atween these two. Sam never leaves 'er, not even to take a breath o' air. He's more dan-g'rous 'n wot she'll be, even if she comes to in 'er right mind."

She bent over the bed and lifted the hand of the sleeper as if to feel the pulse.

"She's wakin'," said Sam, suddenly, in a hushed voice.

The invalid had half opened her eyes, and the lids were quivering with a premonition of complete expansion. Phœbe Ellen bent lower. The movement attracted the attention of the awakening girl, and the eyes fixed upon the down-bent face with an expression of half recognition. This steady gaze continued for a full moment.

"Sis!" cried the sick girl, suddenly—"sis, where's my posies?"

It was the voice Sam remembered to have heard before the accident—the pretty, drawling voice which he had thought of so often since with regret—but with an accent of haste and fear in its utterance.

"Where's my posies?" she repeated, in a high key.

Sam's hopes fell as quickly as they had risen. Had she awakened with her old voice, her old look, but in a new state of delirium? Phœbe Ellen's heart was beating high with the same thought. She did not dare to look into his eyes lest he should read the wicked triumph in her own.

"She's crazy!" she whispered. "She 's woke up 's crazy 's wot she was afore, only dif'rent!"

"My posies, my posies!" repeated the invalid, impa-tiently. "Wot have I done with my posies? If ye've took 'em 'n' hid 'em, bring 'em back!"

Suddenly Sam's heart gave a great jubilant leap.

"She was gatherin' posies fer Dan's grave when the lan'slide overtook 'er!" he cried out. "She's took up 'er life jes' where she left it off that day—thank God!"

And he fell on his knees by the bed and buried his face in the covering.

Anny fixed her eyes on him with a sort of cold wonder.

"Oh, I know," she said, in a quieter voice than she had used before, and therein the old tone and inflection came out fully. "Ye're Sam—the man wot come to the depot fer us."

"Yes—yes!" he answered, lifting his face eagerly.

A slow flush overspread her features and she turned her head away.

"Wot be I doin' 'ere—in bed—with *him* aroun'?" Her eyes met her sister's. "Take me away, sis—wot does it mean?"

Phœbe Ellen's face had hardened as the assurance of her sister's recovery became plain. But she did not lose her self-control.

"Hush!" she said, as gently as she could. "Ye've been sick fer ever so long—ye'll know all 'bout it by-'n'-by!"

The invalid stirred restlessly.

"But why not now—why not now? I'm well, ain't I? Tell me 'bout it—I want to hear!"

"Lay still 'n' rest," said Phœbe Ellen, soothingly.

There was danger now that at any moment the truth about the ownership of the ranch might come out, and such a revelation must never be made, cost what it might. "'Ud it do any harm to give 'er a drop or two o' that morphine, Sam? We don't want 'er to git excited—it might spile the hull bizness."

Sam considered a moment, then rose and measured out the proper amount.

"The Doc said it was allus proper to give morphine arter a operation," he said. "'N' he tole me how much. Ye'll be stronger when ye wake up ag'in," he said to Anny, as she drank from the tumbler which he held for her. "We'll tell ye all 'bout it then. Ye mus' trust it all to us jes' now ; we know best."

"Well," said the girl, drinking obediently. She fixed her eyes upon his in a long, studious gaze. "Ye'll stay with me while I sleep?" she finally asked.

"Shorely—shorely!"

"'N' ye'll be 'ere to tell me when I wake? I'd ruther ye'd tell me 'n sis. See! She has sech a queer look in 'er eyes. Has she been sick, too?"

"No, no," soothed Sam, without taking the trouble to glance in Phœbe Ellen's direction. "Yer eyes see crooked arter bein' sick so long. Only sleep—sleep!"

"Shall I stay with 'er, too?" asked Phœbe Ellen, after the invalid was breathing quietly.

"No, I'll look arter 'er," was Sam's answer. And she left the room and went to her chamber. And when she came down her eyes were burning strangely, and there was something rolled up under her apron which she was trying to conceal.

Sam remained at his wife's bedside for an hour or more. She was sleeping so sweetly, so quietly, that he found himself growing drowsy by sheer force of example. There was no need to watch her; she would not waken for two or three hours at least. Why should he not go out for a little walk in the sunshine? Judy had been brought home, and he could see her out there in the corral, looking wistfully over the logs as if in search of her master. There were a dozen odd jobs that he ought to attend to. Had the boys raked down the mow properly, and not scattered the hay all over the barn in feeding the home cattle? Had Leatherhead tinned up the rat-holes into the granary? Had the saddle been mended that he had flung off in that wild flight to the station? Were the pigs properly "swilled," and had the chickens been kept out of the corn-crib? Pinky, in his capacity as manager of the ranch, had been looking after these things, Sam knew, but his training had not been of the sort to make his oversight thorough. Sam longed to go and see for himself.

He put on his hat and stole quietly out, glancing once at the unconscious sleeper to make sure that all was well.

"I'll be back long afore she wakes," he thought, as he left the house and started across the open between the veranda and the barn.

Phœbe Ellen saw him from the kitchen window, and went at once to the stove, where she bent diligently over something that was stewing in a basin.

"Suthin' fer the little un?" asked Pinky, who was reading a week-old newspaper by the window.

She bent lower over the stove.

"A kind o' a tonic the Doc ordered fer 'er afore he died," she answered.

"Oh," said Pinky, reading on.

Sam had completed his tour of inspection about the barn, and was on the point of returning to the house—he had stopped a moment at the corral to scratch Judy's out-thrust nose—when he was startled by the sound of hurrying footsteps behind him, and Leatherhead's voice rising in a falsetto screech.

"Fer God's sake, hear 'er! Don't ye hear? Come quick! The little un 's woke up clean crazy, 'n' 's bangin' 'er head agin the wall! Pinky's gone to the upper corral —he tole me the missus 'd sent 'im fer suthin'—'n' they ain't nobody 'ere but you. Hear 'er yell? That's her! The missus says it's the operation, 'n' she allus knowed wot 'ud come o' it. She's with 'er now. 'N' ye'd better hurry if ye want to see 'er alive!"

Sam arranged the roustabout's pronouns as best he could, and started for the house on a run. In the chamber where he had left his wife asleep, an awful sight met his gaze—a sight which made him sick and faint and long to run away.

CHAPTER XLI

ANNY was flinging herself from one end of the room to the other like a mad thing. Her countenance had lost all semblance to that of a human being; her features were drawn close together in the middle of her face, where they quivered and shook with a beastly passion. Her teeth showed; she had bitten her lips, and the blood was running down into her bosom. Her breath sounded shrill and irregular, inhaled by jerks and expelled in puffs and gasps, but preserving through all a sound of irrational animal fury. Her eyes had the peculiar bulging, rolling glare of an enraged buffalo; a red light came from them when turned at certain angles.

Phœbe Ellen was cowering in one corner of the room, her teeth chattering.

"I knowed how 'twould be from the fust," she gasped, coming closer to Sam. "Doc Sedgwick didn't know wot he was doin', 'n' this is wot comes o' puttin' a knife in his hand. Look at 'er, 'n' lay the blame where it b'longs." Her voice had grown steadier as Sam's presence gave her assurance of her personal safety. "*I* never cornsented— ye know I never did. She'd better 'a' stayed like she was, *I* say, 'n to have to pass the rest o' her life like this."

Sam gave no sign of hearing. He approached the raving woman and took her by the arm.

"Hush!" he cried, authoritatively. "Hush, I tell ye, 'n' go to the bed 'n' lay down."

He tried to lead her, but she struck at him with her free arm and he was obliged to desist.

"She'll die—she'll die!" cried Phœbe Ellen, forgetting

her own share in this terrible business and thinking only of the deadly horror of it.

Sam was about to lay hands on the raving woman again and try to pinion her arms—he could think of no other means of restraining the mad creature and keeping her from taking her own life—when he was arrested by the sight of Leatherhead's round, pimpled face, its senseless surprise all changed to terror now, peering in at him through the half-open door.

"Git a rope!" cried Phœbe Ellen at this moment. "Anything—only don't let this dretful thing go on. I shall be mad myself in another five minutes jes' to see it!"

"'Ll ye stay with 'er while I go?" asked Sam.

"No! I know where they's one out to the barn," she answered, and she sped past Leatherhead without seeing him and disappeared.

"Sam!" said the roustabout, in a low voice.

Sam's eyes, by a horrid fascination, had returned to the raving woman, but he now faced the door.

"I've got suthin' to say 'bout this 'ere bizness," said the roustabout, in a voice of mingled fright and resolution.

He drew from the side pocket of his jacket a dried leaf of peculiar shape.

"Look at that!" he said, handing it to Sam. "Look at it 's clost 's wot ye ever looked at anything in all yer life. 'N' then tell me wot 'tis."

Sam examined the leaf carefully. Then his eyes met Leatherhead's with a slow, inquiring horror in them.

"It looks like—"

But Leatherhead took up the word with eager triumph.

"Loco. It looks like loco, 'n' *'tis* loco. I come into the kitchen 'bout ten minutes arter ye'd gone out to the barn, 'n' there was the missus bendin' over the stove a-lookin' down at suthin' wot was a-bilin' in a basin. 'It's suthin' fer sis,' she says. 'It's to tone 'er up. It's yarb tea.' I didn't think nothin' more 'bout it, fer it never come into my head as we had the devil 'ere in the house, though I orter 'a' been s'picious arter the way she tried to get red o' the little un that night. By-'n'-by the drink was done. She'd sent Pinky off to the upper corral, so they wa'n't nobody there but me; 'n' she tuck 'n' strained it 'n' emptied the leaves in the fire 'n' kerried the tea up-stairs. Well, even arter the pore little un begun to rave I didn't think nothin', nuther; I jes' made shore the Doc 'd cut too deep, or suthin'; but arter I'd called ye 'n' ye'd gone up-stairs I went back to the kitchen, 'n' there I found this 'ere leaf on the floor 'n' picked it up, thinkin' the wind 'd blowed it in from outside; 'n' I was goin' to throw it into the wood-box when all to wunst I seen wot 'twas. I swear, ye could 'a' knocked me over with a feather, ye could."

"I'm glad Pinky didn't have no hand in it," said Sam, in a voice that hoarsened and broke in his throat.

"I don't b'lieve he did — I swear I don't. It's all 'er own work, the she-devil! I could take my oath to it. 'N' arter the way I've stood by 'er 'n' waited on 'er! She knowed 'bout the Doc's havin' a lot o' that weed dried 'n' spread out up garret las' fall; 'n' she tuck some out 'n' hid it away in case she might need it. Lord! I never seen nothin' clearer in all my life. Ain't it plain ?"

"Come into the room 'ere with me," was Sam's answer. "Has Pinky come back ? No ? I'd like 'im to know the kind o' wife he's got, but that 'll keep. Come! It ain't 's bad 's wot it might be—that is, if Doc Sedgwick's word's good fer anything. Ye won't be afeerd to help me hold 'er while I give 'er some med'cine, will ye ?"

At this moment Phœbe Ellen entered, breathless, with the rope.

"We won't need it," said Sam, quietly. "I've found out wot's the matter—"

In her excitement and horror she had forgotten what

was the matter herself, and the knowledge came back to her now like a blow on the head. She started to speak, but—

"Keep still!" commanded Sam, and she shrank back in scared obedience.

He went to the row of bottles on the table which had remained undisturbed since the doctor's death — undisturbed not by design, but by the accident of that unwillingness which all men feel for disarranging the possessions of the dead — and selected one. Phœbe Ellen's features relaxed into a heavy surprise which quivered into curiosity in her mouth and eyebrows. Sam remembered the bottle well. "Three drops in half a tumbler of water will do the business in half an hour," the doctor had said. Sam had looked and listened too attentively to forget.

"Bring me half a tumbler of water," he said to Leatherhead.

"Wot—wot is it?" stammered Phœbe Ellen, moving forward, and half forgetting the woman who was raging back and forth on the other side of the room.

"Wait 'n' see," was Sam's answer, delivered with a smile as enigmatic as the doctor's own.

In a moment Leatherhead returned with the glass and water. Sam poured out the prescribed medicine with the care of one who has life and death in his hands. Then he said to Leatherhead:

"We must hold 'er—leastways fer a minute or two— till I make 'er drink the stuff. D' ye reckon ye kin manage 'er left arm?"

"I kin try," responded Leatherhead, with tremulous bravery.

"Then I'll 'tend to the rest," said Sam.

The raving woman seemed altogether unconscious of them even after they had seized her, except as an opposing force which, for all she knew, might have been the wall. They grasped her firmly on either side, and, in spite of her shrieks and struggles, bore her to the table where the tumbler of medicine stood. She had already greatly exhausted herself, and between the two men she was passive as if in a clamp. Sam took the tumbler and held it to her lips.

"Drink!" he cried, in a loud voice. "Drink!"

The words forced themselves into her mind without rousing it, but they must have awakened at least some mechanical habit of obedience, some reflex nervous train, for she drank as he commanded, gazing at the ceiling with heavy, unseeing eyes. The glass being emptied, Sam thought best to let her loose again, for he knew not at what moment her ravings might recommence, and in her present state he dreaded less the effect of liberty than coercion. She tottered a few steps, groaning and crying and flinging out her arms; but she was weak with the dreadful strain of her former ravings, and either as a result of that or of the medicine she presently fell in a shapeless heap upon the floor.

She lay quite still, with the exception of an occasional moan, as if the tortured soul were still tossed on the ground-swell of its fury. Sam lifted her very tenderly and placed her on the bed, and she made no resistance. Phœbe Ellen stood in the background watching these proceedings with mingled feelings. She was one of those hard, unyielding natures to whom consequences seldom bring remorse, and she felt only a sort of mental nausea for what she had done. She had never imagined the dreadful details of the action of that drug, and she was almost willing for the moment to take the consequences of her sister's recovery if only for the sake of being relieved of the sight of her torment.

Presently Anny's groans ceased altogether, and she began to talk. Not coherently, but the very disconnection of her words was hopeful as contrasted with her former inarticulate cries, indicating as it did an approach to human consciousness. She imagined strange things, was subject to strange illusions of sight and sound. There were inverted rivers flowing over her, and the sky was below; the bedposts were all talking together, and that made her nervous; there were shooting-stars in the room, and the walls kept falling in and then straightening themselves. Sam watched her through all this with a fierce, anxious joy.

At last the girl lay quite still, breathing irregularly, but otherwise exhibiting no trace of the horror through which she had passed.

"Wonderful!" said Sam, aloud. "Why couldn't the Doc 'a' lived to see this? It 'ud 'a' done 'im 's much good 's the operation."

Phœbe Ellen came close to the bed. She had recovered her composure to a certain extent, and her tongue was up to its old tricks.

"*He* didn't die none too quick," she cut in.

"They's other folks aroun' this ranch 't can't die too quick, either," remarked Sam, significantly. "In fact, they've been altogether too slow 'bout it; 'n' I mean to make a point o' seein' if the law can't hurry 'em up a bit."

And Phœbe Ellen shrank back into silence.

"My posies—my posies!" cried Anny, suddenly opening her eyes. "Who 's took my posies away from me? 'Pears like I'd been wanderin' all over the world sence I picked my posies." Sam was bending over her, and his was the first face she saw. "Where 'd ye say the grave was? Under the pines on the mountain-side? I can't see it from 'ere. Why, I'm in a house! Whose is it? Where's sis?"

"She's 'ere," said Sam, in a tone of gentle assurance. "Come, he said to Phœbe Ellen, in a low voice. "The least ye kin do 's to try to keep 'er calmed down."

Phœbe Ellen approached the bed and knelt.

"Ye're better," she said, in a smothered tone. "Ye've

been sick — ye're powerful weak yit. But ye'll be well afore long, now."

"Have I been sick?"

"Dretful sick. But it's all right. Ye ain't afeerd?"

"No. But I'm so weak. 'N' it seems so queer."

"It 'll come right later. Don't bother now. Ye feel weak 'n' tired?"

"But I'd like to know wot it's all about. My body aches, my bones feels stiff, here's blood on my throat; but my head feels clear. Where's Sam? He'll tell me. He was good to me from the start. Ye needn't stay. They's suthin' wrong with ye." She looked at her sister shrinkingly and with a sudden repulsion. "I don't like yer looks. Ye've changed somehow. Go 'way! Sam 'll tell me wot I want to know."

Phœbe Ellen shrank from the room, and Leatherhead followed her. Then Sam knelt down by his wife's bed and took her hand. He had not intended to go into the details of the accident and the operation and Phœbe Ellen's dreadful act of vengeance—for such he deemed it—not knowing any logical cause for the deed except her unrequited affection for himself; but Anny inquired so rationally about one thing after another, and took his answers with a good sense so quiet and self-possessed, that before many moments she was mistress of all he knew, even to the supreme fact of her wedding. For a wonder, she did not resent it; she flushed a little, was quiet for a time, and then changed the conversation; that was all. And when it came out—as presently it did—that she was the actual owner of the ranch, and that Phœbe Ellen had been usurping her place all these months, Sam understood the misguided woman's final act fully, and in his heart thought better of her than he had done since her hostility to the operation had been made manifest.

How long they talked he never knew, nor just what they talked about; only, whenever he attempted to lead up to the subject of the wedding again, Anny looked so strangely, she flushed so hotly, and turned away so persistently and sought other themes of conversation with such diligence, that he was finally forced to be silent altogether; and presently he fell to wondering why she should seem to care so much about it and yet not be angry. But finally they were interrupted by Leatherhead.

"Well, say!" he began. "They're gone — them two. Yes, her 'n' Pinky. A hour ago. 'N' she had a face on 'er 't 'ud sour vinegar. She says to me, 'We're goin' fer a little ride,' says she, 'n' I never thort it might be fer good, I swear I didn't. 'Ye'll find suthin' in my room fer Mr. Tinker,' says she. 'It's on the beaury. Wait a hour,' says she, 'then go 'n' give it to 'im.' So I waited, 'n' 'ere 'tis. My shape! 'S soon 's I seen 'twas a letter, I knowed they'd jes' nachelly skipped. The last I seen o' Pinky he was goin' up the hill, 'n' he was hittin' the bottle hard. He'll be soakin' drunk afore he gits to the station, I bet a hen!"

Meanwhile Sam was reading the letter.

"Kin I know wot's in it?" asked Anny, when he had finished.

"Yes. They've left fer good—that's the long 'n' short o' it. Gone to Nebrasky. To the old place back there. She says she reckons ye'll let 'em live there 'thout troublin' 'em, even if ye do own half."

"She's my sister," said Anny, belligerent in excuse of her too ready forgiveness.

Sam nodded.

"'N' Nebrasky 's good 'nough fer 'er. Pore Pinky!"

Anny meditated.

"Pore sis, *I* say," she finally retorted. "She had a queer disposition—she couldn't help it. She'll have 'er conscience to deal with. She had one wunst—it 'll come to 'er ag'in when she gits time to think."

Sam smiled.

"Pore Pinky, I still say. Fer he'll have her 'n' her conscience both ; 'n' they're both terrors !"

They were silent for some time.

"It 's turned out all right," remarked Anny at last—"leastways fer *us*. If she hadn't been so wicked—"

"Well, wot then ?"

"I wouldn't 'a' made shore o' the kindest, truest husban' in the world !" she cried, suddenly drawing his face down to hers.

And at this point, though neither of them noticed, Leatherhead left the room, tittering wildly behind his hand.

THE END